RESILIENCE AWAKENING

BRETT HEASTON

ELK LAKE PUBLISHING INC

PUBLISHING THE POSITIVE
Plymouth, Massachusetts

COPYRIGHT NOTICE

Resilience Awakening

Cover and Interior Design: Derinda Babcock

Editor(s): Mary White Johnson, Deb Haggerty

PUBLISHED BY: Elk Lake Publishing, Inc., 35 Dogwood Drive, Plymouth, MA 02360, 2021

Library Cataloging Data

Names: Heaston, Brett (Brett Heaston)

Resilience Awakening / Brett Heaston

328 p. 23cm × 15cm (9in × 6 in.)

ISBN-13: 978-1-64949-283-8 (paperback) | 978-1-64949-284-5 (trade paperback) | 978-1-64949-285-2 (e-book)

Key Words: science fiction; science fiction books; science fiction novels; science fiction other worlds; science fiction kindle; science fiction spaceships; science fiction military space battles

Library of Congress Control Number: 2021940946 Fiction

DEDICATION

To The Voice that created all things,
upholds all things,
and sustains all things.

ACKNOWLEDGMENTS

To The Voice which set everything in motion from the foundation of the galaxies, to the farthest reaches of the cosmos.

Thank you to my faithful wife for supporting me in this incredibly time-consuming passion.

To my daughter Madelyn, my faithful writing companion, brave reader of my first drafts, and engineering specialist.

To the Northwest Christian Writer's Association for freely sharing your gifts and talents.

To my critique group: Pat, Rick, Steve, and Dennis, for saying the hard words no one else was brave enough to say.

To the rejection letters that came with feedback, even those were helpful.

To the King Country Metro Transit Authority.

To that goat that supposedly discovered coffee on the Ethiopian plateau.

CHAPTER ONE

SPACEPORT L32 ORBITING OXYLIUM, THIRD MOON OF PERDUPEO

We would have been smart to find a reliable way off this station before we started the bomb's countdown sequence. But then, starfighters and heroes rarely think before they act. They know that if they do, their hearts might talk them out of being heroes.

I stare at the station café's waitress across the room. She whispers to a Salient deserter and discreetly receives from him an item wrapped in a cloth. With a grin, she turns and saunters away.

Greed never rests.

"What's your plan to get us off this doomed station?" Khal asks from across the table.

I refuse to answer and hold up my hand to silence him. My attention is on the waitress.

"Who do you think you are?" Khal is miffed at my gesture.

I ignore him yet answer the question to myself. *I am Kyvar Astilius. A young, overconfident starfighter pilot who doesn't mind taking risks. I love Ion Drives, the lure of starfighter speed, the Nebula Isles, Hatuerus brew, and being the best and fastest at everything.*

"Need I remind you of the explosives we set?" Khal asks, his voice testy.

I ignore him, eyes still on the waitress. She walks to another table and, after a quick glance around the café, drops the item into the lap of a Covalian trader. "Greed never sleeps," I say.

The comm on my arm vibrates. Thirteen SEGs.

Khal laughs. "Greed? That's your plan?"

I tap my jacket pocket. "Greed always betrays its own."

"Kyvar, I know we are both rookies, but that's not a plan."

"Of course, it's not, Khal." I calmly nod toward the waitress. "*She's* our plan."

The waitress moves toward our table. Her long brown hair is pulled back with numerous blue and black ribbons. She wears a red "L32 Station Café" apron over her clothes and walks with the confidence of a businesswoman. A mischievous thin smile forms on her lips, and her wide green eyes glitter. "Good day, gentlemen. May I take your order?"

I smile. "I must admit the smell of the trigona strips is appealing, but we're in a bit of a rush."

She shrugs her shoulders. "Can I interest you in a few drinks, then?"

"No. We're here for more than food and drink." I pull out a priceless eight-sided diamond Helix from my pocket and hold the stone in front of her. "We're here to trade."

She stares at the stone, worth more than ten Nebula Isles.

"Some believe the stones go back before The Voice caused the eclipse of Erupeo."

The waitress's eyes remain on the Helix. She's not much for conversation, even one related to the ethereal which often works. The second most valuable object in the cosmos has her hypnotized.

"They say the pink ones are perfect." I roll the stone in the palm of my hand. The Helix's rosy shimmer reflects upon my skin. "I prefer the less valuable, transparent ones. Invisibility is power, don't you think?"

She looks at me. "If you don't want it, you can give it to me." She smiles as if I might just do that. Her smile is half charming, but not worth a million illirium.

The comm on my arm vibrates. Twelve SEGs.

Enough amusement. I frown and grab my menu.

The waitress blinks at me as if seeing me for the first time. "Oh, sorry. May I take your order?"

I slide the Helix into my coat pocket where it belongs. We stole only one of them before we set the charges. I turn to Khal and back to her. "We would like some Ale."

Her eyes widen. "Ale?"

"The respectable stuff." Khal says.

"Respectable?" she asks.

Respectable? Where did Khal get that?

"Oxylium Ale," I say, to clarify. A simple pat to my pocket makes the point. "I am willing to pay for it."

She leans forward and motions with a tilt of her head. "See the Kanvarian over there?"

I turn in the direction she's indicated and see the Kanvarian gangster. I swallow my displeasure. It figures she would lead me to one of them. Why couldn't it be some distant trader or naïve broker?

"I can introduce you if you like," she says.

I sit back casually. "That might lead to a nice finder's fee."

She licks her lips and steps back. "An introduction will come shortly." She walks away without taking our order.

Khal frowns. "Not even a drink?"

I shake my head. The only thing Khal likes more than Oxylium Ale is geeking out on engineering and arguing with Ayera. "You call Oxylium Ale respectable?"

The comm on my arm vibrates. Eleven SEGs.

His lips form a crooked grin. "I respect it."

"Nothing in this part of the universe is respectable."

Outside the spherical domed walls of the tiny space station is the blood-red moon of Oxylium. I've come near death twice today—once when we almost detonated the explosives by mistake, and again when our shuttle was jettisoned for leaking noxious gases. I wonder if nearly dying three times in one day is bad luck. I can see the advertisements now—*Visit beautiful volcanic Oxylium—it's thrice the charm.*

I turn to Khal. "Do you know why they asked you to come with me on this adventure?"

He laughs. "I'm the only one capable of fixing whatever starship you break."

"You failed me last time," I say with a sneer.

"I wouldn't call that Caman shuttle a starship."

I laugh. Khal might be a terrible pilot, but he's the best engineer in our galaxy. His dark brown hair and trim beard that covers a large square jaw make him appear almost middle-aged, though he's as young and brash as I am. We are two overconfident Sidonian officers only a few leagues out of advanced flight school, stranded on a doomed space station on the remote side of the cosmos. We really need a ship—and soon. Before the bombs detonate.

"Are you really playing a bluff with a stolen Helix for a case of Ale?"

"It's what they barter around here. We've got to get off this cheapie spaceport."

The comm on my arm vibrates. Ten SEGs.

Khal's eyes widen. "Or it's going to be an early visit to Oupavo."

I am too young for Oupavo. Even my father was too young for Oupavo.

The waitress whispers to the gangster, and he rises out of his seat to approach our table. His narrow eyes beneath his wide forehead and jet-black hair lock on me and glint with bitterness and treachery.

Greed betrays its own, and Kanvarian greed is never satisfied. They buy and sell, steal and kill for anything. They are swindlers of a thousand galaxies. Even *we* fell for it at Tegirium. Ever since, a thread of hatred has separated our galaxies.

Two Kanvarian females flank him, slim and short and scowling. The female Kanvarians always appear to be perpetually angry, with their low brows and tight lips. I've never seen one smile. Ever.

The gangster's hand hovers over a laser pistol at his side. One of the females pulls out a micro cannon. So much for being discreet.

"I heard you would like some Ale." The gangster's voice vibrates from deep within his chest. "Do you want to trade?"

"I do." I pull the Helix stone from my jacket pocket.

The gangster's eyes narrow even further. "That is worth ten cases of Oxylium Ale."

Really? "Do you want to look at it?"

The comm on my arm vibrates. Nine SEGs.

One of the females seizes the stone. She licks her finger, rubs the stone, and examines it, looking for flaws.

I cringe. Why does everyone have to put their spit on my stone?

The pink resonance flickers in her narrow flat face. "It's perfect." She points her micro laser cannon at me. "And it's mine."

4

"Twelve cases," I counter.

"Ten," the gangster responds casually.

"No deal." I touch my comm. The hologram of the Helix disappears from her hand.

"*Gunfrey!*" The gangster spits out a curse.

"Twelve or no deal." I pat my pocket.

"Twelve, then," the gangster says.

I look at Khal and then back at the gangster. This guy is dense. It's only worth five cases. I'm going to enjoy this. I extend my hand to shake with the Kanvarian. His soft padded hand makes for a strange handshake.

He gestures for us to follow. "We will deal."

The comm on my arm vibrates. Eight SEGs.

Khal and I follow the three toward the stellar café's exit. Two Salient deserters try to act like they are not looking at us, some Covalian dealers give us only a glance, and a few officers of the Caman Corporation watch us closely. It's odd to see corporate folk out here, but everyone knows the petrillionaire Caman Corporation owns the mining rights to fragile Oxylium.

The Camans are one of the primary weapons providers of the universe. Most conflicts are fueled by or fought with their weapons. Businessmen with no integrity—this spaceport has it all.

The smell of grilled hides and terro cakes fades as we advance down one of L32s space dock extensions. Through the window of the cylindrical port, the uninhabited planet Perdupeo dwarfs its moon Oxylium. The pale blue planet is in stark contrast to its crimson moon.

Though Oxylium is beautiful from this perspective, below the surface it's a raging inferno. A small group of Caman officers—maybe ten—are stationed on the moon, managing thousands of bots and mining drones. Only one in ten thousand star systems have Oxylium's elemental combination of volcanic hyperactivity and gaseous caverns below its mantle. The aggressive synthesis produces some of the rarest elements in the cosmos—the eight-sided diamond Helix and the minerals that constitute Oxylium Ale. It's no surprise that gangsters, fugitives, and corporate folk alike all lurk here.

The comm on my arm vibrates. Seven SEGs.

The two Kanvarian females strut on either side of me. One pulls out a magnum laser cannon.

Talk about overkill. *Who are these clowns?* "A little extreme, don't you think?"

I receive no reply.

Everyone knows the cheaply built Spaceport L32s leak atmospheric gases. Implosions are commonplace. One squeeze from her cannon would vaporize me and blow a hole in the cabin lock system, sending all of us into space. Who knows, this entire station might collapse upon itself with the airlock seizure.

The gangster carries a CSX H42 pistol, and the other female a Switch H2 micro cannon. Apparently, these guys ditched their own weapons some time ago. They don't even hold their current weapons right. Khal motions for me to look at the gangster, who still has the morphing lock on his H42. Clowns indeed.

We pass five utility vessels and a corporate transport as we approach the end of the dock.

"Where are you taking us? We just want to trade." *And hopefully steal your ship.* I manage an innocent smile.

Through the window at the end of the bay lock, a cobalt blue vTalis freighter waits. The ship's name, *Resilience,* can be seen over the starboard cabin.

It can't be. My heart pounds.

Khal elbows me. "It's just like your father's freighter."

"Where did you get this?" I ask the main goon.

"It's our vessel," he responds in his deep voice. "We've had it for years."

That's not possible. "This is a cobalt vTalis freighter."

"And it's the latest model," Khal adds. "It's custom. I've never seen anything like it."

The gangster leans in like he's listening. One of the females punches him.

I know this model ... *well.* "It goes 10 BURN, Basic Upgraded Relative Nanofire. Four freight bays for supplies or weapons. It's the most maneuverable freighter in the cosmos—capable of scoring against the best."

The comm on my arm vibrates. Six SEGs. We've got to move.

"Looks like Ion Drive upgrades too," Khal adds. "Maybe 11 or 12 BURN."

"This way," the gangster orders. "We'll trade in the ship."

I concede gladly. The starboard corridor leads us down the outside of the vessel towards the bridge. I push down a thousand memories of running these same lines as a kid on my father's ship. Starlight flickers through the corridor windows as the smell of fresh legumna leather reaches for us. We step onto the spacious bridge with its eight seats facing the bridge bay window and the cosmos beyond.

The gangster greets another two females in the cabin. One of them holds a CSX H42 pistol. She swivels in her chair next to two short Shivyuns chained to their sensor seats.

Shivyuns.

They beep and moan as we enter. I acknowledge their existence with a nod, and they reply with a shake of their large heads. They wear their customary thick visors over narrow eyes. Their large legs are chained to their station, allowing movement only with their mole-like hands.

Why does everyone abuse these creatures?

The female with the laser cannon pokes me in the back with it.

"This is your crew?" I ask. "Where's your pilot?"

The Kanvarian female in the chair stands up. "Here," she snarls.

I wave my hands to assure her of my good intent. "Hey, I just came for the Ale. Where's the rest of the crew?"

"Why do you care?" she snaps.

I shrug.

She gives me an insolent look. "We killed them. We found them annoying." She walks past me and speaks to the gangster. "Why are they here?"

"He possesses a perfect Helix," he says.

She faces me. "You do?"

The comm on my arm vibrates. Five SEGs.

The shipboard computer flashes, and another female yelps. "It's working!"

The screen flashes again, and the male voice of the onboard introduces itself. "Welcome. I am Group User Zero One."

"You erased the onboard's memory?" I ask.

One of the female stares at the other, then at me. "It shut off when we killed the captain."

Khal and I glance at each other. "Onboards only reboot when they recognize a new captain," he says. He knows this from flight school.

The pilot looks at the gangster. "When the captain's life readings terminated, the onboard commenced a shutdown." The gangster shrugs, indifferent.

I shake my head in disgust. "I can't believe you actually stole this vessel. You guys are crazy."

Khal's tense stance lets me know he's ready to act, and so am I.

Despite Khal's average build, he is expert in personal combat. Horrible with a rifle, but excellent with his fists and short-range weaponry. Against him, these guys are novices.

Just a little longer.

Khal steps forward. "It's called a vTalis reset. Onboards do it in the case of a S-jacking. You guys didn't S-jack this thing, did you?"

The gangster and the pilot look at each other and back at us. The gangster's face looks like a volcano ready to blow.

"Let's trade for the Helix and end this discussion!" the gangster roars. "Show us the Helix. Now!"

I reach into my coat and pull it out. The pilot seizes it. She puts down her pistol, licks her finger, rubs the stone.

More stone spit. Disgusting.

She examines the Helix with both hands and intense concentration. Khal seizes the moment and leaps into action, kicking her and punching the other female.

I rush the gangster and punch him, but he hardly budges. He steps back, raises his pistol, and pulls the trigger. Nothing happens. He stares at the gun before looking up at me.

The comm on my arm vibrates. Four SEGs.

"Always check your morphing lock," I say, just before I elbow him in the face, kick him, and rip the weapon away from him. I apply the correct grip to the gun to remove the morphing lock.

I turn. The pilot seizes her pistol and turns toward me. I pull the trigger on what had been the gangster's weapon, and a laser beam hits the pilot in the chest.

Khal shoots the female behind him, turns, and drops another. The gangster and the remaining female stare at us. A normal race would step away, but Kanvarians are cruel. When their blood boils, it is nearly impossible to calm them.

The gangster bends down and starts to reach for another weapon.

"Don't do it, big man," I shout. "Don't do it."

The gangster's hand closes on the micro cannon on the ground. I pull the trigger and drop him. The laser tears a hole in his chest.

The final female steps toward Khal, her eyes aflame. I've seen that look before, and it never ends well.

"You don't have to stay here and die," I say.

Ignoring me, she steps behind the Shivyuns to access a weapon but trips and falls. I look at the Shivyuns. They pull back their feet and squeal innocently.

She grabs for a weapon, and Khal blasts a laser through her chest.

I breathe deeply and look around. Only one Kanvarian female clings to life.

"Well done, my friends," I tell the Shivyuns in their language as I walk toward the Kanvarian survivor. She tries to speak. I point my pistol at her and lean forward.

"They will find you." She gropes for the pistol on the ground.

I grit my teeth and smile. "They always do."

"They ..." She fumbles again and grips the pistol. "They will hunt you down."

"I hope the cosmos finds us," I say, and pull the trigger.

CHAPTER TWO

Spaceport L32 orbiting Oxylium, the third moon of Perdupeo
The comm on my arm vibrates. Three SEGs. Time to go.

I push the dead Kanvarian female off the console controls. Nasty creatures. Her limp body thumps on the floor. Green plasma covers the console.

We need to get this remer out of dock. "User Zero One, I am your pilot."

"What is your name?" the onboard queries.

"I am Kyvar Astilius."

No response.

"I am Kyvar Astilius," I repeat, louder.

"Are you my captain?" The onboard's voice is male, metallic and unemotional in its tone.

I always wanted to be a captain. "Yes, I am your captain."

"You're not a captain," Khal whispers.

"I am now. User Zero One, you need a name. How about *Resilience*?"

"That is the name of the vessel."

"You are the vessel. You need a real name and personality. Your name is *Resilience*."

"I like that name," the onboard responds.

I pause. *Did the onboard say that?* Onboards generally don't exhibit emotions, because—well, because they're electronic onboards.

A cabin droid scoots past me and starts cleaning the consoles. Nice touch.

The comm on my arm vibrates. Two SEGs.

"Kyvar, I think I can override the systems." Khal fumbles with his relays.

"No need. *Resilience*, get us out of here. Head to Perdupeo and then turn us toward Oxylium. I will tell you when to face the moon."

"Ion Drives engaged," *Resilience* responds.

A low hum fills the cabin. Ah, the sweet sound of Ion Drives. I've missed it.

"Airlocks released and lift enabled."

I hear the locks reducing. The pressure release makes my ears pop.

The *Resilience* pushes away from the L32 Space Station and heads toward Perdupeo.

I touch my comm on my arm, opening an audio-only feed with the *Impetus*.

"Axton—you're late. We stole a remer."

"A remer?" Axton asks.

"Just get here. The countdown is close." I flick off the line.

I step over to the Shivyuns. "Don't worry, my comrades." I reach down toward the dead Kanvarian and find a lock release for the Shivyuns' chains. "We will get you home."

The male Shivyun stands up. "We are your servants."

"Servants? No. You are friends, and we will get you home."

The male bows, and the female Shivyun stands and follows his lead. I shake their hands as friends, not as their master. In their dogged way, they bow again and focus on their consoles.

Another bot shows up to help the cabin droid with the mess. *How many bots are there?*

"Captain Kyvar, where are we going?" *Resilience* asks.

Captain Kyvar. Sounds a bit corsair, but I like it. Our vector is now well clear of the station. "*Resilience*, set a course for Oxylium."

The comm on my arm vibrates. One SEGs.

"What do you think of Captain Kyvar?" I ask everyone.

The Shivyuns beep.

"I feel the same way. Khal, what do you think?"

"Not the time," Khal says. "We need shields. I'm having trouble with them."

"Captain, are we going to ram the moon?" *Resilience* asks.

I shake my head. "*Resilience*, hold your course."

"Yes, Captain," *Resilience* responds. The blood-red moon centers itself on the screen.

Khal fumbles with the relays.

"*Resilience*, give Khal control of engineering."

Engineering controls rise out of Khal's consoles. "Manual engineering controls engaged, or would you prefer the Holox controls?" the onboard asks.

"Umm, yes, absolutely the Holox, yes." Khal's eyes go wide with surprise and excitement.

The manual controls fold down, and an advanced Holox control system extends itself around his workstation. I see Khal only through projections of the engineering platforms and control relays.

"I have arrived," he beams, swiveling his chair and manipulating virtual control decks.

I move over to the pilot seat. Fortunately there's no blood on it. The seat is unbelievably comfortable. It must be legumna hide. The upgrades in this thing are unreal. They are everywhere, from the titanium frame to the Holox controls.

A droid approaches and offers a glass that contains a dark liquid. I sniff it. Distilled Avantium Mineral Spirit. I take it and down it. I've needed this drink since the restaurant. The droid bows its round blue head and scoots off.

"At some point, *Resilience*, you need to tell me about all these droids."

"There are eight in total. Four servant droids, a military—"

"Not now."

The comm on my arm vibrates. Zero SEGs.

The Shivyuns start to beep and moan. They key frantically on their sensor screens.

Resilience processes their readings. "Captain, the Shivyuns are detecting activity on the moon."

I turn to the Shivyuns. "Friends, you will want to turn down your visors and look away for a few SEGs."

They respond with moans.

"*Resilience*, what is the most valuable object in the cosmos?"

"The nine-sided Helix," *Resilience* replies instantly.

"Everyone knows this," I say. "What is the second most valuable object?"

"The eight-sided diamond Helix," *Resilience* answers.

"What makes it so special?" I ask.

"It's the second hardest object in the galaxy," Khal adds.

"It has no melting point," *Resilience* states, "making it one of only three items in the universe without one. It has survived the eons in its original form. The originator of our—"

"Tell me, *Resilience*, would Helix stones survive a cataclysm?"

Oxylium grows in proportion as we grow near.

"Yes," *Resilience* responds. "Even a supernova cannot destroy the stones."

"I hope so," Khal murmurs. "Kyvar, I still can't get the shields up."

I phrase my words as a command. "*Resilience*, raise the shields."

"Why?" *Resilience* responds.

"Do it!" I demand. "And do not question my orders again."

"Shields raised."

Invisible shields stretch before us. The only indicator is a flashing light on the bottom left of the screen. "Push them all toward the front, all facing the moon."

The Shivyuns flinch as if struck by an object. Such intuitive creatures.

Flashes blossom on the moon's surface.

"Sensors indicate a disturbance on the moon," *Resilience* reports. "It appears detonations are going off on the surface, potentially volcanic in nature."

Flareups ripple along the length of the moon's cavernous rift.

"Sensors detect explosions at the drone mine and along the Contravenes Lava River," *Resilience* continues.

"I know."

"You know?" *Resilience* asks.

"*Resilience*, quit asking questions, or I am going to shut you down."

"Yes, Captain."

The Shivyuns turn their heads as if they've been hit again. They squeak and moan.

"Fire has detonated a series of other mines below the river," *Resilience* states. "The fire river is collapsing into the gas caverns. I am measuring earthquakes and volcanic rifts of seismic proportions. The crust is rupturing."

Shuttles scramble from the surface. The few Caman officers on the moon are attempting to flee. A spacelift crumbles, pulling down a hovering Caman drone mining cruiser. The cable is cut to keep the cruiser from descending into the maelstrom. The cruiser stabilizes and its engines fire as it attempts to escape.

Additional lava lines and volcanic explosions tear apart the fragile dwarf moon. Its primary volcano collapses into its own gas cavern.

The lava mixes with the explosive gases and detonates half the moon. The Shivyuns hide under their controls. The explosion fragments half the moon in the direction of the cruiser and L32 spaceport.

"*Resilience,* make sure all those shields are to the front. *All* of them."

"Yes, Captain."

The moon's shuttles disappear in the spray of fire, red sands, and black mantle rock. The cruiser and Spaceport L32 disintegrate in the blast of planet fragments, and all of the shuttles and spacecraft attached to the spaceport explode.

Our vector protects us from bearing the bulk of the detonation, but sideward projectiles come our way. Our shields take the brunt of the red debris with ease until the black mantle fragments fly toward us.

A massive black chunk of rock smashes into the shields. The vessel rocks from the shield impact. "Shields at seventy-seven percent. Seventy-six percent..." *Resilience* intones.

I grunt. "*Resilience,* tell me when we are down to fifty percent."

The pelting continues. A massive mantle block collides with the shields.

"Shields at fifty percent."

"Already?"

"I suggest we BURN out of here," Khal cries.

A shrill bang rocks the vessel and red collision lighting floods the cabin.

"*Resilience,* what was that?" I demand.

"We have a hull breach," *Resilience* answers.

"*Gunfrey* knows!" Khal yells. "The hull is compromised. The impact is in the bays. Securing them now!"

"Impossible," I declare. "Nothing can pierce Corian shields."

Well, not exactly *nothing*. Only repeated force will drop its ratings until it cannot hold.

Khal groans. "Something did. I'm sealing the bays and ending the leakage."

"Stabilizing atmospheric levels," *Resilience* announces.

"What percent are the shields holding?" I ask.

"Still at fifty percent."

No bearing on the shields? That doesn't make sense.

The red wash dissipates, clearing our view. "*Resilience*, track the charred mantle pieces and maneuver us through the particle fields."

Our Ion Drives roar over the pelting red sands as *Resilience* steers a safer route. The tracking of the mantle pieces displays on the screen. Most of them are in the direction of the spaceport and annihilated cruiser. Showers of red dirt harmlessly push away along the length of the shields. No mantle pieces are in our immediate vicinity.

The *Resilience* slowly presses forward through the space wreckage and particle field. Between masses of floating rocks, the remains of Oxylium appear. One entire side of the moon is no more. In its place is a rubble-filled void, a mass of asteroids, debris and wrecked space equipment. The mangled mass starts to rotate, searching for a new axis. Perdupeo's blue ambient glow shears through the belching orange fires on Oxylium's desecrated moonscape. The scorching heat from the moon's exposed core rages as red sands alight on its edges. Fissures cause burning land masses to separate and float off into space.

"The core ..." Khal's tone is one of utter astonishment.

Oxylium's core glows a molten bronze. Tongues of fire flicker along its length.

"Maybe it's true," Khal adds. "Maybe the cores truly reveal the original."

The original nova was the Cataclysm of Erupeo. The mass that populated the cosmos, when The Voice spoke and created millions of worlds for our exo-existence from just one moment, according to the legend.

I unconsciously reach for the talisman that hangs from my neck, separating the smooth obsidian from the chain. It appears to contain the same bronze swirl. I don't believe the legends, though I've begun to suspect I carry a relic of one. Maybe my father was right. I would ask him now if he was here. Alive.

"*Resilience*," I say.

"Yes, Captain."

"Can your sensors identify Helix stones?"

"Yes."

"Please identify."

The Shivyuns stand up and return to their sensors. Tiny Holox squares appear over thousands of pink and transparent Helix stones. The Shivyuns squeal as rivers of priceless stones float aimlessly before the brilliant blue and orange conflagration. The Cataclysm of Oxylium and its horde lay before us.

CHAPTER THREE

ORBIT OF PERDUPEO

I touch the comm on my arm. "Axton, did you see the show?"

The line crackles with Axton's reply from the *Impetus*. "Kyvar, we suffered damage."

"Damage? You were out of the blast zone."

The screen flickers. Axton's large Gundarian face is oddly granulated on the screen. Even as he mentions damage, Axton is calm. He is always calm, as a good med officer and master of weapon arrays must be.

"Captain, would you like me to display?" *Resilience* asks.

"Uh, sure." Normally this would take a command or an encryption key. *This onboard is good.*

Axton's big olive-green face and hazel eyes no longer appear distorted. "Our Aux engines are gone. The freighter bays were breached and are now untenable."

"Gunfrey!" Khal swears.

"You didn't have to blow the moon!" spits an angry voice. The feed adjusts to show Ayera, our communications officer, sitting beside Axton. Her human-like Hytilian face gleams with a bluish complexion. Gills on her neck flare, a mark of her stress. She scowls angrily at me.

"She's torqued," Khal whispers. "Whenever her skin changes to that color, you just know."

No kidding. I say nothing.

Ayera's glare deepens. "You didn't have to set explosives under the Contravenes—"

"Axton," Khal interrupts. "What's the damage to the Aux engines?"

"We believe we were hit by floaters."

Random floaters are just an excuse for bad pilots. "It couldn't have been floaters," I argue.

"It has to be," Axton replies. "Shields are still at one hundred percent."

What in the galaxies?

"And the engines?" Khal asks.

Axton fumbles with his screen. "Sending you the damage report. The solar infractor is shattered, the differential is in pieces, and the stabilizers are gone."

Resilience displays the damage report from the *Impetus*.

Khal stands up. "We can live with the solar board ruined. The differential will take some time, but how bad are the stabilizers?"

"Unusable," Axton replies.

The vessel will be limited to slow and careful flying without stabilizers. I never enjoy slow flying, much less being careful. The *Impetus* was already slow. No way we are making it home now.

"How about the shuttles? Can you help with the extraction?" I ask.

"We have one operable shuttle," Axton answers.

"Do you have any idea what you have done?" Ayera starts again. "Floaters or no floaters, we will be wanted by the cosmos for this incident. We must—"

"We were forced to do it," Khal says.

I look at Khal and frown. *Not really.*

Ayera's rant continues. "As the political and science officer, I cannot tell you the consequences of your presumption in detonating that moon. The Caman Corporation will restrain the CSX Corporation and keep vTalis support from coming to our aid. Most likely we will be under investigation for many leaps."

"She gets so wordy when she's angry," Khal whispers.

Ayera continues. "And the portentous presage notions of uncovering ancient cores. Please tell me the core isn't exposed." Her gills flare further, and her thick skin is getting hot. You can always tell by the color. She's pale when she's calm. She's far from pale now.

"It's not that bad," I lie.

"I hope you didn't rupture its core. You know what happens to those who rupture cores."

Ah, yes. The rest of the legend. *A lifetime of misfortune befalls those who disrupt cores.* Cataclysms are not reserved for the living. That role is reserved for those outside our dimension.

She knows we are lying. "You know the planetary council outlawed core digs and exposures. It's a heinous crime to the cosmos."

"I guess you will have to see for yourself—" Khal hopes to end the discussion.

I go to flick the comm off, but Axton interrupts. "What vessel are you on, anyway?"

I smile. "I told you. We stole a remer."

Axton smiles, his white teeth in contrast to his olive green, gray-spotted skin. "That's way beyond some first-class vessel. It looks like your father's ship."

"It's amazing." Khal extends his hands over the engineering panels. "Check out the upgrades."

My smile widens. "It even has the new starship smell."

Axton gives an admiring whistle. "Is that Holox, Khal?"

"*Everything* is Holox!" Khal exclaims.

"Even the weapons?" Axton's voice has shifted toward total disbelief.

I turn my head toward the empty co-pilot and weapons platform seat and nod. "Even the weapons platform."

Axton pumps a fist in the air. "Yes!"

"Children, let's get over your fascinations," Ayera intervenes. "Need I remind you that we are now wanted criminals of three syndicates for our actions?"

Yes, Mother. "No one knows that we did this, Ayera. We are two quadrants from any feed relays."

Ayera frowns. "They *will* find out."

"We'll discuss our plans when you get here." I turn off the feed and turn to Khal.

"She's furious." Khal stands up. "Flick me the recovery plans. I'll start gearing up."

"*Resilience*, set a countdown of half a leap. This is our allotment before we must be at the Perdupeo Gate."

"Countdown started." A series of spools and dials appear on the upper left of the screen.

"*Resilience*, map the most productive means to retrieve the Helix stones. We'll use the countdown to collect as many stones as possible."

The screen flashes as *Resilience* conducts the calculations and systematically plots the course of the extractions.

"Shivyuns," I say, "can you fly a shuttle?"

They both rise and pull off their visors. The hint of a smile shows below their beady eyes. Mining is a Shivyun's favorite thing. I wave a hand over them and declare, "Today, I commission you as space miners."

They beep and hum as they waddle off toward the shuttle bay.

Flashes of mathematic computations and formulas show on the screen.

"*Resilience*, work in the background."

The screen goes blank.

"*Resilience*, tell me about the crew of this ship."

"This vessel has eight droids: two service droids, a procedural droid, one in the weapons room, one in the engine room, one serving solely in the Ion Drive compartment, and one in the freighter bay. There is one in the armory that you might find of interest. His name is Xander."

"A military droid?" I ask.

"Yes, but more. He maintains the weapons and serves as the captain's bodyguard."

How awesome is that? I have a bodyguard. Xander's profile appears on the screen. Gray military armor covers his robotics, and an iron helmet covers his electric eyes. A lengthy list of armaments accompanies his photo to the right. I pull out my pad and peek at some of his skills: integrated personality chip, thirteen languages, strategy formulative design chips, upgraded Ion packs, internalized rocket launcher ...

Xander appears to be quite talented. I put the pad down. The entire list can wait until later. "*Resilience*, pull the feed to the freighter bays and the shuttle room."

Various parts of the vessel appear on the screen. In one section of the feed, the Shivyuns work to prepare the shuttles. In another, Khal is running around setting up the extraction routines. Eight other screens appear, showing the storage bays.

Bay One contains stacks of cases of Oxylium Ale, the expensive cosmic beverage with peculiar side effects. The Kanvarians had stolen this vessel loaded with a score of what is literally bottled truth serum.

"How many cases of Ale are in Bay One?" I ask.

"Ninety-six."

I sit back in my seat. Enough serum to produce truth for a year in a galaxy. What would happen if it we pumped it into the atmosphere of a planet, or maybe a biosphere?

Bay Two is empty. Soon it will be filled with crates of Helix stones. What a thought.

Oddly, Bays Three through Six have an obstructed view. "*Resilience*, what's in those bays?"

"Missiles."

"Um ... what kind, exactly?"

"Thirty-four Type 97.5 Ion Drive magnetic pulse general purpose warheads, eight Type 97.6 Ion Drive magnetic pulse engine seekers, four Type 97.7 Ion Drive anti-personnel warheads—"

"List them onscreen."

The warheads immediately appear on the screen. Sure enough, there are ninety-six total warheads.

This is no freighter. Someone has retrofitted this thing into a starfighter. My father would have freaked. A starfighter stolen from Kanvarians, who stole it themselves filled with Oxylium Ale. This thing is slick, fast and loaded.

"Do you want the plans for the recovery of the Helix stones?" *Resilience* interrupts my thoughts.

"Yes, please." I refocus and suppress my irritation at the onboard's intrusion.

Work orders display on the screen with micro-schedules of timelines and estimates for productivity. I touch my comm. "Shivyuns."

The Shivyuns beep in response.

"*Resilience* is sending the plans to you. Please proceed."

The screen feeds show the shuttles, and Xander as he walks into the second shuttle.

"*Resilience*, why is Xander going?"

"He is the most capable of our droids."

Remembering what I read, I suppose the onboard is right.

A soft chime alerts us to the approach of the *Impetus*. The screen displays the vessel. The soft lines of the intergalactic starship show great distress, and sear marks scar her underbelly.

"Open the line to the *Impetus*," I command.

Ayera and Axton appear onscreen.

"You guys look terrible."

Ayera sneers at me.

"Sorry. The *Impetus* looks terrible," I say by way of correction.

Axton answers. "Kyvar, the controls don't respond the same. We're hurting. Khal's got to work on her. Our old bird may not make it."

The *Impetus* got us to the farthest reaches of the universe. It's now in a sad state, with its damaged solar arrays, sear marks, and off-kilter alignment. She seems to sag to port as if she wants to sink beneath the waves.

"You've made a mess of the ship." Ayera scowls.

I shrug. "Oxylium was unstable."

Ayera narrows her eyes. "*You* are unstable. How many were on the moon?"

"What?"

"Who or what died in the blast?"

"The moon was mined by drones and there were only the handlers on the surface."

"How many on the cruiser and the station?"

I shrug my shoulders.

She narrows her eyes. "I hope it was worth it."

The Camans supply the arms to our enemy. Of course, it was worth it.

"Who did you steal the vessel from?" Axton asks.

"We stole it from some Kanvarians, who stole it from who knows who."

"I hate those guys." Axton shakes his head.

"Me, too," I agree.

Axton looks at Ayera and back at me. "Does the onboard know who they stole it from?"

"No. It did a vTalis reset."

"Are there any Kanvarians still alive?" Axton continues.

"Nope," I answer.

"Anyone else?"

"There are two Shivyuns and lots of droids," I respond.

"Great. Shivyuns never talk. They can hardly see, much less speak. Maybe they will tell you, but only you, because you know their language. You still can speak it, can't you?"

I nod. "I did get them to assist with the excavation. It's their shuttles you see."

"You have Shivyuns helping with the extraction?" Axton asks.

"Yes, and Khal is already out there with them."

Axton laughs. "Only you would recruit blind dwarf creatures to help with our excavation efforts." Axton releases his resistor belt and stands up. "Ayera and I will join you soon." The feed ceases.

I reach over and disconnect the Holox Pad from my console. "*Resilience*, find my personal files in the *Impetus* and relay them to this console."

"Your files have already been relayed," *Resilience* responds.

I almost drop my Pad. This onboard is good. *Too* good.

The Holox Pad illuminates, revealing the same formatting and settings from my last Gen Pad on the *Impetus*. I go to my encrypted orders from Admiral Astoye. The process pauses for a security scan of my retina, and the packets appear. I flick away the immaterial and open the packets labeled CONFIDENTIAL ORDERS.

Admiral Astoye's grizzled face appears onscreen. The recorded feed, from many leaps ago, starts with him glaring at me for a few mSEGs before he speaks. I wince. His large frame, solar burnt face, and thick, scarred neck always intimidate me. His many battle scars document his long history of defending our galaxy.

His recorded voice is as rough as his appearance.

"Kyvar, the Vidor are getting more aggressive. They've extended their siege lines to surround our entire galaxy. We will be subject to starvation without supplies. Relief is required, and you must find our allies out there.

"Here are your orders. Go to Asatyria and retrieve the Stellar Gates by any means necessary. Then you and the crew of the *Impetus* are to venture to vTalis and Trasilium. You are to petition for their relief of the siege, as your father did many times before you. Your name will carry weight in vTalis and Trasilium. Return via the Stellar Gates."

The feed ceases.

What an impossible plan. We are only a few rookies, a few leagues out of flight school. I mean, I'm good, but certainly the Admiral knows I am not my father.

Resilience displays the shuttles retrieving the Helix stones. I sit back and smile. At least we can now pay for the Stellar Gates. Only a cluster of eight stones is enough to buy the secret coordinates of the Stellar Gates.

"*Resilience*, calculate the net value of the Helix stones that we will recover."

The screen flickers as *Resilience* begins its calculations.

"Cancel that!" I shout.

"Yes, Captain."

I unconsciously rub my talisman, feeling the etched details. I don't need to know the value. I don't *want* to know. Sometimes it's best to remain in the dark.

CHAPTER FOUR

ORBIT OF PERDUPEO

The final shuttle arrives, and the side lift opens. Xander sits in the front seat, and Khal beams at me from among the numerous crates lining the shuttle's interior. Khal's eyes shine as he pulls back one of the lids. "Kyvar, we've fumbled onto more than just a horde."

Countless heaps of Helix stones glitter. I run my hand through the layers of eight-sided stones. Their pink iridescence shimmers against my fingers, and my heartbeat pounds in my ears at the sheen and intensity of the haul. Mesmerized, I want to stare longer and ponder again the potential net worth of the stones, yet I shake loose even the thought of it.

Khal's eyes gleam with the reflection of obscene wealth.

"Close it," I order. "Come on. We're running tight on time."

He closes the lid. I grab the case and head toward Bay Two.

"I see how it works, Captain." Khal says. "Hurry away with your billion illirium."

I turn around and walk backwards. "What's a billion illirium?"

He ignores me. "Xander, this is how you carry it." Khal picks up a singular trunk of Helix stones.

Xander emerges from the other side of the shuttle holding two stacked trunks.

We approach the cargo bays. "Ever imagine a billion illirium to be so light?" Khal asks.

I smile and lower my container. Khal strains as he sets his down, while Xander lowers his with little effort.

I rub my hands together to brush away the particle dust. Khal does the same and Xander watches, then mimics us.

"You're a funny creature," I say.

Xander turns toward me. "I am a droid made for your protection."

I laugh and start back toward the shuttle. "I never ordered you, nor do we need your protection. But we welcome you as part of the crew."

Khal follows. "Come along, Xander. You are one of us now."

"I do not understand." The droid trails behind us.

"You will," I say.

"You will understand our ways in time," Khal adds.

Xander rounds to the other side of the shuttle.

"You know he has a personality chip," I whisper to Khal outside the droid's range.

Khal whispers back, "I figured he did. He went through shutdown with the vTalis reset."

I nod and pick up another crate. I peer through the shuttle and see the droid on the other side. "Xander, we consider you one of the crew. You aren't a slave or servant. You are equal to us."

"I am a protection droid," he responds mechanically. "It is my programming."

"Lighten up," Khal speaks casually. "You're one of us."

"I am not one of you."

"Of course not," I clarify. "Neither is Ayera or Axton, but you are one of *us*. One of our group."

We continue the banter until we complete unloading the stones. Service bots arrive and continue the process of inventorying the stones, allowing us to head back toward the bridge down the port gangway.

As we walk, I ponder the oddity of Xander, our psychologically stubborn combat synthetic. His reputed military skills and fighting ability seem to be surpassed only by his perplexity with his crew members. There's something else odd about him, too, something I can't yet put my finger on.

Ayera approaches us. She's smiling, yet I frown. She's been irritated with us endlessly during the recovery. Hytilians have their strengths and weaknesses. In her case, they are one and the same. The Hytilian's powerful emotional makeup makes her both the crew's conscience *and* advocate.

"Thanks for the new jewelry." She stops in front of us next to the bridge bay window. She is cool again. Her white teeth reflect the amber light of the fiery spinning core. She is quite pale, and her gills are invisible. I could almost mistake her for human.

"What is it?" I ask, caught off guard by her mood swing, though thankful it is now positive.

"You know how The Voice works?" Ayera asks.

I frown.

"What?" I don't believe in the legends.

She is unperturbed. "The Voice works all things for good." She opens her hands to expose a fragment of obsidian. "It's a piece of the core."

"I thought the old legend says, 'cursed is anyone who participates in destroying worlds?' "

"Ayera, after all you put us through ..." Khal moans.

"We're already cursed." She smiles innocently. "The scientist in me couldn't help herself."

The rock is surprisingly weighty. "It's heavy."

She laughs. "It's solid core. It has the heaviest density of all solids."

A fiery swirl appears solidified within the confines of the hardened rock. "It looks like the molten fire was frozen in place."

"Cryo-coolant will do that," Khal says. "It's instantaneous."

"Now compare it to the talisman around your neck," Ayera says.

I pull out my talisman and hold it beside Ayera's rock. They are identical.

She smiles again. "I always told you it was a part of a core. Do you know what this means?"

"No ..."

"It means your father destroyed a planet too."

"My father?"

She grins, walking past us to the shuttle bay. "Yes, Kyvar. He gave you that talisman, didn't he?"

Khal laughs. "Destroyer of worlds. It runs in your family."

I frown. Father seems to have had more secrets than I knew. He never told me the talisman was a core sample.

Khal and I continue to the bridge and take our seats next to the Shivyuns. On the screen, the highlighted Helix stones number far fewer now. The bulk that remains is clustered in the solid core of the moon, which remains like a giant asteroid. The oblong shape of Oxylium will eventually cause it to lose orbit. Solar winds will push it out into space, or it will drift into nearby Perdupeo's gravity field and crash.

We wait until the last of the shuttles arrive on the *Impetus*.

"*Resilience*, set a course at 8 BURN for the Perdupeo Gate." The Ion Drives ignite as we turn away into deep space.

I stare out between the floating mantle rocks and wrecked space equipment at Oxylium's exposed core. The flame and flicker of the molten core draws my attention like a bonfire at night or perhaps the eyes of a woman. The fiery core leaps in geysers of flame through the mantle fissures. A mantle section breaks off and floats away. Other dismembered pieces fall into the core, instantly vaporizing.

I hold my talisman. *What where you doing, Father? Why did you give me a core sample?* Mining of cores was outlawed by the planetary council ages ago. The curse of the cosmos is upon us. *Were you cursed, Father? And did you pass the curse to me?*

The *Resilience* turns away, and the brilliant orange conflagration gives way to the deep darkness of space. I breathe deeply as the Ion Drives fire, and we head away from the raging inferno.

CHAPTER FIVE

DEEP SPACE—34TH QUADRANT

The silk sands of the Bay of Qantac fold under my feet. The heat from Stella 312 warms my neck and shoulders. The gentle lapping of the sea fills my ears and floods my heart.

I surrender to the tireless rolling waters. Nothing can disturb my inner peace as I advance along the beach onto an obsidian and basalt pier. I let my feet dangle in the cool waters. This is where I go to get away from it all and hide where no one can find me. I could sit here for hours under the heat, listening to the waves and staring into the emerald bay.

A sleek, shimmering fish floats in the depths. Its bright colors— sharp blue and silver with two dots of radiant yellow just behind its eyes—glow as it feeds on the bottom. After it feeds, it moves on in a peculiar corkscrew motion.

I hear a sound behind me. There's nothing as far as I can see to the tall trees looming at the beach's termination. The only sounds are those of the sea, distant birds, and echoes from the cosmos high above.

Above the planet's surface and just beyond its horizon, orange Nilius looms with its triple rings. The cold dead moon gleams in Stella 312's luminescence. High above the moon, starships and frontier activities range. My heart does not yearn like it normally does for the galaxies. Instead, I am pulled by the simplicity of the fish. A simple life in the smooth waters. The simple life I left long ago.

"My son."

I did hear something. I turn to face my father and acknowledge him with a smile as he sits next to me.

"Sometimes," I say, looking out into the sea, "I come here to get away from it all."

His large suntanned face beams at me through a tightly trimmed, black and gray beard. "I prefer it here as well."

"What are you doing here?"

He ignores my question. "The locals call him the meanderer because of the way he swims." He points to the fish. "See how he goes from side to side."

I refuse to look. I've looked enough at the fish. "Father? How did you get here?"

His smile only grows. "The fish does this because its eyes are always trained forward, causing him to lack peripheral vision. Thus, he swims in a twisting motion."

The fish swims in a corkscrew formation as it turns right and left, watching its surroundings. I wonder what point Father is trying to make.

He continues. "When the fish is outside his normal habitat, he swims like this. When he returns to the safety of his sea cave, he swims straight again. Outside his normal habitat, he understands that enemies await him."

I laugh. "I come here to hide from it all, and you come here to tell me about a fish." I laugh again. "Am I the fish?"

He looks away, laughs loudly, and adds his typical sense of humor. "And you are out of water."

I smile. "Dad ..." I look up at Nilius.

"My son. You will make unexpected friends, but out here, you must watch out for enemies, like our friend the meanderer here. They are—"

Nilius starts to pulse and flash. I open my eyes and the moon's orange reflection turns into a strobing light.

The voice of *Resilience* surprises me out of sleep. "Captain."

"Yes," I mumble.

"Sensors detect Kanvarian starfighters at the Tpoint."

"How long do we have?"

"Two SEGs. The *Impetus* is three SEGs behind us."

I grope for my uniform and struggle to get into it. "*Resilience*, I just had the strangest dream."

"According to my understanding, dreams come from the frontal lobe of the human brain that invites processing when the brain is at rest."

I run my fingers through my hair. "I think I just spoke with my father."

No response.

"*Resilience*, do you ever dream?"

"Onboards are subject to neutral processing inside their neural mappings that are caused by overlap with personality chips at low settings. This low setting processing impacts even—"

"Kyvar!" Khal yells. "Kanvarians are waiting on us at the Tpoint."

I rush to the bridge and my seat. Khal takes his seat. Three more seats remain empty. We need more crew.

I look to the Shivyuns. "Shivyuns, my friends, are you well?"

The mole-like creatures nod their heads as they focus on their instrument panels.

The swirling wormhole projects a bluish hue through the screen. Periodic white flashes pulse between swirls.

A bridge bot brings me a distilled spirit.

"Why, thank you." It responds with a few beeps and a bow and departs.

"Khal, remember when we stole my father's trainer and escaped?"

He laughs. "When you threw up in his seat?"

"No. You threw up when I yanked the stick at 5 BURN." I laugh. "What did they always say at the academy?"

"Never turn over 5 BURN," Khal answers.

"The flight mantra of mantras. 'Never turn over 5 BURN.' *Resilience*, give me the helm."

Instantly, the instrument panels slide to the sides, and the onboard flight system controls rise and push into my lap. I stare at the polished chrome levers, padded sensors, and ignition light triggers. They shine as though no one has ever touched them. No time to ask that question. *Resilience* won't remember anyway.

I breathe deeply and lower my hands toward the controls. I remember an old veteran starfighter who told us at academy to *never touch the controls too quickly*. I've never forgotten it. My left hand hovers over the steering column, while my right hand hangs near the Hammer, starfighter slang for the ship's throttle. Just below my fingertips, the power pulls and strains like a war stallion, battle-armored and ready to charge on my command.

Between the pulsating white flashes, the wormhole is fading. "Approaching the Tpoint," *Resilience* announces.

"*Resilience*, display our adversary."

Two Kanvarian starfighters appear on the screen. Their profiles and statistics display to the right. The first starfighter is a Kanvarian F36c *Sluggards Plenty* Class, capable of 10 BURN and armed with missiles, space charges and lasers. A worthy adversary by itself, much less with the accompanying armed freighter Kanvarian C12b, also a *Sluggards Bounty* Class. The freighter carries a variety of missiles and lasers.

I cringe and touch the side consoles. "*Resilience*, you might lose that new starship paint job after this one."

"Kyvar, these guys are heavies," Khal says.

"I know."

Okay, Resilience, let's see what you're made of. I close my eyes and grasp the controls. The swirl terminates in a thinning mist. We discharge from the wormhole like a surfer on the last stretch of a wave, and the *Resilience* floats as we drift into space.

The Kanvarians hail us. I ignore them as I drop the Hammer to 8 BURN.

The Ion Drives aren't subtle this time. A rumbling fire rages deep within the ship, throwing us back into our seats. My face melts into my headrest, until the stabilizer light shines on my console. I pull my head forward and log a mental note to wait for the stabilizer light before dropping the Hammer next time. *Never do that again.*

The Kanvarians continue to hail us.

"*Resilience*, open the line."

A large Kanvarian glares at us with his small eyes and growls, "Identify yourself."

"I am Kyvar Astilius of the *Resilience*. Who are you?"

"The *Resilience* is a Kanvarian vessel," he snarls through the comm. "Surrender the vessel and the Ale that you stole, or we will open fire."

"*You* stole the Ale, just like you stole the *Resilience*. You S-jacked this vessel. This is a Cobalt vTalis class freighter, not a Kanvarian craft."

"Give us the Ale!" he screams.

"Don't push it," Khal whispers.

"Surrender, or we will destroy you!" The Kanvarian's face turns a strange green.

"I will give you your Ale if you tell me where you got this ship." His face turns into a grimace. "Surrender or die!"

"Who did you steal this ship from?" I shout.

The line goes dead and weapons-lock red lighting flashes from the back of the cabin.

"Captain, missiles incoming. Four of them."

The Shivyuns squeal as if we have already been hit.

I fumble with the relays. We have the range, yet the first missile slams into our rear shields and heaves us forward. My back and neck ache from the lurch. I grit my teeth and pop my neck.

"Shields at eighty-five percent," *Resilience* announces.

Time to go manual. I press the side button on the Hammer and pull it out with my right hand, then slow the *Resilience* to 5 BURN and yank the vessel right.

"Release mags," I shout.

Magnetic alternating gravity shells—mags for short—spray from the hull. The second and third missiles explode upon impact with the mags. Shrapnel rocks the ship just as the fourth missile slams the shields.

"Shields are at sixty-nine percent."

I moan. "Come on!" I scream. "Khal, work on recharging the shields."

"I'm on it," he yells. "But get us out of here."

Both Kanvarian vessels close in, ripping with cannons and lasers.

"*Resilience*, engage them with the lasers." I need a weapons officer. Empty seats are everywhere. For once, I wish Shivyuns used weapons.

The shrill sound of our lasers whine over the grating sound of Kanvarian lasers spraying off our shields. They are too close for missiles.

"Shields at fifty-five percent."

I must outrun them and get away—somewhere, anywhere. I turn the *Resilience* multiple times, but the raking continues. I pull the Hammer up, level out, look for the stabilizer light, and drop the Hammer to the floor. The *Resilience* tears away. 7 BURN, 8 BURN, 9 BURN, and finally 10 BURN.

Then we continue accelerating past 10 BURN.

"*Resilience*, what's going on?"

"We can achieve 12 BURN if you like," *Resilience* answers.

"12 BURN?" I ask. "Seriously?"

"Yes."

"Do it." We scream away. I expect missiles, but they don't come. "*Resilience*, display the Kanvarians."

The screen reveals the Kanvarians have been temporarily distracted by the *Impetus* emerging from the wormhole. The *Impetus* blasts away but struggles as they turn on her. I picture my friends fighting for their lives as I watch the explosions and their shields sustaining damage.

I yank the Hammer hard left, and my vision blurs as the rest of my body goes into immediate sensory overload.

"Kyvar, what are you—"

My lungs stop working. Dizziness overtakes me, and my surroundings fade to gray. As if the vessel is aware of the problem, *Resilience* slows to 5 BURN to complete the turn. Once the turn is done, my nervous system rights itself, and I can function again. I can hear Khal screaming.

"*Gunfrey*, Kyvar. Never turn above 5 BURN. You almost blinded us." He's not joking this time.

"The human body cannot withstand turns above 5 BURN," *Resilience* announces. "I corrected your course before you lost consciousness."

"Thank you," I mumble.

The *Resilience* heads back toward the conflict. One Kanvarian vessel is damaged, with its shields nearly gone. The *Impetus* is disengaging. The two Kanvarians vessels are angling toward her to finish her off.

"The *Impetus's* shields are down," *Resilience* declares. "Their hull is breached."

"*Resilience*, target the damaged Kanvarian and take out its shields with lasers. Target its bridge with missiles."

Lasers rip at the wounded Kanvarian vessel. Our cargo bay, converted into a missile repository, rolls out a deadly cylindrical tube. The rocket tube extends fins and ignites an Ion Rocket Booster. The missile smashes into the Kanvarian vessel, ripping into its bridge and detonating its forward cabin.

The larger Kanvarian vessel turns away from the *Impetus*. Immediately, lasers grate and cannons rumble against our shields.

We pull away from the scene, but not too far.

"Shields at forty-five percent, forty percent ..."

I drop the Hammer to 5 BURN. The Ion Dives roar. The grating continues as the Kanvarian trails us.

"*Resilience*. Fire lasers and keep them busy."

Three-second shrill laser bursts continue through the sound of the grating on our shields.

"*Resilience*, analyze their shields."

"Their shields are all to the front."

"*Resilience*, can you reset a missile to voice-activated control?"

"Yes."

"Do it, and then tell me when you are set. Target their Ion Drives."

I shake off their fire with more magnetic chaff, but their lasers continue chipping away at the shields.

"Ready?" I ask *Resilience*.

"Ready."

I dip the *Resilience* and scream. "Release!"

The missile releases and I pull up and drop the Hammer to 8 BURN. The missile harmlessly drops below the Kanvarian starfighter and receives its targeting. It extends its fins. The feed on the screen shows from the warhead.

"Fire!"

The Ion Rocket drive ignites its nanofuels, sending the missile directly into the shieldless rear of the freighter. The missile explodes and cripples the Kanvarian freighter.

"Sensors show their back is broken and their engines are destroyed."

I slow the vessel and turn to rescue the *Impetus*. "Axton, everyone okay?"

Axton appears on the screen. His forehead is bleeding. "Kyvar, the hull was breached, but it's now sealed. The engines are gone. We are hopeless out here." Sadness colors his words. "I am afraid we can't save her."

I stare at the *Impetus*, the brave vessel which got us to this remote place, with her Hytilian lines and powerful engines. Her fate is sealed, but she will die with honor.

"Captain, shall I prep a shuttle?" *Resilience* asks.

"Yes."

"Kyvar," Khal says, "I'll go. I'll get the stuff we left behind."

Moments later, the shuttle pulls away and docks at the *Impetus*. I know that it's with sadness the crew is boarding the shuttle to come here. And Khal will make sure nothing valuable is left behind.

When the shuttle eventually returns, Axton steps onto the bridge. His face carries grief.

"I'm sorry, Axton."

He hangs his head. He loves the *Impetus* like the rest of us, probably more.

"Join me." I point to the seat adjoining mine as Khal comes onto the bridge.

Axton sits and immediately recognizes the luxury afforded in the *Resilience*. It's not consolation, but he does smile. "Well, at least these aren't bad accommodations."

Ayera sits in the Science Officer's seat behind the Shivyuns. "This is quite nice. Quite fitting."

"Agreed, my friends." Khal smiles.

"Welcome to the *Resilience*." I look solemnly at Axton. "Ax, you know what must be done?"

Axton nods, and I gesture toward the screen where the shell of the *Impetus* floats, waiting. "The duty—and the honor—are yours."

"*Resilience*." Axton's voice is emotionless. "Fire."

"My programming prohibits firing upon a friendly vessel," *Resilience* says.

I shake my head, walk over to the weapons console, and set the bearings. I back away and nod to Axton.

Ax breathes deeply and operates the laser fire control. Lasers leap from our undercarriage mounts and tear apart the *Impetus* from stem to stern. When the laser hits the reactor, it explodes, and the *Impetus* is no more.

A silence fills the cabin as we cruise away, past the disabled Kanvarian starfighter.

The screen flickers. "Captain, the Kanvarian crew is suffering. Their reactor is leaking noxious Ion gases."

The worst fears for any star pilot are being trapped in space or being exposed to reactor meltdowns.

"Have mercy on them," Ayera cries.

"Agreed," I mutter, oddly sympathetic towards the Kanvarians that tried to kill us.

The *Resilience* rocks from the recoil of two cannon blasts. The first blast tears through the enemy ship's cabin and the second ripples the aft deck against itself. The leaked reactor gases ignite in a fireball.

I did not issue an order to fire.

Aloud, I ask, "*Resilience*? Was that a cannon blast?"

"Yes."

"Were you directly ordered to fire on that ship?"

Silence.

I decide not to push it for the moment. Instead, I ask about the weapons.

"When were you going to tell me this vessel has cannon upgrades?"

"When you asked."

"At some point," I say, "we are going to restore that memory of yours."

CHAPTER SIX

DEEP SPACE—33RD QUADRANT

The Shivyuns beep and moan.

"A Caman Corporation Cruiser approaches," *Resilience* interprets.

The right side of the screen displays the profile of a Caman S3 Cruiser. The cruiser is sleek and fast, with a max speed of 12 BURN. It carries standard weaponry and a crew of seventeen.

I raise the Hammer to 8 BURN.

The Camans took longer than I expected. They must be losing their edge. We are well ahead of the last Gate. Any suspicions about our involvement in Oxylium should be nullified by our distance from the wormhole.

The screen flickers.

"Display," I order.

A Caman officer appears on the screen. He stands stiffly and wears the standard orange and cerulean uniform. His face shows irritation. No one really wants to go to Oxylium.

"Hail, vTalis CSX Freighter, I am Captain Morellis of the *Excellence*. Our feed shows you are the *Resilience*."

"I am Captain Kyvar Astilius of the *Resilience*. We are returning from delivering cargo to Spaceport L32 at Oxylium."

"You come from Oxylium?" Morellis asks.

"Business as usual. Nothing out of the ordinary." I try my best fake vTalis all-business accent. "As long as you don't threaten your life on the cheapie or on the surface of the inferno, it's just another long-haul, high-paying delivery run."

"What did you deliver?"

"Tetirus Gas."

He frowns. The fact the CSX Corporation has the monopoly on Tetirus Gas has annoyed the Camans for ages. The Captain looks back at one of his men. He apparently wants to confirm CSX trades Tetirus Gas as far away as Oxylium. He receives an apparent confirmation and turns back toward us.

"We have lost contact with our installation at Oxylium and Spaceport L32. Did a meteor shower or solar interference occur when you were there?"

"No." I look away as if I am thinking of something. "There were a few flickers on the scopes when we were approaching the Gate, but we made nothing of it."

"Very well. Thank you for informing us. It's probably just interference."

"Safe travels, Caman friends."

The cruiser travels past us, and the comm line fades out.

"He's going to be furious," Khal whispers.

"Especially when he finds the stones missing." The thought makes me smile as a droid moves up to offer me a distilled Antillean Elixir.

"Thank you, er, sir." I like this droid. He bows, beeps, and rolls away.

"*Resilience*. Set a course for the Embra Gate and Asatyria. 12 BURN."

"Yes, Captain."

"Also, before we hit the Embra Gate, make sure the bays are cloaked. No one needs to know what we carry. Make it look like Tetirus Gas."

Should have done that earlier.

"Approaching the Tpoint," *Resilience* announces.

The blue wormhole swirl thins.

"I've been doing some research," Ayera looks up from her Holox Pad. "I've learned more about the Asatruans. I think Khal's suspicions are true."

"They are?" Khal asks. He sounds shocked.

"Most of the feeds state the Asatruans were once human. They may have come from a generation vessel ages ago, and over the eons they have engineered the survival of their species."

Interesting. Maybe we'll find out more during our trip. The *Resilience* exits the Embra Gate. The Ion Drives light up, and the familiar hum fills the bridge.

"Entering the Embra Galaxy," *Resilience* says.

The Embra Galaxy spreads before us. The galaxy is wide and flat with a spherical rise in the center. As we enter the galactic edges of their system, in a BURN toward the system's center, we lose sight of the galaxy's shape, and we capture our first glimpses of Asatyria. It rides at orbit four planets from the Embra system's only star. Swirling yellow and blue clouds appear to cover the planet, with pulsating effervescent light gleaming outward.

We press through the first atmospheric level of Asatyria. *Resilience* registers the change. "We have entered the oxygen biosphere. Adjusting biometrics and refreshing the onboard oxygen tanks."

The right of the screen displays Asatyria. The sensors dissect its many planetary biospheres and artificial atmospheres. A plot of our course shows on the screen through the atmospheric layers.

The next layer, a blue creamy substance, flows over the vessel as we enter it. "We are entering the temperature-controlled biosphere. Biometrics adjusted accordingly."

A blue tint takes over, shrouding everything in azure light. Floating islands start to appear, connected with bio-cables into the next layer.

"We are entering the final layer, the controlled gravity biosphere."

Lighting returns to normal, and the blue tint disappears.

Khal points to Asatyria. "What a tiny world."

"It's considered a dwarf planet," Ayera says.

Despite its micro-size, or due to it, atmospheric layers extend the livable territories of their planet tenfold. Biospheres and iceberg-shaped floating islands surround us, connected only by biometric cables which glow with energy currents. Other floating islands extend along the bio-cabling to the extent of the first biodome.

"Millions live on the planetary extensions," Ayera continues. "The inhabitable surface holds only a small portion of their population."

Magnetic auleon chutes carry inhabitants to and from the planet and the floating islands.

The crystal-shaped Asatruan library comes into view. "*Resilience*. Park it in the gold zone."

"Access is denied to the gold zone," *Resilience* responds.

I smile. "Trust me. Park there."

We cruise pass the standard landing zone and hover over the golden platform reserved for dignitaries, presidents of corporations, and official viziers.

The screen flickers.

"Display," I say.

An annoyed female Asatruan stares at us. She is young for an Asatruan, yet she carries the same enlarged head and thinning hair.

"CSX Freighter *Resilience*, you do not have permission to land at the premium platforms."

"We come with payment," I declare.

"Our scans reveal no preauthorization."

"How about Helix stones?" I ask.

There is a pause while she stares at us.

She looks down at her controls. "Our scans reveal no Helix stones onboard."

I touch my comm and pull out a singular Helix stone and raise it high. "Try again."

She looks down and back up and gives me a dazzling smile.

"*Resilience*, permission granted to land." Her voice is much kinder this time. "A premium shuttle will arrive shortly."

We land next to ambassadorial shuttles and diplomatic craft. As we prepare to leave, one of the droids arrives with a tightly wrapped eight-fold Helix cluster. I slowly put the cluster in my pocket and tap it. "Eight million illirium goes right here."

Khal smiles. "Enough to buy a small galaxy. A very small galaxy, but a galaxy nevertheless."

Ayera, Khal, Axton and I exit the *Resilience*. Xander must stay for obvious reasons.

"I would feel better with a blaster." Khal remarks.

"You know they are pacifists," Ayera says. "Their ethereal science religion prevents them from shedding blood."

Khal frowns. "Yes, I'm aware of their distaste for violence, and I also know the average age of an Asatruan is one hundred and sixty years old. We went through all this the last time we came here."

I laugh. "When they rejected us for *not* having Helix stones."

Ayera eyes me. "And you expect them to just *give* us the Hgate secrets?"

"Of course."

Ayera rolls her eyes, then grows thoughtful. "That's what I don't understand. They used to be less interested in such things. Their revelations and discoveries have changed the galaxies. It was the Asatruans who published the cosmos's complete mapping of the JUMP Gates. What do they call them?" She looks off, trying to remember the moniker.

I look at Khal. He shakes his head.

Ayera snaps her fingers and continues. "The Jasper Upstream Mapping Protocols. That's what they named them. To date, they've published three hundred thirty-nine of them."

Khal frowns at her. "Yes, but the newer Hgates, the invisible ones—they only give those away for a price."

"And we need *those* Hgate mappings to lift the siege," I say.

We sit down on a bench and wait for the shuttle. Chutes and lateral bio-pulse lines surge with energy.

"They say each time the pulse comes, the Asatruans have another revelation," Ayera's tone is factual, with a tinge of nerd, or possibly sarcasm.

"I don't doubt it. These guys are science freaks," I say.

She rolls her eyes at me again.

"Sorry. I meant science geniuses."

She frowns.

A shuttle arrives and the door slides open for us to step onto its platform. Soft indirect lighting, silver lining, and plush lagumna hide benches welcome us. Inside, a lean, elderly Asatruan smiles at us. His white teeth shine through a polished humanlike face. His swollen head is typical of the race whose brains have enlarged to accommodate endless amounts of data. His hair is sparse, revealing his stretched cranium.

"Greetings, adventurers. I am the chief librarian here at Asatyria. You may call me Ustande."

CHAPTER SEVEN

Asatyria

After a short flight, Ustande steps out of the shuttle. He seems to float while he walks. His polished cheeks gleam. Even his scanty hair doesn't move despite the stellar winds, and the stretched cranium underneath seems to twitch at unpredictable intervals.

"Come this way." His accent is unusual, as though he has been stuck in space for too long. His consonants drag out and his pronunciation is odd.

He leads us to the edge of the platform that floats far above the library. The edge separates itself from the platform and drops down to a holodeck. The glass-walled holodeck is empty except for a few instrument panels on the walls and an instrument console in the center. The floor has a translucent glass sheen except for a circular transparent area near the center console.

Pulsating lights strobe into the holodeck. Ustande walks to the center instrument panel and pulls out two energy lines from the console. The energy lines pulsate in his hands. "Do you prefer to travel by light or as energy?"

Oh no. Absolutely not.

Khal beats me to it. "Ustande, we prefer to travel as humans."

Ustande smiles methodically. "As first-class visitors, you are entitled to travel as we do."

I start to walk back to the lift and Ustande follows. "We prefer to keep our mitochondria intact," I say.

"I am living proof that your DNA will remain intact," he says, stuttering. "It is perfectly safe."

Sure, it is. I am not willing to risk my life for some thrill ride with an old, tampered human. Even Ayera, lover of science, would agree. "We prefer the old-fashioned way."

Ustande turns his head. He doesn't understand us.

"We prefer it the *human* way," I insist.

"Ah." He nods. "I understand."

We walk back to the lift and our shuttle. The shuttle maneuvers around the bionic lift cords until we arrive at the cylindrical library shuttle bay. As we walk into the library, the transparency and brilliant light of the hall is a marvelous sight. Ayera gazes in all directions, taking in the wonders of the structure, and Ustande engages her curiosity.

"Our ultimate goal is to be the repository of all of the knowledge in the cosmos. We are converting this knowledge into energy. Our present goal is to evolve data into a transferable form. Your DNA can absorb energy, but not data. Your mind comprehends and learns data, but energy—" He laughs and shakes his head. "Energy can be absorbed, and knowledge is the natural result. Learning is instantaneous. A pulse of energy can be your next transpondence."

Natural? There is nothing natural about this. *Transpondence?*

Ayera steps forward. "You cannot absorb energy without impacting the rest of your DNA."

"Yes, you can." Ustande appears shocked.

"The transpondence must be treated like any other ..."

I zone out the science talk. I look at Khal. He carries the same disgusted look.

We are suspicious of tampering with the human body. Bioengineering was outlawed in our galaxy long ago. Life forms should remain as such—life forms. Tampering with life takes away life. Unfortunately, the rest of the cosmos doesn't abide by our suspicions.

Khal points toward one of the endless rows of sieves where a diplomat examines an energy catalog. Where data cards exist in our libraries, here endless iridescent light cartridges pulse, begging for retrieval.

Ustande is drawn by our attention. "The dignitary is on a search for knowledge like the rest of you."

The dignitary pulls a cartridge.

"Watch how he pulls the knowledge and places it in a sieved repository." The dignitary inserts the cartridge and energy shoots a neon transfer the length of the structure through a nanotube. "When he leaves, he will receive an energy transfer. The knowledge now becomes part of his DNA."

I grimace.

Tampering with DNA leads to the loss of originality. Identity is lost, and slowly the heart wanders from its origins and the soul becomes corrupt. It is no wonder this race now requires payment for their technology.

Ustande leads us to a podium where he stands as if he has stood there a thousand times. "Welcome to the Library of Asatyria." His tone seems rehearsed, like we haven't talked before.

Khal, looking to my left, stares dumbfounded. I turn my head. Another dozen podiums have a man standing at each of them. Each of them looks exactly like Ustande.

I turn to Ustande. "You're a *clone*."

"I am the Librarian of Asatyria."

I hate clones, especially unexpected ones, and would love to use my fist to introduce a different kind of data into his DNA.

"I understand you have come to retrieve data on Jump points."

"That is why *we* came," I snarl.

"Data can be provided for a fee."

I stare at him, wondering what I should do. *Never deal with a clone, right?*

"The cost is one Helix per JUMP," he intones.

"Are we sure we want to do this?" Ayera asks.

I look to Khal. He is equally clueless. *I don't know. Do you deal with a clone?* I've never done so, but now we must. That's why we came—to retrieve the JUMP Gates, to relieve the siege.

I reluctantly pull one Helix stone from my pocket and put it on the podium.

Ustande stares at me, ignoring the Helix. He puts his hand out, palm facing me. He closes his eyes as though he is trying to read me. My head balloons from the inside, enlarging uncontrollably, tilting toward Ustande. I grasp at the memory of a friend who told me how to beat this feeling. He advised that I should think of what I wanted them to see.

I quickly remember something ... star racing back in the day. My mind drifts to star racing and my many championships. I smile, super-confident, until my mind drifts to my disaster at Serius. My head pulls back, and Ustande opens his eyes.

"You have brought a Helix to pay for JUMP coordinates and you have a star race on your mind. You want the coordinates to beat Castor Rilius?"

It worked. At least I think it did.

Ayera laughs. "I think Axton and I will check out the library— the data section only."

"You were thinking of Serius at *this* moment?" Khal asks.

Ustande laughs aloud. His ancient facial lines don't move as he laughs. *Creepy.*

Another Asatruan glides up to the right of Ustande. "Adventurers, welcome to Asatyria." He is dressed in a silver robe with multiple silk cape lines stretching behind him for ten steps. The robe shines with sparkles of light woven through the lining. He is clearly someone of influence.

He stares at me as though he knows me. His eyes are large with veins around the pupils, and they look through me as if through water.

"My name is Ackbray," he says running his hands through the sparse hair crowning his head. "I am the keeper of the knowledge of these systems."

"Are you a clone as well?" Khal asks.

"No, but I enjoyed your reaction to Ustande. Your disgust of our culture is quite obvious."

His face forms a smile, but the smile does not reach his eyes, and no lines contour his pale cheeks. His face is only a stiff countenance with white teeth. He picks up the Helix stone, peers at it, and nods his head. "One Helix stone for a new coordinate?"

"We are looking for more than just one coordinate," I declare.

He smiles again. "Of course, you are good for it. This I know." He starts to turn around. "Let us go to the JUMP repository."

We walk with Ackbray down a glass corridor.

"For a cluster, you may have a galactic mapping," he says.

I smile. "That is why we are here."

"Looking at your records, we see that you visited not long ago and asked about the Hydrogen Gates. You were refused."

"Correct."

"You still desire them?"

"We do," Khal says and then he gets snarky. "I remember once that the Asatruans were more interested in knowledge and sharing with the galaxies than selling their secrets."

Ackbray stops in the corridor near a window. He turns toward us and looks through me again, making me want to turn around to see who he's looking at. But I don't.

His head has a peculiar twitch. "Where did you come by your stones?" he asks.

I smile. "We have come by a collection of them."

He looks out the window of the corridor. High above the transfer lines, the *Resilience* rests upon a platform.

"A collection?" he asks.

"Yes. A collection."

A vein on his forehead stands out as another facial muscle twitches. "The heat signature of your starfighter reveals you came from deep space around Oxylium."

Impossible. No one can detect and track heat signatures.

He smiles and starts to walk again. "I have heard Oxylium was ignited from within. The only thing that remains of the moon is a cratered asteroid, with most of its Helix stones missing."

How does he know this? I tighten my jaw to show no emotion.

"Is that why you cloak the cabin bays of your freighter?" he says, with the faintest hint of a sneer.

Unbelievable.

"Come this way." He leads us into a domed room. As we enter, soft lighting fills the room. We stand together in the center. "What is it you desire?" Ackbray asks as the lights dim, making it harder to see.

"We desire information about your wormholes, specifically those leading to our home galaxy."

He holds out his deathly white hand, palm up. I pull out the diamond Helix cluster and hand it to him.

"What is your infatuation with the Helix?" I ask.

He smiles. "Our fascination lies in its secrets."

"What secrets?"

"We believe the stones have the power to unlock the secrets of the universe."

"What secrets of the universe?"

He stares at me a moment and then artfully changes the subject.

"Let us see what the stellar winds have for you." He raises his hands and pulls them down. The interstellar mapping follows the motions of his right hand. Planetary and system nebulas come down into the room. Stellar systems and nebulous colors illuminate different corners.

"Want to see the wormholes?" he asks.

"Yes," Khal and I say in unison.

He snaps his fingers and thin, nearly transparent lines of wormholes appear in the galactic mapping.

My eyes widen.

The different colors show what appear to be different types of wormholes with lines designating their start and positions, with coordinates and elemental settings to open and close the Gates.

"We are looking for wormholes measuring back to Hytilium, Sardis and our Home Nebula."

"I believe the stellar winds blow there as well."

I don't fully understand his terminology, but I follow his hand motions.

He stretches his hand. He pulls on the cosmos, which moves from right to left until we are almost disoriented.

Shivyia, vTalis, Phaelon, Navaria, Gaxi, Trasilium ... quadrant after quadrant races past. Dizziness is overtaking me, whirling my thoughts.

Hundreds of galaxies and a thousand worlds pass before us. The lights blur, until the planets become dots and shadows. My head begins to swell again. I look left and see a flash of light around Ackbray. His eyes are closed now, and his hand is out, palm up. *Oh, no.*

I look at Khal. He's out on the ground.

My mind pulls toward Ackbray. My arms aren't responding. Some part of me moves in mid-air toward him. This is no game with the clone librarian. I cannot think of anything on my own. I want to close my eyes, but I know better. I must keep my eyes open. It's difficult.

I look up at the stellar systems. The whirl of motion has stopped on my home system. Lines glow across the seams, and I believe I see what we came for. My mind is pulled, puffed, and I cannot concentrate. Images begin to form behind my eyelids. I blink and blink, until I lose the strength to open my eyes again.

CHAPTER EIGHT

ASATYRIA

My mother's gentle face turns toward me. She puts her hand on mine and smiles. "We tell you these things because we want you to pick yourself up every time you fall down."

"I understand," I say, with a little humility.

"I know you will." She removes her hand.

My father looks at me. His large face beams. "Son, I see it in your eyes. You have that Astilius spirit. Once you learn how to funnel your energies, you will do great things."

"Father, I hope I can achieve half of what you've done."

"No, Son." He shakes his head. "You will greatly exceed me in all things."

My father's face fades out into a bright inland scene. I now stand on the rocky banks of an iridescent blue-green lake. Tall trees rise behind me. A gentle breeze kisses the shore.

My six-year-old sister plays in the water.

"Come on, Brother. Get in." She splashes me.

I step into the water and splash her. She runs and jumps on her raft and starts to paddle away.

I swim and splash her. She paddles away again.

"You can't catch me."

I swim under her raft, pick her up, and dump her in the water. I swim away and regain my footing, yet I don't hear my sister scrambling out of the water.

She is struggling with a salligataur which has seized her arm and has pulled her underwater.

I grab her leg and pull. The creature refuses to let go. I put my two fists together and slam the head of the salligataur. The creature releases her arm and flees, stunned. I yank my sister out of the water. She coughs and catches her breath.

I hold her tight. "Are you okay?"

She nods her head.

"Your arm?" I grab her arm and look at it. She's bleeding, but nothing major. The young salligataur swims away.

My sister is shaking. I look her in the eyes. "Look at me."

She looks up. Her eyes are wild with fear.

"I will never let anything happen to you."

The waters blur and swirl into the blackness of space. Stars replace the sparkle of the water and darkness permeates everything. White stellar dots populate the background, and neon flashing lights reflect upon my glass.

I sit at the helm of a single-engine Ion starfighter. I edge it downward, and a monstrous purple planet comes into view. An entire fleet of enemy warships is headed in the direction of the planet.

My comm crackles. "Kyvar, we have scrambled their sensors and they don't see us. Remember, our targets are the five transports. Ignore the three destroyers."

I look to the right and left. I am one of six starfighters.

"Everyone take out one transport," I shout.

I pull out the Hammer and extract it. Going manual.

"Everyone mark your targets through the comm."

The targeting screen displays our targets and angle of attack. I drop the Hammer to 5 BURN and tear ahead of the other starfighters.

My lasers blast through the thin hull of the first transport. Its hull is torn through and ruptures as I scream past. Another transport explodes, and cannons and lasers flash around me. One of our starfighters detonates. Cannon bursts flare around me. I yank on the Hammer left and right and reverse course.

A transport explodes. I target another one with lasers and its cabin disintigrates. Two more of our starfighters are hit with cannons. Missiles destroy another two of our fighters.

I rage past the enemy fleet. One transport remains, and the three destroyers target me. Lasers and cannon fire flash around me. Three missiles are incoming.

I have no chance. I drop the Hammer to 6 BURN and veer until I complete a turn. The missiles overshoot me. I target the final transport. I roll the starfighter to evade the cannon fire and blast away until it explodes.

The lights dim, and the star systems fade away, revealing our virtual training room. My entire class stares at me. I look at the other five stations. No one else is at their station.

"How did you evade the lasers?" a student asks.

"And the missiles?" another inquires.

I smile. "It's simple. The system is—"

Master Praetor walks between me and the class. "Kyvar knows you cannot turn over 5 BURN. Yet he does it in my classroom."

"Fighters can handle it. It's the pilots that cannot."

A loud singular laughter fills the classroom. Its sound seems to originate from outside the classroom, yet it doesn't seem to interrupt anyone.

"You broke the rules," Praetor declares. "You know the simulator has limitations to enemy fire at 5 BURN, yet you know the governor was not installed in our starfighters for this simulation."

"Then why does the application allow for turns over 5 BURN?" I look to the class. "I succeeded in the mission! No one has ever completed this mission. I have, on this very day!"

Praetor glares at me. He walks closely to me. "Kyvar, look me in the eyes."

I look at the teacher.

He removes an external lens from his left eye. I had no idea he wore an external contact lens. A milky dead left pupil shows in the place of his perfectly brown left pupil before.

"Kyvar. Never turn over 5 BURN."

The classroom morphs into the vibrant scene of the tropical planet of Mrunal. The deep shades of the room have been replaced with moss-covered walls and green vegetation. I hand my father a military case. "This is the last of it, Father."

"Thanks."

My sister runs by. She is carrying her bags.

"I will miss this place," Mother mutters between tears.

"Sister!" I shout. "What's the rush, we have three days?"

"Son. We must be prepared in case the Vidor come early. They aren't your normal enemy. They are ruthless, they consume entire worlds. We have to leave early and not play it close."

"Yes, Father."

I look at our home and can't believe we cannot find a way to keep it. Mother's tearful eyes are too much. I walk to her and hold her tight. My sister and father join us.

A thunderous boom nearly knocks us off our feet. I stumble and step out of the house and look up, with Father right behind me. The swirl of a wormhole is opening above the planet's atmosphere.

"We have to get to the transports!" my father screams, something he rarely does. "Run!"

We run to the machine tracks and board our speed waver. Father has never gone this fast. We nearly fall off as he slams the hyper-brakes when we arrive at the transports. The enemy ships swirl above us. Solar laser platforms splash light upon the assembling Vidor fleet. Starfighters soar into the atmosphere to confront them, to give the transports time to lift off. The ground shakes from blasts from battle cruisers and artillery barges.

My father hustles us to the nearest shuttle with its engines rumbling, prepared for launch. The sliding gate is up. Mother is the first in, and Sister follows.

"Son. You must know something."

"Yes, Father."

"It's in our DNA to save our race. It is who we are. Today, I must stay to fight."

"No, Father. I'm coming."

"You need to see to your mother and sister."

"No, Father."

"There is no time to argue." He casts a quick look over his shoulder at the wormhole, and then turns back to look straight at me. "No matter what happens, we will survive and persist, and all must go on." He steps back. "Today is my victory, my son. Tomorrow's fight belongs to you."

He hits the sliding gate release, and the gate slams shut between us.

I reach for the release button and the manual overrides, but the Ion Drives immediately lift the transport. I slam the manual override with my fist.

"Land this thing!" I scream. I hit the comm. "There is a mistake. We must land."

A voice comes over the comm. "I am under orders of General Astilius. No one disembarks."

I punch the override again, over and over.

"Kyvar," my mom pleads, and finally says, "Kyvar, that's enough." She puts her hand on my shoulder.

I kick the wall and look toward the window.

Today is my victory, my son. Tomorrow's fight belongs to you. *His last words echo in my mind as I stare out the transport window, an angry young starfighter-to-be and unwilling refugee in the escape from Mrunal. My father got us onto the transport but refused to let me go with him, and all I can do now is witness his skill—and hopefully his survival—with his vessel, the vTalis freighter* Resolute.

A stream of vessels follows our rescue ship, fleeing Mrunal, as the monstrous Vidor fleet forms out of a wormhole. Their multiple solar laser platforms waste no time extending and charging their arrays. Vidor fighters swarm in our direction.

"The fighters," a woman cries. "They are coming for us."

I see Father's ship and his battle squadron heading toward the rear of the Vidor fighters as more of the Vidor fleet exits the Hgate. Father's squadron targets the nearest laser platform, blasting it into thousands of brilliant shards. A Vidor destroyer takes note and focuses on our fighters. A missile impacts Father's vessel while the enemy's lasers tear away at the Resolute's *shields.*

Father's squadron targets another laser platform. I lose my line of sight when a rippling explosion annihilates the platform's panels. Many of our fighters vanish into and around the explosion. I lose sight of Father's ship again as more Vidor fighters surround the Resolute *and its squadron, until Father pulls away at what looks like 6 BURN. The Vidor fighters cannot keep up with him, but their battle fleet targets his vessel. Cannons explode around him. His shields must be gone by now.*

Father, get out!

He makes a wide sweep in the direction of the Vidor's final solar laser platform as it takes aim at the Capitol. I know he won't tear away until it is destroyed.

Father! Get out!

He completes his turn and heads for the platform, straight into the face of withering enemy fire.

The raging space battle fades. "That was the last time I saw my father ..." I mumble.

"If you would just open your eyes ..."

I am on my knees before Ackbray. He stares at me. *You creep.* How long was I in that place? *How dare he?* This time I might just tear apart his pretty plastic face and squeeze that nasty swollen brain of his.

I stand up to punch him, but stumble instead, and slump down to the floor, held up by a wall at my back.

Ackbray laughs. "So eager. Stay there. Your strength will return in one SEG."

"You wretched creature," Khal cries out. I look at Khal. We could take him together quite easily if I wasn't in such a state.

Ackbray looks at me. "Your race has such a fascinating capacity for pain. This capacity must be what pushes your limits and creates a stubbornness of character." He looks away trying to find the words. "Your value for life is the persistence of your survival. That is what impresses me."

Khal tries to get up, but he stumbles as well.

Ackbray squats in front of me. "You are so much like him."

"Who?"

He just stares at me, his forehead twitching.

Whatever.

He smiles. "Your race will push its limits. You could reinvent yourselves, but you do not. You just improve what you have. You break new capacities of endurance almost daily." He looks away. "Remarkable, quite remarkable."

I feel enough strength to stand. Khal is moving upward as well.

"May this help you." Ackbray points above him. Sardis, Hytilium and the Home Nebula are above us.

My thoughts of brutalizing this creature disappear. I rise to my feet. It's been a long time since I've been home. Even the Nebula Isles are there. Valerie waits on me back home. I miss her. Numerous JUMP points and relay lines show from distant galaxies as expected. Everything and more than we needed. I gape. Maybe I won't squeeze his nasty brain after all.

Ackbray smiles, stretching his seamless face. He raises his hand, and the stars, planets, and nebulae fold themselves into a solid drive. "This should be all you need." He hands me the drive.

He walks as he instructs us. There is an increase in his pace, as if he wants to hurry before he changes his mind.

"The Hydrogen Gates, the Hgates, are open for only five sections. They are the most common and will get you where you need to go."

"How do they work?"

"The Hydrogen JUMPs require an activator. Pump elemental hydrogen concentrations into the location of the JUMP zone or Tpoint and the Gate will appear."

"Are there other types of Gates?" I ask.

"We did provide three Lithium Gates in your mapping. The problem with Lithium Gates is that they are only open for one section. They close before you can complete the JUMP. If you miss the termination of the JUMP, everyone will perish, or at least we believe so."

"How do you know?"

He stares at me. I know that look.

"There is one ION Gate," Ackbray continued. "The Gate will open up for twenty sections, but you never want to take the ION Gate. No one has ever survived an ION JUMP."

I don't ask this time.

"You must hurry. We have provided more than you need for your journey to be successful." He looks at me with an unusual compassion. "I am sorry about your father."

How dare he?

"Now go. Understand there are great dangers on your journey. Speed is of the essence, and you will have constant pursuers across the galaxy."

I stare at him, nod, and mumble, "Thank you, Ackbray."

Khal and I walk away and find Axton and Ayera in the library sitting on a couch.

"Find anything good?" I ask.

"I did. Look." Ayera hands me three small datacards. "Axton found the compilation on wormholes and Helix stones, and I found the compilation on Oxylium Ale."

Khal laughs. "You got a compilation on Oxylium Ale?"

"I did," Ayera again responds. "I had to refuse the energy load, since I don't want them to install one of those wicked ports in the back of my head—like that guy." She points to a man walking by with a dataport in the back of his head.

"Ugh," Khal blurts.

"And guess what?" Ayera asks.

"What?" I ask.

"They charged me more for the data versions."

"Of course, they did."

CHAPTER NINE

ASATYRIA

"*Resilience*, get us out of here. Destination Shivyia."

The Shivyuns beep, moan, and softly squeal.

"Yes, my friends," I say in their language. "We are taking you home."

They make shrill excited sounds and lower their heads.

"Don't worry. It's for your protection."

The Ion Drives ignite with a familiar guttural churn that rumbles my stomach and makes me smile with anticipation. I plug Ackbray's drive into the port.

"*Resilience*, map these wormholes." Screens flicker as *Resilience* processes the new mapping. A list of fifty wormholes appears on the screen.

"That's a lot more than we paid for," Khal says, pleased.

"I know." I am only half-listening to him as I concentrate on the map.

The *Resilience* lifts above the platform and turns away from Asatyria.

"I can't believe you let him mind-melt you," Ayera says.

"Kyvar thought he would just think of something," Khal says.

"Like Serius?" Ayera laughs.

I grunt.

Axton turns to me. "He mind-melted you?"

I nod my head reluctantly.

The *Resilience* passes by floating islands and landing platforms. Pulsating lights flash through the bridge bay window.

"I heard it is very unpleasant," Axton says, "like your brain is getting pulled out of your skull."

"That's what it felt like to me," Khal says. "I had in mind to permanently remove that twitch from Ackbray's forehead until he gave us the mappings."

"I have a strange feeling we'll see him again," I utter.

Khal grunts. "I don't like your strange feelings."

"Me neither," Ayera says.

Resilience's voice interrupts our conversation. "Mapping complete."

I reposition in my seat. "*Resilience*, display the wormholes and routes from vTalis to Hytilium."

Please tell me this was worth it.

The screen flickers again with *Resilience*'s calculations, and we all watch in anticipation. Relief corridors with new wormhole mappings could help abate the Vidor's siege.

The screen populates with very favorable routes, and a sigh of relief fills the bridge.

Ayera speaks my thoughts. "This makes the trip out here worth it."

"And worthy of being mind-melted." Khal snickers.

"Not sure about that," I say, cringing at the visualization of my brain being sucked through my eye sockets.

I examine the routes. Multiple options allow for supplies to come in and out of Hytilium while bypassing the Kurkursh Asteroid Belt and battle lines.

"Oxylium Ale on me!" Khal says.

"I might just take you on up on that, but first let's see how we get home. *Resilience*, calculate our routes home."

The relief routes disappear and the screen flickers as *Resilience* pushes through the biometric atmospheric layer. A blue hue fills the cabin.

"Mapping complete. I have calculated two routes," the onboard says. "The fastest option and the safest option."

"Display the fastest."

Instantly, the screen reveals two-dimensional interstellar mapping of the route home but processing the map in this format is far too difficult. "Fill the bridge in 3D."

The bridge lights and screens dim as the cabin fills with galaxies. Each galaxy has a faint gray line marking its borders.

A light red dotted line indicates the route. Tags and legends reveal timelines for each of the legs. The JUMPs have elemental concentrations below them. In the upper right of the bridge, a chart displays with detailed legs and timelines. The total time—twelve sections. "Way too fast!" I mumble.

I pull down on the first leg to magnify it.

Resilience provides commentary. "The first leg takes us from Asatyria to—"

"Understandable," I interrupt. "Asatyria to vTalis. Got it."

I extend my hand, pushing back on the first leg to the full view, and pull down on the second leg.

Resilience continues. "The second leg takes us from vTalis through the Phaelon and Navaria galaxies using the Sartav Hole."

"What?" Ayera says.

"That can't be what he provided," Khal says.

I push back the mapping. A dotted line goes from the Sartav black hole to the next leg. I pull back, expanding the third leg.

"No," I mutter.

Resilience provides details of the third leg. "The next JUMP arrives directly at the Demilitarized Galactic Zone of the colliding galaxies of Fraxinus and Gaxi."

"That's the worst place in the cosmos," I declare.

"It's an asteroid zone, and it's filled with unexploded magnetic mines. Only a fool would venture there," Axton says, and Khal nods in agreement.

I push back the map. Out of curiosity, I pull out the fourth leg.

Resilience concludes. "The fourth leg starts in Trasilium and goes through Vidor territory."

I can't help shouting. "Discard this mapping." *Absurd.*

"Maybe Ackbray wants to kill us," Khal says.

"I think he would have already done that," Axton dryly remarks.

My head is beginning to hurt.

"We don't even know if the Hgates work," Ayera says.

Khal throws up his arms in an exaggerated gesture of frustration. "Ayera, Hgates work," he says. "You know this."

"No. We *don't* know this."

"*Resilience.*" I speak a little louder than necessary, to forestall the impending argument between Ayera and Khal. "Display the safer route."

The room dims again, and the galactic mapping displays in the cabin. I look to the top right corner. Total time—seventy-eight sections. Far too slow.

"Does *Resilience* think we're immortal?" Khal quips.

Ayera laughs and replies, "Let's hope it's not too late."

I slouch in my seat and pull down different legs of the route. Each leg is safe. Even the galaxies and stops are boring, not even a good place to eat.

A droid approaches and extends a glass that contains a creamy dark red liquid. I sip it. Lugose Brew with jargos spice. I nod to the bot. Nice touch.

The droid bows its round blue head, beeps, and scoots off.

I watch as the *Resilience* pushes through the final Asatruan atmospheric layer.

"Accelerating to 8 BURN toward Shivyia," *Resilience* says.

"Make it 12 BURN."

"Yes, Captain."

I smile. *Captain.* I'm not sure if I will ever tire of that.

The Ion Drives roar as the *Resilience* hurls itself away from Asatyria.

The blackness of space seems to fill the cabin, and the crew falls silent. We have a long journey ahead of us. I pull my Holox Pad and play with the legs and segments, thinking of how to shave time off the journey. Maybe we can slip through the GMZ and JUMP around other hotspots?

"*Resilience*, display the other options."

To the right of the screen, a list of all of the routes display. The fastest is three times faster than all of the others, yet it's insanely dangerous. I slam the console with my fist.

"Think that helps?" Axton asks in his deep Gundarian voice.

"No." I frown. "What are you looking at?"

Axton smiles and shows me his Holox Pad. "I am reading about Oxylium Ale."

Khal laughs. "I am reading about wormholes, and you have a compilation on Oxylium Ale. Do share."

"*Resilience*, you've processed it." Axton says. "Display a summary of the work?"

Instantly, the screen is filled with a one-sheet review of the work. The data is extensive, but the uses of Oxylium Ale are highlighted and easy to find.

"Bring the uses closer," Khal says.

The section on *Uses of Oxylium Ale* come before us.

"'Entertainment.'" Khal chuckles as he reads. "'False Inebriation.'"

I laugh along with him. "That would have kept you out of trouble back in the day, Khal."

"Or get me into trouble," Khal retorts. "The third use is 'Truth Agent.'"

"*Resilience*, what makes the Ale a truth agent?" Ayera asks. *She's been listening. Really?*

Resilience answers. "According to the compilation, the chemicals in the crushed crystals, when dissolved, give the illusion of inebriation to the brain. In fact, it states in one study that one feels inebriated, yet their mind is quickened. Compounds inside the ale interact with the cortex in the human brain to cause natural decision making and speech."

"Natural decision making?" I say.

"I think it means they cannot lie," Khal says with a smug look.

I sit back further. A truth serum, then—and we have cases of it. I smile.

Khal continues. "Other uses are for medical purposes, brain cognitive improvements and improvements in neuro mental mappings."

"What are the impacts on non-humans?" I ask.

"Tests were only conducted on humans," *Resilience* answers. "No data is available."

"What about mind-melting?" Khal asks.

"There was one article suggesting mind-melting could be prevented by such serums."

"Really," I say.

Khal laughs. "You won't have to worry about thinking about Serius again."

I groan. I don't like even the memory of that memory.

The Shivyuns beep and moan. I turn toward them.

"The Shivyuns have detected a vessel following us," *Resilience* says. "It's an Asatruan Starship Model 5P."

The vessel shows on the screen with a rendering of its make and class. The Asatruan Model 5P is the latest in their class of starships. In the center of the warship is a rotating plasma core. Listed to the right are the standard statistics, yet in every category the results are unknown.

"It has followed us since we left Asatyria," *Resilience* adds.

"You think a clone is flying it?" Khal says. "Maybe Mr. Waxy Face?"

I laugh. "Let's not be totally obvious," I say, "but let's lose them in the Estrous Nebula ahead. *Resilience*, make your course through the Nebula."

The *Resilience* veers toward the Nebula.

"What about the Helix stones?" I turn around. "Khal, can you process the Helix stone compilation?"

He fumbles around and inserts the drive.

The screen flickers as *Resilience* processes the data and displays the uses of Helix stones on the right of the screen. The top four are highlighted and in red. Luxury goods, mining, wormhole Centennial research, and weapons development.

"Weapons development?" I ask.

We enter the Estrous Nebula, and strong tints of orange fill the cabin.

"*Resilience*, 5 BURN, please."

"Yes, Captain." The onboard pauses. "There is little data on the Helix weapons development, yet there is one military academy study."

The clouds of orange gases dissolve as we pass through them.

"There is an article written by a professor at the Military Academy of Exetrius regarding the destructive ability of Helix-tipped warheads upon capital ships, atmospheres and shields. He concluded his article with the following comment: 'One may never know the true military effectiveness of this rare and exhaustible gift to the cosmos. No one would dare tip a warhead with a million illirium.'"

What if a galaxy's survival depended on it?

The Shivyuns beep.

"Captain, sensors indicate two starfighters in this sector," *Resilience* declares.

"What?"

"On the opposite side of the Nebula, sensors reveal two Kanvarian craft. CR052 Class."

Their image and data display. Two-seaters. Max Speed 10 BURN. Missiles and lasers. Not what I wanted to see.

A break in the clouds reveals Estrous. The lifeless purple star floats where a living stellar once controlled its own galaxy. A swirling host of asteroids and planets orbit around the inert mass. A few droid ships can be seen salvaging stones and claiming residual gases.

"*Resilience*, give me the helm."

Instantly, the controls of the vessel are before me.

I lower my hands toward the controls and feel the power beckoning me. I put my left hand to the relay and my right to the Hammer.

A sudden warmth spreads through my body. It feels like home.

CHAPTER TEN

Estrous Nebula

I smile, studying my adversary. Cheaply built starfighters always sacrifice defense and maneuverability for weaponry. As I consider their slow max BURN and their weak shields, my smile turns wicked.

"*Resilience*, prepare a current overhead."

The screen flickers and the upper left corner reveals a sensor-created overhead view of the Estrous system, reflecting its dead sun, its stellar objects, and the closing starfighters.

I breathe deeply and push the Hammer to 5 BURN, the max speed for turning and firing missiles. The screen fills with an orange wash as the *Resilience* ranges through more gaseous vapors. The clouds thicken and eventually the hue dissipates. A dark blue moon passes our left side as the screen shows targeting data for the starfighters.

"*Resilience*, raise shields."

A crimson light blinks on the bottom left of the screen. "Shields activated."

To my right, Axton smiles as he preps his station to convert into a Holox weapons platform. "I'm ready." He slides down his Holox weapons helmet over his face.

"Hold on. I don't want to alarm our friends yet."

He lifts off his helmet, muttering. "You're no fun."

"Just go manual for now. I'll tell you when." Looking at Khal, I say, "Oversee engineering."

"I'm on it."

"Shivyuns," I call out. "Let me know if you sense anything."

They nod and beep.

"Ayera and *Resilience*, make sure I don't do anything stupid."

"Like turn over 5 BURN?" Khal adds.

"Yes. Like that," I mutter.

"You turned over 5 BURN?" Ayera asks.

I ignore her. The starfighters continue to close.

The Shivyuns moan and beep.

"Captain, the Shivyuns detect the Asatruan starship just outside our sensors."

The overhead reveals the starship at the extreme edge of the system. This is getting complicated. Why is an Asatruan vessel following us? I would prefer not to have cutting-edge Model 5P roaming around, especially one with advanced plasma systems.

I bank the *Resilience* in a tight turn around the deceased star in the center of the nebula. A purple plume drifts out of the surface of the star.

The screen flickers. "Open the comm."

A large Kanvarian male appears on the screen. He has the same looks of the gangster from Spaceport L32—the same black hair, unshaven appearance, and clothing. His shoulders are enormous. I can't imagine how Kanvarians fit in those starfighters.

"Hail." His accent is thick.

I slow further and increase the vector of the turn. A feed displays the Kanvarian fighters' approach.

"Hail," I reply. I can play dumb for a while. Ayera will tell me it seems to come naturally anyway.

"Identify yourself." His accent is execrable.

I smile. "We are a freighter from vTalis. Your feed will show we are the *Resilience*, and I am Captain Kyvar Astilius."

"But you're not a captain," Khal whispers.

"Not the time," Ayera hisses, motioning Khal back with a fierce hand gesture.

The Kanvarian's face turns into a scowl. "You are not the captain of *that* vessel. We command you to halt!"

I hear Ayera stifle a chuckle.

Best to keep playing dumb. "Why?" I ask.

He seems to loom larger in the screen, like his shoulders are getting bigger. I still can't believe these guys fit in those little starfighters. I think one of their smaller but meaner females would be better suited for flying the vessel.

As if on cue, a new feed of a scowling Kanvarian female in the other starfighter appears on the screen. I cringe. Though she looks more comfortable in the starfighter, I am taken aback by her ruffled brow and protruding teeth.

"Our captain commanded that very vessel!" she snarls. "Surrender, or we will engage *you*." She draws out her syllables for effect and it works. I cringe again, not out of fear, but her appearance. I think I prefer the huge male.

The starfighters fall in behind us. Red laser lock lights flash in the rear of the bridge.

"What are you doing? This is a vTalis freighter. Turn off your weapons!" I slow the *Resilience*.

The male snarls at me. "We know that you stole that vessel and you have stolen our Oxylium Ale."

I try my innocent look. "I am not aware of any Oxylium Ale."

"We have recovered the remains of our crews from the 34th Quadrant," the female rages. "You engaged them. The captain was my sister," she shouts. Veins protrude from her neck.

I quickly recall the captain's face from Spaceport L32. I see the resemblance in my mind and then I remember Khal's blaster. "My condolences."

"Give us our Ale!" the male bellows.

His screaming shakes me away from any compassion I might have felt. "See, that's the problem ..."

"What's the problem?" the two Kanvarians shout in unison.

I tighten the turn, shortening the vector again. The red lights stop flashing as the starfighters struggle to keep up.

"The problem is—"

I look at Khal. He is smiling.

"The problem is—"

"—we drank it!" Khal and I shout at the same time.

I kill the feed.

"You children!" Ayera scolds.

I ignore her and turn to Axton. "*Now!*"

Axton angles the cannons and lasers and fires at the nearest starfighter. The three-mSEG bursts of lasers tear away at their shields. The *Resilience* rocks from the cannons' recoil.

Axton converts his station into a Holox weapons platform.

The virtual swivel control deck wraps around him, even while he continues firing on the starfighters.

I drop the Hammer to 2 BURN and tear toward the dead sun. We disappear into the purple gases.

The screen targeting data reveals the blasted starfighters' shields are at twenty percent.

I straighten the helm as we burst out of the purple mist. The starfighters veer for another pass. Before they can obtain lock, I drop the Hammer to 10 BURN.

We range through the center of the nebula between gaseous purple plumes and orange clouds. We approach the nearest planet—Selerium, a blue gas plum. I raise the Hammer to 1 BURN and begin a tight orbit of the planet.

We enter a large orange cloud and I slow the *Resilience* further, waiting just inside the fringes of the cloud bank. "Axton, target them when they emerge."

The starfighters emerge into the clearing and sear past us. They are flying by sight only, ignoring their instruments. *Novices.*

Axton fires and again the ship recoils from cannon blasts. Flashes erupt around the two starfighters, and they peel off.

I drop the Hammer to 5 BURN and complete the orbit of Selerium. The Kanvarians come back around for another pass, so I drop the Hammer to 10 BURN and scream back toward Estrous.

The starfighters struggle to keep us on visuals through the gaseous vapor clouds. I slow the *Resilience* and begin an orbit of Estrous. We have the distance on the starfighters, but we need a little more before we exit this system.

The overhead shows the starfighters orbiting the far side of the star at 4.5 BURN.

"*Resilience*, let's see what you can do," I think aloud.

"What?" Axton asks.

I ignore him, extract the Hammer, and pull it close. I notch the Hammer down to 5.1 BURN. I watch the stabilizer light start to flicker. Stabilizers always lose traction above 5 BURN, causing the weight of spatial forces to flow through the Hammer.

The stabilizer light turns off and stays off. I grip the Hammer with all my strength. I can feel weightlessness in my chest, a tightening in my core, and a burning sensation in my throat. I drop the Hammer to 5.2 BURN and literally feel the Ion Drive's fire in my hands. The vessel starts to rattle, and the Hammer takes the brunt. My ribs are compressing my chest with the violent vibrations. I grit my teeth and squeeze. My left hand gradually grows numb.

Axton stares at me. "I don't want to die today. I think we have them. What are you doing?"

"Kyvar!" Ayera shouts.

Both my hands grow numb and my head is fuzzy. I shove the Hammer back to 5 BURN. The stabilizer light turns on and I breathe deeply. Feeling returns to my fingers, and my chest returns to normal.

Axton stares at me and my health readings. "I trust you will explain yourself later."

I breathe deeply and nod. I know better. It's not required, and these guys are already beat. But I want to, I *have* to! I want to slam my fist into my console, but I can hardly feel it.

We continue the tight turn around Estrous. I see the end of the orbit and I level out the *Resilience* in a sharp swift move.

The Shivyuns squeal.

I drop the Hammer to 12 BURN and melt into my seat as the Ion Drives scream to full capacity. I see the stabilizer light is off, and I suddenly understand.

The ship didn't complete the orbit around Estrous. We were still turning when I went to 12 BURN.

My face is morphing through the back of my head. I try to pull my chest forward to no avail.

The stabilizer light remains off.

"Correcting the cabin stabilizers," *Resilience* announces.

I manage to look over at Axton. His face is peeled back to his seat. He looks like he is having trouble breathing.

"Stabilizers corrected."

The stabilizer light winks on. I sit up in my seat and breathe deeply. The pain in my chest starts to subside.

Axton sits up in his seat. "Kyvar, you didn't let the stabilizers settle after your turn."

"You almost killed us," Ayera protests.

"That was a rush!" Khal adds.

"I thought it a bit of a thrill myself," I say with a sheepish grin. It's only a partial truth, but they don't need to know that.

"Not funny, Kyvar," Ayera yells, one hand on her neck. "I

could have gone without the whiplash."

Axton frowns at me. *Oh, great ... here comes more instruction.*

"Next time," he says, "wait for the mSEG for the stabilizers to settle. Never turn over 5 BURN and wait on turns before you drop the Hammer."

I nod. That was stupid, stupid indeed. I let the spatial forces go to my head.

"*Resilience*, set a course for the Narrus Space Gate," I say. "We'll lose them in the Gate. No one would be foolish enough to start a shooting war inside the vTalis Neutral Zone."

"Yes, Captain."

The starfighters round Estrous. Red lights again flash to the rear of the bridge.

"Six missiles are away, two at extreme range." *Resilience* displays a feed of the missiles. The screen shows their trajectory. No need to evade them. The extreme range is enough defense.

"Axton, deal with them." I grab my Holox Pad and relax in my seat.

I watch passively as the first two missiles close. Axton releases magnetic flak which collapses itself upon the first missile. The missile's warhead detonates, assuming it has struck its target. The second missile collides into the fireball and also detonates.

"Two down." Axton is satisfied with himself.

"Target the next two with lasers and cannons."

Axton starts with lasers. The light beams tear into the first rocket and it veers off, leaking fluids until it explodes. The second rocket is hit repeatedly, yet it explodes close enough to hit the shields. The *Resilience* shakes in the pressure wave.

"Shields at ninety-six percent."

The final two missiles burn out and fall limp. I can't imagine the harm in two more pieces of unexploded ordnance floating aimlessly in the galaxies.

"Axton, try some target practice."

He nods and tries to hit the fading missiles, but to no avail.

"Can I give it a go?" Khal asks.

"Sure." Axton gets out of his seat and Khal slides into his Holox weapons system. Khal goes wild with cannon fire and hits nothing.

Axton laughs. "Khal doesn't have game."

Khal returns the laugh as he gets out of the seat. "Never did."

"May I try?" *Resilience* asks.

Onboards aren't supposed to speak out of turn.

"Sure," I answer.

The ship recoils from a single cannon blast and both missiles explode.

Silence fills the bridge and Khal breaks it. "Outgunned by the onboard, eh, Axton?"

I laugh.

"Who are you laughing at?" Axton says. "Next, *Resilience* will want to fly itself."

That's never going to happen. *Or will it?*

The Shivyuns squeal.

"Captain, the Asatruan is still following us," *Resilience* informs.

"How is that possible? We are going 12 BURN."

The Shivyuns beep.

"The Asatruan is approaching at 20 BURN."

"Impossible!" I look to the overhead. While the starfighters are falling behind, the Asatruan is closing.

"*Resilience*, double check. Nothing can go over 15 BURN."

I stare at the screen, then at Axton. "Can you believe this?"

The Shivyuns squeal.

I turn to them. "What is it?"

"Captain, the Shivyuns have detected another ship."

I look at the overhead. An object appears in front of the Narrus Gate. "What the heck is that?"

"Sensors indicate a Kanvarian cruiser blocks the Gate." *Resilience* populates data on the Kanvarian Model Y cruiser. It's fast and fully armed, with multiple missile bays, lasers and solar infractors.

"*Gunfrey!*" I curse. "No ... no!" I slam my fist into the console. My hand is numb again.

In my urgency, I have flown us within missile range of a Kanvarian cruiser. I push the Hammer to 2 BURN, but it's too late.

Red lights flash in the front and then in the rear of the bridge. We are surrounded. I stop the *Resilience*.

The cruiser hails.

CHAPTER ELEVEN

13TH QUADRANT

"*Resilience*, I need strategy."

"Calculating." The screen flickers as *Resilience* runs through possibilities and probabilities. If it's anything close to twenty-five percent, I will take my chances. Even in simulations, twenty-five percent is more like fifty percent. Escaping death has become my specialty.

The cruiser hails again.

"Open the comm," I say.

A stiff Caman Corporation officer appears. *What is a Caman officer doing on a Kanvarian cruiser?*

"Hail, *Resilience*. I am Captain Geisler of the Cruiser *Eutrier*. I see you are—" He looks down at his instrument panel and back up. "—Captain Kyvar Astilius. Is that correct?"

The officer wears the standard Caman orange and cerulean. He's got the same tight haircut and pursed lips like the rest of them. Another rich puppet.

I grit my teeth. "I am Kyvar Astilius of the *Resilience* and this is my crew. Can I ask why a Caman Corporation officer is operating a Kanvarian cruiser?"

He smiles. "We are on a trade mission."

"Then why is my bridge lit up?"

He looks down at his fingernails. "Because you fired on my friends," he says casually.

"Your friends, the Kanvarians?" I demand.

"Why, yes." He raises his hand like it is nothing. "Any trade partner of the Caman Corporation is a friend. Is there anything you would like to trade?"

"I am willing to trade," I say.

"We are?" Ayera whispers.

Come on, Resilience, I think. *Hurry.*

Geisler's tone changes. "You want to trade?" He raises his hand and looks at his weapons officer and the weapons lock indicators stop flashing. "We are willing to trade. Our trade is your lives for the cargo of Ale in your possession."

Resilience's calculations appear on the screen. Three scenarios appear: fight scenario–13 percent, flee scenario–28 percent, or fight and flee–32 percent. Good enough. I was expecting worse. I grip the Hammer.

Axton stares a hole in me. "You are *not*!" he mumbles.

"What's it going to be?" Geisler asks.

I breathe deeply and prepare myself.

"I am an impatient businessman," the Caman declares.

I close my eyes.

"We are prepared to open fire and board your vessel if you choose to not trade."

The Shivyuns mumble.

"Don't do this," Axton says in an undertone.

"Give us back our Ale," Geisler demands.

The Shivyuns squeal and hide under their consoles.

"Last chance, Kyvar!"

My mind sends the signal to my hand to drop the Hammer to 12 BURN. Before I can act, a brilliant white flash floods the screen like an exploding sun, and the Shivyuns scream.

"*Resilience*, tint screen," I say.

"Screen tinted."

A laser tears through the cruiser's shields, searing a hole through its bridge. Secondary explosions from armed missiles spray fire around the helpless vessel.

I count five mSEGs. How is that possible? No laser can remain active over three mSEGs without melting down its delivery system.

Another flash. The flash is shorter, with another in succession. The starfighters explode behind us.

"*Resilience*, what is going on?"

"The Asatruan is still headed our way at 20 BURN."

"What?" I demand.

"The laser came from the starship," *Resilience* replies.

"A plasma laser?" Axton asks in awe.

Khal shakes his head. "Impossible."

Resilience displays the Asatruan Model 5P, and the vessel's data—previously proprietary and unknown—populates the screen. Asatruan Enlighten Class Corvette *Stellar Wind*. Max speed: 20 BURN. Beta Plethora shields. Weaponry: plasma laser.

"The data was provided by the Asatruan vessel's onboard," *Resilience* adds.

"They provided us their data," Ayera says. "Kyvar, it's a message of friendship."

"That gives me some comfort," Khal says. "I don't want to be on the receiving end of *that* laser."

"Sensors indicate the reactor of the Kanvarian cruiser is melting down." The screen shows noxious plumes drifting from the shattered ship. *Resilience*'s display indicates thirty-seven life forms onboard. We should find a way to help them if it's not too late.

The screen flickers. The Asatruan vessel hails.

"Accept."

Ackbray's face appears on the screen.

"Unbelievable!" Khal says.

"It's you!" I yell at the same time.

"Greetings, adventurers."

"Greetings, my *pacifist* Asatruan friend." I smile.

Ackbray's large face shows on the feed, overlaying the image of the broken cruiser.

"May I interest your crew in coming over for a meal?" he asks. As he speaks, the cruiser detonates. The explosion ripples the length of the vessel and ignites the noxious cloud. *Resilience* updates the life readings on the vessel to zero.

"A meal? Sure. I'm quite hungry." It's a lie, and I cringe at the thought, but is there any choice? I look around toward the crew. "You guys hungry?"

"Sure ..." Ayera mumbles, horrified at the explosion.

Khal gives a smug smile. "I always have room for plasma-grilled steaks."

"Gundarians are always hungry," Axton says with a nod.

"To what, Ackbray, do we owe this honor?" I ask.

Ackbray smiles. His plastic face carries a lower brow. He's hiding something. No, he's hiding *everything*. "Let's just say I am interested in trading with my new friends."

"I thought so," I reply.

"One more thing," Khal adds.

"Whatever you ask." Ackbray smiles.

"We provide the drink."

The Asatruan bows his head. "I would have expected nothing less."

The screen flickers out.

◉◉◉

Khal, Axton, Ayera and I head down to the weather deck via the side corridor. Xander approaches from the other end. His frame is imposing, filling the hall like a military barrier.

"Captain." Xander's mechanical voice echoes down the corridor.

"Yes."

"Are you in need of my assistance?"

I shake my head. "Not this time. You can sit this one out."

"Very well." He nods. "I will reset my charges until needed." He turns and walks back toward the weapons room.

We take the lift to the weather deck and shuttle bay. Each of us has put on our officer's dress uniform. Even Ayera wears her Hytilium adapted uniform. The high collar hides her gills, while slits in the uniform allow her to breathe. Only a subtle pale blue beneath her skin reveals her race.

Ayera boards the shuttle. "What's your plan, Kyvar?"

"My plan *was* originally suggested by *Resilience*—fight and flee. Considering what Khal is now holding—"

Khal grins and holds up two bottles of Oxylium Ale. He accidentally clinks them together. The sound causes me to wince. Fortunately, they don't shatter.

"The plan *now* is to enjoy some Ale, unless Khal ruins our meal."

She moans. "And my role is to babysit ...?"

I smile. "Yes, please, and hopefully we will extract some secrets from Ackbray."

A deep frown shadows her face. "I don't know if I like this idea."

Our shuttle exits the dock and heads toward the *Stellar Wind*. Its steely gray sides glisten with a red and black micro starlight diagonal checkering. The design continues even through its rotating center hull.

"How exactly do we plan to extract secrets from him?" Axton asks.

"We tell the truth." Khal's smile gleams.

"And what happens if you tell the truth about the Helix stones?" Ayera asks.

The shuttle passes the rotating plasma hull. An ultramarine light glows from its windows. "From the looks of things, he has more secrets than us." I pull up my collar and smooth down my uniform. "Khal, how do I look?"

He laughs. "Like you've been in space too long."

I grin. "Good. I was born in space."

"You were?" Axton asks, unaware of my birth during the evacuation of the Vestral Moons.

Khal nods. "He's a true citizen of space."

Axton laughs. "That's your problem. Your mind is always in the cosmos."

"When it should be right here, right now," Ayera chides.

The shuttle lands in the *Stellar Wind*'s cargo bay and the door opens. A Class F2 protocol droid bows and greets us. "Come. Ackbray is expecting you."

We step onto the shuttle bay platform. The surface is new, very new. It appears to be seamed bronze with specks of Gregorian silver. No sear marks, nothing, not a single scratch. This vessel must be fresh off the docks. It even has that new starship smell.

The droid escorts us into a long glass corridor.

Khal elbows me and points. "Look."

Outside the window, the *Resilience* rests off the starboard side of the *Stellar Wind*. I marvel at her beautiful lines. The bow folds like a remer, and the linear marks show her upgrade from small freighter to starship.

Khal whistles. "What a beauty. They cut the lines to make her faster." He points to her stern. "See the Ion Drives."

I look aft. Her Ion Drives are wrapped in gold with cobalt stellar markings. I stare at the *Resilience*. I feel bonded to this vessel, like I've known it my whole life, though it's only been a few leaps.

We arrive at a sealed silver door which opens before us.

A deep blue, almost purple, glow floods the corridor. We advance onto a metal floating bridge and I blink to adjust to the lighting. Perforated blue iridescence flashes through the grating and around us. The opposite chamber wall pulsates from purple streaks within the plasma core.

An Asatruan appears on the opposite side of the bridge and smiles at us. He appears to be an engineer, according to his uniform. "What you are seeing is our newest model plasma core. The liquid core insulates the living plasma and feeds the Ion Drives."

I glance at Khal. His eyes are aglow. Plasma cores are not supposed to exist.

"How do you keep the liquid core stabilized?" I ask.

The engineer stares at me with disinterested eyes.

I know that look. It's the famous Asatruan "I am not going to answer you" stare.

"How do you feed the Ion Drive without destroying its capacity?" Khal asks anyway.

The engineer smiles, bows his head, and turns. "Please continue this way."

Annoying secret keepers.

The droid dismisses itself, and the engineer leads us across the bridge and around the corner to an elevated window platform. We stop at a table set for five. Our full names are printed on folded napkins at the chairs where we are to sit.

The engineer turns and leaves.

"Creepy." Khal sits down on the far left, on the other side of the table. "How does he know all our names?"

"Creepy indeed," I agree, taking my place at the middle of the table on my side. Ackbray will be to my left and Axton to my right.

"I think it is a nice touch." Ayera picks up her napkin and sits down next to Khal, opposite me. "This is how you do it, children." She lays her napkin in her lap.

We grumble and follow suit.

Wonderful smells come from silver trays and lids before us. Khal peeks under the lid. "Looks like he's been cooking all day."

The smell of fresh cooked meats and grilled vegetables—a delicacy in space—floods the room.

"Adventurers!" Ackbray appears from around the corner and walks toward us. He wears a silver checkered formal suit, much like the colors of his vessel. He is joined by three other Asatruans. They are shorter yet dressed in a similar fashion.

I stand, and the crew follows. "Thank you for the invitation."

He continues toward us. "I hope you like our newest starship?"

"We do!"

He turns to his three lieutenants and whispers to them. They turn and walk off.

I smile and motion toward my crew. "Let me introduce my friends. You already know Khal. This is Axton, a Gundarian. He is our co-pilot and weapons officer."

Axton grins. "It is a pleasure."

"And this is Ayera, our social liaison, science officer, and ethereal and spiritual resource officer."

Ayera smiles. Her white teeth seem exaggerated as the lighting of the room enhances and almost matches her currently pale blue complexion.

"I am quite fond of science and the spirit," Ackbray says. "We merge them and call them the ethereal."

"We Hytilians separate the two," she says, always a firm believer in The Voice.

Ackbray nods. "Yes, we used to do the same. Let me give you my introduction. I am General Ackbray of the Asatruan Peace Force."

"A general?" I ask.

"Yes, and I have more titles."

More titles? "Such as ...?"

"Royal Vizier, Chief Architect and Lead Ethereal Officer for the Ethereal Realm."

"Royal Vizier?" Ayera inquires.

"We have three Royal Viziers. Each of them is guaranteed a place in our government. It is a lifetime appointment for those who desire to rule one day." He looks down toward the silver trays. "Shall we?"

A host droid approaches. The droid removes the lids of the silver dishes and says, "We have roast mutton from the Oyun Belt."

I lick my lips. "They have the best mutton."

"There are grilled local vegetables from Maritausia."

Nice touch.

"And we have sautéed Galactic Hexapod Rings."

Axton beams. He loves those.

Ackbray's own plate only has vegetables and some form of nasty-looking soft Saju melt.

Khal eyes me. Why does Ackbray not eat what we're eating? *Is this hospitality or poison?* I consider switching plates, but looking at his dish, maybe I would prefer poison. I give Khal a half nod and a grin.

Ackbray catches me eyeing his food. He puts his hand on his stomach. "I have a sensitive stomach."

Fair enough. It is well known the bioengineered have sub-par appetites.

The droid reaches for a silver carafe. "For drink, we have—"

"No." Khal interrupts the droid. "We promised drink." Khal pulls the two bottles of Oxylium Ale from under the table. The dark liquid glows rich amber through the bottle.

Ackbray's large eyes widen further.

Khal removes the lid and leans over toward the Asatruan's glass, but he puts his hand over the glass's mouth. "You know I cannot have this Ale."

Khal grins. "We insist. No one talks business without sharing a drink in our culture."

Clever Khal.

Ackbray looks at the rest of us. "Is this true?"

"Oh, yes," I lie.

He removes his hand and sits back. "Very well. As trade partners, this is part of our business."

Khal pours the golden liquid into his glass as the host droid leaves the table.

Ackbray takes a drink.

Khal fills the remaining glasses. I take a drink, close my eyes, and take in the flavor of one of the galaxy's rare substances. My body seems to drift, yet I am not moving. My mind is all over the place. I shake my head and open my eyes.

I see Ackbray's large eyes are closed. This is going to be fun.

CHAPTER TWELVE

13TH QUADRANT

I roll my fork with the mutton in the Tarqay rice gravy and take a savory bite. My mouth explodes with flavor as the steamed meat mixes with the cool rice over the spiced gravy. I close my eyes, wondering if I've ever tasted anything so good. Someone must have steamed it all day with crusted yehmi. I lick my lips. *Remarkable.*

Ackbray turns to me. "You like the mutton?"

"The best I have ever tasted." That statement doesn't require truth serum.

He grins. "We have cultivated our tastes over the ages."

Khal roughly puts down his glass. "I do believe this is the best drink in the cosmos."

"And the most expensive," Axton adds.

I seize my glass and gulp down half the amber liquid. The effects of the Ale rush to my brain. My eyes feel like they are about to pop. My heart races. I feel dizzy, yet my mind is completely alive and active.

I look at Ackbray. He seems to have three heads. Khal has three heads as well. *Better not say anything just now.* I look out the window for a bit.

Ayera stares at me, knowing she has to carry the conversation. "General Ackbray, tell us about the *Stellar Wind.*"

"This is our latest creation." He turns and points to the plasma core. "The liquid-cooled core allows for ionization, macro speeds and coolant for the laser cannons."

"What is the coolant?" Khal asks.

Ackbray doesn't answer. I am sure Khal will ask him again later. He's probably giving Khal the Asatruan stare that implies *I won't answer your stupid questions.*

I gaze out the window. The wrecked parts of the cruiser and starfighters float in space. What an extraordinary turn of events! Eating mutton and drinking Ale when only a chapter ago in my life, death was a strong calculation. My mind starts to return to normal, or as normal as it gets. *Won't do that again.* I focus on the conversation. Khal and Ackbray each have one head now. This Ale is a sip-only beverage. *Sip* only.

"General, how many of these starships are at your disposal?" Axton asks.

"There are three prototypes currently in use. This was our first 'go' at it, as you would say. A definite success. Would you agree?"

"Agreed." Axton nods.

"Though this is the first trial run of our new flagship class, I took this vessel out on more of a personal accord."

"Personal accord?" I ask.

Ackbray looks at me without flinching. "I am here to trade."

I've heard that before. "That's what everyone keeps saying."

"My offer of trade is to my friends at this table." His forehead starts to twitch. "I do not come on the official business of the Asatruan state."

Interesting. This guy is being dodgy. I might just like him.

"The attack on the Kanvarians was personal?" I very slowly sip the Ale.

"No."

Puzzling. "Then what will you do when the Camans find out you destroyed their ally's vessels?"

He sits back and examines his unusually long fingernails. "I don't believe anyone will attribute this to me." He grins. "I was out of range. The recovery of the vessels will show *you* as the real hazard. Your dangerous attacks were directed upon them. No. I believe this attack will be attributed to you."

Gunfrey! A stinking set-up.

Ayera drops her fork. "Hey—"

Ackbray holds up his hand, cutting off Ayera. "This adds to your list of very deadly actions recently: the destruction of Oxylium, plus Spaceport L32. Then there was the Caman cruiser, plus two Kanvarian spaceships, plus two Kanvarian starfighters. And most recently, a Kanvarian cruiser piloted by a Caman captain. I think you are becoming quite a legend, BURNing through the galaxies, escaping with the Horde of Oxylium and this amazing Oxylium Ale."

Now he's really dodgy. I am not sure if I want to punch him in his stretched face or thank him for saving us. I do like the idea of being a legend.

"You have no proof of any of this," Ayera implies.

"Your heat signature tells where you came from, one of your bays is cloaked, and I just witnessed the destruction of three ships."

I wonder why he's telling us this. He could have already destroyed us. I shrug my shoulders at Ayera and ignore the stare she sends back at me. Time to change the subject.

"Ackbray," I begin, "you are very kind to have us over for a meal. Let us have a toast." I hold up my glass. "To friends."

"To friends," Ackbray says, and takes a drink. After the toast, I look over at Khal. His face is flushed, and his glass is empty. I scowl at him and Ayera follows. *Too fast, Khal.*

Ackbray smiles. "Tell me. What do you think of us Asatruans?"

I look at Ayera. Now is a good time to test her theory.

She breathes deeply. "We believe your people come from the Taurus system. We could be considered neighbors. When your stellar melted, a generational vessel was slingshotted into deep space with the pledge to renew the capsules when the technology was available for retrieval and cultivation."

He nods. "Very good. You know our people. The leader of the group was?"

Ayera looks off trying to recall the name. "Aluzera, I believe."

"Correct." He smiles. "Once the tech existed for recovery, teams were sent out to recover the Generation craft and its cryochambers. The extreme space challenges led them to found a colony in the farthest reaches, on the planet of Asatyria."

I am normally bored by history but will make an exception this time. He does have the greatest tech in the cosmos. I take a bite of the savory mutton and listen.

Ackbray continues. "I was one of the first to be unfrozen—"

"One of the first?" Ayera interrupts.

He smiles. "I am Aluzera."

I can feel my own eyebrows rise. I wasn't expecting that bombshell.

He continues. "Our teams have worked on our bioengineering to extend the lives of everyone on the initial crew. We are considered the founders of a neo-civilization. We Asatruans change our names once we achieve a milestone in our transpondence. Since then, I have changed my name three times."

Transpondence? Who does he think he is?

"You must be at least a hundred and eighty years old!" Ayera blurts.

He smiles. "At least."

Unbelievable. Okay, that's old, real old. No, that's *ancient.* This guy is ancient.

"Our people are founded on ethereal technology. We thrive on the latest advances and this is why you, my friends, have something we desire."

"The stones," I mutter.

"Yes. The stones."

I notice he has only drunk two-thirds of his glass. "Let us drink to new business partners."

"Yes." Khal stands up and tops off everyone's glass. "To new business partners."

We all drink and Ackbray takes a surprisingly large gulp. His plastic face starts to turn a bit pink.

"What is so valuable about the Helix?" I ask.

The twitch on his forehead resumes. "The Helix stones present a milestone in tech breakthroughs."

"Such as ...?"

"Swords and mining, for one," he says casually.

Boring answer. "Yes, we know that."

Ackbray's normal pasty face continues to become flushed. He seems to want to guard his words, yet his mouth opens again, speaking fast. "There are warship uses, the intergalactic Gate openings, starGate wormhole uses and the military usage on the battlefield. These things I offer you as part of our deal. This is part of our arrangement."

"The Horde for the advancement that follows?" I simplify his offer.

He smiles, his ivory white teeth contrasting with his pink face. "That's not all. There's more."

Like what? A timeshare in the ivory moons? "More?" I ask.

His tone softens as he whispers, "I offer you *life*."

"Life?" Ayera beats me to the question.

He responds with a crooked grin. "I don't look bad for at least a hundred and eighty years old, do I?"

"Truthfully?" Khal answers. "Yes, you do. You look terrible. Your eyes are huge, and your head is disproportionate." Khal puts his hand over his mouth. Ayera and I stare at him. *Oh no, the Ale ... the truth serum ...*

"I have to agree," Axton adds. "You do look terrible."

Ackbray turns toward me with a glare in his eyes.

"You'd be fine if it wasn't for that twitch on your forehead." The words unconsciously come from my mouth. This Ale is worse than I thought.

He looks away, refusing to be frustrated with us.

Ayera scowls at me and holds up her hand. "Forgive us, Ackbray. Blame the Ale, for it made them say those things. You are a bit aloof and odd in your mannerisms, though." She quickly covers her mouth, shocked by her own words. Her gills flare under the slits in her uniform and her skin shades blue.

Ackbray breathes deeply, as if refusing to be irritated with us. Finally, he says, "I am an adventurer like you. I am an original. A human, but now in ethereal form. Give or take the next few hundred years, our race—"

"If you call it that," my mouth blurts. My face feels like it's on fire. *How do I prevent this?*

He continues despite our disrespect. "Our race is an intergalactic race of people that have harnessed the ethereal and its breakthroughs and are becoming one with—"

"One with?" Ayera interrupts.

Ackbray ignores her question. "I offer this to you."

"Are you insane?" Khal declares.

He faces Khal. "Even to you, Khal, I offer the opportunity to become one of us. I offer you a chance to be ethereal."

"Forgive us for our challenges," Ayera intercedes. "The Ale speaks too much. Kyvar asked me to come along to make sure this didn't happen. I believe this is a poor time for business."

Ackbray sits back and examines his fingernails again. "Take all the time you need. Time has never been an issue to me."

I summon all my limited self-control to not speak of his appearance. "Why do you offer us this?"

"Because you remind me of myself." Ackbray's tone is sincere.

Interesting. "When you were younger?"

"And better looking?" Khal blurts. His face is red.

"Yes, and better looking," Ackbray concedes.

I laugh to myself. He knows he's freaky looking. "Is that why you call us adventurers?"

"I do. I was once like you."

"Do you miss it?" Ayera asks.

"I will always miss my youth." He winces like he doesn't want to say those words. He quickly adds, "Doesn't everyone?"

If I was one hundred and eighty, yeah, I'd probably miss my youth, too. I say, "Tell us about the warship uses of the Helix."

He winces again. He seems to go distant for an mSEG as the Ale takes hold of him. The twitch on his forehead develops into a spasm. A few veins start to show in the sclera of his eyes.

I persist. "What are the military uses of the Helix, especially related to starships?"

He leans forward. "Very well. We are friends, yes?"

"Yes." I take a sip of the Ale, probably a bad idea.

"The stones have passed every military test. Every test for strength, hardness and melting point. They are an element unto themselves." He talks softer. "Do you understand elemental materials?"

"We do," Khal looks at me. "Right, Kyvar?"

I nod my head like I know what he is talking about. "Right," I manage to mutter.

"The stones redefine them. The entire organization of elements must be thrown out. Weapon-makers pattern hardness tests to kinetic testing in labs. The labs report back on the hardness and calibrations required for designations. The Helix stones break every chart ever created. Any Helix-enhanced weapon gives it greater penetration than any weapon in the cosmos. This is why I want to trade for the stones. There are not many Asatruans. I offer you the chance to become like me—an eternal being. Be a part of us. You provide the stones, and I offer you our biological breakthroughs. In turn, we develop the stones."

I smile at this being that was once human. "Thank you, Ackbray. You know we came to Asatyria some leaps ago to purchase the wormhole data."

"I know," he concedes, "and we regretfully turned you away and requested Helix stones."

"You did."

He smiles. "And you went away, and mined and half-destroyed them in the deep universe. Now you possess more than enough to revolutionize the cosmos."

I smile like I have a clue how to revolutionize anything.

He looks away and his face seems to change back to pasty normal. The flushness of his face seems to be leaving. "Kyvar, you've asked your questions. I think it is time for mine."

He holds up his hand, palm facing us. His brow lowers as he focuses his mental strength through his hand. I stare at him like he is crazy. He is trying to mind-melt us. I smile. Not today, no mind games when Oxylium Ale is present. The truth comes out on its own, with no need for further extraction.

He extends his hand further and winces as he tries again.

"Not gonna work this time," I say.

Puzzled, he pulls his hand back and withdraws into normal conversation. The conversation continues as we finish the mutton and the rest of the meal and have half a bottle of Ale remaining. Ayera asks about the latest in science discoveries. Khal inquiries into the plasma coolant. Ackbray answers them ... truthfully.

In some strange way, I am growing in my appreciation for him, as if I've known him for some time. Conversation shifts down the history route and I check out, while even Ackbray seems to be passively participating. His eyes drift out toward the *Resilience* just outside the window.

I should at least say something to try to mend the offense from earlier. "Ackbray, thank you for your offer. We would love to consider it, but we have a galaxy that needs us. Please understand we cannot trade stones for our own immortality when our galaxy's future is in peril."

He nods. "This I understand."

Khal pours out the remaining Ale into everyone's glass and conversation shifts to our plans and our journey home, yet Ackbray seems distant, shifting his focus toward space.

I finish my glass and regard him. "What's on your mind, Ackbray? Why do you keep looking out toward the *Resilience*?"

He scratches the twitch on his forehead. "I can't tell you. I made a promise."

"What promise?"

He stares at me, refusing to answer.

Cagey. I try again. "What promise?"

He looks up as if he is searching for words. "Do you have any idea who you are?" His voice carries through the chamber.

I look around, wondering where this came from. *Bizarre.* "We are the crew of the *Resilience*. We are on a journey to—"

"Do you have any idea who *you* yourself are?" He raises his voice.

I am taken back by the aggressiveness of the question. Is this some kind of a game? "For the sake of conversation, let's say that's a hard no."

He points to the *Resilience*. "You don't have any idea what you have on board, either?" He points to us. "And none of you have any idea who you are?"

I stare at him. His tone is different, and he seems aggressive yet oddly kind. Even his words carry a strange weight.

"Tell us, Ackbray."

He faces me and stares for a moment. "I can't," he says abruptly, and then his voice is normal again. "It's not mine to share."

What? *Who is this guy?*

He swirls the Ale in his glass. "You must learn who you are and what you possess. When you find yourself, I will come to your aid." He puts down the glass, pulls out cards from his pocket, and lays four of them on the table before us, gesturing toward them.

Ayera picks up a card but doesn't look at it. "Ackbray, I've had the least amount of Ale, yet I don't understand you right now."

He laughs loudly. "You will."

I grab the card with a plasma tint to it and put it in my pocket, then politely scoot my chair back. "Thank you for the meal. How long does your offer stand?"

"As long as you like." He smiles his plastic 180-year-old smile. "I don't age."

Liar.

Khal restrains himself for once. I start to stand up. I lose my balance and catch myself. *Wow.* That was strong Ale. I am having an out-of-body experience. I catch myself with the nearest chair and slowly push myself upward.

I pull out a diamond Helix eight-stone cluster and put the cluster on the table. "Thanks for saving us. We were about to enter a fight with a low chance of survival. We appreciate your kindness. The mutton was delicious." I turn around. "Did everyone enjoy it?"

"I did," Axton answers.

"Oh yes," Khal pushes himself out of his chair. "It was glorious. On another occasion, you will have to tell me how you slow-roasted mutton while going 20 BURN."

Ackbray stares at the cluster. A greedy streak flickers in his bloodshot eyes. "You know, I could take the rest of your Helix stones by force."

The room goes silent as if a hundred phasma rifle scopes are leveled at our heads. But ... I know better.

I smile and nod. "I know you can, but I'm pretty sure there's something inside you that believes in our cause and wants us to succeed. Right?"

Ackbray stares at me and the crew. His stare is endless and unnerving, and even the twitch on his forehead seems to cease. After a moment, he laughs, and his bellicose laughter fills the chamber. "Spoken like true adventurers!"

CHAPTER THIRTEEN

NARUS GATE

"Captain."

I open my eyes and sit up. I run hands through my hair and consider lying back down. I could sleep another two m-leaps.

"Captain," *Resilience* repeats.

"Yes, *Resilience.*"

"We are five SEGs from the Tpoint."

"Thank you, *Resilience.*" The trick to waking up is getting out of bed. I walk over to a basin and splash water in my face. This works, too. The cold water jolts the sleep from my mind.

Only Ayera and the Shivyuns are on the bridge. The Shivyuns greet me with beeps and moans. I nod and smile in return.

"How was your nap?" Ayera asks.

Pink and red memory fragments echo in my mind. "Vivid," I answer, trying to bring together the fragments into a complete memory. "I had the most intense dream."

"I can imagine!" Ayera swivels in her chair. "The Ale activates membranes which supercharge your neurons. I drank very little, yet I'm exhilarated."

Khal walks onto the bridge smiling. "Hey, we get news from home at the Tpoint."

"I know." Ayera presses her consoles. "I've been tracking the feeds, hoping a few messages made it through the four-wormhole cap, but nothing's come through yet."

Khal sits down and starts to extract his relays. "They never do."

Axton saunters in, and I turn to him. "Hey, Ax, how did you sleep?"

"Too short. I was in total dreamland." He shakes his head and runs his hands through his hair.

"Same here." The resolute fragments of my dream merge together, and I shift back to the screen. "*Resilience*, display the destruction of Oxylium again."

The screen flickers as *Resilience* locates and pulls the archived footage. The feed displays on the screen. Our recorded voices sound hollow as we re-live the destruction.

"Sensors indicate a disturbance on the moon," Resilience's voice begins.

Bright white flashes flicker on the planet from multiple locations. I remember those.

"It appears detonations are going off on the surface, potentially volcanic in nature."

Fires. Ripples of explosions in succession roll across the surface just where we put the explosives.

"Sensors detect explosions at the drone mine and along the Contravenes Lava River."

"I know." That was a good one.

"You know?" Resilience asks.

"Resilience, quit asking questions or I am going to shut you down."

"Yes, Captain."

There are squeaks and moans from the Shivyuns, and then Resilience's voice continues. "Fire has detonated a series of other mines below the river. The fire river is collapsing into its gas caverns."

The Shivyuns turn their heads as if they've been hit. They squeal and moan. How did they know it was coming?

In present time, I seize my Holox pad and forward the feed. The feed bleeds the scenes together until I reset the feed.

My voice booms in the replay.

"Resilience, make sure all those shields are to the front. All of them."

"Yes, Captain."

The moon's shuttles disappear in the spray of fire, red sands, and black mantle rock. The cruiser and Spaceport L32 both disintegrate in the blast. Every shuttle and spacecraft attached to the spaceport explodes.

Projectiles come our way. The shield takes the brunt of the red debris with ease until the black mantle pieces appear. A massive black chunk of rock smashes into the shields.

The vessel rocks from the shield impact. "Shields at seventy-seven percent. Seventy-six percent ..." *Resilience announces.*

"Resilience, tell me when we are down to fifty percent."

The pelting continues. A massive mantle block collides with the shields.

"Shields at fifty percent."

I forward the feed again and reset it, and the replay continues.

"Resilience, track the charred mantle pieces and maneuver us through the particle fields."

A shrill bang rocks the vessel.

"There," I say. I grab my Holox pad and slowly pull back the feed. I compress the feed to the lower corner.

"What is it?" Khal asks. "I don't see anything."

Axton leans forward. "A floater?"

"No, not a floater," I say. I take the feed even closer. "There." I point to the corner, at a small white flash with a pink tint.

"Still don't see much," Khal says as he peers at the image.

I drag it closer, losing definition. "*Resilience*, enhance!"

The Shivyuns squeal and start to sway.

"What are you flipping out over?" Khal asks the Shivyuns.

"*Resilience*, flip the screen imagery profiles until you obtain clarity." The screen imagery changes modes until the object comes clear. The object has a pink discoloration. I pull the feed in and out and replay the scene.

"It's a Helix," Ayera says.

"Watch what it does."

When the Helix impacts the shields, it creates a light vortex, a defragmentation around the Corian shields. "That's what impacted the cargo bay." I turn to Axton. "That's why you almost lost the *Impetus*. You were in the spray of that Helix blast."

"The Helix stones pierce shields?" Axton sits back in his seat, mouth open, stunned.

"Khal, remember when we were cadets. What did they say?"

"Nothing can pierce Corian shields," Khal says, imitating the old crusty wing commander from flight school.

"They lied," I declare. "*Resilience*, how many Helix stones do we have?"

"Xander has counted them. There are 5,621 stones."

"Are you kidding me?" Khal says.

"The cosmos supply was once estimated at 10,000. A better estimate would be 12,261."

"And to think our friend Ackbray let us go," Ayera murmurs.

I know we will encounter him again, but that's not important now.

"*Resilience*, measure the vortex the Helix created."

The two-dimensional measurement appears on the screen. I pull it out with my pad and spin it three-dimensionally in front of me.

"*Resilience*, summon Xander."

"Xander summoned."

The screen flickers. "Approaching Tpoint."

I dismiss the imagery of the vortex. "Helm, please." The controls are brought before me.

The *Resilience* exits the Gate. Like a surfer ending a wave, the rush is over and it's time to get back to shore. I ease down the Hammer to pick up speed.

The right edge of the screen fills with incoming messages, news from home. I push the messages away from the screen, even though I see Valerie's face. It's been a long time. *Focus, Kyvar!*

"About time ..." I hear Khal grab his pad.

Axton seizes his as well. "Oh, my clan."

No multi-tasking for me. Two steely gray space stations flash their lights in our direction. The screen flickers as the nearest hails us.

"Guys, I might need some help here."

Axton snickers at me. He's caught the first image of his wife and kids that he hasn't seen for leaps. News from home is more important to them ... I look back. Khal and Ayera are intent on their Holox Pads. Only the Shivyuns keep focus.

"Open the comm," I say.

The comm opens. A CSX Officer appears. His standard navy-blue uniform carries a cadet insignia from the academy. Cadets seem to be getting younger and younger. This one in particular is small and skinny. Regardless, I'm thankful he's not a Caman. They co-run this sector.

Getting through the vTalis defense sectors can only happen with authorization, and technically a stolen armed freighter is *not* authorization.

The CSX officer looks down and up. "Greetings. Our sensors reveal you are the *Resilience* out of vTalis, registered to an Atilio Astilius."

What? My father?

My face must have registered my disbelief and shock. The officer shakes his head. "Sorry, my mistake. I see it is registered to a Senator Nashtech." His tone changes. The officer sits up straighter. "Welcome to the vTalis Sector. Welcome home. Access granted." The comm closes.

I release my controls in amazement. We are in. My reputation has preceded me, or rather, my father's reputation. Nashtech was one of my father's friends. Its sounds like he has paved a course for us, but how does he know we are here?

"*Resilience*, set a course for Shivyia and ease us up slowly to 10 BURN."

The two Shivyuns mumble.

Xander approaches me from my blind side. I turn and flinch. His iron plating and militaristic posture startles me. "Xander, can you please lighten up? A less stern demeanor would be less startling."

"It is my programming."

Khal stands up. "You've got to chill. Hang a shoulder like this." He stands up to shows him. "Or walk with a strut." Khal demonstrates. "Who knows if a lady bot is around the corner?"

I laugh. I stand and move across the room with a bit of swagger. "Now, you try."

Xander hangs his shoulder and walks across the room. He seems to limp. He even tries to smile. "It is a start."

Khal laughs.

Ayera smiles. "You *children*."

I put my arm on Xander's shoulder. "Don't worry, you'll get it." I direct him into the privacy of the corridor.

The lights from the vTalis stations flicker through the port windows and glint on Xander's iron plating. I give him confidential orders, and he rubs his robotic hands together as if I'd just bestowed a gift on him. "I am trusting you with this assignment," I say. "Do you understand?"

"Yes, Captain." He nods his head and moves off to perform his deadly task.

I go back to my seat and sprawl. I still get weirded-out feelings from the Ale now and then. A servant bot appears behind me with cold water. *How does he know I am not fully hydrated?*

I accept the water and thank him, and he bows, beeps, and scoots off.

I grab my Holox Pad. The messages stack one on top of each other. "*Resilience*, prioritize my messages and display the highest priority."

"*Resilience*, start with this one," Ayera says, her voice cracking.

I turn around. Tears fill her eyes.

"You okay?"

"No."

The feed starts. Queen Amytilius of Hytilium appears on the screen. Her body glows a deep blue beneath her pale skin. Her gills flare out. A deep gash mars her cheek. She stands tall, her gaze proud despite her appearance. She appears to be in a very small craft. A fire smokes behind her, but it's hard to see exactly what is burning.

"The Vidor have consumed one galaxy after another. Our elders have been killed, and our youth have fallen. With ruthless intent, they commit murder for the wealth of *their* peoples. I plead with you. I call upon the might and arm of the cosmos. We are in a struggle for our existence." She wipes tears from her eyes. "*This* is what they are capable of."

The feed shifts to a raging blaze and slowly shifts outward.

"What is it?" Khal asks.

"Just watch," Ayera says, her voice heavy with emotion.

The conflagration appears to be a starbase, until the visual moves outward to reveal an entire city on fire. "What is that?" I demand.

"It looks like Waupus!" Khal says.

Axton peers at the screen. "It *is* Waupus."

The feed continues outward, revealing more burning cities. Flaming craters litter the planet. The feed moves away from the broken atmosphere until numerous Vidor solar laser platforms can be seen, hot from their deadly work.

The Queen reappears on the feed from what now appears to be an escape pod. Tears stream down her face. Her jaw locks, and her skin tone shades to a deeper blue. "The Vidor have broken every covenant." Her voice turns to steel. "I, Queen Amytilius of Hytilium, invoke galactic justice."

The feed ceases.

Waupus. A thousand memories flash before me, from the moment I met Valerie to any number of a thousand days at the flight academy.

"How did they get past the ADZ?" Axton asks. "That was our guarantee of survival."

"*Resilience*, play the feeds on the Asteroid Defense Zone assault," Khal says, his voice filled with rare emotion.

The feeds appear from reports from multiple agencies on the screen. They merge as *Resilience* splices them together.

The merged feed reveals the Vidor assault on the ADZ. Their vessels appear from multiple sectors. Thousands of defensive lasers and projectiles and solar weapons rush into the asteroid belt, destroying one Vidor vessel after another.

The screen looks like business as usual. Direct attacks like these have always been beaten off. Our network of overlapping fire is one of the best in the cosmos. The ADZ is reliable and dependable. Nothing can pierce the defenses.

"No!" Khal yells. "The Belt. Waupus. Now the *Antiphilous!*"

What? I turn and see him watching his feed ahead of us. I turn back to the screen. Vidor vessels have appeared out of a wormhole behind the ADZ. They target the center of the defense system, the cruiser *Antiphilous*. Five Vidor battle cruisers engage the ship. Solar laser platforms emerge and target Waupus. The *Antiphilous* takes down two of the Vidor cruisers before it is overwhelmed and explodes. Multiple-angled feeds show its horrifying final moments before its obliteration.

I whirl to face Khal. "Was he on it?" I demand.

"You know he was. He never leaves his post," Khal answers.

Our friend Altrio was a lieutenant on the *Antiphilous*. Or he had been, until a few moments ago. One of over five thousand crewmen.

"*Resilience*, stop the feed!" I command.

The feed halts.

Khal scowls. "They came out of a wormhole behind our line of defense."

"Then they have the mapping as well." I look away and grimace.

Ackbray.

The room goes silent. I sit in my seat, chilled to the core. This changes everything. Our original mission was to obtain the Stellar Gates and find allies to lift the siege. With our defenses compromised or destroyed, the siege is no longer the issue.

This has become a battle for survival.

The silence on the bridge is only interrupted with the Ion Drive's hum and the Shivyuns' soft pads on their instruments can be heard. It's quiet enough to hear Axton breathing.

Altrio's face flashes in my mind. My old buddy. Khal, Altrio and I were always together all through academy. Khal was the sarcastic one, I was the hot-shot hero's son, and Altrio was the funny one. The most popular kid in flight academy. A crack shot at everything, the expert of gunnery experts. And he always shot from the hip with a laser and a joke, always smiling and laughing.

I try to fight back the tears and fail. I lose track of time, remembering Waupus and Altrio and so many others, so many fighters whose families would never see each other again.

A sinking sensation overcomes me at the realization that even as our galaxy is now in a fight for its very existence, we are here, still so far away.

We have to go home.

The Shivyuns squeal.

The screen flickers. *Resilience*'s voice sounds loud in the silence, "Approaching Shivyia."

The Shivyuns start to sway and hum strange sounds.

CHAPTER FOURTEEN

SHIVYIA

The russet mining moon of Shivyia dominates our view. No stations or towers hail us. Living in the shadow of nearby superplanet vTalis is enough security for the Shivyuns, so they need no monitored checkpoints.

"*Resilience*, take us into the base crater."

"Yes, Captain."

We break through their artificial atmosphere and descend. The *Resilience* lands next to an assortment of small vessels and freighters. The limited facilities make small craft and freighters the best and sometimes only option here.

I stand and look around. Axton, Ayera, and Khal are still engrossed in their Holox pads. The Shivyuns gleam up at me through their visors.

I smile. "I guess it's just us three. Come on."

The short creatures hobble off with me. They mumble with an excitement I have never seen in Shivyuns. They beep, moan, and squeal a bit. They even sway and hop around, which is new to me.

"Let's get you home."

We exit the *Resilience*. I take a few steps, and then squat down and feel the soil. It's just like Father said—the soil crumbles. It's dirt, but it's soft as snow. Heavy and solid when compacted, yet with the consistency of powder when raked and separated. The perfect terrain for a Shivyun.

The Shivyuns stand above me. They have removed their visors, and they regard me with their small eyes. They turn their heads, beep and continue scooting. We pass by other Shivyuns servicing other freighters and guides carrying crates on skids.

After all the injustices committed in the past against the Shivyuns, an innocent, naïve race, I am happy to see a solid working civilization here. There are no chains here, no slave traders, no torture from stronger, meaner races.

Recent changes in the vTalis sector protect them now, and they are now given autonomy over *Our Rock,* as they call their cavern-network home.

We exit the crater and enter a causeway tunnel labeled for dignitaries, where we step onto a rectangular slab of crystal. One of the Shivyuns touches the wall and the slab slides along through the tunnel. A few beams of light from the surface stream down as we move, revealing converging passages into an underground cavern city. The slab comes to a stop at the end of the tunnel, and the city is revealed.

"Asokoro City." My father spoke of this place many times. The gateway city for the moon. A hundred other tunnels can be seen at different levels all through the cavern. Huts and buildings lay alongside one central road leading to a palace at the end of the road.

The busy moles are everywhere as we walk through the city. We pass by a shopkeeper, who squints his small eyes as he arranges his wares. He stops, looks up, and stares at me.

Every one of the Shivyuns stares at me as I walk by.

"What is it?" I ask my friends.

"They sense something about you."

"What is it?"

"The same thing we sense."

"And what is that?"

They beep and moan and snicker to each other but won't answer. I guess I'll find out soon enough.

The palace is carved from the obsidian volcanic core of the planet. I remember Father saying the actual core of Shivyia is not a perfect sphere, but has a lateral vein reaching toward its mantle. This palace was constructed from the highest part of the vein. I remember a legend that the rock was the founding gem of this galaxy, but then every galaxy has that legend.

Two imposing black stone doors rise above us. An iron-helmeted guard with a pickaxe accosts us. "What is your business?"

"We are—" I start to speak.

The male Shivyun interrupts me with a higher than usual shrill voice. "This Excellency saved our lives from slavery. We desire to share his goodwill."

The guard bows. "You are welcome to the palace."

The palace walls are pure black, with strips of inlaid ivory. The only light is three beams coming into the structure from infracted light rays through the thermal vents.

We advance to a long corridor filled with dignitaries from different races waiting to get to in. There are Thyritityrians, Miramkars, Kraenians, Naterians, and even a Kanvarian. Each of them watches us. I even see the Kanvarian speak into his comm. *Great.*

The Shivyuns waddle ahead of me at a surprising pace as we continue to walk. They mumble and murmur and beep.

"We have access?" I ask.

"We do," they mumble.

I don't question further.

The next door is guarded by a broad-chested Shivyun that I could have mistaken for a dwarf. He looks at me with dubious eyes.

The Shivyuns bow before him. "This is Kyvar Astilius. He saved our life."

The austere guard smiles and bows low. "Enter our Gates."

The line of waiting dignitaries appear resentful as we leave them behind. We enter the door, only to find another group of waiting dignitaries, this time Caman Corporation and Inovian representatives. We bypass them in the same manner.

The final room is a waiting room with only one representative, a finely dressed Zairian preparing to conduct business. We bypass him as well.

"My friends," I say. "You know this is unnecessary."

"It is necessary. All of it," they mumble, as they lower their visors. "Prepare yourself."

"For what?"

I look at them as the last door is flung open. I am blinded by a brilliant light, and I'm forced to look away. The light is only a direction beam, however, and once we pass the beam, the room is pitch dark.

"What is this?" I ask my friends.

"It is the light that deters those that don't belong," a strong male Shivyun-human voice booms out of the darkness.

I struggle to see its source.

"Is it hard to see in the dark?" the voice asks.

I turn to the right and can't see. I look in front of me. Nothing. The Shivyuns are missing. Behind me is the directional light ray and to the left is darkness.

My eyes start to adjust.

"You humans only know what you can see. You know nothing now, do you?" He laughs.

Not sure if I want to engage with whoever this is, but I do. "Because you turned off the lights."

The voice laughs again. "No. Because your eyes are not adjusted to our ways. Focus on the darkness in the room."

I concentrate ahead, toward the darkest part of the room.

"Good! Sometimes, you expect a brilliant light to direct you, but other times you need to trust your instincts."

I have instincts. I am a starfighter pilot.

I start to see gray shadows ahead of me and figures to the right and left.

"I see you." I laugh. "I didn't know I had arrived at your council."

The voice laughs with me as thin lighting illuminates the council room of Shivyia. The elders of the land sit along two benches on opposite sides. The judge standing at the end of the council benches is the one who spoke. He is half human and half Shivyun. He is almost my height yet has a Shivyun appearance.

"I understand you rescued two of our own," the judge says. "Is this true?"

"It is true. I wanted to return them to your care."

The two Shivyuns from the *Resilience* beep in appreciation. The judge bows. "Our people are indebted to you."

"I love your people. My father always employed a Shivyun on his crew."

The two Shivyuns whisper and giggle to each other.

"What is your name?" The judge's deep voice ranges through the room.

"Kyvar Astilius."

One of the elders stands up and speaks slowly. "Astil ... ius?"

"Yes. Kyvar Astilius. My father was a friend to your people."

The elder responds slowly, very slowly. "Your father ... was a friend of mine. He was a follower of The Voice."

"He always told me if I was in trouble, I should locate a Shivyun named Lothun and ask for his help."

"I am he," the elder responds. "And you? Do you follow The Voice?"

I refuse to answer. "Judge. May I approach the bench?"

"Please." The judge steps aside.

I walk to the front and stand at the judge's seat, turning to face the Shivyun elders.

I nod in respect to Lothun. "Lothun, and esteemed Shivyuns! My father loved your people. He found refuge here during many of his journeys to vTalis. I come now because my people are suffering, facing annihilation. We seek your assistance—"

The judge interrupts. "We are not a people of war." He turns toward his people and then back to me. "We know of your suffering. Our sadness is with you, but we are not a people of war. We can provide basic needs and support for you. We are miners and a race of *Our Rock*. I wish there was more we could do."

I smile and look around the vast cavern. I rub my hands together. "There is one thing that you can do for me."

The elder rubs his chin, the Shivyuns from the vessel sway, and the judge leans in. "If it is not related to conflict and war, what do you have in mind? ..."

CHAPTER FIFTEEN

vTalis Sector

"*Resilience*, set course for vTalis."

"Yes, Captain."

I look left and see the empty Shivyun seats. I'm glad we got them home, but I will surely miss them.

I grab my Holox Pad and examine the feeds. I see the grizzled face of Admiral Astoye. He stands on the bridge of the Sidonian flagship *Virtuous*. I flick it to the screen.

"Kyvar. Here are your new orders. Investigate the Gates. Proceed with all possible speed to vTalis and Trasilium and locate our allies. They are out there." He takes a deep breath, and his voice softens. "I *know* our friends are out there, and I know you will find them. Your father never let us down. I know you will succeed."

The feed ceases.

Gunfrey!

"No pressure," Khal mumbles.

How annoying. "He knows I am not my father."

"No pressure at all," Axton echoes.

The screen flickers. "Kyvar, everyone knows you are not your father."

Now the onboard is commenting without prompting. More annoyance.

"Yeah," I agree. "Even *Resilience* knows."

"Kyvar, onboards aren't supposed to do that," Khal says.

"Do what?" Ayera asks Khal.

"Interrupt the conversation," Khal says. "Onboards aren't supposed to have their own opinion. It's against protocol for onboards to have unique identities. The councils mandate it."

The councils did mandate it ages ago. I pull out *Resilience*'s specs from my Holox Pad and maneuver the screens to find data on the onboard. The entry for the personality chip's make and model is missing. Odd. I look at the screen.

Resilience, what are you?

The screen flickers, giving me the impression that I've just been brushed off by the onboard. "Entering the vTalis Industrial Zone."

Floating platforms flash instructions as we ease into a shield corridor. There is only one route through this zone. Stations scan our vessel, and other vessels form into a line. A CSX medium freighter is before us and a luxury cruiser behind us.

"*Resilience*, remove the cloaking from Bay One."

"Yes, Captain."

Micro-gravity manufacturing facilities stretch before us on both sides. A giant CSX logo displays on a gravity platform. Hundreds of structures and craft in different stages of construction cover the platform. Thousands of workers attend to their assignments. Space lifts and robotic ancillaries swarm the vessels.

"We could use one of those at home." Khal drools.

"That's just for the small craft." Axton points ahead.

A container vessel floats in dry dock. Its length exceeds the entire gravity platform. Thousands of other vessels line the path. Endless activities stretch through the zone. One would wonder why the galaxy isn't full of starships yet. All shapes and sizes are in the yards, many of them crested with the CSX or Caman emblems.

Ayera whistles. "I get it now. I see why the CSX and Caman Corporations consider themselves rivals to the entire universe."

We pass another station which scans our vessel. Even the weapon locks flash in error.

Axton looks around as if the scanners could see through him. "These guys are serious about security."

Our credentials get us through the defenses. I look at the latest station, whose armaments include lasers and cannons. Hundreds of similar stations float alongside the shield barrier.

"I don't think the Vidor will ever threaten these guys. Their defenses are unreal."

Axton gapes at the endless fortifications. "Never seen anything like it."

"Especially since they make the Vidor's vessels." Ayera points to the nearest facility.

A Vidor supercarrier is before us. I grit my teeth. "I hate those guys."

"*Gunfrey*," Khal exclaims.

"Look at the size of that thing." Axton continues to gape.

The length of the vessel dwarfs even the battle cruiser next to it. With thirteen hangar bays with ports and three bridges, I conclude the supercarrier with its thirteen fighter squadrons of one hundred fighters each is probably the deadliest warship in the galaxy.

The screen flickers. "Captain, we have a comm from the surface."

"Display."

Nashtech's face appears before the screen. The medium-aged black-haired tradesman-turned-senator stares at us with his pale azure eyes. "Kyvar Astilius of the *Resilience*."

"Nashtech. My father spoke highly of you."

He smiles and nods. "I miss your father."

Me too. "We all do."

"He was a good man. He visited here six or seven times over the course of the Lumina Dark Wars. I enjoyed his company every time. He was a great man with a heart of persistence that I'd never before seen. He seemed to be fueled by rejection." He looks away and back. "Unbelievable character."

I nod. It was true. Father loved a challenge and strangely welcomed the impossible, as well as every chance to be a hero. Me? I find myself helpless most of the time, always facing something incredulous. It's the curse of the Astilius family—impossible odds.

"It is good to meet my friend's son. He spoke only wonderful things about you. Just wish our meeting was under different circumstances." He straightens his suit and posture. "What brings you to our galaxy?"

"We come to ask for your help in our cause."

"That's what I expected." His tone turns austere.

"Our galaxy is in trouble and we must turn to you for support."

"I have given my credentials for you to get to vTalis. Take these coordinates and come directly to my hangar. Transmitting now." A pin registers on the screen with coordinates. "Understand, the Caman Corporation is watching you. They suspect you detonated Oxylium, and they are missing one of their cruisers. We have a lot to discuss."

"I—"

The screen flickers out, cutting me off.

Axton turns to me. "This is going to be fun."

Khal laughs. "I think he liked your father more than you."

The endless industrial yards cease, giving way to multiple traffic lines all leading to the mammoth planet vTalis. The planet's lime-green surface powers the colorful luminescence that fills the cabin.

Ayera moans in pleasure. "It's so alive!" she declares, as the lush planet looms ahead. "It is so ethereal."

"It is ..." Axton echoes.

"It's because they outlawed industry years ago," I say.

"No industry?" Khal asks.

"None," I respond. "Industry's not allowed on the surface."

The shield barriers open up and traffic disperses in a dozen different directions. We continue along the path orchestrated by Nashtech. The *Resilience* continues to slow as we break vTalis's atmosphere.

The bridge is filled with the glowing green tapestries of the planet. The surface stretches of green and blue are interrupted only by mountains, large vertical cities, and the organized intersections of gray maglev lines.

"It's more beautiful than I imagined," Ayera says softly. A blue swirl springs under her skin, revealing her ecstatic emotions. Hytilians are passionate about all things green.

Khal shakes his head. "Let's not get too excited. We are also entering the cosmos's ego. The gardens here are but a shadow of the businessman's tailored suit."

I laugh to myself and turn around.

We pass the city of Tylium. Its structures etch into a nearby mountain's skyline. Shadow lifts and sky elevators soar upward through the clouds. We break from the traffic line and descend toward the capital of vTali.

The comm flickers.

"Open."

A Caman Officer appears on the screen.

Oh, no.

His eyes are flinty, his tone stern. "*Resilience.* You have clearance to land at the Senatorial Deck. The coordinates are here."

Coordinates appear on the screen and the comm ceases. I breathe deeply.

The screen flickers. "Redirecting landing to the coordinates provided."

We approach the starport, passing over a few billionaire bronze starships and elite Corian Starfighters. The starport's raised platform is made of transparent glass encircled with a gold and green border.

Axton leans over. "Kyvar, you might want to be more careful with your landing. There are some beauties down there. You can't just fix bronze starships."

"I can," Khal says proudly, and Axton and I exchange a look.

Our designated spot leaves us in an assembly of vessels that include a silver jump jet, a few ambassadorial transports, and a Varian private charter. It isn't a bad look. The *Resilience* can carry her own next to the billionaires of the day, especially with her upgrades.

"He's waiting on you." Ayera points.

Nashtech and two others stand nearby. His demeanor is one of impatience. He appears to be accompanied by a Ghathran and an Ethander.

Ayera stands up. "I will go with you."

"Yes, please."

Ayera and I step off the *Resilience.*

Nashtech nods, turns and begins to walk, and we walk alongside. There are no introductions. "I trust your journey was good." His hands are behind his back.

I smile. "It was good, yes. Some challenges, but we are here."

He avoids looking at me. "Welcome to vTalis. This will be home until we figure things out with *you.*" He takes two steps ahead and turns with a scowl. "You show up here after destroying Oxylium and want my friendship?"

"We are here to ask for your assistance," I respond innocently. "Our people are suffering."

He steps into my personal space while the Ghathran watches us intently. "Did you destroy the mining planet?" Nashtech asks.

"I didn't come here to discuss mining," I respond.

"Did you destroy it?" The Ghathran snarls as he speaks. His breath is abominable.

"We were on a shipment run," I say, "and we exited the system when the solar flares blurred our receptors. Don't blame me and my crew for a solar anomaly."

"That's what I thought. You didn't have anything to do with it." Nashtech turns toward the Ghathran. "That's what I told *you*. He had nothing to do with it."

The Ghathran bows and stalks off.

Nashtech turns and walks slowly. He whispers now. "Good answer. I didn't have time to warn you. He was just testing you. You even called it an anomaly." He laughs. "They like a good pun here. Ghathrans run the feeds for Caman. You might just pull this off."

I'm not so sure. This is going to be complicated. "We don't know anything about Oxylium."

"Certainly, you do. I can read your heat signature."

Irritating. "Heat signature? There is no such thing."

"Of course not," he answers aloud, as if he knows that's what I expect to hear. "But I do know there are reports of a CSX Freighter as the last known contact around Oxylium and its spaceport. There is talk of missing Kanvarian starships and a Caman cruiser. You've left a long list of destruction in your crusade across the galaxies. You are becoming quite the legend."

I swallow deeply, wondering if I should play his game. I remain silent. *But I do like the sound of being a legend.*

We walk through a glass corridor and onto a lift. I look at the Ethander next to him.

Nashtech smiles. "Forgive me for not introducing you. The Ghathran threw me off. Please let me introduce my assistant Tyria, an expert in the laws of vTalis."

The albino Ethander smiles.

I turn to Ayera. "This is Ayera, our science and cultural officer."

"It is a pleasure." Ayera smiles curtly.

I look at Tyria. Her white teeth are the same color as her skin and hair. The only bit of color about her is her crystal green eyes. "Nice to meet you both. I have studied the law and understand there are some loopholes that will allow you to petition your cause and elevate your guilt."

What? "My guilt? I didn't come here to be on trial."

Nashtech laughs. The sound bounces off the walls of the lift. "Oh, Kyvar ... you will be on trial."

CHAPTER SIXTEEN

vTALIS

I stare out of the shuttle window, an unwilling refugee in the escape from Mrunal. My father got us onto the shuttle but refused to let me go with him, and all I can do now is witness his skill—and hopefully his victory—with his ship, the Resolute. *My mother and sister are whispering together, occupied with each other, and they do not watch the battle.*

A stream of crafts follows us, escaping Mrunal. The Vidor fleet is forming out of a wormhole. Multiple solar laser platforms waste no time extending and charging their arrays. Vidor fighters swarm in our direction.

"The fighters," a lady cries. "They are coming for us."

I see Father's vTalis freighter and his fighter squadron tear out of the atmosphere, targeting the rear of the Vidor fighters.

"Father is coming to save us. There." I point out the window.

Many Vidor fighters explode or spiral out of control upon his sudden arrival. Father's squadron turns away at tremendous speed and targets the rest of the Vidor fleet. The Vidor fighters turn away from us and the other defenseless shuttles.

"Atilio saved us," the lady declares.

"Atilio always saves us," another says.

I just wish I could join him.

More of the Vidor fleet exits the Hgate. Father's squadron targets the nearest laser platform. The platform disintegrates into a million light shards illuminating the assembling fleet. A Vidor destroyer focuses on our fighters. A missile impacts the Resolute, *Father's vTalis freighter. Other lasers tear away at his shields.*

Father's squadron targets another laser platform. I lose my line of sight when a rippling explosion annihilates its panels. Many of our fighters fall in the process. I see the Resolute *turn away.*

I lose my line of sight again as more Vidor fighters surround the Resolute *and its squadron. Father pulls away at what looks like 6 BURN. The Vidor fighters cannot keep up with him, yet their battle fleet concentrates on his vessel. Cannons explode around him. His shields must be out by now.*

Father, get out!

He turns and heads toward the final solar laser platform, whose target is the Capitol. I know he won't tear away until it is destroyed.

Father—get out!

He completes his turn and targets the platform, despite the enemy fire.

"Father—get out!" I scream and wake myself.

I sit up and run my hands through my hair. Why do I keep having this dream? I rarely did before. The bitter taste of my father's death is on my tongue.

I should be glad my father is a hero, happy he saved us all. Nearly all of Mrunal escaped. We all got away because of him, but it is no consolation. It never helps. He left me. He abandoned me when I needed him most.

I get out of bed, get dressed, and step out of the guest suite of Nashtech's home into the main room. The back door slides open at my approach.

The morning heat from vTalis's lone stellar surprises me, even at sunrise. Its bright light measures the nearby mountains and Tylium, casting a shadow over the nearby caldera of Lake Ventyra.

I sit on one of the deck chairs. On a different day, I would soak up this paradise, but not today, with the image of my father's death in my mind. Very little could improve my mood.

The door opens. A servant bot approaches, interrupting my private thoughts, and offers a tray with a steaming drink. I grab it and smell it. Hatuerus Brew—the best beans in the cosmos. I smile and nod at the bot.

The bot beeps, nods in return and departs.

I smell the beans, drink again and smile. It's true that very little could improve my mood, except maybe this mug of steaming Hatuerus Brew.

Another noise, and Nashtech steps out of the house in a gold and silver robe. "Good morning."

"Morning. Sleep much?" I ask.

"No. I don't usually sleep much." He gives a dry chuckle. "It's common here in vTalis for the successful to lose sleep." He pops his neck loudly. "It's the nature of the vTali. No good business is ever conducted without a measure of lost sleep."

Yes ... sleep. "I had a dream last night that I cannot get out of my mind."

Nashtech sits opposite me. "Tell me."

"It was my father's last moment."

He frowns.

"I've had the dream since his death. I normally have it every thirty leaps or so. Now I have it every leap."

"Sounds like trauma." He looks at me like my father used to. "Have you dealt with it?"

Gunfrey! I look away. *Why I am here?*

"Kyvar." Nashtech's voice carries compassion. "No one can understand the human heart when it incurs trauma."

I stare away. I'm not here for therapy. I would like to get out of here, but where?

The bot shows up and brings Nashtech a loaded plum blister, the usual choice of the rich and powerful. I consider the drink too rich, in more ways than one.

"Kyvar, look. Your father was the best man I ever knew, but that doesn't change—"

"He *was* the best," I echo.

He frowns and looks off, then takes another conversational tack. "Let me tell you about your father. When I first met him, you were in the thick of the Illicium Dark War. He showed up without invitation here. He was given my name by a random broker and he came pleading for help."

"Without invitation?" I ask.

He nods. "I sent him away."

"You sent him away?"

"It is normal to reject the uninvited. It is culturally unacceptable to just show up and plead with a Senator."

"But he was in need?" I ask.

"I don't care. We don't care if you have a need. We, vTali, don't care."

"Surely you do?" I plead.

He laughs. "You are just like him. It's not right to come unannounced."

"And it's not right to turn down those in need."

He nods. "Very well, if you say so. Still, we don't care about you or him."

I laugh. "But you did help him."

"That's the problem. He came back the next leap and I rejected him again. He rented a place nearby and came by every single leap and petitioned me. Annoyingly persistent."

I smile. "He was always stubborn."

"I finally listened to him. We arranged for him to buy a cruiser and that thing he called the *Steadfast,* and I connected him with a Phaelon broker for a handful of fighters." He laughs. "Instead, he goes to Phaelon and works them over for two red dragon fighter squadrons."

No way. Really? "And that's when he showed up at the Battle of Carax with the reinforcements at the last minute."

Nashtech smiles. "Your people gave me the Citizen's Award after the victory." He nods in the direction of the house. "The award is on the shelf."

"You *do* care."

"I have to admit, I started liking your father a bit more after that. He would show up every time a conflict broke out. Remember the *Claymore* incident?"

I nod. "I do."

Nashtech shakes his head. "We loaned him a cruiser and you guys wrecked it. The Camans placed him under investigation. That's the last thing you want. Investigations are the legal term for business death."

"And that's when he fled to Shivyia?"

He nods. "It took me ages to clean up that mess, but of course, your father returned again and again. That's the problem with you Sidonians. There is no illirium in you." He takes a drink. "Until now ..." he mumbles.

I pull out a diamond cluster of eight Helix stones and place it on the table in front of him. His blue-green eyes show a sudden glow, and he nearly spits out his drink before he can recover his composure enough to speak. "So it's true."

I nod.

He picks up the cluster and examines it. He holds it in the light and his eyes engage every angle. "They are perfect in every way. Beautiful." He sits back in his seat amazed.

"Keep them. It's my gift."

"A gift?" he asks.

"Yes. My gift to you."

"Do you know what this is worth?" he bellows incredulously.

"I do."

"You understand my descendants wouldn't have to work or labor at anything for the next ten GENs?"

I nod. "There is more, much more, if you support our cause."

He puts the diamond cluster down. He pulls his head back. "I wish it was that simple."

"But it is."

"No! It's not. You can't buy your way out of this. Our people have never been to war. Our people have no idea what war is about. We make starships, freighters, cruisers—"

"For everyone else," I interrupt. "You build warships and sell them to the highest bidder, even the Vidor. You have no loyalties but to yourself."

"Hey," he raises his voice. "That's low." He takes a drink. "But it's true. I told you, we don't sleep much."

"We need help. My people are facing annihilation."

He frowns. "Don't forget the Asatruans who sell the JUMP coordinates to whoever can pay, a fact that impacts your defenses."

"Tell me you are not like the Asatruans." I say it, even though I know better.

He smiles at me and shakes his head. "You are such an Astilius. I remember sitting in the same seats with your father in many visits to our Congress. You know the challenges with our government, right?"

"Only what Father told me."

"It's been a while, and it's far more complicated now since Oxylium." He eyes me. "We are a trade oligarchy. Two companies run the planet. Everything functions as a republic, yet the ruling parties are two companies. While some governments have shadow ruling parties or companies that rule via proxy, we rule directly. My party, the CSX party, has command of the government, but if we make poor decisions, we can lose power. As we prepare for our presentation to the Senate, I am very concerned how you have alienated the ally you were supposed to make—the Camans."

He takes a drink and looks at me.

"Don't answer this. Why did you have to blow Oxylium?"

"I—"

"We are glad you did, but that's off the record," he says quietly. "The problem is our constitution. We are in league with an opposing company, yet we are forbidden to wage war. We cannot support you. Even to support you with arms could potentially go against other trade deals."

"Then provide us starships, at least."

"I *do* plan to propose new trade deals with your people."

"That's a start." I grab my drink and sit back in my seat. The brew's temperature is perfect now. I sip and savor the flavor, looking over Lake Ventrya. The sunrise shadow has moved, revealing the water's clarity, and the incandescent waves shimmer with the day's fresh light. "You have a beautiful view of the lake."

He takes a drink. "I spend leaps out here taking it in. My favorite place in all the galaxies is right here."

I concede with a nod. At least we have a potential trade deal.

"Before we start planning for Congress, I have a question for you." Nashtech inflects his voice to a softer tone.

I look over at Nashtech. "You may BURN it by me."

His jaw is set, and he looks fixedly at me. "Where did you get the *Resilience*? I remember a boring Class C Freighter called the *Impetus* bypassing our system. Now you have a souped-up converted freighter turned starship. When I heard about your alleged escapades, I looked up your vessel. Guess what I found?"

"What?" I mumble.

"The only record of a vessel with the name *Resilience* was originally ordered by an Atilio Astilius from our space yards."

"When?" I ask.

"Three leagues ago."

I scratch my head. "That doesn't make sense. He died three leagues ago."

"How is this possible?"

"I don't know."

"I was rather hoping you did. It might answer a lot of questions."

CHAPTER SEVENTEEN

vTALIS

"You are not listening!" Nashtech's face is red. "Tyria keeps explaining the legal situation. Your only option is to plead guilty."

We are conferring with Nashtech and his legal assistant before we attend the meeting of Congress. The conference, so far, has only high marks in the category of unproductivity.

"You know we can't do this." Ayera's gills flare up. "A guilty plea counters our Queen's call for galactic justice."

Nashtech shakes his head. "You don't understand our customs. We, vTali, don't care about galactic justice. Any call for galactic justice has no relevance on this end of the cosmos. Any non-guilty party gets no audience with our Senate in their final decisions. No one will listen to you. If you are guilty, you have an audience. Use the guilty plea to squeeze the deals from them. If—"

"That's why you must plead guilty and ask for a lesser judgment," Tyria adds.

"And this plea opens the door for you to have a platform. *Then* you speak of justice," Nashtech concludes.

"Why have any judgment at all?" I ask.

Nashtech stares at me. "Because we don't care about people who are not guilty. You don't get it. Our kind doesn't care about your kind."

Tyria levels at me. "Confess you blew up the moon because of the injustices of the Caman Corporation."

"*Then* plead your case," Nashtech confirms again. "They will demand all of the stones and you will give them over. Or at least some of them."

I shake my head. "It doesn't work that way."

"You said yourself there were more on the moon than anyone ever estimated. Keep what you need, let a warrant be issued, issue your payment as settlement, and everything is over."

"All while our people are slaughtered. No!" I shout.

Nashtech frowns. He shakes his head. "You're such an Astilius ..." He takes a bite from a spiced laterik roll.

Tyria settles down easily. "This isn't Sidonia. You must plead guilty in our system to receive justice."

An angry blue swirl spirals under Ayera's chin. "We can't do that. It's not our nature."

Tyria provides an annoying smile. "Nature is all around. It's *our* nature. Guilt here is defined in different ways. It's a measure of half-truth combined with the capacity of your conscience to stomach it."

"What?" I ask. "We don't throw away integrity for business deals."

Nashtech sneers at me. "But you are wrong! You shouldn't have blown Oxylium. You can't deny this."

"I can for now." I grab a spiced roll and smile.

"What happens if they call for an investigation?" Tyria asks.

"That's my biggest fear," Nashtech murmurs.

"I don't believe arguing is the best course of action." Tyria is as tactful as she is pale. "I believe your best approach is confession."

"No," Ayera says.

Nashtech looks skyward in frustration. "We've been here half a leap and haven't agreed on anything."

"We did agree to a proposed trade deal," I say.

Nashtech moans. "*After* you confess your guilt and pay off, say, eighty-three percent of it."

I shake my head. "I can't do that."

"Then you're not going to get your deal." Nashtech stands up. "Let's just go."

We prepare to leave.

Nashtech looks at me. "I'd bet you feel you are ready, yet you are going to do the same thing your father did. Plead the humanitarian card and point out genocides, injustices, all that. Right?"

"Right," I respond. "Our people are suffering, and the armaments of the cosmos are here, right here."

"We are pacifist. You know this?" Nashtech asks.

I've heard that before. I look away, grabbing my bag. "Have you ever met an Asatruan named Ackbray?" I ask.

I gather my things, yet no one answers for a moment. I look at Nashtech and his face is still. Tyria is staring at him.

Nashtech eventually responds. "Why do you ask?"

"I met him in Asatyria. That's exactly what he said."

He clenched his jaw. "I've never heard of him."

"Just curious."

He's answered my question without even realizing it.

We prepare our things and step toward the lift. The door opens and we step in.

"Take your places." Nashtech points to the floor.

I look down. There are Holox squares on the floor. I didn't realize this was a maglift. We step into our positions without comment.

The lift takes us down four floors where ambient lighting kicks in. The lift slowly turns ninety degrees as the floor moves under us. Seats come up out of the floor in the place of the squares. I ease myself into the emerging seat. The seats are quite comfortable. Legumna leather no less.

The lift slides onto a maglev track and the ceiling flickers into a transparent film. We push forward toward the lake and the surface, and then merge into a shared maglev line with other maglifts. We seamlessly run ahead until it halts at the lake.

"We now wait for the bridge."

"There is no bridge over the lake." I state.

"It's gotten slower these days."

The maglev starts to move and advance across the lake. I look over the side, wondering where the bridge came from.

Nashtech laughs. "It rises once a day to allow traffic."

We move across Lake Ventyra and over the rise of the extinct volcano. We round a few corners and venture over the next rise. I am blinded by the light of the sun when we descend to another crater.

The next caldera holds Lake Thallium, which flashes the evening sunrays in our direction. Another glaring light beams from a structure on a whitewashed island.

"This is where we meet." Tyria points ahead.

The isolated congressional seat of vTalis sits alone on the island. The Senatorial complex is impressive with its wide porcelain wash and electrum dome. The columns are studded with gold, and the steps glitter with silver. Everything has gilded undertones, even the ripples from the green lake. It looks gawdy and earthy, inviting yet daunting. Everything you would expect from the vTali.

Another bridge rises, and the maglev passes over to the island. We step out of our transport onto a transparent walkway. The sheen of the green waters reflects upward.

"Please excuse me a moment." Nashtech walks away to multiple dignitaries awaiting him.

"I will show you around." Tyria leads us to the guest chambers which overlook the Senate. Her pale skin, white hair, and crystal eyes are a contrast to the lean tan features of the vTali. A few Shivyuns waddle around, and there are a few notaries from Atheares.

We sit down on stools overlooking the assembly.

"When you go to speak, be aggressive," Tyria says.

"Aggressive?" Ayera asks.

The assembly comes together.

"We respect confidence. What Nashtech liked about your father was his confidence and resolution. You, I guess, will be the resilient one." She looks away. "Which means you will fail a lot. Ah ..." She looks back at me. "But you rise again. I hope today is one of your rising occasions."

Her crystal eyes penetrate me. She is a bit too intuitive. Unfortunately, I don't get the feeling that today will be a rising occasion.

"Look." She points to the assembly. "There are twenty-two seats in the assembly. Each has a vote. If the trade vote comes up, you only have to have a simple majority."

"That's it?" Ayera asks.

"That's it. Sometimes ... there is a sway vote though."

"Sway vote?" I ask.

"The sway vote will occur if there is a tie. Then the vote is measured by two new members of the council. There is one vote by the Shivyuns and one by my people."

"Really?" I ask.

"Yes. It was the result of the Camans wanting to dilute CSX power."

"Has it worked?"

"No. Quite the opposite so far."

The speaker starts to make announcements. Tyria angles for us to start walking. "They will call you soon. If you can win the CSX vote and the sway voters, you have support for your cause. That is, of course, if no one asks for an investigation."

We arrive at the entrance and top of the chamber. "Let's wait here."

The speaker proceeds with announcing all the members of the Senate. I hear my name and I start to step forward.

"Not yet." Tyria puts out her pale hand. "Wait for Nashtech."

I see Nashtech heading up the walkway toward me.

"The Voice will guide you," Ayera says.

I shake my head.

"One more thing," Tyria adds. "See the lean gangly Caman over there?"

"The tall one?"

"Yes, him. His name is Tlaagon. Don't even look at him. He's a firebrand and a troublemaker."

So am I. "I will try."

"Come." Nashtech holds out his hand, inviting us down the stairs. He turns as I approach, and we walk down together. "You will be expected to deliver your message soon. Are you ready?"

"I will be when I start speaking."

Nashtech smiles. "I usually feel the same way."

Many of the Camans eye me, some with no small amount of hate.

"Nashtech, there is one thing I haven't shared yet with you."

"What is it?" he whispers as we walk.

"You know I have the Hgates?"

"The Hgates?" he asks. "You got them from ...?"

"The Asatruans," I whisper.

"And you tell me now?"

"I figured it was best to give you some warning."

He laughs. "You Astilius."

We sit.

The speaker of the assembly stands up. "Honored guest—Kyvar Astilius. Please stand and address this assembly."

I stand and breathe deeply. "Prestigious members of the vTalis Council, I come on behalf of the Kopernian Confederation and our two respective star systems, the Sardis and Hytilian systems. Our planets and peoples are in a war of extermination by the Vidor. The Vidor have broken every galactic law and treaty. They have destroyed cities and planets and have now broken through our system's defenses with new Hgates."

"Can you prove this?" a CSX man asks.

"We can. Particle analysis shows the elemental applications involved. Many of you may know my father Atilio Astilius. In previous wars, he visited vTalis, calling for aid. Many times, you came through with supplies and starships, and I believe once, in proxy, your actual starships were piloted by my people."

A few Senators whisper to each other.

"I remember another time when your father was ostracized from our planet," a Caman yells. It is the gangly character Tlaagon. I try not to look at him.

"Yes. I remember the incident. I do remember he was given another opportunity in which your Excellencies granted him favor."

"You know we are pacifist?" shouted a CSX man.

"No one can look the other way when harm comes. No one can turn the other way when atrocities are being committed, or planets are being destroyed."

Nashtech moans.

A Caman man laughs. "It happens every day. This is vTalis. We are businessmen. It's just business."

A CSX man stands up. "Agreed. Why you? What do you have worth defending on the remote side of the cosmos?"

"Billions of souls, and the fate of future GENs."

"We don't care about your GENs," a different Caman adds. He is seated next to Tlaagon. "I propose we move to end this discussion."

"We will pay for your assistance."

"With what?" Tlaagon blasts the question.

Nashtech shakes his head. "No, no, no," he whispers.

I look to both sides of the Senate. "We desire your friendship, and a treaty of goodwill and an alliance."

Tlaagon receives a message from a courier. He stands up and unfolds the message. "An alliance?"

I look to the CSX side. "We can pay for your assistance. In many ways we lack what you possess in armaments and warships."

"Even if we support your people, we will not engage with the Vidor," a CSX man shouts.

"What if I told you we had JUMP mappings to bypass the Vidor system? Would your people be interesting in securing passage?"

Many of them whisper to each other.

"You mean you have JUMP mappings from the Asatruans?" the same CSX man asks.

Nashtech smiles. He seems to like this approach, at least a little.

"They can be provided."

"To what extent? How many routes?" another CSX man asks.

I smile. "Enough to secure a long-term caravan bypassing the Vidor."

Nashtech stands up. All their heads, even the Camans', turn toward him. "I vote we continue this discussion and the details. I consider this a deep dive proposal for business opportunities and trade routes with concessions."

Tlaagon grunts in disgust. "Tell us how you will pay for this support."

"We have funds," I answer.

"I say again, Kyvar, how do you propose to pay for all of this?"

"Our people are prepared to transfer all of our wealth if need be," I lie.

"That's going too far. We don't do business with slaves." He looks at his Caman friends. "We have more ethics than this. I propose you have another avenue of wealth you do not speak of."

"What is this?" Nashtech asks Tlaagon.

Tlaagon looks at his note again. "We all know you are Kyvar Astilius. A CSX Freighter was last seen in the region of Oxylium when the mining planet exploded. I have confirmation with a Captain Morellis that you were leaving the area when he went to investigate. You possess data on Gates that could only be afforded with Helix stones, and there are the issues of heat signature."

Gunfrey! Why does everyone test me with the heat signature? Is it really a thing?

"And you come here with a request for military aid. You declare you have wealth commitments that don't exist in your silly remote two-star system."

"As stated to Captain Morellis, we were in route with a trade shipment."

Tlaagon smiles. "I propose we continue our deep dive analysis into our business relationship with the Kopernians. In addition, we push forward with an investigation into the mysterious CSX Freighter *Resilience*. The same vessel and its crew which appeared out of hyperspace as the last potential witnesses of the Oxylium solar flare disaster, as you called it."

His fellow Senators stand up and shout for an investigation. The rage of their support of him is loud and irrevocable.

The Speaker of the Chamber stands up. "In light of these accusations, there must be an investigation into Kyvar Astilius, his crew, and their connection with the Oxylium incident."

Nashtech scowls at me. "I demand an immediate search of the *Resilience*." He sits down.

I stare at the Speaker. "I aggressively disagree with your assertion, Speaker, and your need for an investigation." I turn toward Tlaagon. "But if it behooves you to search my vessel, you may comb the *Resilience* for anything of value."

Tlaagon snarls at me. "We will begin our investigation immediately." He nods to one of his agents, who turns and makes for the exit, speaking into his comm. "Are you done, Kyvar?"

"I am." I look at the Speaker. "I look forward to your deliberations into our innocence. We are here for support and for galactic justice."

CHAPTER EIGHTEEN

vTali Senatorial Lounge

"Kyvar, the name is Talecium." A tall, lean, polished CSX political officer sits down between Nashtech and me. He holds out his hand.

I shake his hand. "Nice to meet you."

"Is it true?" he asks. He has the look of an intelligence officer more than a shipping captain or political player. His chiseled cheekbones and tight haircut give it away.

I don't answer. Maybe I learned something from Ackbray.

He comes in closer and speaks in a barely audible voice. "If it is, it was the greatest thing that ever happened to us. Well done." He pats me on the back and walks off.

I turn to Nashtech. "Is he one of your shadow guys?" I remember my father telling me about their shadow wars across the galaxies.

Nashtech looks at me, grabs his drink, and smiles. "We are pacifist, my dear friend."

Heard that before. "Are you sure you don't know Ackbray?"

He clenches his jaw, just as he did the last time I asked. "No, I don't."

I take a drink of Trasilium Ale. The flavor is rich. It's been brewed all day. I glance out the window at the Senatorial complex. The rich palladium architecture reflects vTalis's dim purple sunset.

Another man approaches. He looks like a gaudy caravan merchant, all covered in rich garments and jewelry. He comes in close. "If you possess the Horde of Oxylium, I will personally send a fleet of warships to stall the Vidor. It won't be enough to stop them, but it will slow them until your allies arrive."

Sounds appealing. I look at Nashtech. He slightly shakes his head with pursed lips.

"Thank you for the offer," I say. "I believe we will be coming to an arrangement soon enough."

"Very well." He lays down his ID card and walks off.

I slide the ID card to the stack of ID cards on the far side of the table.

"Let's just say he's a swindler," Nashtech whispers. "He's only allowed in here because he's the owner's nephew."

Other dignitaries visit us and pay their homage to Nashtech. I sense he loves this, where everyone seeks him out and gives him reverence. And all in these luxurious seats and accommodations—the brew, the Grehem ribs and the mashed roumgala. This is living, but I've had my fill. I am sure Ayera, at another table with Tyria, is ready to go as well.

"Nashtech. You know we leave soon?"

"Kyvar." He speaks with his hands. "Stay. You have the wealth of the cosmos, and I am honestly enjoying seeing everyone drool over you. They figure maybe you can just drop a few Helix stones in their bag for their kindness."

I shake my head. "Our galaxy is in danger."

His face sobers instantly. "You must stay to face the deliberations."

"How long, a few leaps?

"More like twenty. This is a governmental apparatus. We are slow in government and rapid in business."

"I've noticed," I say, in my driest tone. "We are leaving once the inspectors are done with the *Resilience*."

"Please. You will turn the tide. You did reasonably well today." He lies.

"No, I didn't. That goon got the best of me."

He concedes and nods. "Perhaps."

"Nashtech. I thank you for your hospitality. If you deliberate in our favor, we receive it and will pay for it. If not, I am truly sorry." I hand him a drive of the JUMP Coordinates. "Take this, and you have instructions on how to bypass our battle lines."

His eyes widen. The Hgate coordinates are worth their wealth in transportation costs and labor fees alone. For traders, it's like giving them free fuel expenses for a lifetime, along with new express routes for commerce.

"Kyvar. These alone are worth our partnership." His face carries concern. "I honestly don't think we can get you the support you need in time."

I set my jaw. "Do what you can."

✪✪✪

Nashtech and I walk toward a private commissary market. A gold sign reads *vTali Politico*. Khal waits at the entrance.

"This is your engineer?" Nashtech asks.

"This is Khal, the best engineer in our galaxy."

"Nice to make your acquaintance." Khal bows.

"Grab whatever you need," Nashtech says. "I am paying."

Khal's eyes widen. "Anything?"

"Anything."

"He does own the place," I add.

We walk through a digitized wall. The wall flickers as we walk through it. The morning heat dissipates instantly, and the smells of exotic perfumes and fresh foods flood the senses. To the right is a saloon with open air couches and a fragrance department. It's not like the normal commissaries with flashing lights and tracking retinal scanners.

"This commissary is an exclusive market for the Senators, ambassadors and other upscale politicians. Its stock is limited, but everything is first-class." He whispers, "They pay better."

I turn toward the food department.

"No need for food, Kyvar," Khal says. "I raided the local markets yesterday. Best Lombardy chips, Terra wings and Ranger Ale I've ever had." He grabs a drift cart, and we move in the direction of the hardware and engineering backrooms.

Nashtech checks his comm. "Gentlemen, if you don't mind, I will catch up with you." He walks off.

"Are you having fun on this planet?" Khal asks.

I shake my head. "I can't stand politics."

We get to the hardware section, and Khal brainlessly drops numerous items on the cart. Invisible walls on the cart rise to keep the items from falling. "Love shopping with others' money though ..."

I laugh.

We advance to the Ion battery isle. The entire isle is dedicated to the remarkable Ion cells. Khal grabs a case. He checks the expiration date. "Still freaks me out how these babies power everything, from a starship to this cheap cart." He kicks the drift cart. It shakes and resumes its hovering. "Kind of took the fun out of engineering."

"And the only difference is the engine," I add.

He smirks. "Spoken like an engineer."

We head to the comm isle and grab some extra line feeds and updated star map drives.

"Why are you grabbing map drives for the Vidor System?" I ask.

"I noticed *Resilience* has some holes in its mapping."

"It does?"

"There are a number of gaps. Just filling in the dead spots. I remember Vidor territory and the Starduc System."

"I get Vidor, because it's not shared, but why Starduc?"

"No idea. Because there is nothing there, maybe?"

We advance to the health section and grab stellar sleep regulator pills.

"Don't forget slags for Ayera," Khal reminds me.

"Why does she take those?"

"I don't know. Just grab them." He tosses them on the cart. The cart walls rise again to contain our purchases.

"I forgot laser casings, and as long as our rich friend is paying, we need cartridges for the lateral mags."

I shake my head. Cartridges are a luxury. "Just go."

The cart is quite full. I turn toward the exit, where Nashtech stands, looking annoyed as I approach.

"Kyvar, I have word they found nothing in the *Resilience*. Suspiciously innocent you are, they say. Where did you hide them?"

I stare at him and say nothing.

He shakes his head. "You are learning almost too much here."

"There was no way I was going to plead guilty before your people."

"You still don't understand, but that's over now. What matters is that Tlaagon is after you. I have received word they are issuing a bounty on you. Must you go without our support?"

"We must."

"Then know this. If you leave, I never had this conversation with you, nor did I warn you. No one has ever broken out of our system. The station perimeter is invulnerable. I can't promise you that I can protect you."

"I understand."

"No, you don't." He raises his voice. "I can only stall them. I have issued orders for all stations to be manned by CSX personnel, but that doesn't guarantee your safety. Kyvar, are you sure you want to do this?"

I nod.

"*Gunfrey!*" he shouts. "If you do break out, you will be attacked from all sides. They will be waiting for you. The Camans have friends throughout the cosmos. With a price on your head, bounty hunters, the slime of the universe, all of them will be after you. Are you *sure*, Kyvar?"

I am growing more annoyed. "Yes."

"Just like your father." He flings his arms into the air in a gesture of frustration. "And if you survive, the Camans will come after you with starships, battle cruisers and *their* drone frigates. They might very well join forces with the Vidor and force your submission."

I smile. "That would never happen without approval from your council."

"It doesn't work that way."

"Sure, it does."

He regards me in silence for a moment, then says, "I see more of your father every single time I speak with you."

Khal walks up with the laser casings and mag cartridges.

"Those are my favorite," Nashtech points at the mag cartridges.

Khal nods. "The Anticlines make the best cartridges."

As we head out, Nashtech gives me one more bit of advice.

"One thing, Kyvar. Though I don't approve of your reckless approach, I do think fondly of that freighter of yours. Take care of her. She will take care of you."

CHAPTER NINETEEN

vTALIS

"Welcome back, Captain." *Resilience* speaks through the comm system as I advance down the corridor. "Caman agents scoured the vessel. I gave them our mockup records and flight history as you requested."

"Well done, *Resilience*." I step onto the bridge. "Axton, how did it go?"

"We put on a good show," Ayera says. Axton swivels in his seat. "They were angry. Very angry. There were lots of threats about what would happen if they discovered Helix stones. One of them was particularly nasty—"

"Yeah, some tall, lanky politician." Ayera points toward the weapons room. "I had to call in Xander."

Axton laughs. "When he walked onto the bridge, everyone was fairly nice again."

I sit down and smile, recalling Xander's list of detailed weaponry. A military bot has its advantages.

"One of the Camans still kept swearing and mocking us, though. He had a strange name Tla ...Tlagoo—"

"Tlaagon." I grit my teeth. "Anything else?"

"I picked up something in the corridor as well," *Resilience* adds. "I heard them say they would never support any sorties against the Vidor, because the Vidor are their second largest business partner."

"Of course," Ayera adds. "Their integrity *is* their business."

"*Resilience*, get us out of here," I order.

The Ion Drives ignite, the airlocks seal, and the freighter lifts off the platform.

A servant bot brings me a pink petrolyte drink. "I was just thinking I was thirsty." I take a sip and give the bot a nod in acknowledgment. "How does he do this?"

Axton nods his head and holds the same drink.

Ayera provides the scientific answer. "He senses your hydration levels. It's his primary function. He's even learned your preferences at different times of the day. He is constantly logging our eating habits."

"Remarkable. Creepy, but remarkable." Axton salutes the bot with his drink.

I address the bot just as it scoots off. "What is your name?"

It beeps.

"Does anyone know its name?" I ask the crew.

No one answers.

"We'll call you Hydrobot."

He beeps and seems to like the attention, but maybe not the name.

"*Resilience*, set a course for Shivyia."

On Shivyia's loading platform, Lathan, the Shivyun, removes his visor. He gleams at me with his tiny eyes. "Here are your ..."

He speaks so slow that I struggle putting his words together. "Stones?"

"Stones ... yes." He scratches his forehead. "We played ..." He fumbles with his words. "They dig well." His face forms into a toothless grin.

I grab a handful of Helix stones from a crate. I take his hand, form it into an open palm, and release the stones. "Take more, please."

"Thank you." He mumbles and nods.

"Thank *you* for watching our stones." I bow.

The two Shivyuns from Oxylium waddle up from behind him.

"Captain ..." They reach for me and put their arms around me. They give me an uncomfortable Shivyun hug. It's a bit too soft for my comfort and awkwardly low. My arms rest on their soft fat shoulders, making for the strangest hug in the cosmos.

"We will help you to the vessel." The male waddles past me.

The female agrees with beeps and moans.

I help them with the first crate and the crew arrives to grab the other crates. The crates are loaded one by one into *Resilience's* Bay Two.

I turn to Lathan. "Thank you again for trusting my father and me."

He bows. "We are indebted ... to the Astilius clan." He holds his hand to his heart, bows, turns, and waddles off.

The two from Oxylium remain. They stare at me with pleading eyes that seem to water. They speak quickly compared to Lathan. "If you will allow us, we would like to return to your crew."

No. "I can't allow you to come. We are headed home, to the farthest reaches of the cosmos. We may *all* be killed."

The Shivyuns moan and start to kneel.

"Don't do that." I grab them and pull them up. *This is crazy.* "It's just ... I don't want you two to die."

"We are willing," they mumble.

"It's dangerous out there," I plead with them.

They sag down and start to squeal softly. Their squeal is pitiful, and it jars my ears.

Ayera walks up behind me. She puts her arm on my shoulder. "Kyvar, let them come."

I lower my head and level at them. "You know we may die before we even get home?"

They beep, moan, and stare at me with pleading eyes.

"Okay, then, let's get on with it," I say, in reluctant acquiescence. Their quiet squeals turn into an excited hum and they start to hop strangely.

Ayera smiles. "Come on, you two. The cosmos is calling."

❂❂❂

We exit the artificial atmosphere of Shivyia, and I turn my chair around.

"So ... how do we get home?"

No response.

I turn back around. "*Resilience*, display our routes home using all available means."

The screen flickers for a few mSEGs until it populates with the top ten routes home. The hazardous first option remains twelve leaps. The next closest option is seventy-eight leaps.

Option One is listed in detail on the right of the screen. The route starts at the Elextrious Gate just outside the vTalis sector. Each of the legs has its challenges, and survival is hardly certain. Impossibilities are everywhere. It involves six wormholes, one black hole, a leg through enemy Vidor Territory, and another through the Demilitarized Galactic Zone.

This is absurd. I run my hands through my hair and sit back in my seat. Axton is fixed on the screen. Ayera's eyes stare ahead with a relentless green. A blue swirl appears under her skin, and her gills are inflamed, and she seems to be speechless.

"Khal?"

"We have no option," he answers, for once without sarcasm.

Ayera takes her eyes off the screen. Luminescent tears flow down her check. She nods her head. I looked at the Shivyuns, and they mumble in agreement. They are good with whatever we decide. Axton just frowns and nods.

I run my hands through my hair again. "Why? *Why* does the most dangerous route have to *always* be the only option?"

Ayera mumbles a quote from a Hytilium poet. "'When death calls, we must face it head on—'"

"'—lest it surprise us.'" I complete the verse.

"If we don't take the short route home, there may be no home," Khal adds.

I turn around. "*Resilience*, calculate our chances of survival."

"Kyvar, you know you shouldn't do that," Khal says, with a rueful smile.

The screen flickers until a solid red 0.37% appears on the bottom left corner.

"Care to see the detail of the calculations?" *Resilience* asks.

"No," I reply firmly. "*Resilience*, set a course for the Elextrious Gate."

"*Gunfrey!*" I curse and complain at the traffic, "These shield perimeters ..."

We pass a station. It displays the pitifully slow maximum

speed of BURN 1 and our weapons lock lighting erroneously flickers.

Nashtech's credentials automatically push us through, and a new cloaking setting holds over *Resilience's* Bay Two.

We pass more stations. Some of them have tractor beams setting max pace governors to reduce traffic. We are wedged among starships, luxury liners and space barges when traffic starts to finally give way. A nearby station displays max BURN 3.

I edge the *Resilience* into another lane and ease down the Hammer. Certain vessels seem to be appearing repetitively on the feeds.

"*Resilience*, are we being followed?"

"Two starfighters, Caman Model 14s." Their make and model appear on the screen. Single seaters. Max Speed 10 BURN. Lasers.

"Hail them."

The screen flickers a few times. No response.

"Keep hailing them."

The screen flickers a few more times until our hail is finally accepted.

A Caman lieutenant answers. He wears the standard orange and blue. His face is flushed, and he looks young, very young. "Hail," he answers.

"Hey buddy, I feel like you are following us. What's up?"

The young pilot doesn't answer.

"I am Kyvar Astilius of the *Resilience*. And yourself?"

"I am Lieutenant Shives of the *Growler*."

"My sensors indicate you have been behind us since we passed vTalis."

His smile is small and cold. "You must be mistaken."

Whatever. I flick off the comm. "*Resilience*, keep an eye on them. I am sure they will fall off a bit and come back. And summon Xander."

"Yes, Captain."

We pass another station and increase to 5 BURN. The *Resilience* ranges past slower traffic. We pass another two stations, the governors are lifted, and the shield vestiges expand.

"*Resilience*, take us to 10 BURN slowly."

The trailing starfighters fade behind us.

Xander approaches the bridge. He marches in, appearing as though prepared for battle. His hands are by his side and his martial air is evident. He stands at attention. "Captain, you called?"

"Did you do what I asked?"

"All is prepared," he answers, rubbing his hands together.
Good.

Khal shakes his head. "You've got to stop this."

"Come on ..." Xander responds with human flair.
Where did he pick that up?

Khal shakes his head again. "You come in all tough and *then* you have style. I like it, but you have to have the swagger to go with it. Drop a shoulder at least."

Xander drops a shoulder. "Come on ..."

Awkward, but better.

Khal laughs. "Keep that up."

"Xander," I ask, "where do you stay when you're not on the bridge?"

"In the weapons room."

"What do you do there?" Khal asks.

"I prep the weapons, wait for orders, and charge."

"Xander, please sit over there next to Axton when you are not working." I point to the empty seat.

"Now?" he responds mechanically.

"Just sit," Khal answers.

Xander sits in the empty chair, and Axton smiles at him. "Just like part of the crew."

I look over at Xander. All the seats are occupied now. I nod as a strange satisfaction washed over me. "How does it feel, Xander?"

He smiles and sits back in the soft lagumna hide leather seat. "I could get used to this."

The Shivyuns beep and moan.

The screen flickers. "Captain, my long-range sensors indicate a cluster of Caman vessels at the last station centered around a drone frigate, and the starfighters are trailing us at 10 BURN."
Gunfrey!

The screen displays a list of vessels. Class C Drone Frigate, with ninety auto-cannon drones. advanced ancillary Corian shields, missiles, lasers. Two additional Caman Model 14s and a missile-armed version of the same starfighter.

I grunt. I hate drones, especially the auto-cannon models. I've see them tear vessels apart worse than Vidor swarms. This is no small trap.

"Axton, thoughts?"

He says little as a rendering of the vessels appear on the screen.

"Khal, ideas?"

"You're the crazy one," Khal responds. "Do your thing!"

We pass the second-to-last station. One more before the sector ends.

"Xander, are you sure everything is ready?" I ask.

He nods. "Everything is ready."

Axton stares at me. "What is ready?"

I ignore him. "Ayera?"

No response.

"Ayera?"

"Do your thing ..." She mumbles. She gets quiet when she is worried.

We approach the drone frigate with the three starships flanking it. Weapons lock indicators flash in the cabin.

Traffic starts to thin and move in other directions until there are no obstacles between the Camans and our freighter. I push up the Hammer to 1 BURN.

"Hail the bridge of the station." Maybe I can convince the laser cannon- bearing station to intervene.

The screen flickers.

A Caman officer appears on the screen. *Gunfrey*! He wears a scowl. "Kyvar Astilius of the *Resilience*. Your vessel is not allowed to leave the vTalis Protective Zone. You and your vessel are currently under investigation. According to Mandate 51.23b, 'no persons or peoples that are currently under investigation are allowed to leave the vTalis sector.'"

"Why is there a Caman Corporation officer in control of this station?" I demand. "Your kind is not over the vTalis sector."

The officer stares at me. "Our *kind* ... desire you to be safe during the investigation."

The feed of the station officer is trumped by another feed. The face of Senator Tlaagon appears. "Kyvar Astilius. I never liked your father, nor do I like you." I can almost feel the hatred in his voice. "We know what you did. Surrender your vessel."

I slow the vessel further.

"Kyvar, do you know what I love about drones?"

I scowl at the Senator. "Entertain me, goon."

His face turns red. "They have the ability to rip apart your vessel piece by piece, leaving me with the precious stones and you and your friends to the pitiful expanse of space."

A squadron of drones leaves the frigate. In my head I can almost hear the silent malicious hum and nasty rotation of their autocannons.

The two rear starfighters line up in firing position behind us. Lights flicker throughout the bridge.

Tlaagon levels at me. "Surrender your vessel for inspection."

"You reviewed the vessel earlier," I say.

"We know you hid the stones in Shivyia, and you have them on board. Like your father, you took refuge in Shivyia. You are just like him." The Senator's lips start to foam. "A coward hiding underground."

What an angry beast of a man.

"You are surrounded, Kyvar." Tlaagon screams. "Surrender!"

Red laser-lock lights flash to the front, starfighters assume battle formation in the rear, and the drones are incoming. We haven't even left the vTalis sector yet. This is going to be a long journey home.

CHAPTER TWENTY

15TH QUADRANT

"My drones will cut you to—"

I flick off the comm. "*Resilience,* target the frigate's bridge and control tower."

I wink at Xander and he tries to wink back.

Targeting registers on the screen. "Fire."

I extract the Hammer and drop it to 5 BURN. The Ion Drives roar, and we turn away from the frigate toward the shield perimeter.

The Shivyuns squeal.

Axton transforms his station into a Holox weapons control center and targets the starfighters behind us.

Shrill lasers pepper the shields.

"Shields at ninety-seven percent."

Drones and missiles race toward us. I yank hard on the Hammer to prevent us from crashing into the shield perimeter.

"Release mags," I shout.

The Shivyuns squirm in their seats, beeping and moaning.

Magnetic decoys throw off a few missiles, which slam into the shield perimeter. Lasers continue to tear at the shields. "Shields at ninety-four percent."

The vessel rocks when a missile slams into the shields. "Shields at eighty-two percent."

"Come on, Axton," I say.

I yank the Hammer again.

"This isn't exactly a steady platform," he complains.

The ship recoils from our cannon blasts. One of the Caman starfighters peels away after being hit.

"The drones are closing in. Slow them down!"

Axton turns in his seat and focuses on the short-range drones. He picks off a few of them before they get into range.

"Take them out!"

"There are only ninety of them," Axton says sourly as he cranks away with laser and cannons.

I angle the *Resilience* back toward the frigate. This will be a real test. The frigate has the strongest individual Corian shields in the cosmos.

I open the comm. "Tlaagon, you want the Helix stones?"

"Give them to us!" His hand is in a fist.

"I am sending one your way."

The Senator laughs. "You fool. I will—"

I kill the feed.

The missile hits the frigate's shield in a white microburst, followed by successive bursts until it strikes home. The missile flies through the glass bridge and detonates inside the cabin, rupturing its hull, and breaking off its control tower.

The drones fall limp. One of them breaks apart against our shields.

The ship rocks from a pulsating mSEG laser blast.

"Shields at seventy-four percent." A missile slams against our shields and cannons shells explode around us. "Shields at sixty-two percent."

I roll the *Resilience*, release mags, dip below the disabled frigate, and drop the hammer to 12 BURN. We tear away from the scene, exiting the vTalis sector.

The screen flickers. "Four missiles incoming—I can deal with them."

Axton stares at me, but I shrug my shoulders. Why not allow the onboard to 'deal with them'?

Axton nods his head and grabs his Holox pad casually. Even gunners can take a break.

At 10 BURN, the starfighters won't be able to keep up until we get to the heavily trafficked Elextrious Gate. I sit back and breathe deeply before I look over at Xander.

"Well done. The Helix stones created the vortex we were looking for."

The bot smiles.

Axton turns toward me. "You put a Helix stone on a missile?"

I nod.

"Brilliant!" Khal exclaims.

"No one would dare tip a warhead with a million illirium ..." Ayera mumbles, quoting the Exetrius professor from the Asatruan library Helix compilation. "The Voice even speaks through mortal men."

"Only you, Kyvar." Axton smiles. "Only you."

Khal laughs. "We might just make it home."

The ship rocks as *Resilience* commences fire at the missiles, which all explode in succession.

I look to Xander. "Please head back to the weapons room and add Helix tips to every missile warhead," I glance at Axton, "and cannon shell."

"Yes, sir," he responds informally, and departs for the weapons room.

"Even cannon shells?" Axton asks.

"Why not?" I answer.

"I don't like how the station fired at us." Ayera says. "They will accuse us of attacking them. How did the Caman officer get in that position?"

"Tlaagon probably forced the change," Khal responds.

"It doesn't matter, though. We killed a vTalis Senator," Ayera replies. "Technically, you declared war on vTalis."

"I didn't have a choice."

"It doesn't matter. Now we're *all* wanted fugitives."

The Elextrious Gate comes into view. Its blue swirl and pulsating red light dominates the vantage. Space particles shimmer with the unpredictable lighting. I ease up on our speed to 1 BURN. Traffic lines start to form again around the directional station. We pass multiple craft and a cargo vessel. I edge our way through the traffic, until I am forced to fall in line behind a heavy freighter.

We are now seventh in line for the Gate.

I look to the feeds. The starfighters are closing. "Come on ..."

The dull gray directional station reflects the blue and red swirl from the Gate. Despite its directional purpose, it does have a swivel cannon hanging below it. Hopefully no Caman officers are manning this one.

The feeds reveal the Caman starfighters edging closer. No one would reasonably engage with this much traffic. I settle the

Resilience even closer to the heavy freighter and hold the ship's controls tightly. "Come on, we don't have all leap ..." I gripe.

"Patience, Kyvar," Ayera says.

I moan. I am not patient. Why should I be?

We are now sixth in line.

One of the starfighters, a Caman Model 14s, hails us.

"Open the line," I say.

An angry Caman officer glares at us. "Kyvar Astilius, halt your vessel. You are wanted for the destruction of Caman vessels and an attack on a vTalis station."

"Who are you?" I demand.

"Captain vSteven of the *Maverick*." The Captain is middle-aged, not a young kid out of diapers this time. His jaw is locked, and his eyes narrow—he probably lost friends on the frigate.

"Why do you threaten an innocent vessel?"

"I will open fire if you don't comply." His eyes go down to slits.

I return his glare. "If you open fire, your death is certain." Axton slides down his Holox helmet and turns the cannons toward him.

The Captain's scowl softens as his pupils grow. He's angry, but not stupid.

"I suggest you stand down and withdraw while you can," I say.

The *Maverick* angles itself into a different firing position. Other Caman fighters show up. Three-to-one odds now. What fun. Weapons lock indicators flicker on the bridge.

We are now fifth in line behind a civilian transport, a container ship, a diplomatic vessel and the heavy freighter.

Let's try this again. "*Resilience*, summon the station."

A CSX Corporation officer answers the hail. He wears a tight blue uniform and has a confident air about him.

The officer smiles. "I am Captain Magheus. Welcome to the Elextrious Gate. Kyvar Astilius, what can we do for you?"

"Oupavo does answer," Ayera whispers.

"We are having a problem with some fellow vTalis starfighters."

"Nashtech said you might need some help." He smiles. "Let me hail them."

The comm flickers until it includes vSteven. Meanwhile, the civilian transport hits the JUMP. We are now fourth in line.

"Caman vessel *Maverick*, why are you targeting a vTalis freighter?" Magheus demands.

I like this guy.

"Because they are wanted for the murder of Senator Tlaagon," vSteven answers.

"Is this true?" Magheus asks me.

"No."

Magheus turns toward the feed with vSteven. "Your accusations don't give you the right to target innocent vessels." The station's cannon turns toward the *Maverick*.

I *really* like this guy.

The container ship hits the JUMP. We are now third in line.

I speak to Captain vSteven. "I don't think this is the place to discuss our differences."

He's angry, shaken, and stuck. The starfighters don't have the firepower to stop us without the support of the station. He wasn't prepared for the station's aggressive posture. Beyond this, there is something about the captain—something I recognize.

"Stand down, Captain!" I shout.

He scowls at us, but not like Tlaagon. I see not fear in his eyes, but something else.

The diplomatic transport hits the JUMP. We are now second in line.

"Captain vSteven, stand down or this station is prepared to fire," Magheus demands.

A few of the missile lock indicators stop flashing, but not all of them.

I look at the captain. What is it about him? Something that drives him, something more important than this investigation. "Captain vSteven, you know we are going home. Our galaxy is currently under assault by the Vidor and we desperately need help."

He fake-yawns his supposed disinterest. "I am under orders to take you down."

A heavy freighter hits the JUMP. We are next in line.

I glare at him. The revelation comes to me. His determination is obvious, his greed is personal, and his vice is evident. Greed always betrays its own. "If it's the stones you want, you can have them."

A crooked grin appears on his angry face and the lights in the cabin stop flashing. "You have the stones?"

"Enough to fill a galaxy."

"Kyvar, do not hit the JUMP. Pull aside and we can discuss."

I smile. "We can discuss when you come and help our galaxy."

"Kyvar—"

The *Resilience* rushes into hyperspace.

CHAPTER TWENTY-ONE

PHAELON

The swirling Elextrious JUMP starts to thin, revealing streams of starship traffic.

"More traffic," I complain. "*Resilience*, controls."

The flight controls rise and push into my lap.

"Kyvar, I've been studying the Phaelon Galaxy." Ayera speaks quickly in her cultural research tone. "I don't think we should expect too many unfriendlies here. The Phaelon are in league with the CSX Corporation and they are openly against the Camans."

The Gate ceases in a fine mist and we float into the Phaelon Galaxy. Three traffic lines converge, guided by shield perimeters, to a station checkpoint.

"They are definitely friends with Nashtech." I point to lines of heavy freighters and cargo barges carrying the CSX logo.

"Let's just hope he has prepared the way for us," Khal says.

We fall in line behind the same heavy freighter from the previous galaxy.

"Glad we're not in a rush," Khal says.

"We are if the Camans show up." I look at the feeds. A cargo barge is now behind us. No Caman fighters have passed through the Gate yet.

"So, we just wait for clearance from the cheapie up there?" Khal points to the L32 station.

"Yep." I frown.

"Maybe we should just blow it up like the last one," Khal retorts.

"Wouldn't take much," Axton adds. "I can't believe these guys haven't upgraded, or it hasn't imploded yet. The L32s are the cheapest stations in the cosmos."

"The Phaelons have always been poor." Khal plays with his relays.

Ayera crosses her arms. "Yet the King is one of the richest in the galaxies. He has basically enslaved everyone. They work for nothing in his factories."

The feed shows the *Maverick* is now through the Gate a few vessels back.

The screen flickers. "Captain—"

"I know."

"We enter the state of the dragon fist." Khal points to the L32 station flanked by two red fighters. The station and fighters carry a bright red dragon fist emblem.

"What's with the dragon fist?" Axton asks.

"It's their galactic emblem." Ayera is quick to answer on anything related to culture and science. "It comes from a legend that every Phaelon king must face off with the red dragon before taking the throne. Now the king demands the emblem on every vessel in his galaxy."

Khal laughs. "Archaic."

"You would say that," Ayera lifts her head. "Unappreciative of culture."

The comm flickers. The station hails us.

"Patch 'em through."

A tall, lean Phaelon displays on the screen. He is dressed in red with a dragon emblem on his chest. He has black hair, a wide mouth, and a typical large Phaelon nose.

"Kyvar Astilius and crew of the *Resilience*, I am Captain Phraius. Welcome to Phaelon. We have been expecting you. Senator Nashtech sent word of your journey. We have a fighter escort for you through our system."

Yes!

"Come ahead of the freighters and continue your journey." The shield vestiges flicker and provide us a new path.

The comm flickers out.

"The royal treatment." Khal puts his arms behind his back.

I pull the *Resilience* out of line and push through their checkpoint as two dragon fisted Phaelon fighters slide to either wing. The screen displays the Phaelon Dragon 2 fighter. Single seater. Maneuverable max 10 BURN. Armament—cannons and lasers.

The comm flickers.

"Accept."

"Kyvar Astilius of the *Resilience*. I am Lieutenant Phaxylius of *Dragon's Teeth*. We will escort you through the system."

"Thank you, Lieutenant. You can probably see some of the Camans are trailing us."

He smiles. "We will make sure to stall them for you." He glances down a moment, then back up. "Kyvar, our king sends his regards. He has recorded a feed for you. Sending now."

The screen flickers, and King Phaseolus of Phaelon appears on the screen. He wears a silver threaded breastplate over a black pin-stripe suit. The breastplate is emboldened by the emblem of a red dragon. He wears a red crown over a silver head covering.

"Kyvar, my condolences for the loss of Waupus." He frowns and bows, showing respect. "Nashtech has informed me of your journey. He speaks of a trade deal. As you know, I have been more than favorable in the past with your father." He pauses and bows again.

"We are encouraged with another potential arrangement. We pledge military arms in your support, assuming you pay well." He rubs his hands together and smiles. "Unfortunately, we must wait for the trade deliberations to come out of vTalis. Once they arrive at an outcome, we will be the first to come to your aid. We are always willing to volunteer our dragon squadrons to the assistance of the Kopernians."

The comm ceases and the lieutenant appears.

"Phaxylius, please pass the word to your king that I look forward to meeting with him personally one day. As for trade negotiations, know we will make payment guarantees in Helix stones."

The lieutenant's eyes grow.

"Phaxylius, please forward this message to your king personally and know that Helix stones are available to you as well if you help us with the deliverance of our people."

He smiles, exposing every single tooth in his mouth. "Kyvar, you have my commitment to deliver your message, and hopefully I can personally assist with the defense of your people."

"Thank you."

The comm ceases as the Phaelon fighters pull ahead of us, leading us through another shield passageway. We pass a dignitary transport and a few civil service vessels. The pace increases to 5 BURN.

I smile as we race past many lines of starship traffic on the opposite side of the shield vestiges.

"Yes!" Ayera erupts.

I turn around and see her smile, a blue swirl flickering beneath her pale skin.

"What's up with you?" Khal asks.

"I found the public feeds in their system. They are blocked in vTalis, but here, the underground is ripe. I have broadcast the cries of my Queen for galactic justice to all the feed outlets. The plight of our race will be loosed even in this oppressed system."

"Brilliant!"

"How do you know the underground is ripe?" Khal asks.

She smiles and looks at her screens. "I checked the feed captures and there are thousands of them received almost instantly."

"Let me see," Khal demands.

She pulls out the feed summaries from her Holox pad, spins it, tosses it to him and he examines it on his controls.

Khal narrows his eyes and studies the data. "The geos are everywhere. All of the three inhabited planets, the moons and every one of their geodomes."

Ayera beams. "They are starving for feeds out here."

"I like it, Ayera. Keep it up." I turn around in my chair. The news of the loss of Waupus may instill anger on behalf of their citizens.

We surge past a few uninhabited planets until we pass Phaelon itself. The planet reflects a mix of dull green and burnt orange.

"What happened?" I ask. "Father always said it was very fertile."

"It's currently under a scorching," Khal answers.

Oh, yes. I'd forgotten Phaelon is an elliptical, the challenge of two stellar orbits. The elliptical orbits cause some planets to incur periodic scorching or freezing, based upon the orbit cycles. These conditions are excellent for farming of some stellar crops, but ruinous for livable habitations, forcing inhabitants to flee into biospheres or underground.

A few stellar lifts shoot toward two modern stations orbiting the planet. The stations appear on the screen. Phrale I has four long wings accommodating thousands of ships. Phrale II is the civil and military station—thousands of dragon fist vessels litter the decks.

"Glad these guys are on our side," Khal adds.

Axton looks back at Khal. "It's all teeth, though. Lots of lights and flash, but little armor. Most of their fighters don't even have shields."

"Now *that's* cheap." Khal whistles. "There are no second chances without shields. We would've already been dead three times."

We approach Seteria, the inhabited moon of the ringed planet of Agoura. The small moon glistens from a thousand factory biodomes reflecting the solar rays of its nearby sun.

"That's where they say the dragons come from." Ayera points to the dark brown moon speckled with green.

"Really?" Khal asks.

"I believe there are beasts down there. The legends are probably fabricated to elevate the king's stature, but yes, I believe the beasts are based in truth."

Khal frowns.

We pass Phaelon's second sun. The smaller, younger star blazes a brilliant white compared to its counterpart's sharp yellow. We continue at 5 BURN until we merge back into thin traffic lines. The blackness of empty space slowly takes over our vantage.

The comm flickers.

"Open the line."

Lieutenant Phaxylius appears. "Kyvar, this is where your escort must return to base. Know we have stalled the Camans, and they have been detained for right of course without permit." He smiles.

"Thank you, Phaxylius."

"It is twelve sectors until the Jewel System. Please continue your course." He bows, and the comm flickers out.

The dragon fist fighters sear ahead of us and turn back toward us. As they pass overhead, we see what looks like dragon's teeth painted below their cockpits.

"Good show, my friends." I like those guys.

I guess they don't know there is an Hgate only a few sectors from here. I drop the Hammer to 10 BURN. The Ion Drives roar and the *Resilience* tears away. "*Resilience*, take it up to 12 BURN once we are out of sensor range."

I pull out my Holox pad and put my feet up. I watch the feeds from Valerie again, not that I haven't watched them a few times already.

Xander walks onto the bridge. He hangs a shoulder and has a crooked smile.

"Captain. The warheads have been upgraded."

I smile and nod. He sits in his seat and puts his feet up.

"Xander. Don't get too comfortable. I need you to arm a cannon shell with the hydrogen concentrations from the Asatyria. I've flicked them to your station in the weapons room already."

He gets out of his seat. "I will set the charges." He casually walks off.

"It's a good look." Khal smiles. "I like the casual approach."

"You are prepping the elements?" Ayera asks with elements of doubt.

I turn toward her. "Yes. It's what we have to do to open the Hgates."

Khal stares at her. "Do we have to go through it for you again, Ayera? The Hgates are safe."

Ayera frowns. "They haven't been proven."

Khal fumbles with his controls. "I've been reading up on the Gate compilations from Asatyria. Here is what I've found. *Resilience*, display a summary."

The screen flickers, and the three types of Gates appear on the screen.

The Hgates have a slow closure rate. It's potentially enough for a small battle fleet to come through. The closure occurs when the hydrogen level is insufficient to keep the Gate open.

The Lgates close three times faster. The Lgates are opened by releasing lithium into the opening point in the concentrations determined by our Asatruan friends.

I join the discussion. "We all know the Lithium Gates are never open long enough for a JUMP."

"Correct, unless it's a short JUMP," Khal adds.

"Let's make sure we stay away from the Lgates." I skim the write-up on the ION Gates. No one has ever successfully navigated an ION Gate, even drones. "And let's never take an ION Gate, either."

"Yes, Kyvar." Khal is annoyed. "We only take Hgates."

Good, that's cleared up.

"*Resilience*, does the compilation speak of any accidents with any of these Gates?" Ayera asks.

The screen flickers and *Resilience* displays a photo and a couple of paragraphs of information. "The only reference found is an event with a freighter carrying lithium. It had a hull leak. Unknown to the freighter, it stopped for repairs near a hidden Lgate. The leakage caused the Gate to open, drawing in the freighter."

"And?" Ayera asks.

"Their starship and crew were never found again," *Resilience* answers.

Ayera moans. "This doesn't reassure me at all."

Me neither.

CHAPTER TWENTY-TWO

PHAELON HGATE

"We have arrived at the first Hgate," *Resilience* declares. The Ion Drive's hum ceases as we drift into empty space.

I look up from my Holox pad. There is nothing but dead black space. "There is nothing out here."

"Nothing," Khal agrees.

I touch my comm. "Xander, tell us when you are ready."

"Yes, Captain," he responds with an almost human-like tone. His personality chip, which was reset with *Resilience*, has been updating. "I will need 4 SEGs."

I flick off the comm.

"We have all of the requirements?" Ayera asks.

Khal regards her and nods. "We do. The requirements are pretty basic."

"Are we sure we want to trust these Asatruans?" Ayera continues her questioning. "All of their data is created and supported by them. In my studies, everything I have learned doesn't back up *any* of their data."

"Then we are going to die today?" Axton asks, in a faintly acid tone.

"What concerns me is the hyper vortex," Ayera rattles away. "You know hyperspace is the realm of the ethereal. Its not our place."

Why does she have to do this? She always gets weird about the Hgates.

Ayera continues. "Wormholes are anomalies in the universe. They've always existed for eons. Drone testing has always been a proven method of directional attributes. I see no record of drone testing. All I see is mathematics proving the existence of the Hgates."

She turns her Holox pad around. She flicks out a four-dimensional hyper-frozen particle condensate chain.

I glance at it and it makes my brain hurt. I fly by instinct and survive on clever strategies and minute manipulations. I leave the heavy science to others.

"Let me see that," Khal demands. "You're our science and political officer. This one is for *my* head."

She throws the chain to Khal.

"I think you are looking at it like a chemist and through the lens of physics. You must view these as inventive, creative—this needs an engineer. Chemical elements open up the Gate, but the connections within them are inter-dimensional. This, right here, deals with hyper—"

I drift back into my thoughts. I can't believe they can banter on like this about science versus engineering for leaps. They are the same to me. I grab my Holox pad and open the message from Valerie, the one I've watched so many times. Her light hair blows in the wind. Her face is flushed from crying, yet she glows in the midday sun. I do miss her.

I turn on the feed, hold up my comm to my ear, tap it twice and the audio plays softly for only me to hear.

"Kyvar, we have lost Waupus. Nearly everyone got out when the platforms showed. I watched it all." She frowns. "The Queen was one of the last to escape." Remember the leaps at Alza Mare ..." A single tear streams down her face. "I watched it burn." Other tears follow. She wipes them with her sleeve. "We have been moved to Nasgreun. Please hurry home. I know you are making a difference, but we need you here ... I miss you dearly." She tries to smile. "Meet you at Nebula Beach."

The feed ceases as Khal continues his discourse with Ayera.

"—formulas are driven by a millennium plane that is not one of our understanding. That's your problem. But without the millennial code, we cannot understand it. Everything here is based upon a new code for millennial—"

I look at the male Shivyun. "What do you think of these guys? Brainy, eh?"

He beeps and moans.

"I agree."

"So then you're saying that they've remapped wormholes based upon a new discovery of the millennial plane?" Ayera asks.

Khal continues in a tone of controlled impatience. "No. Their algorithm for the millennial plane allows for uncovering new data points and Gates that are primed for opening. I think they've gone way beyond our dimensional understanding."

"I still don't understand how you reevaluate interdimensional planes," Ayera responds.

"You have to—"

I touch my comm. "Xander, how are we doing?"

"Hurry up!" Khal yells. "Ayera is driving me crazy with her questions."

"Close, Captain," he says mechanically.

"Say it normal, at least," I add.

"Would you prefer I say no problem or no worries?" Xander responds.

"Yes."

"No worries," he says.

"Much better."

"How about this?" A shrill bang echoes from the weapons room. "No worries, man." The shrill sound of metal-to-metal impact. "Let me just click this and that." The sound of loud cranking followed by a poly-lever. "All good, man. The Hshell is ready."

Dumbfounded, I stare for a moment at the comm speaker before I can think of what to say next.

"Ready?" I ask.

"Ready, Captain."

Ayera continues to examine the spiral. "I don't doubt the vortex will tear open, but the question is, will it tear us apart? We aren't Asatruans."

Khal stares at her. "Ayera. It's not science, it's interdimensional engineering."

"Can you prove we will not be torn into space particles?"

I look at Axton. He's had enough too.

Xander walks onto the bridge. He provides a crooked smile and walks in with a strut. "I just worked on the Hshells for your Tpoints."

I look at him.

"Now you can open your foolish Gate."

I laugh.

He sits in his chair and turns in my direction. "Maybe I prep some Lshells?"

"No, Xander—never," I respond.

He laughs. His leathery laugh has traces of personality to it. Khal's smiling. Xander is getting it.

"Are you children done?" Ayera asks.

Khal smiles. "We are done as long as you stop looking for science answers to engineering questions."

"That's the problem—you're trying to reveal the truth about science through your lack of—"

I look at Axton. We've had enough of their rambling. I check the sensor readings and see only deep space and this giant void of nothingness. Even the Shivyuns appear bored. The only threats are of our own design ... each other.

Khal and Ayera continue to debate, and Axton and I ignore them.

The Shivyuns squeal.

"Fire," I command.

The cannon shell explodes. A gaseous flash rips apart the darkness. The ship shakes from a shockwave and the crew falls silent. *Resilience* powers the Ion Drives and its resonance fills the cabin.

A swirling blue gaseous cloud forms in the darkness. Its spiral is twice the width and pace of a normal wormhole and it continues to grow.

"Let's not do this," Ayera squirms. "What good are we dead?"

The swirl widens further. The ship starts to move toward the Gate.

"Kyvar, don't do this," Ayera begs.

The *Resilience* moves deeper into the Hgate.

"Are we sure about this?" Ayera asks.

"I haven't been sure about anything in a long time."

The Shivyuns squeal again.

With a jolt, the *Resilience* enters the swirling vortex. The entire cabin vibrates rapidly. The wide blue sweeps of the Gate dissipate in thin light blue burning tongues. Hyperspace sucks around us and whips us around.

The *Resilience* is yanked around as the vortex spins and pulls us from side to side. My unsecured Holox pad flies to the ground and I grit my teeth.

"This is excessive," Khal yells over the vibration.

"*Resilience*," I shout. "Can you adjust the stabilizers to the new vibration levels?"

The screen flickers. "Processing data." Calculations show on the screen.

My console rattles. I'm dizzy from the shaking.

"What's that smell?" Ayera yells.

"The Hgate chemicals are leaking through," Khal answers.

"I will work to neutralize," *Resilience* adds. Another set of calculations roll on the screen.

Formulas flash on the left side of the screen followed by the right. "Stabilizers adjusted. Vacuum seals adjusted—Ayera's favorite fragrance inserted."

I hold my jaw, happy to not be grinding my teeth anymore. The rotten smell of chemicals is soon replaced with a strong sweet smell.

"Oh, not that stuff ..." Khal moans. "My family is going to find my rotting space corpse one day and their first response will be, 'He sure smells good.'"

"What's wrong with you guys? I love it." Ayera's tone is light and airy, like she spent the afternoon shopping with her friends.

I look at her. "Ayera, did you really give *Resilience* perfume to inject?"

She smiles. "You guys needed a female touch."

Khal grunts.

I shake my head, turn around, and relax in my seat, watching the erratic aggressive blue swirls. The pulsating lights shimmer off the consoles. A quiet pervades the crew. I ponder the long trip home and the insanity of it all.

I see a shimmer to my right and see a micro light particle reflecting the Hgate churn.

I follow the particle and look behind. The cabin is full of particles, floating with the weightlessness of feathers.

"I've never seen synthopies." Ayera touches one near her and it falls to the ground.

"Is that what these are?" Axton asks.

Ayera nods. "Synthopies are rare elemental anomalies only seen within JUMPs."

"*Resilience*, what causes them?" Khal asks.

"The elemental forces in the Gates cause the loose particles to converge," *Resilience* answers. "The micro reactions cause the light to shimmer through them. They are very rare and occur in one in ten thousand elemental combinations."

The Shivyuns mumble. They examine one of the particles hovering over their console. They take off their visors and raise their padded hands toward it. They touch the particle and moan as it falls. Their moan turns into a squeal as it disappears.

I laugh to myself and sit back. "Ayera, remind me, what do they say about the synthopies?"

"Some call them signs of good fortune. Others swear they are for the cursed."

Khal laughs. "Sounds like us."

"What part?" I ask.

"Both."

CHAPTER TWENTY-THREE

NAVARIA

The lights flicker.

"Tpoint in five SEGs," *Resilience* announces.

I open my eyes and close them, lingering in the unconsciousness of sleep.

"Wake up," Ayera says.

I should have taken my nap in the cabin. I open my eyes and see Hydrobot holding a fresh cup of vollinium juice. I reach for it and take hold of the cup.

Hydrobot bows and scoots off.

The chill drink is cold to my hands. I sit up, drink it, and feel the sugars rush through my system.

"Captain."

"Yes, *Resilience*," I mumble.

"Your health sensors indicate the lack of sleep is wearing on you."

No gunfrey. I run my hand through my hair. "I know."

Axton leans over. "Kyvar, your readings are bad. You haven't been sleeping much at all." He turns his pad toward me. "Your cognitive functions will suffer unless you get more sleep."

I look to the bridge screen, where the blast of blue and red swirls invades the cabin. "It's kind of hard to truly rest in this hydrogen-sucking hyperspace wormhole."

"I get the same med readings," Khal adds.

"You're another story." Axton smiles.

"Ayera, do you have one of those pills?" Khal asks.

"Which one?"

"The slags."

Axton looks at Khal. "That's not going to help. Ayera takes them because she isn't human. Her anatomy can handle them. You can't."

"Hey, Khal," Ayera holds up a pill. "If I give you this, peace treaty for earlier?"

He nods his head. She tosses him the pill.

"Slags only trick the brain," Axton says. "They only take off the edge."

"What if you have no edge like Khal?" I smile.

Khal frowns at me.

"Don't do it," Axton pleads.

"Just this one." Khal swallows the pill, and Axton shakes his head.

Hydrobot scoots up to Khal and provides a drink. Hydrobot is good, really good. The small droid beeps and scoots away.

Enough of the slags. "Ayera, what have you learned about Navaria?"

She pauses, and I ask the same question a different way. "What should we expect on the other side?"

Ayera stands up. "*Resilience.*"

"Yes, Lieutenant Ayera."

"Display Navaria."

The planet Navaria displays on the screen. The medium sized blue and green planet is partially obscured by red clouds.

"What I have learned is that you are my slaves." Ayera's tone is demanding.

"Really," I mutter.

"First you bargain a slag for a peace treaty, and now this?" Khal mumbles.

"It's the only way," she says. "These Navarians are descendants of the Naphtali Mission."

"They are?" Axton asks.

"The Nova Fire Storm?" Khal adds.

"Yes. They keep the males around as slaves, but the females blame the death of their original civilization on the males. They rule over them. *Resilience*, show the context."

The feed shifts to show the entirety of the small Navarian system. Stellar Emertral blazes in the center of the small system. Navaria is the second of only three planets circling the star.

"*Resilience*, further out," Ayera commands.

The perspective pulls back until the Navaria system can be viewed next to an adjacent system littered with thousands of objects. Ayera pulls the display mapping into the room. To the right is the Navaria system. Next to it is an asteroid belt encircling a black void. She points to the black area. "Queen Amytilius rules Navaria, but they originally came from there."

"The void?" Axton asks.

Ayera nods. "That's Naphtali 3s."

"That can't be," I declare.

"When Stellar Naphtali went nova, they escaped to the nearest system and the planet of Navaria."

"You mean the black hole was their sun?" I ask.

"Yes," Ayera answers. "The Naphtali mission landed on Navaria, and it is run by females only."

Khal crosses his arms. "Long live the female race of the Naphtali."

"*Resilience*, display Queen Amytilius." Ayera's voice is confident.

The Queen's face appears on the screen with a write-up next to her. She has a long neck covered in layers of golden necklaces. A silver robe covers a silk jewel encrusted terra. Her hair is bundled with golden ribbons. She wears no smile and, judging from the shape of her jaw, she has no teeth. An oddly well-dressed, serious Queen.

"Queen Amytilius hates males." Ayera says.

"Let's just go around this place," Khal suggests.

"No time," I mutter.

Ayera continues. "She really hates males. She blames the death of her world on them. Males are only kept around to serve the females and work."

This is going to be fun.

"The only way we can justify coming to this remote galaxy is the Queen's Prize. She has offered anyone a great prize if they are willing to venture to the fading asteroids." She points to the closest rocks to the black hole. "According to the queen, she believes these rocks are from her ancient planet and they contain lost heirlooms from her world. Anyone retrieving items considered of value to the queen will receive a reward."

"*Resilience*, display the Queen's Prize."

The Queen's Prize appears on the screen.

Join the Recovery of the Naphtali Mission. A great reward is offered to adventurers willing to recover lost items. Pursue this endeavor and the great Queen will reward you for life. Females only.

"Females only." Khal's tone is sour.

"I guess I can't help, then," Xander states casually.

Khal laughs.

I smile. "Good one, Xander." This is interesting. "What kind of items?" I ask *Resilience*.

The screen displays a list of the Queen's Prize items and their reward. Family data book–five thousand illirium. Flower seeds from the surface–one thousand illirium. Images and even nasal captures–one hundred illirium ...

"Weird," Khal says. "Who knows, we might come back with a data book filled with males and the smell of body odor."

Everyone laughs except Ayera. Even Xander tries a metallic giggle, and the Shivyuns cobble together some chuckles. Khal pushes out his fist toward Xander, who stares at him.

"You're supposed to bump it with your fist."

Xander stares at him.

Khal shakes his head.

"Get your act together, slaves," Ayera demands.

"Yes, honey," Khal mumbles.

"Honey?" Ayera snarls, and then smiles.

The Hgate thins until the Tpoint is achieved, and we float into the Navaria Galaxy. There is very little space traffic, yet a string of solar arrays glitter Emertral's light in our direction. "*Resilience*. Tint."

We see Navaria and her sister planets. In the distance is an endless range of asteroids rotating around the looming blackness.

"*Resilience*, let's push it to 1 BURN." The Ion Drives ignite and a familiar hum fills the cabin.

Laser light finders light up the room.

The screen flickers. "Captain, we are getting pinged with laser sensors."

They know we are here.

"It's their solar array," Ayera states. "They use it to regulate their weather. They are terrified of another cataclysm."

"It's also their weapons platform," Axton adds.

What?

"Weapons platform?" I ask.

Ayera answers. "They don't have a lot of defenses except something no one else has figured out. They refract light from their sun. The refraction can be angled to become their weapon by magnifying Emertral's rays. It's not a laser as much as an infraction weapon. They use them to annihilate space rocks venturing into their system. They've also destroyed entire cruisers before."

Oh.

The screen flickers. We are being hailed.

"*Resilience*, open the comm."

"No!" Ayera yells. "You don't get it. They *hate* males. I'm telling you no one is allowed here, including us. Well, at least you." Ayera walks over to me. "Get up, slave."

Who is she?

She smiles and bows. "Get up." She winks. "You are my slave."

I notice her light blue skin tone has a sheen to it. Her gills are flaring. An indication of stress. She seems to like this, but not really. I get up, and she takes my seat.

Another hail comes in as she sits. She breathes deeply and doesn't answer at first.

I sit in her seat.

"Accept," Ayera declares.

A long necked Navarian appears. She wears a tight red tunic, with numerous gold necklaces around her neck.

"Who comes to the Navarian system unannounced?" she demands.

"I am Ayera Agreya of the *Resilience*, with my slave crew."

I try to act like a slave and not look the Navarian in the eyes.

"What is your business in Navaria?"

The solar arrays start to turn toward us, and their infraction starts to build, evident by a glowing on their wings.

"You can do this, Ayera," I whisper under my breath.

"I am here for two things. I am searching for genizah stones, and I would like to participate in the Queen's Prize."

The Navarian's eyes narrow, studying Ayera and the rest of us. "Ayera Agreya, permission granted to land at our orbit station. Coordinates are being sent now."

The coordinates appear on the screen and the comm fades out.

Ayera links her fingers together behind her neck. "*Resilience,* set the course."

"Yes, Captain."

Resilience did not *just call her Captain.*

Ayera turns to the right. "Xander."

"Yes," he answers without formality.

"That's the spirit." Khal extends his fist again, and Xander bumps it with his own, provoking a smile from Khal.

"Xander, fetch me a Helix stone," Ayera orders.

"Yes, Captain," he answers and walks off, all the while grimacing at me in his version of a smile.

"Xander," Ayera calls to him, "make it a cluster."

"Yes, Captain Ayera," he repeats.

Khal laughs. "Kyvar, look out. She's gonna take your position and *your* stones."

Everyone laughs except me.

CHAPTER TWENTY-FOUR

NAVARIA STARBASE I

The *Resilience* slows on approach to Navaria Starbase I. The station is more like a platform with a large bridge on its edge. An endless planetary tow cable drifts down to the surface, where a maglev elevator ascends upon it. A stream of drone mining shuttles leave the platform, heading toward the asteroid belt.

Axton's gaze is fixed on the drones. "It's sad they mine their old galaxy."

"Very sad." Ayera's tone is compassionate. "Their ancestors' remains are now their economic lifeblood."

The Shivyuns adjust their visors just prior to a strong infraction flickering into our cabin. I turn my head. The Navarians are not polite with their solar tech.

"Dim the screen," Ayera shouts.

Resilience dims the screen.

"Come on, slaves," Ayera insists. "We are approaching the apron."

"Do you have to yell at us?" Khal says.

"Let her be," I reply. "She's getting into her mode."

"Mode?"

I look over at Khal. "Do as she says."

"Fine!" Khal bellows.

I turn back to Ayera. "Ayera, as much as Khal wants to go, I think he and Xander should stay in case things go—" I hesitate.

"Go?"

"—cataclysmic." I smile.

Khal and Xander each nod their heads.

She crosses her arms. "Fine. As long as I can convince them that I have you tied up."

Ayera, Axton and I walk out of the *Resilience* onto the apron of Navaria Starbase I. A singular uniformed Navarian officer stands before us. Her neck is longer than the Queen's—much longer. She must be bioengineered.

"Greetings," the officer says. "Come with me."

"Come, slaves." Ayera pulls the chain she hung around our necks at the last minute.

We walk into the bridge structure down a narrow gray hallway. We stop at a solitary room. "Wait here," the officer orders.

"Thank you." Ayera bows.

We enter the room. The Navarian closes and locks the door.

"This is great," Axton complains. "We are locked up here."

"Silence, slave." Ayera slaps him. Then she whispers, "They are watching."

I turn. The wall has a sheen to it. They *are* watching us to see who we really are.

"Sit there," Ayera demands.

Axton and I sit down against a wall, while she sits with dignity in a chair.

We wait for an inordinate amount of time. Getting impatient, I stand up, forgetting my place.

"Sit down!" Ayera screams.

I sit.

The door opens and the officer walks in. "Uninvited guests— you come to mine and explore?"

"I—"

"You understand our Queen is not interested in visitors, yet she asks for adventurers. You know what this means?" The officer eyes us.

"No," Ayera answers.

She scowls at Ayera. "I have to deal with the likes of you." The officer examines Ayera. "What are you?"

"I am Hytilian," Ayera answers. Her light skin has a bluish tint, revealing her irritation. Her six small gills flip upward. She is stressed, but only we know this about her. "I have gold to pay in exchange."

The Navarian pauses.

"I also have silver."

The Navarian lowers her head in acknowledgment.

Ayera smiles. "I can give you some now, and the rest when we return with our ores."

The Navarian relaxes a bit. "Then we may be friends." She smiles. "Very well. Come with me." She walks to the door and opens it.

"Get up, slaves," Ayera snarls. She's convincing, and quite disturbing at that.

"I am Nartinia, a servant to the Queen," the officer says.

I walk faster to hear their exchange. This chain around my neck is quite irritating.

Nartinia slows. "I want to understand our arrangement."

Ayera answers fast—far too fast. "We provide gold for access to the belt. Half now and the rest when we—"

"That is the Queen's share. What is *my* share?"

"How about thirty percent of our mining finds?"

"Fifty percent," Nartinia counters.

What is Ayera thinking? You never start at thirty percent.

Ayera stops. "How about forty percent?"

Nartinia bows her head in apparent agreement to the terms.

At the bridge, the galaxy opens up in a wide sweeping view of the asteroid belt. Twenty workstations face the cosmos. I grit my teeth when I see most of the seats filled with Shivyuns chained to their posts. Guards walk around with laser whips. Some of the Shivyuns have scars on the backs of their heads. My blood boils.

"You know these Shivyuns recognized your heat signature as far away as the stargate?"

Heat signature again? That's not a thing. I walk faster to hear the dialogue.

Ayera laughs. "Heat signature? Very funny."

Nartinia scowls at Ayera. "You laugh at me." She pulls out her staff and it starts to flick phasma surges.

Ayera is filled with resolve, despite the other's lack of composure. "I laugh because I have always been told heat signature is not a *real* thing."

Nartinia smiles and pulls back her staff. She steps over to one of the stations. "Shivyuns can diagnose a heat signature when you allow them to look at their sensors with ultraviolet radiation scopes."

No way. When did this happen? I push my way forward to look at the scopes of the station. Not paying attention, Ayera allows it. Nartinia stares at me and back at Ayera, who finally recognizes what is going on.

"Slave, know your place," Ayera growls, pulling hard on the chains, "or I will put you in it."

I hang my head and step backward.

Other Navarians walk around with phasma spears as we move to the center of the bridge, where Nartinia sits on a stool, her own phasma spear in her hand.

Nartinia eyes Ayera. "I don't believe you are telling me everything."

Despite the blue swirl of stress drifting under the surface of Ayera's skin, she answers with great confidence. "I have told you everything."

"Who do you think you are?" Nartinia persists.

"I am Ayera Agreya."

"Let me share with you what happens to those who lie to us." Nartinia turns her head and shouts orders. "Prep the arrays."

We stare out into the galaxy. A nearby solar collection tank turns reveals a giant C for the Caman Corporation. *I should have known. This is bad, really bad. We should get out of here.*

Other solar arrays turn, infracting Emertral's light into a collecting station. The refractor tank gathers the light.

"Controls," Nartinia orders. She slides on a Holox helmet as the Holox weapons control system encases her seat. "Now we just need a target." She angles the target of the infractor toward the *Resilience.*

I don't think so. "No," I scream.

Ayera punches me and I fall to one knee. I've forgotten how hard Hytilians can punch.

The weapons control glows red as the charge accumulates. Nartinia looks at us and smiles maniacally. "As much as I would like to blow up your vessel, someone wants it more than I."

She alters the aim of the infractor, targeting the nearest asteroid. She touches the invisible screen in front of her, closes the Holox controls, and steps out of her seat. The laser infraction releases particles of light toward the asteroid. The laser pierces the asteroid and continues through, tearing apart rocks and creating waves of floating debris.

I stand up as Nartinia walks toward me.

"That is what we do to uninvited guests." She snarls at me. "Kyvar Astilius, do you not think we know you? Everyone knows you. You are wanted in thirteen galaxies." She flips out her phasma spear and shoves it into my chest.

Everything vibrates, and my vision goes out. I fall to my knees, feel sharp bursts of pain in my head, my ear, and a tingling in my hands and feet.

Axton pulls me to my feet, yet I stumble.

"I can't feel my —"

"The phasma affects your nervous system, but it's only temporary," Axton whispers. "Stay calm."

My feet regain feeling, but not my toes. I try to stand again, but stumble. My teeth chatter. My lips burn. My jaw hurts.

"Stop that chatter," Axton says.

I try to speak, but my teeth only chatter with more violence.

Nartinia laughs and looks at Ayera. "We have disrupted his nervous system. The infamous Kyvar Astilius, unable to speak." She laughs louder. "You think you can just come here and lie to us. You are my prisoner until the Camans arrive."

CHAPTER TWENTY-FIVE

Tempura, mining asteroid in the Naphtali Asteroid Belt

"In all your researching, you *never* found an alliance between the Camans and the Navarians?" Axton asks Ayera.

I try to speak, but my jaw hurts too much.

"No," Ayera says. "Even the cruiser that was destroyed was theirs. The Queen ordered its destruction with the infractor." She stands up and paces the detention cell. "They hate strangers. I don't understand this ..."

"They are obviously in league with each other." Axton examines the iron and electric gates. He shakes the iron handle. It rattles but doesn't budge. "*Gunfrey!*"

"It doesn't make sense. They must be secret business partners."

I lean against a jagged wall.

"It doesn't make sense ..." Ayera repeats.

"Ayera, it doesn't matter, if we can't get out of here." Axton kicks the iron handle.

My teeth start to chatter again. I picture the lady and her electric pincer walking toward me again. I had no idea it would hurt so bad.

Axton walks over. "Try to not bite your tongue. Your nervous system is on overload due to the shock." He tears off the edge of his shirt and folds it a few times. "Bite this instead."

I put the makeshift bandage into my mouth and let my teeth chatter on it. *Miserable.* My head and shoulder throb from additional blows on the way here. I try to stretch my shoulder, but it only strings out the pain.

"I bet they didn't even destroy the cruiser," Axton speaks over me.

"That's it. It's part of the cover. This must be part of the Shadow Wars between the Camans and CSX Corporation. The Camans don't want the—"

A resonating explosion shakes the detention cell, startling us all, and then Axton smiles. "It's the *Resilience*."

I believe I can hear Ion Drives in the distance.

"Khal is coming to rescue us," Ayera shouts.

"I doubt ..."I try to speak through the bandage.

"No, that's Xander," Axton finishes my thought.

Another explosion. Laser guns and the sound of a rapid-fire autocannon. Many voices screaming. Metal doors banging. More screams. An explosion. A laser pistol in a hallway. No sharp *ting* sounds of the phasma spears, only projectile weapons. I don't think they bargained for a space marine in deep space—nor did we.

The sound of a heavy-stepping droid at the door, and then a metallic fist hammering on it.

"Get away from the door, guys." Khal's voice. "Xander, blow it!"

We scurry backward just before the door handle impacts against the opposite wall. Xander peers through and Khal steps into the cell.

"Khal ..." I manage to say.

Khal runs to me. He's carrying a machine pistol and grenades are connected to his vest. "You okay?"

"I am—" My teeth start to chatter again.

He looks to Axton, who explains the problem. "He was phasma shocked. It's only temporary."

I bite my tongue again and taste blood. *Gunfrey.* I stand up and wobble, still dizzy.

"Come on, Kyvar." Khal tries to carry me and doesn't make it very far.

Xander storms in, picks me up, and throws me over his shoulder. The metal beefcake is earning his keep. I close my eyes as I struggle with consciousness. Even standing up is too much.

I fall out of consciousness, only to be awakened by periodic flashes of gunfire. The hallway blazes with autocannons, lasers—even a phasma spear is thrown at us.

We make our way out of the hallway to the darkened lobby entrance. The only lighting comes from an upper room. The Navarians are waiting on us, two rows of them. There is screaming, and demands are made.

"We must—" My bandage falls out of my mouth and my teeth chatter again. My mouth bleeds as I involuntarily munch my tongue. The pain jars me completely conscious as I stare at Navarians around us.

"Surrender," Nartinia demands. "Put down your weapons. My Queen demands it."

"Kill her," I mumble to Xander.

Nartinia advances with her sparking spear. "Put down your weapons."

Xander points his cannon at Nartinia. She narrows her eyes and hits him in the chest with her phasma spear. It does nothing to him.

He shoots out the light in the upper room and the room falls dark. Xander opens fire. A series of bursts echo from his autocannon until every Navarian is on the ground.

"Nice work," Khal declares.

Xander turns, blasts through multiple sealed doors, and carries me to the *Resilience*.

The *Resilience's* Ion Drives are alight. Xander runs me to the captain's chair and folds me into my seat. Two smaller service bots arrive behind him. Hydrobot brings a petrolyte drink. I take a sip, ignoring the floating tendrils of blood from my mouth. *So thirsty.*

Axton hands me a fresh piece of real gauze as he takes the helm.

The *Resilience* rises, and I sit up straight as if I know what I am doing. We cruise toward the asteroid belt until a brilliant laser flickers near us. Axton rolls, driving us straight into the thickest part of the asteroid belt.

I stare ahead and know I can do better. "*Resilience*, controls."

The controls rise and push into my lap.

"What are you doing?" Axton asks. "You are in no state to fly."

"I am, too," I mumble through the gauze.

We head toward an asteroid and go in close. I have enough time to cut it close, but impact-warning lights flash.

The Shivyuns squeal.

"Kyvar!" Ayera yells.

I yank on the helm to turn, but it is too late. The ship rocks as the shield takes the bulk of the impact.

"Shields at seventy-four percent."

"*Resilience!*" Axton shouts. "Take away his controls. Give me the helm."

My controls fold into the floor.

"What are—" I mumble.

"Captain, your health levels are out of whack. If you need to know the science of your mental state, Ayera can tell you as well."

I moan.

"Very well, Kyvar, phasma shock impacts the entirety of your ancillary functions. They are required to—"

I raise my hand to cut her off. I cross my arms. My teeth chatter on the gauze. *This is insane.*

Axton steers the *Resilience* into the flow of the asteroid belt. A brilliant laser tears into an asteroid near us. Shrapnel rocks the ship.

"Shields at fifty-four percent."

I moan again. "Come *on.*"

"Phasma shocks also put a trap on your short-term memory," Axton instructs me as he pilots the *Resilience*. "Your response times are curtailed, and your cognitive abilities are fried. Want to know more?"

No, I don't, because he's right. I scowl. *I'll just keep chewing on this wonderful gauze.*

The *Resilience* continues to dodge asteroids as the powerful infractor blast fires into the belt, until we are finally beyond the infractor's range. We edge around an asteroid and see a clearing of the space rocks. We have fallen into the gravitational pull of the dreadful void.

Everyone falls silent.

I grit my teeth through the gauze. My body is doing strange things. My chest and head hurt. My temperature is out of control. I rub my head as if doing so will remove the pain. I focus on the screen and try to ignore my uncomfortable state.

"Ayera. Can you get me one of those slags?" Axton asks.

"I thought you hated those," Khal adds.

Axton stares at him.

"Here." Ayera tosses the pill.

"That's supposed to keep him up." Khal won't let it go.

"In Kyvar's state, it will work in the opposite manner," Axton declares.

The *Resilience* slows as we turn toward the swirling mass of nothingness.

"Kyvar, take this." Axton hands me the pill. "Hydrobot, bring Kyvar a drink."

"Why are we doing this?" Ayera squirms in her seat.

"No one has ever survived a journey through a hole." Khal adds.

Hydrobot comes out of nowhere and I gladly take the pill. My head pounds and my teeth continue to chatter.

"One SEG and you will be all right, buddy," Axton whispers. Axton turns to Ayera and Khal.

"As long as Kyvar is in this state, I hold the Hammer and we are going through the void."

They stare at him. I try to speak, but nothing in my mouth works.

Axton sits back. "I know no one in galactic history has ever achieved this, but we have to—"

I seem to have a moment of controlled thought. I grab my Holox pad. I try to flick it three different times and get nowhere. *I can do this.* I focus and flick some directions to *Resilience*.

Immediately, our galactic route is displayed with Holox relay and matching points. Our route is shown with a dimensional quarter-line.

"The other end of the wormhole is the cosmos's junk zone?" Khal asks.

"There is no black hole in the Sartav," Ayera says, to compound the point.

It's invisible. I write it on the Holox Pad and flick it to the screen.

"That's not possible," Ayera retorts.

I write on my pad for *Resilience* to flip the screen to ultraviolet, and immediately the screens are tinted.

My head pounds. My heart hurts as I gnaw on this nasty gauze. The ultraviolet sensors send the Shivyuns into hyper-mode. I guess heat signature is a real thing. They yammer and beep incessantly to each other. It's working.

Resilience picks up their work and layers their heat signature diagrams and mappings to Ackbray's routes. They match.

Khal groans. He hates being wrong.

The Shivyuns yammer incessantly to each other.

"You did—" I try to speak, but it hurts.

The data screens swirl together. Coordinates confirm that asteroids going through the fields come from Navaria. I sit back. The black hole is truly a wormhole.

"According to the Shivyuns' calculations, the black hole is a wormhole of the greatest magnitude in the cosmos." *Resilience* says. "The power of the supernova and the mix of gases tore the hyperspace gap."

"All right, say this is the discovery of the eons. It would be great if it doesn't *end* in a war zone." Khal folds his arms.

Ayera picks up the thread. "And to think the Gaxi and Fraxinus blame each other for crashing asteroids into their galaxy."

"What if they knew it was a wormhole, and not just a void?" Khal asks.

"They might make peace," Ayera answers.

The *Resilience* cruises toward the swirling black hole. The pitch-black swirl can only be captured by the silhouette of fading rocks, objects spinning and spiraling toward it. Normally, we are propelled by a planet or prosperous land, but not this time—just an empty blackness.

Sleep is overtaking me. *That was fast.* I close my eyes and don't want to open them.

"The slags work quick," Axton tells me. "I imagine when you wake up, you won't chatter anymore."

I start to fade as I listen to the crew.

"It looks like death to me," Khal mumbles.

"Must we do this?" Ayera asks.

Axton laughs. "There is a legend that holes get you locked in other dimensions and you lose track of all reality."

"With endless darkness," *Resilience* adds.

Did Resilience say that?

"A place of total darkness and fear," Ayera's voice is fading.

"No better place to face your fears." Axton tries to be encouraging, but his tone has elements of doubt.

Resilience dims the cabin lights as the forward lights are turned on. The Ion Drives reduce as the hole pulls us.

"Must we do this?" Ayera asks again.

We must.

The *Resilience* drifts further into the hole's gravitational pull. Thick darkness is everywhere. Chills of foreboding go up my sleepy spine. There is no blue hyperbolic swirl. No light show. Nothing but an inescapable, impenetrable darkness. Maybe the Shivyuns were right. *When you adjust your sight, you can see the things that have always been there and hidden right before you.*

I stare into the void and try to adjust my focus. My eyes flutter. My heartbeat settles. Pain seems to lift from me, only to be replaced with a fading consciousness. Best to give in and allow deep sleep to overtake me. Maybe in my sleep, I will be able to see the things hidden before me.

CHAPTER TWENTY-SIX

NAVARIA BLACK HOLE

Impact microbursts ripple across the front shields of the Resolute. *Brilliant light floods the cabin.*

"Shields at twenty-three percent," the onboard announces.

Atilio Astilius glares at the incoming host of fighters and narrows his gaze. He slams his right fist on the console, pries open the lid, and extracts the stabilizer wires. He yanks the wires and extends them outward. He pries out a console lid on the left side of the Hammer and shoves the wires in.

He breathes deeply, turns the freighter, and drops the Hammer to 8 BURN.

The ship rocks from more laser blasts. "Shields down to twenty percent."

He roars past the Vidor fighters. He holds down the stabilizer button on the side of the Hammer with the installed wires.

"Manual use of the stabilizers is not—"

"I know."

He reaches deep into his pocket, pulls out a dark object and presses it against the Hammer. He breathes deeply and yanks the Hammer left. The vessel roars in a sharp turn. The stabilizer light flickers.

With each flicker of the light, he screams as he bears the weight of the stabilizers. He lifts from his seat, as his face grows red, yet he presses to complete the turn. He slows to 5 BURN and the stabilizer light stops flickering.

The screen feed crackles. Hytilian Commodore Ardyx appears on the screen. "Atilio, many of the transports are away. The laser arrays are targeting our cities. Most of our fighters have been taken out or fled. You are alone."

"How is my family?" Atilio asks.

"They are safe."

He yanks the Hammer.

"Targeting the arrays!"

He flicks off the feed and targets the nearest array. The array is beginning its deployment, splashing brilliant light in random locations. A cruiser with a fighter escort is nearby. Another cruiser is exiting the wormhole.

Lights flash in the cabin and Vidor fighters scream by.

The screen flashes as a cannon blast deflects off the shields. "Shields at nineteen percent."

"Target the platform and fire," he commands.

Missiles scream ahead, detonating the fragile solar panels in endless rivers of glass shards.

"Not my city!" he roars.

He looks down toward the planet. Lines of shuttles exit the atmosphere, their lives saved.

The screen flashes and the ship rocks from additional laser blasts. "Shields dropping. Eighteen percent, seventeen percent, sixteen ..."

Another laser array starts to churn. Vivid light emanates from the collection panels. It's surrounded by fighters, but it must be destroyed.

He breathes deeply and holds the Hammer. He squeezes the stabilizers, drops the Hammer to 8 BURN and races toward the planet. He grips the Hammer and yanks it. The stabilizer light flickers and with each flash, his face grows red and a vein displays on his neck.

"Gunfrey!" he screams, and he keeps screaming until the turn is complete.

He lowers the Hammer to 5 BURN and breathes deeply.

"Now!" he shouts at Steadfast, the onboard.

The laser array explodes in countless fragments as lasers erupt from the front of the vessel. Fighters tear after him.

He sees another laser array prepping to fire just outside the wormhole.

The ship rocks from laser grating from multiple fighters. "Shields fifteen percent, fourteen percent, thirteen percent..."

Commodore Andryx appears on the screen. "Atilio. It's time to go. Your shields are nearly exhausted. Evacuate. That's an order!"

He squeezes the stabilizers, drops the Hammer to 8 BURN, and tears away while turning. He raises the Hammer to 5 BURN and releases the stabilizers.

"Get out of there," the Commodore commands.

Atilio looks down toward Mrunal. Tarograia hasn't been evacuated yet. "Why have they not left?" he demands. "I see hundreds of transports still on the ground. What's going on?"

Pause.

He looks back. The third infractor is charging. The electric light shimmers to full charge. Where did it come from?

Father breathes deeply, regaining himself. "Why haven't they left?"

Silence.

"Tell me, Commodore," he stresses.

"The warning didn't come in time," Andryx answers.

Atilio grimaces. He starts to turn the Resolute.

"Return to Starbase Nine. That is my order," the Commodore yells.

He looks down. Tarograia, the ancient capital, cannot be destroyed.

Father looks over his shoulder. The array is fully charged. The infraction has been collected and the convergence is tying the particles together for a fully charged blast. It is in its most vulnerable state.

He seizes the Hammer with two hands, completes the turn, and slams the Hammer to 8 BURN.

The ship rocks from a cannon blast from the cruiser. "Shields are eight percent."

Weapons-lock warnings bleed through the cabin. Missiles are incoming.

He turns at 8 BURN, releases mags, and pulls to complete the turn. The vein in his neck pulses. He screams. Two missiles are evaded.

The infractor glows and aims at the city.

The ship rocks from a missile collision. The Resolute rolls and nearly throws him out of his seat.

"Now!" he shouts, but the lasers fail to fire.

"Shields at zero."

"No!" He screams and drops the Hammer to 10 BURN.

Lasers flash in wild arcs. Another missile explodes nearby. A cannon blasts. Orange lights strobe, and warnings echo within the cabin. The infractor's particle light detonates, engulfing the Resolute in a fireball and shrapnel storm as the ship passes out of the infractor's proximity.

"The hull is pierced. Engines are on fire. Aux power is fading."

Another explosion tears at the hull with a jarring whine of metal, like the vessel is crying its last breath. The engines sputter.

Atilio yanks the Hammer, but it has no weight, no bearing.

"Ion Drives are inoperable."

The Resolute glides toward the swirling Hgate. "No!" He slams his hand on the console. "No! Steadfast, do something!"

"Engines have lost power."

"Aux engines?"

"Inoperable."

The smell of sulfur drifts on the air from the ventilation system.

"Reactor leak." Red strobes bleed over the orange in the cabin. "Sealing Ion compartment and jettisoning canisters."

The reactor disengages from the Resolute and drops off as it glides toward the Hgate. The engines are on fire.

"The hull is fractured in the engine compartment."

He hangs his head. "Seal it!"

"The hull leak is sealed off. Engines must be jettisoned as well."

"I know." A tear streams down Atilio's face.

The entire engine compartment disengages and floats to the rear.

Atmospheric levels appear on the screen. Oxygen counts and other vitals display. He breathes deeply.

Commodore Andryx again appears on the feed. He salutes with tears in his eyes. "Atilio. Tarograia has survived." The line fades.

The starship continues to drift.

He breathes deeper. Oxygen levels are dropping.

The starship helplessly glides into the Hgate under an incoming cruiser. The speed of the freighter is enough to propel it in the opposite direction of the flowing Vidorian warships.

Tears stream freely down his face.

"Captain."

"Yes, Steadfast."

"Onboard balancing atmosphere controls were destroyed in the explosion."

The oxygen levels are too low.

"Steadfast. Record this file and save it."

"Recording."

"For my wife, mother of our children. I am recording this message to you because I have lost sufficient life support to be sustained here in deep space." He breathes deep. Tears run down his face and fall onto the bridge and console. *"Remember that day at HelmStat, the day you told me all would be well if I remember that place and that moment."* He pauses. *"The time has come, and I must tell you, you lied!"* He laughs painfully. *"That was forever ago. What I remember is something much different. I remember when we were on the beach of Lacanstal. I remember the night walks on the shore. The escapes away from the children and the fireball moon nights. That's what I miss. To see you again in Oupavo—I dream."*

He swipes his sleeve across his eyes and face.

"My consolation is your safety. You will survive. I will not. The future of our generation is with you. I charge you to lead the next Gen. They will do more than we can imagine." He wipes his eyes again. *"They will be our message to a future we cannot know."*

The oxygen levels are horrible. A putrid smell pervades the cabin. A droid brings water and parks itself next to him. He puts his hand on the droid.

"New recording. To my son, Kyvar, my first-born, I have given you everything that a father can give."

He rubs at his eyes as they burn now. He coughs painfully.

"In so many ways you have failed me, and in so many ways, you have stunned me. You are one of the most fiercely loyal individuals I have ever known. Your curious heart seems to always get you in trouble, but there is a tactical genius in you, a cleverness that scared your peers and teachers, and even me. An inner brilliance that forgets the practical at times. A showy bravado combined with an inward humility that defines you. I will miss our times away from it all when it was just you and me.

"I must confess I made the admiralty promise to not promote you too quickly, because I wanted you to learn the hard way.

Character is more important than promotion. You will understand one day. You will have your chance to save the galaxy, and you will perform greater exploits than I." He coughs, then breathes deeply once more. *"Your name will be the one remembered. My heart—"* he coughs again, harder this time, *"—my heart will go forward with you. Goodbye, my son."*

I awake in the darkness of the Navarius Black Hole Gate. No lights except the running lights in the cabin. No sounds except the Aux Drives as backup steering in the Gate. The screen shows quadrant and sector data on the bottom left. The blackness of space and the empty outer dimensions fill the cabin throughout.

My jaw hurts, my tongue throbs, but my head and shoulder feel better. I no longer want to gnash my teeth, and I have a better sense of awareness about me. I feel almost alive again, and my health sensors confirm improvement.

Everyone else is asleep. I must have been out for a while. I look below the console and remember the dream. The console is the same shape and size of Father's craft. Deep in there are the stabilizer manual controls. He smashed it with his hand while evading Vidor fighters. He had a strange object in his hand as well.

I lean back in my seat remembering Father's last words. He was proud of me and he'd held back my promotion at the same time. *Perhaps one day I'll understand it.*

I dismiss these thoughts and remember his care for me and the times away he spoke of. Tears roll down my face as I remember the climbs up Mount Vsusa and the days at Lake Ganueda. I never thought he remembered those trips until now.

I look out into the deep blackness of space and adjust my eyes to the blackness, and I think I see something. A vapor cloud or an accumulation of particles. I think I see stars in the distant vacuum of space.

It happened out there. Father must have died there, somewhere out there in another wormhole, in another dimension. Alone.

I rub my eyes and turn around. Axton sleeps next to me in his seat. Khal is fast asleep as well. Even Ayera is curled into a ball in her chair. I am amazed to see the Shivyuns cuddled together in a mass, eyes empty as if they are looking into the unknown.

The outer dimension must be talking.

I hear a faint sound to Axton's right. I peer over and see Xander sitting in his chair, watching me.

"Xander. I didn't realize—"

"I thought it best," he says, "to come and guard my friends while they sleep."

I nod my head. An appropriate action. We need it right now.

"The darkness is speaking," he says.

"How long have we been like this?"

"At least a hundred SEGs." He motions to the rest of the crew. "The darkness has taken hold of them."

It has taken hold of me too.

"Xander, why are you not impacted by the—the darkness?"

"I have no soul or flesh."

"This dark hole speaks only to those of the flesh?"

He nods. "It seems so. I believe Ayera was right. What is hidden in you connects with the darkness out here. It's not a torment. Rather, the hidden or unconnected holes in one's mind connect with the emptiness of space and cause things to surface."

Valerie used to say this as well. "What we hide will find us out ..." Father's death found me out here. I haven't yet dealt with it.

Xander looks at Ayera. "Even Ayera has secrets that haunt her."

"I am afraid we all do." The secrets of the unresolved. I know I haven't resolved myself to Father's death. He must have died in that wormhole. It is no wonder no one found his freighter.

"Captain, may I ask you a question?" Xander asks.

"Sure."

"What is The Voice?" Xander's tone is curious.

I frown.

"I have no concept of The Voice," he says. "Ayera speaks of The Voice, and I have no reference."

I concede. "The Voice is a legend. A legend that says the cosmos was created in a single moment in time by an entity called The Voice. That in that moment, the galaxies were formed and continue to be formed at the speed of light."

"A creator of sorts?"

"Yes, and there is more. The Voice is the overriding force of the Cosmos. The Voice in someone's head, a consciousness per se, and the guiding interplanetary ethereal that guides the galaxies." I shrug my shoulders. "That's what they say, if you believe."

"And you don't believe?"

"I don't." *Why should I? He took my father.*

Xander turns toward Ayera. "It seems she has a greater faith than you."

What kind of a response was that? He doesn't get it. "Resilience."

"Yes, Captain."

"What happens when one dies in hyperspace?"

No response.

As if Resilience knows. Where is his body?

"Do you know, Xander?"

No response.

"My father died in an emptiness like this. No burial. No honor. No dignity. Xander, what happens when one dies outside our dimension?"

No response.

As if he knows. As if anyone knows.

No one has ever died in hyperspace before. Not until my father.

CHAPTER TWENTY-SEVEN

THE GALACTIC MILITARIZED ZONE

"Xander, do you wish you had a soul?" I ask.

He smiles. "A soul?" He looks back at Ayera. "I think she is one of the sincerest individuals I have known in my short existence. Does having a soul mean I must sacrifice self-learning circuits for neural emotional inconsistencies?"

I look behind me. Ayera is weeping in her sleep. I had tuned out her cries some time ago. Considering the tears that I shed, it's probably good for all of them.

"You suppose we are a bunch of saps," I say.

He laughs. "Yes, a bunch of sapdragons."

I chuckle. I recognize his phasma chest plate sear marks. I should have noticed them earlier. "Thanks for saving us back there."

"It's what I was made for. Saving you sapdragons ..."

"*Resilience* always said you are the most capable droid. You aren't so bad."

He forms a loose, crooked smile. "Nor are you, Captain."

I put my hand on my sore jaw. I am thankful the phasma scoring was only temporary. My tongue still throbs, and I cannot escape the taste of blood.

The cabin lights turn on. Periodic light flashes indicate the Tpoint is approaching. Only the dead darkness of deep space shows through the screen, yet *Resilience* knows better.

Axton wakes up, rubs his head.

I smile at him. "Welcome back."

Ayera sits up. "I had the worst dream of my family."

"Sounds like the past is haunting you in your dreams," Axton says.

"The empty synapses in your brain connect with the emptiness out here, completing the dark spaces," Xander comments.

Everyone stares at the military bot as if he had no mental capabilities before this point.

Khal sits up. "Xander, that was pretty astute."

He smiles. "Thanks. I gathered this while I watched over my friends."

He's getting it—a sense of family.

"What was that about the dark spaces?" Ayera asks.

"The empty synapses are the—"

"I know that," Ayera interrupts. "What about the dark spaces?"

"They are the incomplete stories, accounts, life experiences, or areas you choose to ignore or forget. Those spots are the dark matter in your brain which connect with the deep darkness out here."

"Brilliant," Axton says.

"How do you know this?" Ayera asks.

"I watched each of you, and I read about it."

"From where?" Khal asks.

"I tapped into Axton's diagrams."

"My stuff?" Axton inquires.

Khal laughs. "Nice touch. Who needs a med officer, eh, Axton?"

Axton frowns.

Lights flash. I can see the Tpoint. "*Resilience*, controls."

The controls rise and slide into my lap.

"I was given some answers in my dreams." Ayera wipes her eyes. "Xander, that is a brilliant analysis. Thank you."

Xander nods.

"I dreamed of my father," I announce.

"I actually think I met mine," Khal adds.

The Shivyuns squeal and turn away.

The Tpoint grows before us. Sparkles of light, the first variations of color in many SEGs, flood the cabin. Everyone blinks and turns away from the screen. "Tpoint in 1 SEG."

"*Resilience*, tint."

The screen tints.

"*Resilience*, create an overhead for us to track our progress."

Four-dimensional imagery of the GMZ appears in the cabin. A light dashed line shows our future flight path. The two opposite galaxies appear on differing sides of the cabin. Between them is our path from one end to the other. Galactic asteroids float across the room. On the screen, *Resilience* pulls a feed write-up of the GMZ.

"Read it," I order, to stimulate everyone's mind. I need them awake and prepped for strategic thinking. Now is not the time to talk of the past.

"The Galactic Militarized Zone, or GMZ, is a wasteland of wrecked space parts, asteroids, and debris," *Resilience* intones. "It is radioactive and toxic from unexploded ordnance. Thousands of unexploded magnetic mines litter the belt. The opposing sides have droid bots and laser stations roving free in the belt. After eons of uninterrupted war—"

"That's enough," I say. "*Resilience*, set our climate sensors on alert and prevent any fallout from getting to us."

"Yes, Captain."

I look to the overhead display. Asteroids cloud the Tpoint. It's going to be tight from the start.

"I'm worried about the Gaxi. They just blast away at everyone," Axton states, an unusual tone of uncertainty in his voice. "They have one of the largest fleets in the cosmos. They have thousands of artillery barges that face the asteroid belt separating the Fraxinus and Gaxi galaxies."

I turn around. "Khal. Thoughts?"

"The droids are my biggest worry. There are thousands of them. They are programmed to neutralize anything in the field."

"I am less worried about the droids than I am about the mines," Axton replies. "I am most concerned about the magnetic mines."

I turn to the screen. "*Resilience*, can you highlight the mines?"

Bold black circles enclose sensor-detected mines, and orange faded arcs appear around their magnetic trigger radiuses.

"And their entire blast zones," I add.

Further yellow arcs encompass detonation blast impact ranges.

"Good. *Resilience*, can you highlight the drones?"

"Highlighting the drones is possible only when their engines are engaged."

Gunfrey. That's terrible.

"Ayera, once we get in range, get on the comm and forward our plea. Tell them where we are headed and why. Hopefully, it will help, and not draw the Gaxi out."

"The Gaxi are a furious race," Ayera returns.

"I know."

"I will transmit, regardless," Ayera concedes.

The Tpoint closes, and we drift out of the invisible Gate. This time there is no swirling mist accompanied by vibrant colors. I veer the vessel into the long line of asteroids, push the *Resilience* to 1 BURN, and begin to turn and bank the vessel in and out of the asteroids.

I reach up and throw the overhead onto the screen and slide to the left, taking care to angle the craft between the yellow blast zones on the overhead. All seems rather actionable. I breathe deeply. Where are the droids?

I increase our speed to 2 BURN.

"Captain, sensors indicate droids are headed in our direction."

I look to the screen. Thousands of tiny dots litter the screen. I slow the *Resilience* to look around. This is insane.

"Axton, just fire at will when they come."

Axton converts his station into a Holox weapons control center. He instantly displays targeting data and swivels in his seat and virtual workstation.

"*Resilience*, balance the shields, but keep them in the direction of the attackers."

"Yes, Captain."

Data and types of the droids appear on the screen. The cheap yet deadly G32 models find their strength in numbers. I heard once that a factory worker could churn out one every SEG, with fully functional Ion Drives and lasers. There could be millions out here.

A few scout droids appear in our path. Axton crushes them with lasers.

"I suggest we hug the rocks," Ayera says.

I pull out the Hammer and go manual.

A glittering horde appears before us, a horde made up of thousands of little unpredictable swirling drones with malignant beady sensors.

Here they come.

"Axton, open up with the cannon," I order. "*Resilience*, fire an anti-personnel missile at the center."

The missile fires and detonates in the crowded center. The center disintegrates and the remaining thousands fly toward us with lasers blasting.

"Shields at ninety-three percent, ninety-two percent ..."

I dive the *Resilience* to the nearest asteroid, push it to 2 BURN and maneuver at asteroid surface level. Droids only go 3 BURN.

Lasers grate on the shields. "Shields at ninety percent."

Axton fires his lasers and cannons, and their numbers do not diminish.

I guide the freighter up and around another asteroid. Droids converge around us.

The screen lights up with brilliant flashes of grating laser impacts. "Shields at seventy-eight percent."

I drop the *Resilience* to 3 BURN and nearly crash into another asteroid. I flip the vessel and turn behind another floating rock mass, pushing into the yellow blast zone of a magnetic mine.

"What are you doing?" Axton cries out.

"Kyvar," Khal squirms. "I don't want to die today. You're in a blast zone."

"I know." I slow to 1 BURN and allow the droids to catch up. We approach the orange ignition zone. Anything magnetic within that zone will set off the mine.

The droid horde catches up. Lasers still grate on the shields. "Shields at sixty-nine percent."

I turn the *Resilience* just shy of the orange ignition zone straddling its border.

"*Resilience*, release mags when I order."

"What are you doing?" Ayera demands.

I ignore her. "Release mags ... *now*."

I slam the Hammer to 5 BURN just as the magnetic chaff is released into the ignition zone. The magnetic mine sucks in the elements within the orange detonation region and explodes. The fireball races toward us as we race for the edge of the yellow blast radius.

Red lights flash in the cabin.

"Kyvar!" Ayera screams.

The shockwave throws us into a stream of asteroids. I yank the Hammer and evade some of them, then push up the Hammer to 2 BURN even as we crash against another.

"Shields at forty-five percent."

I maneuver *Resilience* between some large rocks and raise the Hammer to 1 BURN.

Many of the droids are destroyed, yet the feed shows a small number of the horde still tracking us.

"Axton, take them out."

Lasers and cannons roar from the vessel. Many drones explode, yet others push the attack.

White flashes on our shields. "Shields at forty-two percent."

I bank around a large asteroid. The asteroid's size allows me to drop the Hammer to 3 BURN. Axton singles out the drones, and the *Resilience* recoils from his repetitive cannon fire until all the surviving drones are taken out.

I straighten the freighter, breathe deeply, and release the controls.

"Khal, what's the damage?"

"The Corian shields are half gone from the impact." He gets out of his seat. "Let's hope there isn't another run-in with another drone family. Just don't engage anyone for a bit. *Please*." He leaves the bridge.

"I wasn't sure if you were going to kill us or save us." Ayera breathes deeply. "I see you saved us."

The Shivyuns beep and moan.

"Good flying, Captain," Xander says.

"Sometimes you just have to want to live more than they do."

Ayera shakes her head. "And to think I thought the phasma went to your head."

"Be careful or something *will* get to his head," Axton says.

I smile and look to the screen. We're leaving the asteroid belt. The triple stellar Gaxi Galaxy ranges ahead of us. No star traffic is before us—there are no starships, no stations, no defense systems.

But somewhere out there is one of the deadliest battle fleets in the cosmos.

CHAPTER TWENTY-EIGHT

THE GALACTIC MILITARIZED ZONE

"Entering the GMZ," *Resilience* declares.

"Looks peaceable enough," I announce, despite hundreds of anomalies that have just appeared on the overhead.

Khal runs back into the bridge. "I am going to try to relay Aux power to repair the Corian shields. Don't do anything. We aren't ready for another engagement."

"I know."

"Why do you have to say, 'I know' all the time?" Ayera asks.

"Because he knows everything," Khal answers just before he hurries out.

"Or maybe he thinks he knows everything." Ayera crosses her arms.

I look back at her with a smile. "I do."

"You do what? You know everything or you think you know everything?"

"I know."

She shakes her head at me and looks down at her Holox Pad. "I get no readings, and no one has responded to the comms." Ayera says. "I did read the Gaxi accepted peace with the Fraxinus three times, and each time an asteroid was hurled into their system. The first two times they lost habitations. Since then, they have sworn to never make peace with them. They say no watching eyes will ever look away from their system and the belt separating them."

She sits back in her chair. "They don't even know there is a wormhole sending asteroids from Navaria. Ever since the third peace treaty's failure, their battlefleets stand sentry, awaiting another assault." She looks to the screen, not the overhead. "Where is the Gaxi battle fleet?"

I shake my head at Ayera, who never seems to look at the sensors.

"That's the scary part." Axton tweaks his relays. "Hey, Kyvar, what's with all of the objects on the overhead?"

I don't answer. A flicker of light shows on a station in the distance. It hails.

"No hiding the monstrous mine that just exploded, I guess." Axton coughs. "Not to mention the thousands of droid floaters left out there."

I turn to Xander. "Tell me what we should do. Should I just jam a missile and BURN toward our Gate and get out of here?"

"No," he responds.

"I agree," Ayera adds. "Blowing up galaxies might be your thing, but it doesn't make friends."

Khal hurtles back onto the bridge, frustrated. "The Aux engines relay isn't going to work."

I will ask him for fun. "Khal, should we just blow it up?"

"Not now." He sits down at his station. "I am going to try to shelter the core drivers from the motivators to increase our shields. How about BURN? Can I reduce your BURN capability for a bit? I need to amplify the power to the shield grid."

"Sure. If I need it, I'll tell you."

The station hails again.

"Xander, why should I not just blow this station?" I ask.

"The simple answer is you don't know what is behind it."

"*And* we don't just fire missiles at everyone," Ayera adds.

"I agree." These guys are no fun.

Axton grins at me. "Are you sure the phasma didn't go to your brain?"

I drop the Hammer to 4 BURN. "*Resilience*, open the line."

A Gaxi officer appears on our screen, a thin reptilian with a large jaw and tiny eyes.

"You have entered Gaxi territory. Identify yourself," he demands in a deep voice.

"I am Kyvar Astilius of the *Resilience*."

The reptilian fumbles with his controls. His eyes drift, never blinking, from his controls to us. He is slow to respond. What a horrible multi-tasker.

"We are passing between systems, heading back to the Hytilium quadrant and our Home Nebula, through Trasilium."

He coughs. "No one passes through this sector."

"I understand. We have cargo that is needed back home. Our home has been attacked. We are requesting permission to pass through to these coordinates." I flick him the Hgate coordinates.

"Received." The reptilian reads his feed. *What a slow reader.*

I slow the *Resilience*. He looks up and stares at us.

"I wonder how long this guy has been in his station," Ayera whispers.

He continues to stare at us.

"Asking for permission to fly through to these coordinates."

"These coordinates are just inside the border of our system. There is nothing there."

"There is an invisible Hgate in this location."

He looks down to his screens, keys something and looks up again.

"We can prove this to you. The coordinates were given to us by the Asatruans. The Hgate and the data fields will be given to you as a gift, for granting your permission to use the Gate."

He looks at his feed and nods his head. "You are authorized access according to this path." New coordinates flick on the screen.

The *Resilience* cruises past the station. I look to the right and can see the reptilian in the station window as we pass. Same stare. We wave as the feed ceases.

"Space sickness?" I ask Axton.

"Classic signs. He looks like he's been affected by some space radiation out here."

"He looked fried," Khal adds.

"He looked like he hasn't slept in months," Ayera suggests.

"Like you," Khal blurts.

She laughs. "He also has the classic signs of emotional distress. Like they said they wouldn't allow any eyes to be taken from their watch. He must have lost loved ones on the habitations and vowed to stand guard. Little does he know it has destroyed his psyche."

"*Gunfrey,* Ayera. Fried works too." Khal bangs his controls. "Come on, shields." He swivels in his chair. "Let's try the Ion Drive connection." He keys something and slams down a lever.

We all stare at him. Holox controls turn and bars rise indicating the connection.

"This might just work." He stares at the controls. "Come on, *Resilience*. Come on."

The familiar Ion Drive hum softens as the power is redirected. Khal stands to watch the shield count on the screen. "Come on, *Resilience*, you can do this."

The shield rating starts to increase from 42% to 43%.

"Yes!" Khal yells and sits down with his hands behind his head. Hydrobot arrives with a drink for him. "Thank you, my friend."

I smile. "Nice work, Khal. Nice work."

"I told you they sent me to fix your ships." He glares at me. "But ... you *could* quit breaking them."

We continue to move toward the Gate. I look at the overhead. Our advance continues through a cluster of objects. Either *Resilience* has faulty sensors, or an armada flanks us.

"Kyvar, what are your thoughts on the overhead?" Axton asks.

"I think *Resilience* sees what we don't," I respond.

"Something seems wrong out here." Ayera squirms. She never looks at the sensors. She doesn't trust them. "Where's the fleet?"

"They are there." I point to the port. "And there," I point to the starboard. "We are passing between them."

The Shivyuns start thumbing their sensor screen. Axton grabs his pad and examines something. "There!" He turns the Holox Pad toward me. "You can see the asteroids. It's a reflection. It must be between the—"

"Ayera, do you not know what is going on?" Khal asks.

"What is going on?" Ayera inquires.

"Look at the overhead," I point. "The mapping built by *Resilience*."

"I thought it was fried," she responds.

"No," Khal replies. "The Gaxi officer was fried."

"Look again," I suggest.

The tiny black dots on the overhead expand as we pass between them. There are now thousands of them. She stares at the screen.

"How long is it going to take you?" Khal demands. "Axton, our Med officer, has this one figured out."

She looks at Axton, who nods and gives her a smug look.

She loosens her resistor, stands up, and points to the overhead. "You mean the Gaxi fleet is around us. It's invisible?"

"To us. Not to *Resilience*," I say.

"I believe we are approaching the cloaking infraction point. One SEG," Axton specifies.

"Those are all warships?" She stares at the screen.

"You know, Ayera, sometimes you have to trust in more than just your feelings."

She grunts. I laugh.

"Sometimes you should trust your sensors," *Resilience* adds, "as well as your amazing onboard."

We laugh. That's against programming, but that was a smooth response. Disturbing, but smooth.

She frowns.

"Infraction point imminent," *Resilience* details. "Cloaked shields are terminating."

Khal continues to laugh.

"Children, pay attention," Ayera sits back down.

The Shivyuns squeal.

A thin incandescence flashes on both sides of the bridge, blinding us as we exit the Gaxi cloaking field.

"Tint the screen," I demand.

"My emotions tell me to evade that—" Ayera says.

"*Cruiser!*" Axton screams.

The screen tints reveal the terrifying image of a cruiser heading directly for us.

Red strobing collision lights flash in the cabin. The cruiser, not previously visible on the overhead, looms before us. Its size dwarfs even the Vidor cruisers. I grab the controls and yank them upward. The *Resilience* pulls upward as a terrible grating rips at our shields.

The shield rating drops on the screen. "Shields at thirty-five percent."

White flashes gleam through the screen as our shield covering rips away. Ayera falls backward with a scream.

The grating against the shields continues. "Shields at twenty-five percent."

The Ion Drives roar as I pull out the Hammer and yank as hard as I can. The cruiser is enormous, and its extensive forward bridge fills the screen.

"Kyvar!" Khal screams.

We smash into the undercarriage of the cruiser's bridge. A white flash reveals the breaking of the Corian shields and the resistor belt tries to embed itself into my chest. A jarring jolt slams the *Resilience* and propels us away from the cruiser.

Lights flash in the cabin. "Shields at zero percent."

I push up the Hammer as we stall out before the bridge of the Gaxi cruiser.

"*Gunfrey,* Kyvar!" Khal freaks. "*Resilience,* run diagnostics."

The screen fills with extensive damage control reports and endless streaming lines of code.

Axton releases his resistor belt and scrambles to the back of the bridge. "Ayera, are you all right?" He fumbles with his Holox Med Pad, enabling the sensor.

She struggles to get up. "My resistor was jammed. I couldn't secure it in time." She moves past Axton. "I am fine."

She stands in the center of the bridge. Her hair is everywhere, and her face glows a shallow blue. "Kyvar—what happened to your trust in sensors?"

CHAPTER TWENTY-NINE

Gaxi System

I release the resistor belt and sit up. My chest burns, my necks throbs, but nothing hurts worse than my pride. I just piloted into a heavy cruiser. *So much for the best pilot in the cosmos.*

"The cruiser isn't there." I point to the overhead. "It's *not* there."

"Oh, it's there, all right," Khal says.

"Most pilots don't cruise through invisible fleets at 3 BURN." Ayera is furious.

"Glad I repurposed the shields." Khal pats his control. "We would be either space dust or *gunfrey*."

"Disgusting." Ayera walks back to her station.

Xander laughs. "I would rather be space dust."

I just rammed a cruiser. Of all the stupid things.

The comm flickers. I ignore it, but what am I thinking? Our stalled-out freighter literally lies before the Gaxi cruiser's bridge. A tall lean lizard dressed in uniform is smiling at us, looking down into our cabin. I examine him more closely. I do believe he is laughing at us.

The cruiser hails again. "Open the comm," I growl.

A smiling uniformed Gaxi officer appears before us. "Welcome to the Gaxi System. I am Commodore Brauch."

"Thank you," I mumble. I'm not in the mood for smiling Gaxi officers.

"Kyvar Astilius, you are invited to board. We would like to discuss your journey, your purpose in this visit, and this precious cargo of yours."

I stare at him.

"Say something," Ayera whispers.

The Commodore laughs. "My apologies if you didn't see us on your scopes. We are testing our new cloaking shields for our latest cruiser. I assume you didn't see us, is that correct?"

Gunfrey right. I nod.

"I must compliment both the recklessness and skilled piloting you possess. It's a rather rare combination. And thanks to your engineer for increasing your shield capacity—"

"Good to get some credit around here," Khal interjects.

"—because without his skill and yours, you would be space dust."

"We told you," Xander whispers.

I stare at him. I'm *really* not in the mood.

"On behalf of the crew of the *Resilience*," Ayera responds, "we accept your invitation."

The Commodore's eyes peer at her. A soft smile forms on his lips. "Good."

The line ceases.

"Get your act together," Ayera addresses me as she stands up. "Who's coming?"

"I think I'm going to sit this one out, even if it involves Ale." Khal puts on his Holox engineering kit. "I've got to fix what's broken, and I need some help here too."

"I will stay," Xander volunteers.

"No," Ayera responds. "We need your protocol skills in case they are required."

Axton looks at Khal. "I'll stay."

We grab a few Oxylium Ales and a Helix cluster on the way to the shuttle, and then we head for their docking bay. I feel naked as they watch everything we do. Embarrassing for any pilot.

My mood is improving, but Ayera doesn't help with her aggressive certainties. "Kyvar, you know these guys are shell-shocked."

Not that I am not? "Brauch seems pretty self-assured."

"Maybe he is, but they lost two worlds to asteroids. They are in shock. It's madness. The entire industrial might of their galaxy has gone toward these armaments. Look."

I look to both sides. Thousands of artillery barges lay at sentry. Enough weaponry to take on the Vidor. Every gun is pointed at the asteroid belt.

She continues. "You hold that Helix cluster as if it holds value to them."

"It holds value for anyone. You disagree? What do they value, if not this?"

The shuttle enters the cruiser's bay. It slows, hovers and descends.

"Peace," Ayera says quietly. "Kyvar, we have knowledge that will bring them peace."

I shake my head. "I think we have to be more subtle. They have lost too much. They need to find it for themselves."

The back hatch of the shuttle opens for us to disembark.

"I don't agree," Ayera shakes her head. "Peace must be their most important thing." She looks for agreement to Xander, who does not speak but looks out at the cruiser bay. The bay is enormous, with very few other vessels. Just some small freighters and a few shuttles. No fighters.

Commodore Brauch walks up with a large group of attendants. The wide-chested lizard glares at us with narrow, deep-set eyes. He wears a badge-covered red sash over a dark blue tunic. "Welcome to the *Prominence*." His voice is very deep.

"Thank you for welcoming us aboard." I clear my throat. "I am Captain Kyvar Astilius. We come from the Kopernian System. I hail from Sardis. This is Lieutenant Ayera, science and cultural officer, from Hytilium."

She half bows.

He looks her up and down. "What are you?"

"I am Hytilian. Our planet is mostly water, and our species has adapted."

"I've never met a Hytilian." He looks at her almost as if he considers her as food. He licks his lips with a large pink tongue. Disgusting.

"And this is Xander," I say, motioning toward him, "our protocol droid."

Brauch looks at Xander. He eyes the bottles of Oxylium Ale in his hands and smiles.

"Come this way. I must learn of this voyage of yours. If you are not spies, then you are insane enough for me to listen to your story. Did you set off the magnetic mine in the field?"

"That was our doing." Ayera answers.

"I thought so." Brauch leads us to a lift.

"Brauch, where are your fighters?" I inquire about the empty shuttle bay.

He frowns. "My father didn't believe in starfighters. He only built artillery barges. I think differently from my father. This is the first of a new type of warship. We will complement her with fighters. Now, tell me how you made it through the belt?" He gives us a thin smile. "You make me question our defenses."

"We came from the black hole which is at the center of the field," Ayera responds.

I frown. *You never play your cards so quickly.*

"There is no hole there," Brauch snaps.

"There is," Ayera insists, "but it's invisible to the eye and the scopes."

We enter the bridge. Ayera and I advance toward the center of the bridge, while Xander stands sentry at the lift.

"Promontory," Brauch commands his onboard. "Display the journey of the *Resilience*."

The bridge is instantly filled with our track. Projections of floating asteroids fill one side of the room. The fonts and colors show projection styles from another era. These guys are at least a Gen back in their development. From the belt comes a dashed line of our flight path through a series of artillery barges. The line continues towards the far side of the room.

"There," I point. "We came from there. You can't see it. It's the Navaria Black Hole. It formed when Navaria went nova and the Naphtali Mission escaped."

"Naphtali Mission?" Brauch steps aside and whispers to one of his officers.

"The mission to save the Navarians," I continue. "It mostly failed."

He scratches his face, then sits in his chair. "Tell me why you are here again?"

"We are passing through your galaxy. Our galaxy is under attack and we are rushing home. We were given these coordinates by the Asatruans to get home via Hgates."

"Asatruans? I don't know the Asatruans. We have an Hgate here?" he points to the location we provided.

"Correct," I respond. "We are willing to pay for our safe passage and give you the Hgate mappings for your effort."

"As you know, we have cut off association with the outside cosmos since we lost Ikin II." He cringes as if the words hurt. He scratches his face again. "Entertain me, at least. Tell me about this Hgate."

I touch my comm and flick it on the mappings. The elemental allotments, scope, travel density and corridor dimensions display next to the Hgate.

He walks below the mapping of the Hgate and stares upward. "This goes to Trasilium?"

"Correct. From Trasilium, we will venture through Vidor to home."

"Does Trasilium make fighters?"

"The best in the cosmos," I respond with enthusiasm. *I love their fighters but hate their pilots.*

"And we would be only a JUMP away ..." Brauch paces.

"Yes, and Trasilium is known for building strong trade partnerships and working with other galaxies on fighter development."

Brauch smiles. "Kyvar Astilius, I am quite pleased with our friendship."

I step forward toward him. "Then we shall cement our friendship with a gift."

"A gift?" The reptilian licks his lips with a rather large tongue.

"Yes." I hold out a diamond Helix cluster.

Brauch steps backward. "Helix clusters?"

I bow. "Consider it a gift of our friendship."

Brauch looks at the cluster of eight stones. He licks them and I cringe. "They are perfect," he says with a strange drawl, caused by his dry tongue from licking. "Kyvar, I believe we will be most excellent friends."

"One more thing." Ayera steps forward.

No, Ayera, it's not necessary.

"I would like for your most excellent scientists to research the hole and our journey. If we are correct, the asteroids that destroyed your habitations were not from Fraxinus, but from Navaria."

Brauch steps backward and laughs. "Ayera, my dear. If your friend here, Kyvar, didn't just enlighten us with your Helix stones and the answer to my fighter problem, I would question

again a slight suspicion I have about your desire to spy on us."
He turns around and says sharply, "I trust you are not a spy."

I step forward and grab her hand to keep her silent, but the tactic fails.

"I have nothing to lose by investigating," she says with a shrug.

Brauch stares at Ayera, and I squeeze her hand and fake a pleasant expression. "Brauch, thank you for your friendship and time."

He smiles. "We will monitor your journey, and if the Hgates are true, then we will consider your statements about the black hole."

We bow. "May the friendship between our peoples be one of peace and prosperity," I say, in my best formal tone.

Brauch nods. "You are permitted use of the Hgate, and we welcome your gifts. May there always be friendship between us."

We turn to leave. As we approach the lift, Brauch bellows "Xander, what is in your hands?"

He raises the objects. "Oxylium Ale."

A murmur comes from the other officers on the bridge.

"We Gaxi like the Ale." Brauch laughs. The murmur turns into laughter.

Xander advances with the Ale, and Brauch receives it, licking his lips.

"We have much more if you are interested," I add.

More chuckles rumble from his officers.

We bow again and proceed down the lift.

"Ayera, the spy." I say, in my best melodramatic tones.

"I am no spy," she snaps. "Why would he say that?"

"He wasn't ready. He needed to be sure."

"How could he not want peace more than anything?" she asks.

"Because they don't know yet that peace is what they want. Give them time."

She glances toward Xander, once more looking for him to side with her, but he shakes his head and says, "I'm with the Captain on this one."

She frowns. I can tell she wants to engage in some debate. Her skin has a circulating blue gleam. Her gills start to rise.

She's looking for a fight, but she's not going to get it from me.
"I don't disagree," I say. "I just think they have to learn it for themselves."

"Why would anyone refuse to welcome the truth?" she continues.

I frown. "Sometimes the truth can be too much at once."

"Why?" She won't let it go.

The lift stops and Xander steps into the shuttle bay. "Come, children."

I look at Ayera, who glowers at Xander. "That's *my* line."

CHAPTER THIRTY

Gaxi System

I examine the *Resilience* from the window of the shuttle. The vessel looks like it has been shaken and rattled, but there are no sear marks or hull damage. The damage was to the shields and the engineering sector only. We can still get home, but the question is, how fast?

The shuttle enters the bay. I see Khal running around, screaming something.

I stretch my back and try to pop my neck, but it doesn't give. I feel the tightness in my chest. My jaw hurts. My tongue still bleeds, leaving a nasty taste in my mouth.

The shuttle hovers, descends, and lands. The shuttle door opens, and we are barraged with the noise of Khal's furious repairs.

"—and then the resistors were shaken loose." He growls. "Axton, hold this." A shrill metallic sound bounces off the bay walls, followed by a sharp *klink* and Khal's admonition. "Here, don't drop it this time." He comes to us across the shuttle bay.

"What's the damage?" I ask.

"Bad, really bad. Meet me at the bridge."

Khal gets wound up when I break his stuff, but he seems extra annoyed this time. I hear the weakened hum of the Ion Drives, and a putrid smell pervades the ship. That can't be good.

"What's the odor?" Ayera asks.

"*Gunfrey,*" I answer.

"Disgusting."

"It's definitely not your perfume," Xander says.

She smiles at him as we advance to the bridge.

"Here." Khal tosses me his pad.

I look down at the pad and scroll down. My eyes widen. This *is* bad.

"Your small knock, as you probably want to call it, jarred loose a dozen systems and impacted everything." He glares at me. "*Everything.*"

I flick the report from the Holox pad to the screen.

"Just look at the top one. I must confess, the shield redirection I set up sucked our Ion cell reserves. I drained the life from them. I didn't intend to kill our cells. Our range is very limited."

No. "We have to stop in Trasilium ..." I mumble.

"For repairs and Ion cells. Maybe your friend Castor could help us."

I glare at him. "You know I hate that guy."

"That's just the beginning. The cell reduction pushes us down to 7 BURN max."

"Couldn't even outrun a ratspink," I say.

"Or a scrotus." Khal adds to the pain.

He points to the screen. "The stabilizers are done for. I can get us through the Gate, but nothing more. We need a new package. I believe it will take a full install to get this one back in. No crazy flying, not even against the Camans, or you might shake our hull apart."

I grunt.

"Aux engines are out too."

"Aux?" I ask.

Khal continues. "Completely down until the cell counts increase. Ax, lasers are out."

Axton nods. "You told me twice already."

Khal goes on. "The weapons control lens is cracked. Not just the window, but *Resilience*'s targeting is down. We have to rely on Princess's shooting over yours now."

Ayera smiles.

"Too bad the cannon doesn't fire in the direction of the engineer's seat," Axton says dryly.

Khal is not in the mood. "That's just some of it. You don't just ram a cruiser and expect nothing to be wrong. I am afraid she'll never be the same. It's like my first street cruiser. When

I took Wendi on our first date, I wiped out a caravan of spice merchants. No one was hurt except a Wille ranger, but the cruiser, well—it was never the same, as much I worked on it. Never the same, I say. Never the—"

Enough of his rambling. "*Resilience*, display our options."

"Yes, Captain."

A series of options instantly appear.

I look at them and moan. None of them are good enough to prevent a stopover at Trasilium.

"Kyvar, it looks like there's no option but to see your old buddy Castor."

"Isn't Castor the only pilot who ever beat you?" Ayera asks.

"He cheated," I declare.

"Of course, he did," Khal says. "No one could have beaten you. I do believe he took the turn at Serius Canyon at 6 BURN. It's recorded. I know he did it."

"I know," I say. I'm already tired of this conversation.

"You know he beat you?" Ayera asks.

I frown. "I know he cheated."

"And he stole your girl," Khal blurts.

Of course, he did. It's the tradition. The winner kidnaps someone of importance from the opposing team. "Let's just say I rescued her."

"Dashing Kyvar lost his girl ..." Ayera laughs.

"Let's get out of here. The cosmos is calling. Right, Ayera?"

"Right." She agrees for once.

"*Resilience*, get us out of here," I order. "Take us to Trasilium."

The Ion Drives increase, but not to full levels. The familiar static neutralizer of the Aux Engines is missing as well. We wave at our friends on the bridge of the *Prominence*. Captain Brauch hails us. He is holding a bottle.

"Open the line."

Brauch displays on the screen. His green face is flushed.

"Kyvar, this Ale is fantastic. Thank you for the donation to our cause."

"You're welcome," I respond. "Thanks for the friendship."

How much has he drunk?

"Ayera. My men think you are beautiful. We will miss you." He waves creepily.

Charming. "It was great to meet you and your men. We look forward to building ties with your state." I lie, smile, and wave. I am sure Ayera is trying to do the same. I close the comm.

"Positively disgusting," Ayera sniffs.

"I can't figure out if he wants to eat you or date you," Khal says.

"Or both," Axton adds.

Ayera's skin turns a peculiar bluish-purple shade I've never seen before, just before she huffs and turns her back on all of us.

The *Resilience* glides around the *Prominence*. Endless artillery barges flank us for what feels like an entire sector. We finally reach a clearing, and we increase our BURN and achieve the Gate. The explosion from a singular cannon shell seamlessly opens the Hgate and we are through.

The lights flicker. "Tpoint in one SEG."

I yawn. "For once, I could have used a longer JUMP."

"Not long enough, for sure." Khal bangs on his console. "Come on. Lasers and long-range sensors are restored, but Kyvar, I can't get the Ion Drives to uptick to give you the speed you want."

Gunfrey. I *so* wanted Khal to work some miracle to bypass the repairs.

The blue swirl starts to thin, revealing busy Trasilium. Lines of traffic and lights from stations peak through the swirl.

"Crossroads of the galaxies ..." Ayera speaks like a travel guide.

We float through the mist into the Trasilium sector. There is no empty space as far as I can see. One wormhole to the far right and another on the left, traffic lines between.

I process possibilities. We could just melt right into this traffic and BURN away, if it wasn't for our damage.

A space station hails.

Never mind, no dead time in Trasilium. "Open the comm."

A uniformed female officer appears. She smiles and narrows her eyes at me. "Welcome to Trasilium. I am Officer Maritreus."

She looks familiar, very familiar.

"You have entered from an unknown Gate. I see your registration as the *Resilience* out of—"

"We are a vTalis freighter hailing from the Kopernia system."

She looks down on her screen. Her pupils enlarge. The game is up.

"Kyvar Astilius, is that you?" she asks.

"Yes." Admitting it's me makes me cringe.

"So much for being discreet," Khal says under his breath.

"Castor is not going to believe this," Maritreus announces.

I could go without hearing *that* name.

She turns around in her seat. "Can you believe it? It's Kyvar." A few other members of the station walk up behind her. Each is dressed perfectly in their uniforms. I recognize a few of them from the prize runs.

A tall captain steps up and speaks. "Kyvar Astilius. I can't believe it is you. We didn't expect you to come here. Where did you come from? Your heat signature says you came from the Gaxi System?" He turns around. "Is that right?"

"We flew through Gaxi," I answer, and look at Ayera. "We made some friends."

"Not on your life," Ayera says through gritted teeth.

I continue. "Good to see you guys. We are flying through, and we need some help. We had a run-in with some droids, a magnetic mine and a cruiser."

They stare at me.

"It's a long story. I would love to catch up at a repair facility."

The captain flicks us coordinates. I remember how Trasilium makes their starfighter pilots work the stations. "We will escort you, and I am sure Castor would love to catch up."

"Thanks, and one more thing. Can we try to keep this quiet from the Camans?" I ask.

The Captain smiles. "Camans are not known for being quiet and, nor are you. We will send you an escort□best we can do."

The line closes.

"Kyvar, do you remember him?" Khal asks.

"I recognize his face."

"He is one of their starfighter pilots."

"If he is the guy I am thinking of, I roughed him up a few times in competitions."

"You roughed them all up, leading up to Serius," Khal says.

"Serius is the one you lost?" Axton asks.

Khal is quick to tell the whole story. He doesn't care that I don't want to hear it. "Serius Canyon is where Castor Rilius came out of nowhere and defeated Kyvar and stole his girl. Defeated by the king's son ... He even took Valerie away for the evening."

Two stiletto Trasilium fighters ease into a flight pattern on our flanks. I don't even have to look at their stats on the screen. I know these fighters by heart. Arriving at 5 BURN, they cruise effortlessly. While vTalis makes the best freighters, Trasilium manufactures the best fighters—sleek, narrow, maneuverable and deadly☐and their sweptback wings give them an impression of effortless flight. They are loaded with missiles, cannons, and lasers, and capable of 12 BURN.

Single, double, and triple-seater models litter their galaxy in a show of awesomeness. Their unique mix of Ion and hydrogen fuels glow a light blue incineration out the flare ports. The Ion fire flare ports illuminate the stern of the blue and silver polished vessels.

"I don't ever want to engage these guys." Axton gawks. "They match us weapon for weapon. Even the single seaters."

"Best fighters in the galaxy," I mutter.

One of the fighters hails us. I open the comm.

Another Trasilium captain appears before us. He's wearing his helmet and visor. Behind him the cockpit glows from the rich Ion fires. He flicks open his visor. "Lieutenant Kyvar—"

"He knows your real title," Axton snickers.

"—Astilius. I am Captain Mulites Rilius of the *Firespark*. I will escort you to the base station. In case you are wondering, my older brother is Prince Castor."

Gunfrey.

"Even the loser of Serius Canyon needs an escort. Just don't turn over 5 BURN. Only my brother can do that."

Ayera laughs.

"Is it true you have the Horde of Oxylium onboard?"

I give him my best sour look. "Is it true that your brother cheated years ago?"

He smiles. "Yes, he did."

"At least someone agrees with me." I sit back. "Mulites, I like you. These guys don't believe me."

"I answered your question. Now you answer mine. Do you have the Horde of Oxylium aboard?"

"We are headed back home, and we need your help. It is true there was an incident at Oxylium, and we were there."

"And the Horde?"

"Let's say that the Camans don't need to know we're here."

Mulites smiles. "Very well. I will be escorting you to the base station. I will have you know one thing."

"What is that?"

He frowns. "This is Caman Territory."

I nod. "I understand."

"Their Starfleet is on its way looking for you. They should be here in three leaps. My brother is tasked with seizing you and your crew."

CHAPTER THIRTY-ONE

TRASILIUM

Trasilium, or Antilles as the locals call it, spreads out before us. Between the maze of traffic lines and native wormholes, we pass groupings of interstellar worlds and floating habitations. A cargo carrier is behind me and a diplomatic transport is before me. Even my escort must fall in line as traffic lines merge.

I peek at the two starfighters. I could truly make a break for it mixing in with the endless traffic, but reality hits me—they *would* catch me. The *Resilience* can't outrun anyone in its current state.

"Khal, are you absolutely sure we can't BURN out of here?"

"Kyvar, I can't improve the Ion BURN rates anymore."

Ayera coughs. "Next time, think before you ram an invisible cruiser."

I look away. We don't have many options. What if they take us into custody and hand us over to the Camans? What's the point? All this yearning for space has earned me *what*?

I unconsciously hold the talisman around my neck. I consider what Father would do. He would probably petition the king himself and hope Trasilium loyalties are greater to their neighbors than to the Camans. I breathe deeply. Despite my hatred of Castor Rilius, this must be the best option.

I hear Ayera tapping away at her controls, and I turn around.

She gleams. "I love their feed system. It's a true public domain. I have transmitted the message from my Queen about galactic justice, and it's spreading. The feed is being republished everywhere."

"Let me see."

She flicks it to the screen.

I scan the networks and their distribution rates. "I love the offline feed rates."

Ayera sighs. "For some reason, it appears to be the first transmission of the feed."

"I don't think it's completely public, then," Khal says. We pass a Caman freighter. "I believe someone else here has control over the media."

The feed stats continue to multiply, and the rates are staggering.

Ayera taps away at her console. "It's done. I just loaded the message onto every available network." She sits back. "Now, we just hope to Oupavo, the outcry for justice inspires support for us." She wipes the screen of the feed statistical data. The swipe of the screen reveals Inner Trasilium.

"Oh my ..." Khal mutters. "I almost forgot."

Ayera whistles. "I always loved coming here before the war."

"This was the best place to travel for competitions," Khal adds. "Even Kyvar enjoyed it until he lost."

I moan.

"Come on, Kyvar," Ayera urges me. "I know you lost at Serius but look at this place. It's spectacular."

I concede. "It *is* a beautiful system."

Trasilium's two stellar suns are flanked by a host of ringed planets separated by moons, stations and artificial habitations. One of its stars gleams an incandescent white, while the other shines a bright yellow. Streams of endless lines of traffic converge, covering transient scales and lighting from at least five wormholes in opposite directions.

"There is Serius." Khal points.

The fragmented ex-moon floats starboard of our path. Ecospheres litter the surface on opposite sides of a jagged crusted canyon. I stare down and see the place where I felt the BURN of Castor's Antillean fighter.

I moan again.

"Kyvar," Ayera snaps. "*Resilience*, display Serius."

Resilience displays a magnification of Serius. The interstellar moon displays with data and demographics to the right and a feed on the Serius celebration.

I vividly remember their days of celebration. On the final day, officers from the local galaxies would complete. The Serius Prize would be awarded to the best pilot in the Quadrant. I won for three years as an underclassman. It was an embarrassment to all Trasilium. Each year I would beat their best and kidnap someone's girlfriend into deep space. It was the tradition. By the third year, after Valerie and I were a thing, I allowed her to kidnap the ladies of Trasilium into hyperspace on a lady's night instead. It was a real joke until the fourth year.

I sit back in my chair, remembering. "I beat them, I beat them ..."

"Until Castor showed up. Remember?"

I nod. "I do."

Khal is such a downer.

"You mocked him to his father, the king."

"The king?" Axton asks.

"Yes, the king."

"How did he beat you?" Axton keeps asking annoying questions.

"Really? Do we have to go there?" This conversation is beginning to irritate me.

Khal ignores me. "Kyvar rounded the final turn and everyone was clearly behind him. That's when Castor came out of nowhere, pulled off the turn at 6 BURN, and won the race."

"How?" Axton demands.

"I don't know." I shrug. "My father is the only one who has ever turned above 5 BURN."

"Then what?" Ayera asks.

"Seriously, do we *have* to?" I plead.

"We do." Khal smiles.

"Really?"

Khal continues. "Castor then kidnaps Valerie and tears off into deep space."

"He kidnapped her?" Axton asks.

"Yes," I concede, "but I went after her with our entire fleet."

"How long did it take?"

Khal laughs. "A long time ..."

"Castor exhausted his Ion Drives. We couldn't catch him until they burned out."

"Kyvar lost his girl." Ayera laughs.

Khal laughs. "And his pride."

I look at Axton. "See why I don't like this place?"

The display of Serius disappears to reveal Illirium, the cosmos's most valuable mining moon. The fiery moon is the singular home of the nine-sided Helix stones. As a Caman Corporation base, it is the only fully shielded habitation in the cosmos. As we approach, Caman stations litter the subquadrant. A Caman droid cruiser hovers over the moon.

"Looks just like the same model from Oxylium," Khal reminds me.

The breaking up of the Caman cruiser flashes into my mind. The spray of debris. The cruiser's futile attempt at escape by cutting the cable. The mantle rock disintegrating the ship.

"Hey, Kyvar, want to blow this one as well?" Khal asks.

I laugh. "I think one cataclysm is enough for a lifetime."

"You children." Ayera mocks us.

A few orange and blue standard-issue Caman fighters head in our direction. *Great. Here they come.* The game is more than up.

Resilience displays Illirium with facts and demographics, even a write-up on the nine-sided Helix displays.

"*Resilience*. Is Illirium fully mined?" I ask.

"There is only one Helix field remaining on Illirium. It is near the core, and digs are currently underway to mine it. All other fields are exhausted. According to the feeds, this has caused a great rift in the alliance between the Caman Corporation and Trasilium."

"We can exploit this rift," Ayera suggests.

"Yes, and hopefully the rift has become a chasm by the time we arrive."

The *Resilience* cruises past Base Station One. The triple-stacked spherical domed station extends four arms, stretching its capacity wide, with endless berths for travelers.

Annoying Caman logos are everywhere—on transports, fighters, and maintenance vehicles. And somehow, I've missed another four more fighters now escorting us.

We continue to Base Station Two. The station is different, for it carries one large habitation instead of three. It appears almost like a planet, with an artificial atmosphere and floating disconnected docks and platforms. Lift lines connect landing pads with the station.

We orbit until we course through a heavily trafficked section into a brightly lit diplomatic landing for small freighters, shuttles and fighters. *Resilience* takes us in. All of the crew watches the spectacle of the heavily populated station, but my mind is elsewhere.

"Khal, how long do you need for repairs?"

"Ten leaps for a full refit. Enough to get us to flight performance—half a leap. This includes Ion Drive refills, work on the stabilizers with some of their gear, and Aux Engines reinstall. If we can get these, we can BURN out of here."

Half a leap—we can do this.

Two Antillean fighters hover next to us as we descend. The Caman fighters land nearby. I see a consortium of men with blasters leaving the bridge structure, heading in our direction.

"Here they come." I stand.

"Got a plan?" Ayera asks.

"This one is going to have to be impromptu."

"Our lives are in the hands of *Mr. Impromptu*," Ayera cracks. I turn to Xander. "Come with us. Weapons will be on lockdown, though."

"Yes, Captain." His tone is a bit mechanical. Khal eyes him, and Xander smiles.

I turn toward the Shivyuns. "Shivyuns, are you good?"

They mumble their confirmation.

"Then you have the bridge."

The Shivyuns reply with a few beeps and moans.

We exit the *Resilience* and Antillean and Caman officers await us. I recognize Castor at the front. He smiles like a boxer smiles at an opponent he's already beaten. He has the same spiky hair, locked jaw, and customary Antillean features: average height, lean build, large eyes, and round face.

"Welcome, crew of the *Resilience*." Castor half bows. He comes closer and approaches Ayera first. "And who are you?"

Ayera smiles. "I am Ayera Agreya, science and cultural officer."

He looks her up and down. "You're too pretty to fly with this numbracket."

"He's the best pilot in the cosmos."

"Really." He mumbles and turns to me. "Kyvar—the loser of the Serius. Welcome to our world where stolen Helix stones are *not* your property."

I eye him as he advances to Axton.

"And you are?"

"I am Axton."

"Best co-pilot, med officer and gunnery specialist in our galaxy," I add by way of introduction.

"Why haven't I met you before?" Castor asks.

"He was studying medicine when you and I were jockeying around."

"Fair enough." Castor moves on to Khal. "Khal, how's it going?" Castor puts out his hand and Khal accepts the handshake.

"Good." Khal motions toward the *Resilience.* "As you can tell, we ran into some challenges out there."

"I see that." Castor steps toward Xander. "And what's with the space marine?"

"His name is Xander. He is our protocol droid," Ayera says.

"Yeah ... right ..." Castor responds and steps backward. Two Caman officers approach.

"My friends, if your list of crimes didn't precede you, your visit to Trasilium would be a little different. As for now, you must come with me under armed guard."

Axton looks at me. Xander wants to act, but I discreetly shake my head. The officers put phasma chains on my hands. I cringe at the thought of more phasma. My jaw still hurts from the shock only leaps ago, and my tongue has only started to heal.

We walk with Castor between squadrons of starfighters to a lift. The glass lift takes us down past a set of royal administration offices. At the bottom, we reach an ivory chamber with high ceilings and stellar dome windows. Our chains are removed, to my great relief.

Additional Caman officers and a brigade of Antillean starfighter pilots stand to attention. We advance to a large table where Illirium shines through the windows. Stellar traffic and gangway noise are muted by the airtight system controls.

There are fourteen Caman officers and Castor's entire elite starfighter force of fifty pilots. I recognize them by their red striped lapels on their uniforms. The Caman officers point weapons at us. At least five of them have blasters at Xander's head. It's obvious they know his capabilities.

"Sit," Castor orders.

We sit at the table and Castor follows, eyeing the Caman officers. "I think you can lower your weapons now."

The Camans lower their weapons.

Castor points to Xander. "I know your type. The only reason I don't shut you down is that I see you are already in lockdown mode." He faces me. "Either you're stupid, or you're telling me something."

Telling you something stupid. "I set him to lockdown. He cannot be reset without an order from me."

He regards me with a speculative eye. "Very well." He turns to the bay glass. "Open the comm."

The glass wall flickers as the comm opens. Caman Captain vSteven of the *Maverick* appears on the screen, in his Starfighter. Fire flashes from the engines behind him. He must be on full BURN.

"Captain vSteven."

"Greetings, Commander Castor. I trust you have what we are looking for?"

I wave at Captain vSteven.

"Ah. Kyvar Astilius. I trust you have come to your senses now."

"We ran into some complications at Gaxi and need repairs," I say. "Can you assist?"

The captain snarls. "I can assist after you surrender the Helix—"

"We have seized the *Resilience*," Castor interrupts. "It is yours when you get here."

The captain smiles. "Castor, you will be richly rewarded for your loyalty." He laughs maniacally.

"How can I know you will keep your promise?" Castor asks.

"You have my word." vSteven nods to acknowledge his pledge.

I am not convinced.

"Very well," Castor says. "We will make the exchange when you arrive. In the meantime, we will keep the *Resilience* and its crew in confinement."

The comm flickers out.

Castor pulls out his pistol and points it at me. "The plan is to keep you as *my* prisoner. *My* people will be pleased to know Kyvar has been bested again."

"Have you no heart for *our* people?" Ayera pleads.

"Ayera, there is so much more here than concerns about you and your race ..."

Now he's going too far. "And what price are you getting to sell your soul?"

"Have you no decency?" Ayera implores. She stands up and the Caman agents push her down.

"Hey," I say.

Xander shifts in his chair. Castor eyes him and says, "If he even starts to stand up, he's laser dust. I *mean* it."

"How could you even consider this?" Khal speaks.

"The engineer speaks and wants to be heard. Silence!" Castor yells.

I stand up and ten pistols are raised at me.

"Sit down," Castor raises his pistol. "It will be my pleasure to put an end to the scrum of the universe."

I put my hands up.

"Do you want it to end right here, Kyvar?" Castor demands. His face is growing red. "I could blast you right here, you and your entire crew." He steps closer. "Want to die here? Now?"

He's raging, and my blood is up too. I want to grab his small Antillean throat and squeeze. I look around. His fifty officers have stepped closer. Their hands are near their sides. Combat ready. We've got nothing except Xander.

"What's it gonna be, Kyvar, Loser of Serius?" He puts his pistol to my head. "It doesn't matter to the Camans if you're dead or alive."

Castor's face glows red. He steps back. The vein in his neck is bulging. His pistol hand is flexing as if readying to shoot.

"Kyvar Astilius, the famed rogue, found dead in Trasilium." He steps back and pulls the trigger.

CHAPTER THIRTY-TWO

TRASILIUM

Castor's blaster glows hot, and a controlled incendiary beam shears from the barrel. The air before my face vibrates as the laser skims my nose. It tears through the nearest Caman officer in a hollow thump.

"Now!" Castor yells.

Shrill lasers rip across the table. Fifty flares of hot light tear into the Caman officers' bodies, and they crumple in distorted positions. A few try to reach for their weapons. Another round of piercing lasers finishes off the survivors.

Castor looks at me. "I sure had you convinced. I consider you far more a brother then these scrums." He walks over to the guy behind me and spits on him. "I've wanted to do that for the last three leagues. Thank you for killing him." He tosses me his blaster.

I unconsciously catch the blaster. *Gunfrey.* The barrel is on fire. I drop it on the table and shake the burn out of my hands.

He turns to his men. "Good shooting. Nice work."

Castor touches his comm and bots enter the room. "Make it convincing," Castor snarls at the bots.

Castor walks over to one of his men and walks with him toward Khal. "Khal. This is Armstead, our own best engineer. What do you need to fix up the *Resilience*?"

Khal gleams. "I need an Aux reboot package, an Ion Drive install, stabilizers—"

Castor waves his hand. "You two go figure it out. Just direct Armstead and he will get it done for you. But you ..." He puts his hand on Khal's shoulder. "You can't leave yet because you haven't shot your way out of here." He winks.

Khal smiles.

"What is your plan?" Ayera asks.

"My plan? You just did it," he says. "You all shot up the Camans." He sits down. "Then you escape, and we chase you all the way to Kopernia."

He stretches his neck. It pops a few times. He removes his gloves and relaxes in his seat. "Now ... tell me what is going on. You arrive with the cosmos's most valuable cargo, and you haven't really told me anything. Let's start with how you got that sweet ride?"

I laugh. "The *Resilience*?"

"Yes ..." He eyes me like I am being stupid.

"We stole the remer from Kanvarian gangsters."

A bot approaches us. He looks me in the eyes and grabs the blaster. He motions for me to put the blaster in my hand. *Whatever.* I comply, letting my fingerprints bleed into the blaster's handle.

Castor continues. "Kanvarians with a remer. No way."

"After we blew up Oxylium—"

He stares at me. "You really did it?"

"We did."

Castor smiles. "Bold, with a touch of reckless. Just as I remember you."

The bot unfolds a bag and motions for me to put the blaster in the bag.

"Really?" I say. "You're really framing me for his murder?"

"It won't matter. I heard you killed one of their Senators."

I smirk.

Castor motions for me to put the blaster in the bag, and I comply.

He touches his comm again. "Bring the meal." Another door slides open and other bots come in with platters. "Then where did you go?"

"We went to Asatyria to purchase the Hgates."

"You got them?"

"Yes, and there are some additionals for you." I touch my comm and flick the data to his comm.

A bot lowers a platter of spiced legumna hides. Castor chooses one, takes a bite, and touches the comm on his arm to pull the data outward. His eyes glow. He speaks with his mouth full. "You've identified Gates at the Northern Edge and at our Centrura Base." He smiles. "Father will be pleased."

Like you need more Gates, as congested as this place is.

I grab one of the spiced hides. Good flavor. I motion for the crew to eat as well.

Khal and Axton jump at the opportunity. Ayera, however, looks at the bot busily cleaning bloodstains off the floor, and she grimaces. "How can you eat right now?"

My mouth waters at the exceptional flavor. The spiced hides must have been steamed for hours and the spiced ulan peppers bring out the hide's natural flavors. "This is way better than *Resilience's* food."

Castor takes another bite. "The Vidor are expanding even into our territories. They have placed demands upon our moon base at Centrura and our governor has conceded. We have even lost contacts with probes and freighters in the region. They are planning something against us. You know we have no Capital ships?"

I nod.

"It was the strategy of our Kabul to limit Capital ships in our quadrant as a pacifist move. Trasilium—all business and no teeth. Instead, Father invested in fighters."

I raise an eyebrow. "Your fighters *are* the best."

"Hundreds of first-rate fighters are no match for thousands of heavies."

"And the Camans?" I ask.

"My father has had enough of them. He is overstepping the Kabul on this one. But he risks his rule as much as I do. The truth is, we were swindled by the Camans. Scrum. All of them. They offer us their business, their entanglements, and strip Illirium of its treasure. It's a waste."

He bangs the table. "When I heard you tore apart Oxylium, we rejoiced. Brilliant, Kyvar. I've considered blowing Illirium ten times over. Brilliant."

I unconsciously hold my talisman.

He looks at the Caman that he shot. "This is why I used this pretense to get rid of a few of their goons." He looks at me. "Thank you for killing this guy. You served the greater good."

I grin. "My pleasure."

A bot arrives and brings a bottle of Oxylium Ale.

Really?

The bot pours two glasses. "Now we can be honest with each other." Castor takes a huge gulp.

I respond in like manner. Instantly, the rush overcomes my mind. An acceleration. An awakening. My mind is alive, though my body feels fatigued.

"Why do you really hate the Camans?" I ask him before he asks me a question.

"Who doesn't?"

"Good point."

"They swindled Father out of the nine-sided Helix horde. They came, provided their equipment, and reworked our arrangement five times over. You saw our laser system coming in? It's not that good. We had to demand funds and develop our own defense force."

"The fighters?"

"Yes. Everything in our fleet goes 12 BURN."

"Everything?"

"Everything, and that's why we are coming with you."

"Coming with us?"

"My father has ordered us to chase you when you leave." He takes a drink and winks. "I mean, when you escape."

I smile. "Chase me?"

"We are all coming." His tone is matter of fact.

"All of you?"

"All of us—the fifty." He magnanimously extends his hands to include the fifty starfighter pilots hanging around.

"You can't be." Ayera interjects.

"Father orders it. He's ordered us to chase you, but at the same time help you in your cause."

"Yes." *What a relief. All this way and no allies until now.* I smile. "You're not so bad, Castor."

I am in awe. We finally have support. Fifty fighters aren't going to turn the tide, but fifty Antillean fighters can certainly leave a mark. I take another bite of the hides. They taste great in the Antillean spice sauce.

He smiles magnanimously. "I would ask you about the horde if you hadn't already told me. Even the Hgate. Do you have any questions for me?"

I shake my head because I don't.

Ayera coughs and I turn her way. She makes a strange gesture and I don't follow her. I look at Axton. He moves his hand in the form of a turning starship.

Of course. How could I forget? It's troubled me for leagues. "I do have a question. How did you win at Serius? I mean how did you turn at 6 BURN?"

Castor grins. "It's in the owner's manual."

"What?"

"The old school manual. A Gen ago they taught the older pilots to turn over 5 BURN. It was fine back then with the older engines. When the Ion Drives came into being, the G ratios were too much. I found an old manual that explained how to take the stabilizers and insert them into the Hammer as an override. In essence, if you can carry through with it, *you* become the stabilizer."

I pause as the realization hits me. The dream—that was how Father did it, and that's how I tried before.

"It's not easy. It nearly killed me. I just pulled off one turn and I felt like my insides were getting ripped out. I was so wiped I nearly crashed. I managed to steal away Valerie before I hit full BURN and went into a form of temporary catatonic. My body started to shut down. I was in terrible shape."

"Valerie said you were horribly sick. I didn't believe her though ..."

His face twitches. "I remember the pain like yesterday. I will *never* do that again."

✪✪✪

Finally, with all the talk done, it's time to finish this charade of Castor's. I stand with Khal, Axton, Ayera and Xander. This has to look good. I breathe in deeply and exhale. "Xander, blow the door."

Xander folds over his micro cannon and blasts the door. The door fragments off its hinges into the hallway.

"Run."

All of us run toward the lift. The shrill sound of laser pistols pierces the air.

"*Hurry.*"

We enter the lift as voices carry through the hall. As the lift rises through occupied floorspaces, Xander folds up his cannon and we discreetly hide our pistols. The lift stops, and we pull our weapons back out. I take two steps and blast a Caman pilot, and then flip to stun an Antillean maintenance worker reaching for an alarm.

"Stun the locals only. Don't kill them," I order as we run over the platform.

Xander runs ahead and blasts the fuel lines linked to Caman fighters. The fighters belch fire and explode. Smoke billows toward us. We advance to the *Resilience*, while Xander hunts down more parked Caman starfighters. The platform shakes as each fighter detonates.

"Stop them!" Castor screams. His pilots follow him out of the lift. "To the fighters!"

We reach the *Resilience* and run aboard. The platform jolts us as other fighters explode.

"*Resilience*, prep the engines." The Ion Drives light. I can hear their full ignition in the background. *Armstead and Khal did their work.*

I touch my comm. "Xander. Hurry. We've got to get out of here."

Xander sprints across the platform. "There's only one long-range Caman fighter left on the platform. It must be destroyed."

The fighter is out of cannon range, parked on an elevated lift. "Xander, it's too far. Let's go."

"Not too far. It must be destroyed," he repeats. His accent is strangely Spartan.

We watch Xander on the screen as he nears the fighter. A compartment in his right leg opens up. He somersaults, pulls out a rocket launcher, and takes a knee, then freezes, aims, and fires in a smooth ballet of destruction.

We all stand and stare as Xander turns and runs. The rocket tears into the fighter and ignites its Ion Drives. The Ion detonation shakes the entire platform.

"Wow." Ayera is awestruck.

"That's our guy. He sits right there." Axton points to the seat next to him.

"I've got to get one of those," Khal says.

"That was awesome, Xander, just get back here."

The feeds show Caman officers firing lasers at the *Resilience*. Xander takes out a few of them as he runs toward us. Castor and his men continue hustling to their fighters as Xander comes aboard and the airlock closes.

"*Resilience*, controls."

The controls rise and push into my lap. I look at the console as if something inside it is calling me. I ponder how to turn at 6 BURN as I raise up the *Resilience*. I toggle coordinates, prep for sighting, look for stabilization, and drop the Hammer. We tear out of busy Trasilium. Streams of traffic and interstellars range past us.

The screen flickers.

"Open the line."

Castor Rilius appears on the screen. His image is silhouetted against the hydrogen and Ion fire illumination behind him.

"Kyvar Astilius, we saw what you did, and you are ordered to surrender your vessel, and the Helix stones." His fist is in the air. "My entire flight squadron will hunt you to the ends of the galaxies to make you pay for your crimes."

CHAPTER THIRTY-THREE

TRASILIUM

Castor Rilius's feed flickers off and back on. "Our comm is now encrypted." He smiles. "It was fun framing you for murder."

I give a wicked grin. "I never liked him anyway."

"Me neither." Castor laughs.

The mammoth moon Hatuerus comes into focus. Stellar light reflects off the light brown moon. *Resilience* displays the moon, showing the deep inset gorge where Hatuerus beans grow—the best beans in the cosmos. I lick my lips, remembering the rich coffee flavor I experienced in vTalis.

"Khal, did you pick up some beans at the station?"

Khal laughs. "No. I think we were little preoccupied with not getting shot."

Good point.

"Just keep your course." Castor points to a large station reflecting light in a high orbit. "My guys on the station are having sensor issues. They won't even know you're passing by." Castor flicks a data file to us.

The screen displays the station. Dead spots are shown where repairs are being made to their sensors.

"*Resilience*, set your frequencies to ranging, and we should be clear."

The screen flickers. "Absorbing the frequencies into the relays."

Castor looks to his side. "Kyvar, before we BURN out of here. My father has a message for you. Sending your way now."

The comm flickers out and the face of Pharecon Rilius appears. His face is large framed, and his hair is sparse. He looks like an older version of his cocky son with the same eyes, small neck, and Antillean features.

"Kyvar, my condolences to your people for your losses." He holds his hand to his chest and bows slightly. "We are with you. My son and his complement will be the first of the forces we will provide at your disposal. We have always been friends." He smiles slowly, perhaps at old memories.

"I loved your father every time he visited. He encouraged me to break away from the yoke of the Camans. Let's just say his seeds of rebellion are now bearing fruit. Let it be known our friendship and mutual admiration between our galaxies becomes an alliance on this day."

The screen flickers out and Castor appears. "I told you my father is in full support of this."

"You realize—"

"You are declaring war on the both the Camans and the Vidor," Ayera interrupts me to finish my sentence.

He stares at us like we are stupid. "I do. And we are."

We continue past Hatuerus and reach the invisible Hgate. I halt the *Resilience*. Castor's fifty starfighters slow and hover around us in an arrow formation.

"Kyvar. Now what?" Castor asks.

"Are you sure you want to do this?" Ayera asks Castor.

"That's why I stopped, to ask him the same thing," I say. "Castor, are you sure you want to do this?"

Castor grins. The feed crackles, opening wide for all the starfighters. "Hatuerus Squadron, do you read me?"

Fifty voices chime in with their Starfighter call signs.

"Are you ready?" he asks.

Fifty voices answer at once. The voices are garbled, and I make out a good number of customary Antillean salutes.

Castor smiles. "Kyvar, the answer to your question is yes."

"You know you are declaring war," Ayera reminds him. Her tone is almost parental. "And you have little defense against the Vidor."

"I do. Ayera. Don't you worry, we have more than you think."

"Really," I say.

"Really." Castor responds with confidence.

"We'll take your word for it," Ayera says with finality.

"Very well. Castor, we will reconnect near the Tpoint." This Gate is one of the longest Hgates in the galaxies—at least half a leap.

Castor nods his acknowledgment and I flick off the comm.

"Axton, open the Gate."

The *Resilience* recoils, an Hshell explodes, and the Gate begins to swirl.

The swirling blue light fills the cabin, and we pass into the wormhole. A sinking feeling overtakes me. I dismiss it because it's become so common.

"What are we doing?" I accidentally speak aloud. Taking the back door into your enemy's house isn't exactly a good idea. We can label this surprise attack an interdiction, but the odds of surviving this gamble are just like all the rest. Terrible.

Ayera squirms in her seat. "I'm done doubting you, Kyvar. Don't let your confidence fail me now."

Noted, Ayera. I look at her and nod. *I can't guarantee anyone's safety.*

My mother is a cautious woman, my father not so. My father would be proud of me, my mother sick. *Glad ... I am more like my father.*

I release my resistor belt. "Not sure about you guys, but I'm getting some sleep."

"Good idea, Kyvar." Khal releases his resistor belt as well.

I enter my cabin, ease into my bed, and lie down. I feel like I could instantly sleep. Ah ... the simplicity of rest. I close my eyes and picture home and the Nebula Isles. I picture Valerie. She's waiting for me ...

Most of all, I would enjoy sitting by a simple stream or a body of water. I think I could do nothing for the rest of my life. At a minimum, maybe, I could just have a few leaps without seeing my life flash before my eyes. My mind swirls with the memory of so many near-death experiences ... The memory of each of them makes my heart race. How many more can I handle? ...

The deep swirl of hyperspace floods the cabin, brushing light onto Atilio Astilius's waxen face. Consciousness left him some

time ago. His console health readings continue to decline, and red-line conditions show across the board. His heart rate and normal brain functions are slowly declining. Yet...the readings don't flatline—they stabilize at ten percent of normal levels. Atilio has entered a minimal existence, a sort of suspended animation.

In a blinding flash I open my eyes. I blink and see my cabin: my things, my pictures, and the Holox Pad on the desk. Nothing out of the ordinary, except Father. Dreams of Father, always ...

I stand up and stretch. "*Resilience*. Did I dream?" I know the answer, but I want to know his readings.

"A scan of your neural networks shows hyperactivity."

"I know that. Did I dream?"

"Yes."

"I don't think he's dead," I declare.

"Who?"

My father. "*Resilience*, what is the last feed report of my father?"

"According to the feeds, your father's last known location was at Mrunal, fighting off the Vidor. There is no further data from the feed networks."

"I don't think he's dead. *Resilience*, what happens when one dies in hyperspace?"

"No one has ever died in hyperspace."

"I know, but what happens? What *could* happen?" I grumble.

"Perhaps they end up in another dimension, or they go to another galactic plane," *Resilience* suggests.

"No. That doesn't make sense. He was headed through the wormhole to Vidor, just like us. Just like us now. He would have been ejected from the wormhole into Vidor territory. If they'd fired a single shot, he'd have died of exposure."

I sit in a chair and put my head back. I picture my father's vessel exiting the wormhole into Vidor territory. He doesn't answer their hails, and the Vidor attack the vessel.

My mind is filled with the terrible sight of thousands of Vidor fighters swarming my father's vessel. It would have been miserable. I stand up, as though I can banish the image from my head that way. The horde of fighters fills my mind's eye as they gather to destroy his vessel.

I unconsciously hold the talisman around my neck.

"Father!" I yell. "You shouldn't have left us!"

I grab my Holox Pad and throw it to the ground, smash it with my boot. Light continues to gleam from the pad. I smash it again, but it refuses to completely shatter.

"Kyvar?" Khal appears at my cabin door and stares at the Holox Pad. "Come *on*."

I hang my head.

Khal picks up my Holox and walks toward the bridge, and I fall in beside him.

"I started wigging out in my cabin too," he says. "The Vidor are terrible, and I can't believe we're doing this. It seems like all we do is risk our lives. It's freaking me out too, but taking your rage out on a Holox pad?" He looks down at the Pad again. "Those are really nice, and they're the upgraded versions." He looks up at me. "You're gonna make me fix it, aren't you?"

I shake my head.

"*Gunfrey* is what you are, Mister Captain."

On the bridge, we see Axton asleep at his station. He is snoring in the staggered Gundarian way.

"Where's Ayera?" I ask.

"You wouldn't believe it," Khal responds.

"What?"

"She's sleeping."

"Really?"

"I checked on her and she's out. I've never seen her sleep so long before. Even Xander went back to charge. I think he said he exhausted more of his reserves than he expected."

I shake my head. "Makes sense. He *does* have a rocket launcher in his leg."

"I had no idea we had such a powerful bot on board," he laughs, "and we teach him the worst things ..."

I sit down and recline in my chair. "Khal, I dreamed of my father again."

He looks at me. "Again?"

"I think he went into a coma in the wormhole. All of his readings were minimal, but he didn't die."

"You know I don't know anything about medicine, right?" Khal says. "It's like giving our Shivyun friends here pistols."

I look at the Shivyuns. They mumble with the attention.

"I know."

"Look, Kyvar, your dad was a hero. He saved us all and Mrunal would have been cratered without him. He saved millions out there. It was a good way to go."

I shake my head. "I still don't think he's gone."

"Hey, why don't you ask Ax when he gets up if it's possible for those readings you saw to be real? And Ayera may know something about the ethereal."

"I will." I concede to a future conversation with Ayera on the ethereal.

Khal starts fumbling with his console and I turn around. Hydrobot shows up with a Gundaries Infused Malt. "Nice touch, Hydrobot. You're a good bot."

He beeps and bows and turns.

"What were the readings?" Axton put his large green hand on his forehead.

"Maybe ten percent. They just leveled out across the board."

"That's not possible." Axton frowns.

"What's not possible?" Ayera walks into the cabin. Her skin is as pale as I've ever seen it. The sleep must have turned off her overdrive emotions.

Axton regards her. His forest green skin, light green face, and brown hair contrast with Ayera's paleness. "Kyvar dreamed of Atilio again. In the wormhole, Atilio's life readings settled at ten percent."

"That's not possible," she says.

"I agree," Axton replies. "It's not possible. Even twenty to thirty percent is not sustainable."

Ayera looks at me. "As far as I am concerned, he must have gone into a coma or into the ethereal."

"Well, he didn't die." I refuse to believe them.

"If he had life readings, he didn't die," Axton adds. "But that's the thing. No one can survive those ratings."

I look off into the wormhole. He didn't die. "If his life readings were active, the answer isn't ethereal?"

Axton scratches his face. "If it's a coma, he went into a sentry mode. He would've eventually terminated in space without life support."

"Axton." Ayera's tone is one of rebuke, I suspect because Axton used the word 'terminate.' "Kyvar, when things can't be explained, it is the ethereal itself that comes to us. I find when things can't be explained, it's The Voice—"

"Really, Ayera?" I moan.

"If he goes into a coma state, he could survive," Axton says.

"Yes ... but the wormhole took him into Vidor itself," Kyvar adds.

I thought Khal hasn't been listening.

"I don't think there's anything we can do," Khal concludes.

He's *gunfrey* right. I consider the Vidor swarm that probably finished off my father, and I try to dismiss that thought. I look to the wormhole for distraction but find none. My father's resting place is somewhere out there, probably in Vidor territory where we are heading. I breathe deeply and try to find some comfort. He did save millions ... but somehow thinking that never comforts me. He was a hero who left me far too early. Too early, without saying goodbye.

I look away from the brilliant swirl and my eyes are drawn to the consoles. I peer at the seam between the consoles. At some point, I need to break this thing apart. *Why not now?*

I bang the console and the rattle causes the seam to open slightly.

"Kyvar, what are you doing?" Khal demands. "The Holox Pad and now the consoles?"

Through the seam in the console, I see something familiar. I bang it again, more forcefully. The seam opens more.

"What are you doing?" Ayera asks.

I get out of my seat and pull open the console, exposing the insides. Relays, formulators, and wires fill the cavity. Beneath a maze of wires, I recognize the stabilizers from the dream and reach down and pull them out.

Khal moves toward me. I pull on the wires until they are clear of the console.

"Why are you pulling out the stabilizers?" Khal asks calmly, as he might address an unstable maniac wielding a pistol.

I sit down, fray them, and recognize the contacts.

Khal sits down with me. He smiles. "Ah...they hid these from the pilots a Gen ago. They were designed to work, but too many pilots went blind when BURN speeds increased."

I pull out the wires, twist them, and cap them. I pull out a charging pen cap on the Hammer and see where it installs. "It goes right here."

"It does if you want to die," Khal adds. "You heard Castor—it's foolish."

"There has to be a way," I insist.

"The stabilizers require a grounding force to work." Khal adds the details I lack. "A null ground, neither positive nor negative. The vessel can only provide this at certain moments of lock. What is required is something to provide the deadening effect. Man is not polar by nature and can provide the connection, but only for a very brief time."

"Is there nothing else that can level or neutralize its affect?" I ask.

"Nothing that we know of," Khal confirms.

"There has to be something. I have to be able to turn over 5 BURN."

"What about something that has no polar conditions?" Khal processes aloud. "Something raw in its nature, something in its makeup that is neither positive nor negative. A conduit of sorts."

"I like where you are headed."

"We can experiment in a lab." Khal looks me in the eyes. "Not here with our lives."

"That's not going to work," I grumble. "The Vidor have thousands of fighters and they have a max speed of 8 BURN. I can't even turn over 5 BURN."

"We can experiment with metals and neutral carriers and try simulated exchanges." Khal stands up. "The best I can do is formulate it with *Resilience*. *Resilience*, can you assist with metal and composite elemental simulations?"

"Yes," *Resilience* answers.

Khal walks back to his workstation. "Relay them to my workstation and let's get busy on this."

"Sending frequency and relay stabilizer data, Ion exchange requirements, and flight diagnostics to your Holox system."

I look at Khal and his eyes grow wide with the voluminous data displayed.

"*Resilience*, how long do I have?" Khal asks.

"Two SEGs before the Tpoint," *Resilience* answers.

"Impossible," Khal utters.

"Do you what you can," I reply.

CHAPTER THIRTY-FOUR

VIDOR TERRITORY

The stabilizer cords lay tangled on the floor, and I don't trouble to pick them up. "Khal, how goes the research?"

"Nothing yet. There was something about resonance stones that seemed interesting but didn't lead anywhere. There was the exhausted mining and polarity stones article, but nothing tangible."

"Just keep looking." On a normal day, I would look forward to a starfighter engagement, but I'm worn out. I look at my health readings and my fatigue bar grows. Everyone knows it. In fact, everyone's fatigue is rising. Ayera would be pushing back on us, if she didn't have the same issue.

I look up at the overhead, at the interdiction path created by *Resilience*. Sensors have detected a corvette and a starfighter guarding the Tpoint. Dotted arrows show our planned routes. The *Resilience* will run ahead, but not too far ahead as Ayera insists, and target the Ion Power Moon. Castor will lead his squadron and target the solar laser platform station. The route continues through a collection of stations, starships, destroyers, and a cruiser toward a blue marker for the invisible Hgate. A red marker shows an Lgate as provided by Ackbray, and an enemy carrier is stationed near it.

I point to the Lgate. "We are not taking *that* Gate. It's a dead end."

"Literally," Khal adds.

I stare at the Starfleet carrier and its thirteen ports with a hundred starfighters in each port. The carriers are the most terrifying part of the Vidor fleet—they hold virtually unlimited fighters. The key to our survival is to prevent the fighters from scrambling. It's the only way we will survive.

"One run, right, Kyvar?" Ayera insists.

"That's ... what everyone says." One surprise strike is all we agreed to, though I can't help but consider what I would do if I had a chance to take out more of their vessels.

She sees my hesitation. "One slash of the sword is all we agreed to. Anything else will invite their fighters to scramble."

Right.

The screen flickers. "Approaching the Tpoint."

I breathe deeply. I yank out the Hammer and grip it with two hands—going manual. Axton kicks on his Holox weapon system. Ayera tightens herself in. Khal pulls over his engineering controls. The Shivyuns pull down their visors. Xander just stares ahead, his thoughts known only to him.

The Hgate's blue wash thins and mists away until we float out of the wormhole. We are instantly blinded by the light.

"*Resilience*, tint."

The screen tints. I forgot how bright the Vidor system is. Their stellar *must* be aging out.

A Spaceport L32 hails us.

"A cheapie," Khal whispers. "These guys are really in league with the Camans."

"Open the line," I command.

"What?" Axton asks.

"What are you doing?" Ayera is aghast. No one negotiates with the Vidor.

"Open it," I order.

A uniformed pale, almost luminescent, insectoid creature stares at us with large gray multifaceted eyes.

"Break the line," Khal growls. I ignore him.

"Can I kill him?" Axton mutters, half to himself. "I *want* to kill him."

The Vidor officer speaks, its voice metallic, buzzing, edged like a blade. *Resilience* interprets.

"Identify yourself. You are not authorized in this sector. Why have you come to Vidor?"

I lean forward. "I am Kyvar Astilius and no, we are *not* authorized in this sector. We are here for justice."

"Can I kill him?" Axton whispers again, and our eyes meet. I lift one finger where it cannot be seen by the Vidor, to caution Axton to wait.

A larger officer appears on the screen. The arthropod-like creature glows crimson. His eyes morph from gray into obsidian. "Halt your vessel or we will—"

"We seek justice," I say. "Justice for the children of Waupus."

I nod to Axton and drop the hammer to 5 BURN. Axton opens up with lasers and cannons. The L32 implodes with one hit as its airlock seizes. A starfighter near it explodes.

The enemy corvette opens with lasers. The comm remains open as the Vidor officer screams orders in clicks and strident buzzes.

Our vessel shakes with the lasers' impacts. "Shields at ninety-five percent."

"*Resilience*, target their weapons deck and fire."

Two missiles release from our freighter bay just as we range past them.

A feed shows a white flicker and a massive explosion. Hot warheads detonate, causing a rippling explosion, and the feed ceases. "The corvette's hull is leaking. They are losing power."

"Kyvar, I am through." *Resilience* fields Castor's comm and puts his feed on the corner of the screen. "Looks like you made a mess of it." His lasers tear away at the crippled Vidor vessel.

Castor's other officers confirm when they are through the Gate. Antillean lasers target the helpless corvette until it keels over and breaks in two. Its lights flicker off.

"Sensors indicate the corvette's reactor is in meltdown," *Resilience* says.

"Castor, stay clear—that ship's reactor is going to blow."

His fighters veer away toward the solar laser platforms just before the reactor detonates in a red-orange fireball.

I drop the Hammer to 12 BURN and race for the opposite Gate. My line of sight is obstructed by a destroyer, a cruiser and a station at the Hgate. The starfleet carrier isn't far, either. The mammoth carrier starts to block out the brilliant Vidor star, casting a deep shadow over our flight path.

"Don't leave our cover," Ayera demands. "We discussed this."

I nod.

A destroyer looms. *We got this.*

Weapons lock lighting flickers on the bridge. I raise the Hammer to 5 BURN. "*Resilience*. Target the bridge and fire."

Resilience's missile bears down on the destroyer and I roll the freighter. I watch for the stabilizer lock and drop to 12 BURN. The destroyer's lasers fail to target us as we range by.

The missile tears though the shields of the destroyer and explodes in the bridge. I slow the *Resilience* and bank toward the Ion factory moon. Targeting shows on the screen.

"*Resilience*. Fire!" One missile should be enough to detonate it. I turn and drop the Hammer toward the Hgate.

Another destroyer bears down on us.

The Ion factory is hit with the missile and ruptures blue gaseous plumes, but it doesn't explode. *What?*

"Don't do it," Ayera demands. "Don't go back. We don't have cover yet. You've already rushed ahead."

I ignore her and slow the *Resilience* and bank away, taking fire from the destroyer.

The *Resilience* shakes from laser blasts. "We are taking damage. Shields at eighty-four percent." Targeting shows on the screen. The Ion Plant receives my attention.

"*Resilience*. Fire."

I hold true to make sure the impact is significant as we take more damage.

The vessel rocks from shield impacts. "Shields at eighty-two percent. Seventy-nine percent ..."

"Kyvar, let's go!" Ayera shouts.

"Kyvar, turn!" Khal yells.

The missile disappears in the gaseous cloud and erupts with a fiery rage. The Ion factory plant ruptures in billowing plumes of blue flames. Rushes of particles smash the shields as we turn away.

"Ensuring atmospheric controls. Shields at sixty-five percent, sixty-four percent ..."

The vapors and plumes reduce our visibility, yet the destroyer continues to fire as both our ships are buffeted in the Ion cloud.

"*Resilience*, show me the Gate. Sensors only."

Resilience recreates a view virtually from sensor data. I drop the Hammer to 12 BURN and tear toward the Gate. I see a cruiser, a corvette, and a carrier unloading two of its ports with fighters.

"*Resilience*, factor warheads for every vessel."

Targeting appears on the screen with warheads for each vessel though we are not yet in range.

"Kyvar, you are rushing ahead again," Ayera pleads.

"*Resilience*. Fire missiles at every target when we are in range."

A feed of Castor shows on part of the screen. "Kyvar. The platforms are down." A feed of the platform shows Castor has made a wreck of things. The solar charging stations float worthless in their bright reflective orbits. Millions of shards of glass glint light as they hurtle past. Ancillary vessels explode as Castor speaks. "Meet you at the Hgate."

Captain Adain, Castor's second, shows on the screen. "Kyvar. Your support is through. We are headed there at 12 BURN. We will take care of the destroyer behind you and will support your attack on the carrier."

Fifty fighters are headed in our direction, tearing toward us. Our shields are only at sixty-two percent. I shouldn't have gone back to the Ion factory. Too much damage and no fire support.

We achieve range and I slow to 5 BURN. *Resilience* releases twenty Ion Drive missiles, and they streak across Vidor space like hawks pursuing their prey. I smile—what a beautiful sight.

"Go, *Resilience*!" Khal cheers.

Axton opens up with cannons and lasers on the starfighters as they approach. There are too many of them. We dive to evade their lasers, and our shields bear the brunt of their assault. "Shields at fifty-eight percent, fifty-four percent ..."

Antillean fighters show up behind me and blast away. The cheap Vidor fighters are no match for the modern Antillean fighters, but their numbers are the real issue. There are just more of them. Endlessly more of them. I roll the *Resilience* and drop mags to evade missiles, but the shields continue to weaken from the fighters' laser bursts.

Resilience's targeting slams home. A cruiser receives three missile hits, resulting in its bridge catching fire from an incendiary warhead, its reactor melting from an infusion warhead, and its weapons ports being annihilated with fragmentation warheads. I should probably let *Resilience* do the targeting more often. We range past the cruiser and Adain's fighters punish it until it breaks into pieces.

Another destroyer and a corvette are disabled and several of Adain's fighters veer to destroy them as well.

Other missiles impact the carrier ports. Another incendiary warhead scorches one of its three bridges, but fighters continue screaming out of the carrier. The carrier has moved into our flight path and we must go around the beast.

"Get me in close," Axton demands.

I slow and turn the *Resilience*, evading a swarm of Vidor fighters, and run parallel with the carrier. Axton fires Helix-tipped cannon shells into three of the carrier's bays. Explosions erupt along its side. I evade a porthole being emptied of fighters. The carrier is so large it seems endless.

"Kyvar, I've got to get some Helix-tipped warheads," Castor speaks through the comm. "That's spectacular! They go right through the shields."

The Vidor fighters continue to barrel around us. I cannot even count them.

I see some of Castor's fighters are falling. He's lost at least five. I cannot continue to fire on this beast. We must do something different.

The ship shudders with laser impacts. "Shields at forty-five percent, thirty-seven percent ..."

I have failed to see the stream of fighters angling behind me. I drop the Hammer and we push ahead.

"Xander, you prepped the lithium particles into one of the warheads, right?"

"All is prepped," he responds.

"What did you do that for?" Khal asks. "I thought we aren't going in there?"

"We aren't."

I pull back on the Hammer and take us away from the carrier and then roll back. The roll banks me into a swarm of fighters. The vessel bounces from multiple hits on the shields.

"Shields at thirty-five percent, thirty-three percent ..."

The fighters are everywhere.

"*Resilience*. Target the Lgate with the lithium warhead and fire."

"What?" Khal demands.

The *Resilience* recoils as the cannon releases a shell. It detonates on the opposite side of the Vidor carrier's stern, where a creamy purple swirl starts to form.

I rush away from the fighters and drop the hammer to 12 BURN, and my escort follows.

"Kyvar, what did you just do?" Adain asks.

"We opened a Lithium Gate. Hopefully, the carrier will be sucked into it."

"Looks like it's working."

I look at the feed of the carrier. Its stern starts to fade into the purple swirl.

We are clear, but where is Castor? I look to the feeds. Castor's squadron is struggling with an onslaught of fighters. He's lost another ten ships. Hundreds of Vidor fighters surround him. He cannot BURN away.

"Castor, can you shake them?"

Castor's face shows on the screen. His face is red, and he is yanking his controls all over the place. "Kyvar, I'm stuck here. Get out of here. There are too many of them."

"Kyvar, we must go back and help Castor," Adain declares.

"Agreed." I push the Hammer up and turn back toward Castor and slam the Hammer down. "*Resilience*. Take over our missiles. Blanket the Vidor with them."

Missiles tear from the bays and scream toward the swarm of fighters. Fragmentary warheads detonate, taking out masses of them. Axton fires with cannons and lasers.

A small hole appears for Castor to get away and he BURNs out. We tear by the enemy fighters, and I start to bank away when another horde of Vidor fighters heads toward *me*. I start to turn at 5 BURN, and they follow. Hundreds of them angrily blast at us.

The ship rocks. "Shields at twenty-three percent, twenty-one percent ..."

"Khal, now would be a good time to tell me something about the stabilizers."

"I got nothing. Sorry. Maybe there's something to do with a center of an asteroid. I see an article—"

Whatever. I seize the stabilizer, pop the ends and insert them into the Hammer. I drop it to 6 BURN and start the turn.

"Shields at eighteen percent, seventeen percent ..."

The stabilizer light flickers with the inserted stabilizers, but it never remains on. It's only a flicker of a light, a flicker of a hope. Castor has lost twenty-seven starfighters now and the swarm can turn at 5 BURN as well.

"Kyvar. Are you really going to do it?" Khal asks.

"Shields at fourteen percent, thirteen percent ..."

I grip the Hammer with all my strength as it hits me. My body throws itself back in the seat. I grit my teeth and feel my core screaming at me. I see stars, and then my vision turns black. I hear voices yet see nothing. My fingers go numb. My heart is tearing through my chest. I close my eyes. My awareness is shot, and my consciousness is in question.

"Shields at ten percent," *Resilience* intones, calling out the damage.

I hear Khal and Ayera screaming and I feel the *Resilience* turning. I look over and Axton has the controls. I look to the screen. We BURN toward the Hgate. Castor and many of his fighters are away.

"I got it from here," Axton states. "*Resilience*, take away his controls."

My controls are removed from me. I blink my eyes and settle in my seat, consciousness fading.

"*Resilience*, open the Gate," Axton orders.

The ship recoils from a cannon blast and the Hgate starts to swirl. Missiles stream toward us and lights flash in the cabin. The ship rocks from an impact as we enter the Gate.

The blue swirl dominates our vantage and I close my eyes.

"Shields are zero percent. The hull is breached."

"I'm on it." Khal works with his relays.

"Khal, what's the damage?" Axton asks.

"Looks like the missile fried the shield generator and tore into our engine core. Afraid I'm going to have to shut down the Ion Drives."

I open my eyes. The Ion Drives?

"Atmospheric controls kicking in. Balancing measures and systems."

"Seal off the Drives!" Axton orders.

"Are you sure?" I manage to say.

"Do it!" Axton repeats the order.

The Ion Drives go silent and the familiar hum comes to an end as the engine compartment is sealed.

"Looks like it's going to be a slow BURN home on Aux," Khal murmurs.

Axton releases his resistor and grabs his Holox Med Pad. "Kyvar, you okay?"

I roll over.

"You look terrible. He scans my eyes and reads his Holox Pad. "I think you let go at the right time or you would have been blind."

"You almost killed us," Ayera states.

"Honestly, I'm not sure if he saved us or nearly killed us," Axton declares.

"He saved Castor," Khal says.

The feed of Castor shows on the screen. "Kyvar, thank you for bailing me and my squadron out of that mess. You're the best. Hey, are you okay?"

I shake my head.

Axton turns around. "He took the brunt of the 6 BURN turn, but his vitals are good."

"I told you, Kyvar." Castor shakes his head. "I will *never* do that again."

CHAPTER THIRTY-FIVE

12TH QUADRANT

"Open your mouth," Axton's voice seems only half audible through my delusional mind.

I open my mouth, and he shoots stale sensory-induced air deep into my throat. It burns, but at least it tastes like murgan berries.

Axton looks at his pad. "You're fine, just really lightheaded. You'll be messed up for a bit."

"Got that right," Khal echoes. "He left us long ago." He laughs.

"Come on, guys, he just saved Castor." Ayera shows a little compassion. "He nearly finished the complete turn at 6 BURN when he blacked out. Castor only completed a quarter turn at Serius, and it nearly killed him."

They are talking about me like I am not here. Hydrobot brings me a petrolyte drink. I grab it and nearly drop it.

Hydrobot beeps, catches the drink, and sets it between my legs.

"It was actually 7 BURN," Khal adds.

"Not good enough," I mumble.

Axton turns toward me. "You saved Castor for sure."

"Though you weren't supposed to go back." Ayera frowns. Her compassion is over.

I take a drink and feel a surge of energy. "Not good enough!" I yell. "We may have knocked out a carrier, but they have another thirteen of them!" I throw down the drink. "I *have* to be able to turn over 5 BURN, or we are all going to die."

"Hey, man," Khal responds, "I'm trying to figure out what no one in the galaxies has ever done, just for you. Don't be furious with me."

I stand up and promptly collapse.

Axton steps over to me. "*Gunfrey* for brains?"

I frown at him and take his offered hand.

"Don't take it out on us." Axton says. He pulls me to my feet, and I concede with a nod of the head. I wobble away to my cabin.

I splash water on my face and look at myself in the mirror. My eyes are bloodshot and my vision blurry. I collapse into my bed and stare at the ceiling.

How do you do it? How do you turn over 5 BURN? How does one do it? How did my father do it?

"Someone tell me how to turn over 5 BURN?" I groan out loud.

"I believe what you are looking for lies outside the understanding of this Gen."

I grunt at the thought of the onboard listening to me in my cabin. *No, Resilience. I don't need onboard feed jargon.*

"*Resilience.* Don't —" I stop myself. My father was from another Gen. "*Resilience*, my father was from another Gen. Explain."

"Your father's generation was the Ion Generation, when extremely cheap, expendable fuel capable of producing near light speed came into being. According to feeds, when the Ion Drive was first invented, pilots were incurring high rates of losses because of their inability to maneuver over 5 BURN. The planetary councils outlawed starfighter manufacture without speed governors in place. This became standard procedure. A few overrode the systems to achieve greater maneuverability, at great cost. There was a search for metals to override the systems. A true dead net-neutral was required. An element was needed that was capable of forcing stabilization at all times."

"I am aware of this. So is Khal," I mutter.

"What you may not know is that at the same time, the coring of planets was occurring to obtain these types of metals. A few planets were cored until the planetary council outlawed this action. Some systems didn't comply with the planetary council rulings, but most did."

"Are you telling me a core sample is enough to provide the stabilization?"

A pause.

"How do you know this?"

A pause.

"*Resilience*. How do you know this?"

"Feed research connects these data points."

It's almost like *Resilience*'s tone has changed. I thought I heard another voice tone, a humanoid voice, but still the response is a plausible deduction for an amnesic onboard. "*Resilience*. You aren't telling me everything."

"Test the Oxylium core sample." *Resilience* continues with the same tone.

Oxylium? Oh yes, Ayera's Oxylium core sample.

"*Resilience*. When we return home, if you don't tell me your story, we will have to run extensive diagnostics on you."

"Yes, Captain."

I head back to the bridge. "Ayera, do you still have that core sample?"

She stares at me. "From Oxylium?"

"Yes. Bring it to me."

I continue walking and stop at Khal's station. "Sorry. Me jerk—you nice guy. Friends?"

He glares at me. "What?"

I nod my head. I want him to agree and *now*.

He nods. "Sure, *gunfrey* bonehead."

"All good, then?" I ask, nodding again.

"What's up?" He stares at me like I have something wrong with me, which I do.

"Have you considered core deposits?" I ask.

"I considered it, but every scientist at the planetary council declares the folly in it."

That's it. The planetary council doesn't want coring. "Test the core sample Ayera will bring to you shortly."

The Shivyuns screech and moan.

I walk back to my seat. The blue swirl permeates our vantage.

"The Shivyuns have detected Vidor fighters in the Gate," *Resilience* explains.

"What?" I ask.

A feed displays on the screen. Hundreds, maybe thousands of them, are two SEGs behind us.

I frown and breathe deeply. The damage report is on the screen. Shields are out and our Ion Drives are sealed. Max speed is 3 BURN.

"*Resilience.* Open a line with Castor."

Castor's face appears on the screen.

"Castor, do you see this?"

"I do," he replies.

"Castor, your Antillean fighters can outrun them. Rush ahead and save yourselves."

Castor shakes his head. "Not happening. You rescued me." He smiles. "Even if you beat *me* at Serius, I would support you."

We exit the Hgate and float into space. We see nothing ahead of us. Our galaxy is still a long BURN from here. Yet a looming object—the bow bridge of the Vidor carrier—drifts aimlessly to our starboard. I stare at the obtuse object. The Lgate must have closed on it, severing the front bridge from its drives and controls.

"No life readings are located on the carrier," *Resilience* states.

The purple swirl of the Lgate has long since closed. I stare at the uninhabited wreck, once home to thirty-five thousand. Even the front bridge of the carrier is staggering in size. The fate of such an enormous vessel weighs on me as I consider the devastation.

We turn our craft and take our positions outside the Hgate. Test shots are taken to make sure we have the range perfectly.

"Sensors indicate the fighters will arrive in one SEG," *Resilience* says.

I touch my comm. "Castor, hit them when they are vulnerable, when they float out of the Gate."

"Fire perimeter formed," Castor confirms.

"We are in no shape to fight," Khal says. "We don't even have shields. One shot to our bridge will take us out."

"I know."

"Of course, you do," Ayera mutters.

Axton turns on his Holox controls, and his station turns into a weapons control center.

"*Resilience*," I say. "Take over missile control."

"Yes, Captain."

The Vidor fighters begin to emerge. We open fire, destroying the leading vessels. Wrecked spacecraft pile into each other as they are damaged and disabled. A few fighters scramble out, but most collide into each other, folding back into the Gate. Castor's fighters single out the scramblers. The mangled mass of Vidor spacecraft becomes a snare, and the swarm is annihilated.

Axton smiles. "That was like taking down musgraves back home."

"It was fun," *Resilience* agrees.

Did Resilience just say that?

"I think we can do this all day," Khal adds cheerfully.

"I am running very low on cannon shells, and our laser generator is about up." Axton adds a dose of reality to the situation.

We turn and BURN for home at the miserably slow max speed of 3 BURN.

We only make a short distance before *Resilience* announces, "The Hgate is reopening."

No.

"Castor. Just go this time. Go. Leave us."

"No," he spits back.

"What happens if they bring a destroyer through the Gate?"

"We make whatever distance we can before they come again." His voice is calm.

The Shivyuns beep and moan.

"Sensors detect a warship at 15 BURN and closing," *Resilience* says.

"15 BURN?" I ask. "Identify."

Specs shows on the screen. "It's the Asatruan," Khal declares.

"The Asatruan?" Ayera asks.

"Ackbray. It's his starfighter," I mutter.

The comm flickers. Ackbray's big head fills the screen. "Hello, adventurers."

Are you kidding me? "Hello," I mumble. "How did you—"

"Captain, we have a Vidor ship exiting the Hgate," Ackbray says. "Gentlemen, will you clear my vector? You're blocking my fire."

The Shivyuns squeal.

Castor's Antillean fighters veer away. A brilliant phosphorus fire emits from the Asatruan's spiraling hulled vessel. The laser tears into a drone frigate before it can engage its drones. The explosion tears apart other starfighters in the section. The laser ceases.

Ackbray continues past. "Castor, would you please pick off the stragglers?"

"My pleasure." Castor pulls his fighters away and proceeds with eliminating the surviving Vidor fighters.

Ackbray fires his laser again, tearing apart a corvette and more fighters until the Hgate closes.

A random fighter gets close to us and Axton opens with cannons and destroys it.

"Ackbray, how did you get here?" I ask.

"I have my ways. I will be coming aboard with my chief engineer. He will be installing a plasma drive in your ship to get you home."

"What do we owe you?"

He smiles his creepy plastic smile. The centuries haven't done him any favors. "I believe you already have it covered."

I don't know what this means, but maybe the harvesting drone emerging from his starship has something to do with it.

CHAPTER THIRTY-SIX

34TH QUADRANT

"Have you considered my offer?" Ackbray and I walk the *Resilience's* port corridor.

Khal and two Asatruans walk ahead escorting a hovercart transporting a plasma core. The living core moves within its transparent containment. Its glow bathes the corridor in rich blue light.

"I've been sort of busy—"

One of Ackbray's men trips and catches himself from jostling the hovercart.

"Careful," Khal says. "Slightly combustible."

I continue. "I'm not sure if we would have survived the last attack without you. How did you get here?"

Ackbray provides a crooked smile. He is not going to answer. It must come with being Asatruan. *Asatruans and their secrets ...*

"I find when adventurers set off on a quest, they generally need help here and there."

I laugh sarcastically. "I would not call this an adventure— I've almost died five times."

He smiles once more, but it seems less creepy this time, "Sometimes that is what makes the most memorable adventure. It lends sparkle to the wine, you might say."

We stop as Khal and Ackbray's engineers enter the *Resilience's* engine room. The *Stellar Wind* and its rotating hull rests outside the window. Ackbray put his hand on my shoulder. "Your father would be proud."

My father? "You don't know my father."

He removes his hand. His big eyes look away. "I must admit he never travelled to my system in his lifetime."

"Why do you speak of my father?"

"Any father would be proud of you. You've stolen the greatest of priceless hordes, you fractured a peace with the Kanvarians, and vTalis is ablaze with talk of you and your exploits. You've destroyed countless starfighters, frigates, destroyers, and now a carrier. You name is renowned." He puts his hand in the air with a dramatic flair. "Now I offer you something greater than a name—immortality."

I shake my head. "Ackbray, I am human. I will always be human."

Ackbray looks back at me. "Don't be so harsh. It's only an offer."

I look out the window and see his drone excavator pass between our ships.

"You just want the Helix stones." I watch his eyes as I speak, but they reveal nothing. He stretches his mouth into a smile.

"We will use them wisely."

The excavator drone opens its chute and scoops an invisible object.

"*Resilience*, highlight the Helix stones."

"Yes, Captain."

On the glass, tiny Holox squares show where our missiles and cannons once carried Helix stones. "You're harvesting our cannon fire for Helix stones."

He smiles again. "As I said, we will use them wisely. You dropped a load of them in Vidor, but I am not going in there."

"And this is why you are giving me plasma boosters, a tech unknown to us?"

"Ah ... but a tech now known by you. I am not giving you my engines, just boosters to get you home. As a bonus, I will give you fuels to use them a few more times." He bows. "My gift to you."

"For harvesting our gems?"

He bows again. "The least I can do."

"When the Vidor find out what you did, they will engage your entire planet."

He looks at me and shakes his head. "You have more faith in the Vidor than I do." His large eyes hold mine. "They are not stronger than you."

"They outnumber us ten to one. We are but a small system."

"But they are weak," he insists.

"Then teach us how to beat them."

He laughs aloud. "You have everything you need to do that."

"How could—"

"Kyvar!" Khal's voice echoes down the corridor. "You've got to see this."

I walk down to the Engine Room, assuming Ackbray is following.

"Look at this." Khal's face gleams.

The Engine Room glows a soft blue.

"It's reconfigured to run on the plasma core." Khal is ecstatic. "Unless I hooked something up wrong, we should be ready to go home."

"Does it run independent of the systems?" I ask.

"No. It's basically our new fuel," Khal answers. "Everything about it increases capacity and power to all systems."

"There are two things to remember," Ackbray's chief engineer says. "The plasma core's life is limited. You can only use it seven times."

Khal nods. "They only gave us boosters and amp canisters. We don't have regeneration systems. It's basically waste, once it's used up."

"Never wasted." The engineer shakes his head. "Spent plasmas can be regenerated into laser feeds."

"Lasers?" Khal asks.

"Yes. The refining chamber must be redirected to combusts the elements ..."

They continue to talk as I realize Ackbray is still in the hallway. When I get back to the corridor, Ackbray is turned sideways looking out the window. His mouth appears to be moving. I walk closer.

"—will leave it to you, then." Ackbray's voice trails off.

"Who are you talking to?" I ask.

"An old friend."

"I don't see anyone."

He smiles. "That's too bad."

I wonder if he talks to himself all the time. "How do you suggest we fight the Vidor?"

"You are human, right?"

"Yes," I answer.

"Humans don't fight with anger or aggression. You fight with your spirit and tenacity, with an endless willfulness to engage. Pardon the pun—you have *resilience*. You said you've almost died five times. That takes *Resilience*."

He puts his hand on my shoulder again. "You must fight and *win*. That is what sets you apart."

"You just want the stones."

He shakes his head. "No, Kyvar. I need the stones, but there is much more. The cosmos is watching you."

I frown and look away. "I can't even turn over 5 BURN."

"Are you sure about that?" He regards me with his uncomfortable eyes. He seems to look right through me. If I didn't know better, I figure he would mind-melt me, but he probably knows my mental state couldn't handle it right now.

I hear noises behind me as Ackbray's men start to head back down the corridor.

Ackbray stares fixedly at me. "You are equipped for all you need. Remember that. You have *everything* you need."

"Then you will join us to battle the Vidor?" I ask. "There will be plenty of Helix stones to harvest."

He laughs. "We Asatruans don't make alliances." He starts to walk with his men. "Remember Kyvar, we are pacifist."

Gunfrey, right ...

We walk the Asatruans to the shuttle bay and return to the bridge. I sit in my chair, and Hydrobot brings me a petrolyte power drink.

"Thank you, my friend."

Hydrobot bows and beeps.

I turn toward Khal. "Tell me when you are ready."

"Give me one SEG to make sure everything is good."

I relax in my seat and take a drink. I watch Ackbray fire his engines and turn away from us.

"Look at those plasma burners," I murmur.

The scorching blue-purple fire rages from the *Stellar Wind* as it BURNs away and then disappears from our sight in the space of an eyeblink.

What? I drop my drink.

"Did he just JUMP without a wormhole?" Khal asks.

"I saw it too," Axton adds.

"I think he just did, yes," I mutter.

We stare at the empty spot left by the *Stellar Wind*. I can't believe it. That's never been done. He has to be the most dangerous creature in the cosmos.

Khal fills the silence. "All right. I don't know what to make of Cranium Head, but he blessed us with new tech. I am lighting the plasma core. Oupavo, I hope this works. If I wired this wrong, even our remains will be indistinguishable."

A strange smell pervades the cabin.

Resilience is quick to respond. "Atmospheric controls kicking in."

"He said that's normal," Khal adds. "Ayera, no perfume needed this time."

"Are you sure?" Ayera asks.

"Oh, yes ... I am sure."

There is no Ion Drive background noise. Everything is silent, scary silent. "No noise?"

"None," Khal responds.

Ayera smiles. "I love it."

I grunt. "I hate it."

Khal laughs. "Kyvar, you're a bit old-fashioned."

"*Resilience*," I say. "Take us home."

CHAPTER THIRTY-SEVEN

THE SARDIS NEBULA

Valerie holds my hand but thankfully doesn't speak. I don't want to speak or do *anything* for some time. Everyone knows my health readings are off. One could say I've been hit in the head one too many times.

I rub my feet in the sand and stare out at the crystal waters. I could sit here all leap ... maybe even the rest of my life, but then again Nebula Beach only exists at low tide. It's the only time to visit before the tide rolls back in.

I smile and enjoy it while I can—the sun on my back, the sound of innocent birds, and Valerie next to me. She releases my hand and shifts her position. She runs her hands through my hair, both annoying and soothing at the same time.

I hear a hyperlift, a spacelift and a booster igniting, yet I refuse to look up. *Space. What's that?* Not interested—not even close. It only seems to cause me pain and death. The memory of the wrecked carrier flashes before me. Plenty of death.

If I was a better pilot maybe more of the Trasilians would be alive. I'm thankful my crew survived, but I still can't turn above 5 BURN. It makes me feel like a rookie pilot.

Enough of those thoughts. Back to the crystal waters.

I stare at the waves crashing on the shore. I could sit here all day and not think about anything except the clear water.

"I imagine we could see the bottom even at the center of this sea," I say.

"I imagine a lot of things." Valerie's voice is soft and comforting.

She beams with her perfect smile. Her light hair lifts on the ends with the gentle breeze. "What do you imagine?" I ask.

"I imagine," she drifts upward with her gaze, "the Nebula Isles with you and no one else after all of this."

I much prefer the Nebula Isles with Valerie, but I am not looking up with her gaze. I honestly don't even want to see space. I am content right here.

Her eyes remain affixed on the sky. "Imagine the Nebula Isles and it will be so ..." Her tone carries a romantic fervor which causes me to finally look up.

I slowly look upward and follow the path of a space lift to multiple stations. The dotting of stations disappears into the red swirl of the Sardis Nebula. The oval system still carries the red gaseous tint from its supernova many Gens ago. Instead of the death of a star system, rich astro-deposits and existing stars have fueled many civilizations.

I feel the pull. Space is sucking me back into its grip: death, battle, starships, BURNs, secret weapons. I frown and look away. *I can't even turn at 5 BURN. My old man could.*

"What is it?" she asks. Her voice carries concern.

"I so wish we could go right now. Let's just go to the Isles now."

She puts her arm over my shoulder. She smiles. "That is why we imagine. Look up again."

I look up.

"Imagine the riddled islands of Moreh. Our own villa terraformed for eons. Our own mountains to climb and oceans to explore. Just you and me ..."

The riddled islands are extreme ellipticals adjacent to the nebula. There are thousands of them. Like floating atolls, the planets drift along in predicable ellipticals. The mini-planets or isles are prepped for the timing of their temporary livable orbits. Valerie keeps telling me she has one reserved just for us.

"That's my Kyvar. Remember that day in Casamar?"

I nod.

"You were the hotshot son of everyone's hero. You were so dapper. Your head wasn't even in our system. You walked like you were the best. You'd just achieved zero-niner, and you and your friends decided to raid the barracks of the opposing team."

I smile. "Khal was there. It was his fault."

"You let him lead you. What were you thinking?"

I laugh. "He's a brilliant engineer, but a terrible pilot."

"You thought you were going to raid their barracks and ended up at my medical dorm past curfew. *My* dorm. I saw you and your friends out my window. I grabbed a torch and shined it at Khal."

I laugh. "He freaked out."

"I beamed the torch in his eyes, pulled my med scanner, and he thought it was a blaster. Then I turned the light on you and stepped back when I realized it was you."

I smile. "You just stared at me."

"Because everyone knows Kyvar Astilius, our hero's son."

"Hey ..."

"Then you asked for my datacard. What were you thinking? The nerve."

"Why didn't you give it to me?"

"I wasn't going to give my ID to some stranger. Some son of a hero about to raid the ladies' Med dorm."

"But you would blackmail me?"

"I did get into your personal space to intimidate you," she adds, "and I threatened to turn you in."

"That's when Khal freaked out again. He was terrified, because he was already in suspension." I laugh and look out to the waters.

She elbows me. "I should have turned you in."

"Instead, we went on a date," I add.

"The truth is I fell for that hotshot, headstrong son of our galaxy's hero."

I shake my head, too lazy to say any more.

"I think you've become more famous than your father."

That gets my attention, and I look at her.

"You have something you didn't have before." She holds my hand.

"What?"

"You care." She smiles like she does when she figures me out. "You didn't care before. You just flew on instinct. Now you fly because you care. Because you have a destiny to fulfill, a galaxy to save." She runs her hands through my hair again. "That's why you demand more of yourself. You carry your father's weight now. The Voice has guided you to this moment."

I frown.

She is undeterred. "Before, you just did it because you were a dreamer on a remer."

A dreamer on a remer ... She would say that. She was always smarter than I. I look at her pale blue eyes and soft tan skin and put my arm over her shoulder. "You're a keeper."

She smiles and laughs. "You aren't the only jockey on a remer called to save the galaxy. There's an entire ship full of heroes with you."

My comm vibrates.

I ignore it. *How could they ruin this moment?*

"Are you going to answer it?" she asks.

"No," I say.

My comm vibrates again.

"Just act like nothing is going on," I mumble. *Not a care in the world.* I stare at the sea like it will help me at this stage. Like nothing is going on. Nothing is important. The waves crash. The birds sing. The waves roll. My comm vibrates.

"They expect too much of me. They expect too much. *He* expects too much."

"Who?" she asks.

"Father."

"Your father?" she says.

"He trained me to be the best," I say.

"You *are* the best."

"No, I'm not. I should have died so many times."

"I heard about what you did at vTalis and Oxylium. You destroyed a Vidor carrier. No one has ever done that."

My comm vibrates a fourth time. I throw it into the sea. She gets up and retrieves it.

A familiar sound booms overhead. I refuse to look up, but I clearly hear the new Ion Drives of the *Resilience*.

"Come on." She splashes me.

I groan.

She approaches and puts her arms around me.

"Your sister and mother were happy to see you."

"She's aged," I say. "Mother has aged."

"Well ... she thought she'd lost you. I have had to console her many times. Kyvar is a survivor, I tell her. It's what he is, and he is the greatest pilot in the cosmos."

"She always was the cautious one."

She laughs. "And you should learn from her."

I hear sounds behind me, sounds of walking, of movement.

"Just ignore them," I mumble.

Valerie holds the comm in front of my face.

Don't look at them. Ignore them.

She squats down in front of me. Her crystal blue eyes peer just over my head.

Ignore them. I hear more sounds behind me. *I need more time, right here, right now.*

"Kyvar, you can't ignore them."

"Are they all there?" I whisper.

"All of them. Even the Shivyuns."

The Shivyuns ... that's too much.

"You need to go, Kyvar." Shadows of sadness color Valerie's words. "The galaxy is calling for you. I can wait. I *will* wait."

I glance behind me and turn back to face the water. The whole crew approaches us. Khal is smiling his crooked smile. Ayera pleads with me with her eyes. Axton just looks at me as he always does. The Shivyuns moan. Xander grins.

The Shivyuns are the first to come near. They come in close, sit next to me, and rub sand on my feet with their large cumbersome feet and tiny toes. The short plump creatures beep and make shallow hums of encouragement.

Khal sits down on the other side. "I see what you like about it here. I always seem to come when it's underwater. I still prefer Nunday Beach over this one."

"This is beautiful," Ayera exclaims.

"It was more beautiful before you guys came," I mumble.

The Shivyuns moan.

Xander sits down next to Khal. "Mighty good gig you got here."

"You had to ruin this for me, you warhorse."

The bot counters. "It's Xander."

Of course.

"Kyvar, you don't want me flying the *Resilience*, do you?" Khal asks.

You got that right.

Axton sits down next to the Shivyuns. "I've had to take the helm too many times. It's your turn."

I laugh and smile. It feels good to laugh.

Valerie looks me in the eyes. "Go on, Kyvar. I'll meet you at the Nebula Isles."

The Shivyuns beep and moan.

I put my arm over the shoulder of one of the Shivyuns, and the rest join in. The Shivyuns squeal, and we all laugh.

A skylift screams in the distance. We all look toward it as if it was something of importance.

"The entire cosmos is looking for you," Ayera declares.

CHAPTER THIRTY-EIGHT

ZEBULON STARFLEET BASE—SARDIS NEBULA

"*Resilience,* you are clear for Deck Five," the Zebulon base operator says through the comm.

"*Resilience* to base, we copy."

The feed ceases.

"*Resilience,* take us in."

Feeds on the screen show Castor and his fighters descending onto their designated decks.

"Khal, how are we on the shields?"

"Getting there. I refitted the Corian packs, and they will be fully charged by the time we lift again."

I turn to Xander. "Doing well, Xander?"

He pulls out a knife from his metal sleeve. Not sure how he does it, but he twirls it. Impressive.

"Not bad," I say.

"I can do more." He rolls the knife between each finger and sheathes it under his sleeve.

"Troubling," Ayera mutters, "but notable."

The *Resilience* descends amidst a mix of Hytilium luxury cruisers and ambassador craft. Ayera and I prep to head out.

"Kyvar, I analyzed the core sample," Khal informs me.

"And?" I continue packing up my gear while we talk.

"It matches the zero-grid polarity required for it to work."

I turn and stare at him. Is he serious?

"I can't promise you anything, but I'll smelt it down and see if it can be the conduit for the stabilizers."

I have nothing and everything to say at the same time. For once, I choose nothing.

Khal hesitates a moment before he asks, "Kyvar, if this actually works, what gave you the idea to do this?"

"*Resilience.*"

Khal turns to the screen. "*Resilience* told you?"

"Yes," I answer.

I start to leave with Ayera.

Khal stands up, hefts up his belt as if to get down to serious business. "*Resilience*? We need to talk."

We take multiple lifts and movers until we arrive at the Galaxy's Planetary Council, a floating administrative sphere deep within the Zebulon Station. The only connection to the sphere is one bridge. We stop at the edge of the transverse. There are no handrails and I look down at the five-zero drop on either side.

"No railing?" Castor asks.

"Everything here is by design," Ayera answers. "This bridge was designed to put fear into those who choose to cross."

We begin to walk across the bridge. Castor stares at the drops on each side. "It works."

"The purpose is for every decision-maker to understand the gravity of every choice. One of the values of the council is deprioritization of self."

I shake my head. It's a noble yet naïve concept.

We arrive at the opposite side and move through multiple security checkpoints until we reach the council chamber's entrance. Four circles of forty seats face each other underneath the sphere.

"What's with the arrangement?" Castor asks.

"It's intentional," Ayera says. "Everyone is equal. There is no platform or screen in the center. Even feeds are disabled in the chamber."

"Disabled?" he asks.

"Even the feeds," I whisper as we quietly proceed to our seats. We try to be quiet since they are currently in session.

We are escorted to empty seats on the front row. I pause. A small plaque on the seat reads *Atilio Astilius.*

His name is still on it?

I reluctantly sit in my father's seat as council members slide aside for Ayera and Castor.

Nearly every other seat is occupied. I recognize many of the leaders of other civilizations. The Queen of Hytilium is across from us. She is taller than Ayera, and her skin glows a deeper blue. I believe this means she is suffering emotional intensity right now. I look closer. Yes ... her gills are flared up.

The Queen stands. "We have raised our threat system to the highest level. Evacuation has already begun. I fear they will attack Hytilium next. We are virtually defenseless. Please send your fleet to protect us."

I start to stand, but Ayera puts out her hand. "Not yet," she whispers.

The Speaker of the Assembly stands. I recognize him from the public feeds. He has the familiar barrel chest and beard. "My Queen, our fleet has been assembled and we are preparing our defenses."

"I have seen the fleet. It should be at Hytilium *now* to defend us. We are the furthest planet in the system."

"My Queen, I will turn this discussion over to Admiral Astoye." The Speaker slightly bows and rolls his hand toward the Admiral.

Admiral Astoye stands up. He served with my father, and his are the transmitted orders we have been following. "We have ten capital ships and hundreds of fighters. Our plan is to strike them when they assemble, or at whatever wormhole they exit from."

The Queen shakes her head. "You can get there before any bombardment starts."

"If they take the normal Gates, we can. A normal wormhole allows one capital ship at a time. We will strike them when they are weakest."

"And if they show through some unknown Gate?" A blue swirl moves across the Queen's face.

I don't care much for these assemblies. I failed at this in vTalis, but they don't understand the Hgates yet. I stand up and open my mouth. "The Hgate is just outside your moon."

All eyes turn toward me.

"That wasn't the plan," Ayera hisses, but I ignore her.

The Speaker stands again. "Welcome, Kyvar Astilius. Thank you for joining our council." He gestures to the entire council. "You will see he is there, in his father's seat of honor."

A murmur echoes through the chamber.

The Queen looks my way. "Kyvar, how do you know the location of the wormhole?"

"It's on the Stellar mapping we provided." I look toward the Admiral. "Has your team analyzed it?"

He frowns at me. "We have, but it's from the Asatruans."

Everyone is suspicious of them. I get it. I still am, too. "The Hgate is there, and it's the closest to our galaxy. They will come directly to Hytilium first with their entire fleet." I look at the Queen. "I agree with the Admiral's plan. We should attack them once the Gate opens up."

"And the timing?" the Queen asks. "How can you guarantee the survival of my planet?"

"I cannot even guarantee the survival of my own crew." I look at Castor and Ayera. They look back at me, unafraid. "But we can engage them before they get to Hytilium."

The Queen nods her head.

"Admiral, how can we engage them with only ten capital ships?" the Speaker asks.

"We have the support of Antillean fighters." The Admiral holds his hand to his chest, honoring Castor. "No other galaxies have come to our aid."

"How about the CSX Corporation?" the Speaker asks.

A businessman, dressed in CSX Corporation teal, stands up. "We have a message from Senator Nashtech. My colleague here from the Caman Corporation will deliver the message."

A Caman officer, wearing the standard orange and cerulean blue, stands up next to the CSX officer. I can't believe they allowed this individual in our council.

"Due to the investigation into the behavior of Kyvar Astilius, we cannot approve of any actions with vTalis concerns in mind. In addition, there is the reaping of Caman assets at Oxylium and the death of one of our Senators."

A murmur goes through the place.

"This is not the place for accusations and legal matters," the Speaker shouts. "You may take up your issues with the magistrate. Sit down, representatives from vTalis." He turns slowly toward me. "Though this is not the place for legal matters, young Astilius, do you have anything to say?"

I am still standing. I should have sat down. I breathe deeply and look up.

The Speaker gestures with his arm to give me the floor, and he sits.

"Before I started this journey, I thought I could take on the cosmos. I thought I could outfly and outgun anyone." I clasp my hands behind my back. "You all knew my father. He was our champion. When he died, I masked his death and what he meant to me with a self-dependence on my ego."

I look down at Ayera. She wears shock on her face. Unexpected humility will do that.

"Now that I've seen how hopeless our situation is out here, and how we stand little chance of survival, my ego is dead. *Dead.* If I didn't sit in my father's seat right now, I would probably just hide on a beach somewhere and wait for the end." I breathe deeply to center myself before speaking again. "Before I blew up Oxylium—"

Everyone murmurs. The Caman officer stands. "Speaker, we must make legal arrangements."

The Speaker stands and yells, "Take it up with the magistrate!"

"I must petition," the Caman officer pleads.

The Speaker rages back. "I remind you that though you are an invited member of the council as a business partner, we have proof enough of your business dealings with the Vidor that we can investigate *your* practices with *our* enemy."

The Caman officer scowls and sits down. The CSX Officer next to him is almost imperceptibly shaking, and I realize he is chuckling.

"Kyvar, you have the floor." The Speaker waves and sits down.

"After I blew up Oxylium, we went to see the Asatruans and purchased the Stellar Gates. We passed through many galaxies on the way home." I look at the Queen. "We broadcast your plea to the galaxies."

She puts her hand to her chest and nods in acknowledgment.

"I sought out allies at vTalis, but I seem to have made enemies instead. We found friends in the Trasilians." I look toward Castor. "We faced many challenges. The final leg of our journey was through Vidor. We survived making that passage only because we used Helix-tipped warheads and cannon shells."

A rumble in the crowd.

The Caman officer stands up and glares at me.

I return it full force. "You can investigate me but understand this—we are in a battle for our survival. Your petty rocks are worth nothing compared to the civilizations represented here. Every time I feel fear, I imagine their faces, and the faces of my friends." I look at Castor and Ayera. "We have everything we need, all the power and might, to succeed. A friend told me all that we require," and I place my hand over my heart, "is our strength, our courage. Our success lies within us."

I look at the Speaker. "I don't know anything about politics, or much about intergalactic law—"

The Speaker laughs. "Kyvar Astilius, your father used to say precisely that."

"—but we have a plasma laser that we can use only six more times. And we may have cracked the issue with turning over 5 BURN."

The crowd murmurs, and Admiral Astoye's face carries shock. I probably should have told him this already.

"We are hopeless in this fight, but we must *fight*. We must wage this war. We must win. Never in my life did my father give in to an enemy's threats. Nor should we."

CHAPTER THIRTY-NINE

ORBIT OF THE PLANET HYTILIUM

The thing about space battles is the absolute pace of them. The fuels and the men burn out quickly. Advanced weaponry targets even the most skilled of pilots. Few fighter pilots survive. A matter of skill and talent sets pilots apart, yet I am different. While other pilots rely on their abilities, I fly on instinct, a knowing, more than skill or talent. A knowing of what to do and how to do it. I, Kyvar Astilius, fly on instinct alone.

Who am I kidding? Bravado doesn't work anymore. I can't believe this used to hype me up ...

The blue swirls of the Hgate thin as we near its termination. Between the vibrant color bands of the hydrogen wormhole, stars stretch as far as I can see. I ponder the lunacy of our pre-battle rituals. I have my bravado, Axton never touches his controls, Khal has his sarcasm, and Ayera gets super quiet as if she is praying. Have we changed at all?

"*Resilience*, give me the helm," I order.

The onboard flight system controls rise and push into my lap. I breathe deeply and lower my hands toward the controls. *Never touch the controls too early.*

The screen flickers. "Captain."

"Yes, *Resilience*."

"Two starfighters, Vidor Type N5s, await us." Their model, class structure and weaponry appear on the bridge bow window. I look at the screen and the classification of the standard issue Vidor fighter. I skim the displacement and crew and go to weapons and speed. Lasers. No missiles. Max speed 8 BURN.

The Hgate continues to thin. This will be a hot Gate.

I lower my hands to the controls and stop myself. "Ax, are you ready?"

"Yes, Captain." Axton's large light olive-green Gundarian hands hover over the Holox weapons control relays.

I look at Khal. "Khal, let me know if we have any issues."

"We don't have any issues." He laughs. "But you have issues."

I do have issues. I look down at the modifications to the Hammer. A new thin zero-neutral casing has been installed around the Hammer. The casing covers a smelting of the molten core sample over the connection between the stabilizer wires and the Hammer. "Khal. Are you sure about this?"

"No."

I shake my head. He would say that.

"Ayera."

"Yes, Kyvar," she responds.

"You have the first shot, since this one is getting personal."

"Thank you." Her voice carries a quiet, serious tone.

"Xander. Are you ready?"

"Yes," he says, and casually puts his feet on the consoles.

I look pointedly at his feet. "Is this your new pre-battle ritual?"

He grimaces in his droid version of a smile. "It is always good to present yourself calm, even if you are terrified beyond measure."

"Good wisdom," Axton adds.

"Who taught you that?" Khal asks.

Xander points at Ayera. "She's always scared, yet she looks calm on the outside."

We chuckle. Ayera glares at him. "Sometimes I think you're *really* too attentive."

"Xander, are the plasma coils redirected to the lasers?" I ask.

"All is prepped."

I still can't believe we have a plasma-coil redirect to our lasers. I shake my head at the insanity of it all.

The Shivyuns beep and moan, focusing on the controls through their tiny eyes and big visors.

"Let me know if you sense anything," I tell them, and they mumble in response.

A red signal light strobes, indicating the Tpoint. I breathe deeply and pull out the Hammer and go manual. I feel power emanating from the controls.

The *Resilience* floats through the Gate into open space.

Two Vidor starfighters await us. One of them hails us and I ignore them. I look down and the stabilizer light is on, or maybe it never turned off. That's early. I drop the hammer to 5 BURN. The Ion Drives roar and the *Resilience* tears away.

My body is not plastered to my seat. "Khal! Do you think—?"

"I believe it is working. I believe *it is working*!" he yells.

Lasers trace away, and their shrill sound echoes in the ship.

"Fire!" Ayera yells, and the recoil from the swivel cannon rocks the ship.

A small flicker of white shows on one of the starfighters' shields before it explodes. "Nice shot, Ayera," Axton says.

I drop the Hammer to 6 BURN and start the turn. The stabilizer light remains lit.

"You know it's not safe to turn at 5 BURN," Axton says, and smiles at me. "The human body cannot—"

"I know." I grin at the new ability.

We out-turn the remaining starfighter. I sharpen the turn even at 6 BURN and still feel no effects in my body. We complete the turn and I straighten the freighter. The stabilizer light is still lit. I drop the Hammer to 12 BURN, and the enemy fighter is immediately out of range.

"Khal. You did it!" I pull out my Holox Pad, write on it, and flick it on the screen. "*Genius.*"

Axton laughs.

I type *Khal is a super genius!* and I flick it to the screen.

Khal stands up. "I didn't suggest this, nor did I provide the raw materials."

Ayera smirks. "I did insist on the core sample."

"And I suggested the use of it," *Resilience* adds.

A silence fills the cabin. *Did the onboard say that?*

"*Resilience.*" Khal points to the screen. "Onboards are programmed to not burst out like that. It's against governance coding."

No response.

"*Resilience*, remember what I said." I make my tone serious. "When this is over, we are going to have a talk, or you are going to have a full diagnostic run."

No response.

"Acknowledge, *Resilience*," I say, in sterner tones.

No response.

Onboards are not programmed to be stubborn.

The turn puts us on the trajectory of the planet Hytilium. Hytilium's blue surface dominates our vantage, silhouetting the Vidor vanguard's endless stream of menacing gray warships as they advance on the planet. I can feel Ayera's pain. Her planet is next on the list of devastated worlds.

Axton whistles. "It's the entire front line of their fleet."

I breathe deeply, glad the Queen evacuated most of the populace.

"Finding targets certainly won't be a problem," Khal adds.

The targeting computer processes onscreen. *Resilience* charts a list of the warships on the right of the screen. "Sensors indicate one fleet carrier, four battlefleet destroyers, ten cruisers, seventeen support vessels, three guided missile platforms, two solar laser platforms—"

"*Resilience*, we get the point," I say.

Silence overtakes us as *Resilience* processes the voluminous targets before us. The blue reflection of Hytilium splashes through the bow window into the bridge. Azure rays of light flicker among us.

I look to each of the crew. There is no need for words, no need for me to inspire them. Everyone knows their duty. We are as prepared as we ever will be, alone out here in the cosmos.

Though the silence feels right, Khal breaks it in his typical style. "This has been the rush of a lifetime. If we make it out alive, a bottle of Oxylium Ale for everyone."

"Like that's a reward," Ayera cuts in.

We laugh.

The vastness of space stretches behind us, and ahead lies the vanguard of an enemy's battle fleet. Though our galaxy is behind us, no one is foolish enough to *be* here, except us. The crew of the *Resilience* is all alone. But for some reason, after all we have experienced, it seems natural to be here. I wouldn't feel at home anywhere else except here, with my crew and our ship facing the certainty of never returning home.

We tear through space toward the enemy fleet. *Resilience* continues its calculations and targeting on the screen. A percentage calculation appears on the left under a grouping of strategy options. I eye it and laugh.

"*Resilience*. We didn't ask for your assessment."

The calculation disappears.

"*Resilience*, display again," Khal demands. "I've got to see this."

The highest percentage chance of success, 0.97%, reappears on the bottom left corner beneath the target processing. *Zero point nine seven percent.*

"We've faced worse odds and survived," I say.

The cabin lights dim to battle mode. *Resilience* displays targets and separates feeds for display. Weapons lock indicators flash in the cabin as enemy vessels target us. The bright red of a laser platform turns in our direction. Its charging sprays a brilliant light over their battlefleet. Carriers light up, with hundreds of fighters coming in our direction, and a battle cruiser aims its big guns at us.

Resilience's on-screen processing fades. "All targets acquired. All missiles are armed. Favorable cannon and laser targeting has been relayed."

I breathe deeply. The fate of the galaxy now lies in our hands.

CHAPTER FORTY

ORBIT OF THE PLANET HYTILIUM

Resilience displays a mass of incoming fighters.

"*Resilience*, how many?"

"Ninety."

"An entire squadron." I angle the *Resilience* to face the fighters. They stream in a path directly in front of a battle cruiser.

"Ax, clear us a way and take out the nearest battle cruiser."

He smiles and checks his systems. "How does this work?"

I look at him. "Are you serious?"

"I've never fired a plasma laser."

"Axton, the plasma coils are reworked into the laser fire system." Khal says. "Just fire the lasers."

He looks at me. "Now?" he asks.

"Yes, now!"

The Shivyuns squeal.

Axton fires the laser weapon and a blinding phosphorous white light illuminates our screen. *Resilience* tints the screen.

Thank you, Resilience.

The center of the fighter squadron is vaporized. We BURN through their carnage and come close to bringing them within missile range. I raise the Hammer to 5 BURN. "*Resilience*, release the missiles."

I feel the jettison of thirty missiles and see their beautiful Ion Drive trails. Each projectile veers in the direction of *Resilience*'s targeting. What a sight.

The ship rocks from cannon fire. "Shields at ninety-five percent."

I grin. No time to watch the show.

Missile lock indicators flash in the cabin. I drop the Hammer to 7 BURN, releasing mags to draw their missiles.

The stabilizer light holds, and I range past the crippled battle cruiser. The cruiser is broken from stem to stern. Lights flicker as she loses power, and internal explosions reverberate within the confines of her broken hull.

Fighters streak past me. Feeds on the screen show *Resilience's* missiles hitting bridges, armories, shield generators ...

I raise the Hammer, turn left around the battle cruiser, and head toward a carrier and another battle cruiser.

The Shivyuns squeal.

"Ax, hit the escort."

Another blinding phosphorus light emits from the lasers.

Resilience fires three missiles at the carrier's bridges. I yank the Hammer, cross the bow of the carrier, and hook left to pass by its port side. Feeds show a massive elliptical explosive spray coming from the stern of the cruiser. The laser must have hit its armory.

I slow to 2 BURN as we come alongside the carrier.

"Just like before, Ax. A cannon shell for every port."

We pass the first port. The ship shudders from the cannon recoil. The cannon shell enters the first bay and explodes within the carrier, causing a series of fully armed Vidor fighters to explode in a domino effect. The eruptions ripple through its decks and out of the roof of the carrier.

Another blast. The second bay is wrecked.

Our ship reels. "Shields down to eighty-nine percent."

I grunt. "Side cannons. We will weather it."

The third port is destroyed, then the fourth, fifth, sixth, seventh, eighth, until a swarm of fighters turn toward us.

The ship shakes. "Shields down to eighty-five percent."

"Good job, Ax." I drop the Hammer to 7 BURN and turn away. We are immediately out of the range of the fighters. Lights flash in the cabin. I drop the Hammer to 12 BURN.

"Eight missiles are inbound," *Resilience* reports.

Axton takes out a few with cannons. I look down. The stabilizer light is still on. "Khal. Do you think the stabilizers will hold?"

"Why not?"

I turn the *Resilience* at 12 BURN and the missiles cannot make the turn. We head back to the Vidor fleet.

The Shivyuns squeal.

"Ax, take out the rest of the carrier."

"Copy that, Captain." The plasma laser illuminates the screen.

I raise the Hammer to 5 BURN. A battle cruiser is before us. "*Resilience*. Take out her bridge."

A missile streams away toward the cruiser.

Cannon fire explodes around us.

I drop the Hammer to 8 BURN as the missile takes out the controls of the cruiser. Fighters close all around.

Resilience displays the Hgate. "Captain, sensors indicate the Hgate is starting to thin."

This strategy might just actually work.

I drop the Hammer to 6 BURN and rush away. Swarms of Vidor fighters rush toward me.

The screen flickers. Castor's face shows on the screen. "Kyvar, what was that? A plasma laser? When are you going to let me play with some of your new toys?"

I smile. "Here they come." I look at the feed. Five squadrons of Vidor fighters are behind me. I push up the Hammer just outside their laser range.

Captain Seath of the Gundarian fighter bomber squadron appears on the screen. "Kyvar, we will take a run at the fighters and take out the platforms."

"Proceed."

Other fighter groups appear and indicate their directives.

Resilience displays our galaxy's fighter force heading in our direction. Eight squadrons of fighters and bombers and miscellaneous craft scream toward us. I see the path they leave for me in the center. I drop the Hammer and tear through the hole as missiles and lasers erupt around us.

I turn and witness the collision of hundreds of fighters. Lasers blast in all directions. Our bombers veer off to attack the platforms. The comm is wild and incessant.

"*Resilience*. Filter the comm. Leads and immediate range only."

The change is better, but still noisy.

I see what's left of the Vidor vanguard. Vessels are still coming through the Hgate, but it is closing. It will take ten full Gate cycles for them to come through.

Wrecked cruisers litter the vantage. One battle cruiser looks undamaged. Corvettes, artillery barges, and platforms are coming together for protection. The battle cruiser sprays laser and cannon fire in all directions. Cannon shells explode around us.

"Shields at seventy-six percent."

I examine their concentrated formation.

"*Resilience*. Target the cruiser's reactor and fire."

Axton eyes me.

"Missile away."

I veer away. I drop the Hammer to 12 BURN and howl past the cruiser.

The missile tears into the Ion Drive reactor chamber of the cruiser. The explosion sets off a gaseous explosion, wrecking the cruiser. The shockwave tears apart a nearby corvette, a few barges and a frigate.

I slow and turn the *Resilience*. The Vidor fighters are mostly destroyed or fleeing. The platforms are disabled, and their vanguard has been solidly defeated.

The Hgate starts to fizzle into near invisibility. Our fighters turn toward the Gate. Castor joins by my side. Other fighters assemble in our direction, head-on to the Gate.

I watch the Gate spin to a near close.

"*Resilience*. Open a line with Command."

Admiral Astoyes's face shows on the screen.

"Admiral, their vanguard has been destroyed. Please tell the Queen her planet is saved."

"I will pass the word," the grizzled veteran responds with his deep voice. "Good work, Kyvar and crew of the *Resilience*, and excellent work to our fighter wings."

We face the swirling Hgate as the Admiral opens a line with all of the fighter squadron leads and congratulates them, yet the excitement fades. The Hgate doesn't completely dissipate. Instead, it starts to re-swirl. *Impossible*. Gates don't restart. They require a full cycle. What?

The swirl reverses polarity.

"Kyvar. Are you seeing this?" Castor asks.

"I see it and I don't like it." I turn around. "Crew, thoughts?"

"This isn't normal," Khal says.

"Hgates must be closed for regeneration." Ayera stares at her controls. "That's what I read. They can't be reopened. Hgates must have time to rematerialize."

"I don't understand," Castor eyes widen. "How could they—"

The swirl grows until we see Vidor warships edging through.

"*Resilience.* Take out that corvette."

A missile screams toward the corvette before its Drives engage. The warhead explodes in its bridge and it starts to drift.

A destroyer is next through the Gate.

Resilience reads my mind, and a missile screams towards its bridge.

The Hgate continues to open, even larger than normal.

The destroyer's bridge explodes.

A carrier exits the wormhole. *A carrier through a regenerated Gate?*

"Castor. All fighters. Hit it with everything."

Every fighter opens fire on the carrier. The carrier slams into the wrecked corvette and just pushes it aside. Twenty missiles impact the carrier, but it keeps coming as the Gate continues to swirl and widen.

A battle cruiser, with two corvettes, exit the Gate.

"How big is this Gate? *Resilience*, what's in the Gate?"

The screen flickers and displays a sensor-created overhead of the Vidor vessels in the Gate.

"It's their entire fleet," Axton mutters.

Their vanguard was nothing compared to this fleet. We don't even have enough missiles for these targets. Another five Vidor vessels exit the widening Gate, now six times the size of a normal Gate and growing.

The Shivyuns squeal.

I look at them. "Ax, take out the carrier."

Blinding light fills the screen.

"*Resilience*, take out the engines of the corvettes and the bridge of the cruiser."

I feel the jettison of the missiles from the *Resilience.*

The ship shakes with cannon fire. "Shields at seventy percent." Another hard shake. "Sixty-eight percent."

Our missiles detonate in the engine compartments of the corvettes and the cruiser.

The ship shakes again. "Shields at sixty-five percent, sixty-two percent." More vessels are exiting above us. We are getting hit from multiple angles. The Hgate has grown monstrous, planet sized.

We are losing fighters.

I see another carrier exit the Gate in the distance.

The Shivyuns squeal.

"Ax, hit it."

A blinding searing light fills the screen.

Fresh out of secret weapons. "Time to get gone." I open a comm with the fighters. "This is Kyvar Astilius. All fighters withdraw."

CHAPTER FORTY-ONE

ORBIT OF THE PLANET HYTILIUM

Our fighters streak away toward Hytilium.

"Castor, how is your fighter wing?"

"We lost some good pilots." His face is grave. "We are low on shells and out of missiles. Do you plan to re-engage?"

I stare at him. "This is the battle for our galaxy. If we lose here, we lose all."

I rush ahead and turn the *Resilience* back toward the Vidor fleet. Castor's force and around a hundred other fighters trail me. We dodge wrecked craft and the remains of the Vidor's vanguard.

"*Resilience*, open a line with the Admiral."

Admiral Astoye's face shows on the screen.

"Kyvar, what happened with the Gate?"

"I can only guess they reversed the polarity, which has never been done before, and the reversal increased its scope. Our sensors indicate the entirety of their fleet is passing through this regenerated Gate. I can only advise we hit them hard and withdraw to the Kopernia Triangle."

"Kyvar, your father used to say something when his plans fell apart."

"What?"

"He said, 'I know.'"

Ayera laughs.

"Why did he say that?" I ask.

The Admiral smiles. "Because he never actually knew what was going to happen." His face turns stern. "Kyvar. It's been a pleasure." He puts his fist to his chest. "See you in Oupavo."

He turns toward his commanders. His voice is iron. "*Open up the Gates of Tartarus!*"

The line flickers out, and the feed reveals the combined home fleet of ten capital ships opening fire on the emerging Vidor battlefleet. The cannon, laser and missile fire of the home fleet brings pride to my heart. Never have they worked together so well before...but what did he say?

"See you in Oupavo? What was that?" I ask aloud, to no one in particular.

"I've heard him say it before," Khal answers.

"It gave me the chills." As I say it, another chill ripples across my scalp and down my back.

"Me too," Ayera adds. "I think he meant it this time."

Holox targeting coordinates fill the screen.

"*Resilience*, take out their shields on my command. Use every remaining missile."

Axton examines his reserves. "We will be running low on shells soon *and* stones."

Khal laughs. "Makes no difference if we're dead."

"It makes a difference to me if I *am* dead," Ayera says, and turns to me. "Kyvar, we *will* survive this battle. We have to."

I look at the endless stream of warships. "I'm not so sure about this one."

The screen shows the fire between the opposing capital ships. Our fighters will engage from another vector, a brilliant strategy if we had more fighters.

I breathe deeply and look down at the stabilizer light. It holds.

I look at the Vidor formation and come up with an idea. "Let's do something stupid," I think out loud.

"What?" Khal asks.

"I don't think you meant to say that," Axton says, low-key.

I drop the Hammer to 12 BURN and close within range of a carrier, a guided missile cruiser, and a battle cruiser.

Lights flash in the bridge, yet I hold the course.

"Eight missiles inbound."

I grip the Hammer and yank it to the right. The missiles lose their bearing and overshoot. I dip the *Resilience* and slide underneath the Vidor fleet. I straighten the *Resilience* and end up facing the bellies of the Vidor ships. I push up the Hammer to 5 BURN. Thirty Vidor capital ships are in our line of sight.

"All missiles away! *Now!*"

The entirety of our bays empty, and missile trails stream toward the Vidor ships.

Cannon shells explode around us.

"Shields at fifty-nine percent, fifty-seven percent."

I angle toward the nearest carrier and drop the Hammer to 12 BURN.

Missile lock indicators flash in the cabin and I yank the Hammer, shaking loose the pursuing missiles. I clear us away from the Vidor fleet and circle back. More cannon shells detonate near us. "Shields at fifty-five percent."

The *Resilience's* missiles connect with their targets. Shield generators, bridges and armories explode. Flashes and explosions occur everywhere.

Fighters stream out of a nearby carrier. Axton opens with cannons and the ship shudders. Vidor laser fire grates on the Corian shields. "Shields at forty-six percent."

I angle away and drop the Hammer to 12 BURN. A corvette and its missiles immediately come after us.

Castor and the fighters engage the Vidor fighter squadrons. I see another squadron go after Castor. Another five squadrons leave their carriers and head toward us.

"Castor. Get out of there. There are too many of them."

I turn, evade the missiles, and rush past the madness of the fighters. Axton initiates more cannon fire. A fighter lashes at us with lasers. "Shields at forty-three percent."

Three more squadrons of Vidor fighters head our way. "Castor, get out!"

A battle cruiser explodes nearby, and its death fireball leaps above the line of warships. Artillery shells fire into the fleet and over the fleet. Streams of heavy missiles rage through and around the Vidor formation.

A feed shows one of our battle cruisers receiving multiple hits. A corvette detonates and ignites nearby escorts. Streams of Vidor fighters head in the direction of our capital ships.

"Castor, the fleet needs us."

His face shows on the screen. He's surrounded and his lasers are firing. The veins on his neck are swollen. His face shows extreme pain from the erratic maneuvers.

"Kyvar, we are surrounded," Castor pleads.

It's true. We've lost most of our fighters.

"All fighters withdraw to the home fleet." I yank the Hammer and Axton clears a path through the disorder. "Follow me." I drop the Hammer to 12 BURN, and I count only thirty fighters escaping the melee.

Castor's face shows on the screen. "Kyvar, my laser exchange is fried. I've got nothing. Steering is whacked. No weapons. I am disengaging."

Gunfrey. "See you in Oupavo." I pause for only a moment. "All squadrons, assist the home fleet. I am going to make another pass."

I yank the Hammer and turn back toward the Vidor fleet.

Admiral Astoye's flagship, the *Negotiator*, is the Vidor's primary target. The big guns of the battle cruisers are all targeting it. The vessel's bow is already torn through. It's hopeless.

"Sensors indicate the *Negotiator's* hull is compromised." *Resilience* displays the cruiser's damage reports. "The superstructure is bending."

"Open the comm."

The Admiral appears onscreen.

"Admiral Astoye, abandon your vessel," I demand.

"Never, Kyvar. We have them." He turns to his commanders. "Target all your firepower on that carrier."

I look at the carrier. It is nearly crippled, but so is the *Negotiator.*

"Admiral. *Evacuate.*"

"Never," he responds.

Four Vidor battle cruisers fire on the *Negotiator.* Their shells penetrate the bridge and explode. The Admiral's feed goes dead.

"No!" My scream echoes in my ears and all through the *Resilience*'s bridge.

See you in Oupavo.

Additional shells tear into the *Negotiator's* superstructure, and the vessel shudders with a deep internal explosion. A deadening silence fills the comm line and the fleet.

Other Vidor vessels emerge from the Gate and open fire on the home fleet. One of our destroyers explodes. Another cruiser disengages after receiving direct hits. A corvette flees.

"No! Stop them!" Ayera screams. She sees Vidor battle cruisers and solar laser platforms rush toward Hytilium. We can do nothing. We have no way to stop them.

We approach the Vidor fleet. I have no missiles or plasma lasers. *This is stupid.* Lights strobe on the bridge, indicating we've been targeted.

"Incoming missiles."

They seem to come from every vessel. My angle of attack is terrible, but maybe I can dive below them. The vessel shakes from a missile impact. "Shields at thirty-three percent." Bad idea.

Missiles seem to be everywhere. I yank the Hammer to evade the missiles, reversing course. I pull away to try another approach.

A missile corvette explodes. A cruiser is incapacitated. Our few remaining capital vessels keep firing on the Vidor. I must stall them. I turn toward the Vidor fleet and more lights flash in the bridge.

"Missiles incoming."

I release mags, roll the *Resilience*, and turn.

"Axton, fire when you are in range."

Axton opens fire and tears into the nearest cruiser.

A wall of cannon fire erupts around of us. The ship rocks. "Shields at twenty-nine percent. Twenty-five percent. Nineteen percent." This isn't working.

I grunt and yank the Hammer to withdraw. The ship shudders when a returning missile slams against our shields. "Shields at nine percent."

I drop the Hammer to 12 BURN in the direction of our fleet.

Squadrons of Vidor fighters surround our surviving capital ships. Five more Vidor squadrons head toward our fleet. Our fighters have long been driven off or obliterated.

The destroyer *Infamous* is holdings its own with two escorts, but only one of its three Ion Drives glows. I yank the Hammer and Axton opens up on a Vidor squadron.

The ship rocks from a rear impact. "Shields at seven percent."

"How did I miss them?" I ask.

"They were behind us," Axton answers.

Not good enough. My mind is not keeping up anymore. Battle fatigue.

I yank the Hammer to fend off a Vidor fighter targeting the destroyer's engine. Axton takes down the fighter, but we are too late.

"Kyvar, we need to get out of here!" Khal yells.

I yank the Hammer and fail to see an entire squadron coming toward us from the side.

"Kyvar!" Ayera screams.

The impact of so many lasers immediately overwhelms the capacity of the Corian shields. The impact strikes the Ion Drive chamber, and we spin out of control. The remaining squadron flies by to attack the destroyer.

I grab the Hammer and drop it. Nothing happens. *No!*

"Fire in the Ion Chamber," Khal declares. "Sealing and ejecting the Ion Drives."

No. No. This is not happening.

I feel the release of the Ion Drives compartment, and the familiar hum is no more.

"Aux Engines?"

"Gone."

The lights flicker on the bridge until reserve atmosphere and comm feeds are restored. We have become helpless witnesses to the final massacre.

I watch the Vidor squadron make its second pass on the destroyer, whose armory detonates in an elliptical portside explosion.

The other squadrons attack the remaining escorts until they are broken apart. Our fleet has been essentially obliterated.

In the distance, a feed shows the solar laser platforms scorching Hytilium.

"No!" Ayera screams and cries at the same time.

We float aimlessly, defenseless, and a squadron of Vidor fighters turn toward us.

This is the end of our journey, our lives. I look to the enormous Gate. The remainder of the Vidor fleet has now completely cleared the swirls of the wormhole.

See you in Oupavo.

CHAPTER FORTY-TWO

Orbit of the planet Hytilium

The Vidor fighters are coming for us.

I close my eyes. The journey ends here. Everything flashes before me. The crazy idea of blowing Oxylium, stepping aboard the *Resilience*, Ackbray, vTalis, Shivyuns, Navaria, Phaelon, Trasilium, Vidor, and now this, to this end.

I think of Valerie and the Nebula Isles. I will never make it, and a hole forms deep inside my heart, for her and for myself.

I unconsciously hold the talisman and think of Father. I think of his big face and I laugh. Yes, absolutely, he would be proud of us.

I look at Xander and Axton. Xander is motionless. Axton has disengaged his Holox controls. Each of them have few words to say.

"We gave it our all, Kyvar," Khal declares. "We did *good*."

"More than anyone else could have," Ayera hiccups the words through her sobbing. Her skin glows a shallow light blue-green.

I look at the Shivyuns. They don't have final words—they rarely have words. Instead, they squeal.

What? I turn to face the screen.

Just as the Vidor squadron comes within range, a brilliant light fills the cabin and illuminates our vision. I look to the scopes, and the fighters are exploding, spinning away, breaking apart. A Vidor battle cruiser buckles from a plasma blast. Visibility returns, and another flash fills the screen.

Resilience tints the screen. A rotating hulled Asatruan vessel ranges past the bridge. The screen flickers, and a familiar thin pasty face appears.

"Adventurers, I see you have exhausted the cosmos's supply of Helix stones in a *single* battle."

An excavator drone ejects from his starship. A hundred questions fill my mind. I choose poorly. "How did you get here?"

Ackbray calmly regards me. "Kyvar, I made a promise to watch over you." The line ceases.

What does that mean?

The *Stellar Wind* blasts another battle cruiser. Another Asatruan plasma warship passes by. Four Plasma Drives glow purple as the warship presses toward the Vidor fleet.

The Vidor fighters start to re-form and direct themselves toward Ackbray's starships.

A red fighter flashes by. "The Phaelons!" Ayera shouts.

"What?" Axton asks.

"See the dragon?" Khal points to their dragon emblem on the fighter.

More red fighters rage past the bridge, joined by blue Antillean fighters. Both the Phaelons and Antillean fighters provide cover for Ackbray.

Another plasma laser flashes.

A contingent of orange fighter ships stream past the bridge. The lead fighter angles itself into firing position.

The screen flickers, and Caman Captain vSteven's face appears on the screen. He wears a memorable scowl.

"Kyvar Astilius, you look pathetic. One blast would end your story."

I almost laugh. "We've been resigned to death for some time. Right, guys?" I look over my shoulder, and everyone nods their head.

To vSteven I say, with no small amount of sarcasm, "What other news, *Captain*?"

He frowns. He doesn't even get to have the simple joy of instilling fear.

"I won't blast you now, for two reasons," he says. "You could have destroyed me leaps ago and you chose not to. Then there is the intergalactic binding where we are sworn to defend you in exchange for the Horde." He smiles a thin, sour smile. "Blasting you would be bad for business, and for *me*." He slowly pushes a button in his cockpit. The line ceases.

The feed shows a drone sweeper exit the side of his vessel. The drone moves slowly toward something, about to receive it.

"*Resilience*. Display the Helix stones."

Holox squares appears all over the battlefield. One of them is swooped up by the sweeper.

"*Resilience*, identify all other sweepers."

The sweepers have a different color square on the screen. I shake my head. There must be at least fifteen of them crossing the battlefield.

"They want the stones," Khal says. "Unbelievable."

Ackbray's lasers have destroyed three of the Vidor battle cruisers. A carrier lists from a plasma blast. Vidor fighters retreat to their fleet. Another plasma laser sears across the lines and ruins a Vidor frigate.

The Vidor fleet fires artillery and long-range missiles. The artillery is absorbed by an extensive shield around the Asatruan vessels.

"Another Gate is opening," Khal points behind the Vidor fleet.

"Display."

The feed reveals volumes of CSX Corporation fighters streaming out of the Gate. Additional Vidor fighters peel off to meet them.

"*Resilience*, why did you not pick up the Gate?"

"It is an unknown Gate type."

Of course.

A large CSX battle cruiser exits the Gate. The screen flickers. Nashtech's face shows on the screen. He is dressed in his Admiralty uniform.

"Kyvar, how are you?"

"We are on emergency systems. No weapons or shields, but we are covered now."

He turns his head toward his captain. "Focus your firepower on the lead carrier." He turns back toward us. "The Senate had every desire to destroy you. But in the end, I convinced them the Horde was better with us than with the Vidor."

Nashtech's feed shakes from direct hits.

"Take out that corvette!" He yells at the captain and then looks at me. "Kyvar, stay safe. This fight is ours now." The line ceases.

"Over there," Axton points toward Hytilium.

Another Gate swirls a lime green. Artillery shells descend upon the Vidor fleet.

"The Gaxi," I mutter, surprised.

The screen flickers. Captain Brauch of the Gaxi shows on the screen. "Kyvar, my men have been persuaded to assist you in your crusade. Please make sure you stay clear. Not all my men are target marksmen, and our fleet is a bit aged."

I laugh quietly. His barges hurl space mortars toward the Vidor fleet.

"Brauch, we will stay clear. We aren't going anywhere."

Brauch grins and looks at Ayera. He waves at her and the feed ceases.

"Positively creepy." She scowls.

"You should be thankful for that creep right now," Khal scolds. "I certainly am."

I look in the direction of the CSX Fleet. Fighter bombers, squadrons of them, target the nearest Vidor carrier. The distant silhouettes resemble the model line of the *Resilience*. I smile, watching what looks like us from a distance.

vTalis freighters converted to bombers arrive in multiple squadrons. Each of them releases magnetic mines targeting the Vidor bridges and fighter bays. The carrier resists the attacks, until its shields flicker out. Seeing weakness, the squadrons descend like hornets, conducting bombing runs, tearing apart the infrastructure, until the massive carrier explodes and breaks into pieces.

A wing of Phaelon fighters take out the Vidor laser platforms and artillery frigates near Hytilium. Sweeper drones are everywhere now. There must be over a hundred now. *Greed in the midst of battle.*

Ackbray's starships withdraw to our location. Their threat is replaced by the deployment of a CSX solar laser platform squadron. One of the laser platforms explodes, compounding an infusion of light in the center of the CSX fleet. CSX battle cruisers advance next to the platforms to provide cover. Two more waves of fighters rush out of the CSX Gate. The CSX

Corporation solar laser platforms hammer the Vidor fleet, tearing through a frigate and cutting a carrier in half.

The Gaxi fleet sends endless barrages of space mortars into the Vidor fleet. The Vidor capital vessels start to lose their cohesion. A Vidor corvette detonates. As the Gaxi continue their barrage, the Vidor battle cruisers target them. One of the barges explodes, setting off munitions in multiple directions. The explosion rocks another barge which detonates. In response, the Gaxi target the Vidor heavy cruisers in a massive assault with every weapon in their arsenal.

The heavy Vidor battle cruisers receive hits on their shields until they are torn through. The repeat shelling scours the insides of the vessels, severing the cruisers' infrastructures.

The murderers of Admiral Astoye are no more.

More fighters fly by our bridge—another wing of Phaelon, Antillean and Caman fighters. A Caman drone frigate passes by, deploying its drones.

The Vidor are forced into a rough formation surrounded by three waves of attackers. They attempt to cumulatively boost their shields, but the incessant Gaxi barrage prevents them from successfully recharging. The CSX platforms destroy another battle cruiser, and its bombers take out another carrier.

Hydrobot brings me a petrolyte drink. I smile. "Thank you."

He beeps and turns around.

I put my feet up and enjoy the drink. This is different. I'm not the one destroying something for once.

The screen flickers. Ackbray's face appears.

"Adventurers, want to join the fight?"

I hold up my drink. "Not really. I'm done blowing stuff up for a while. How about you?"

He laughs. "Our plasma coils are done."

Behind his vessel, I can see Vidor ships detonating and the combined fleets pressing their final attack. "We used ours up a long time ago."

"Kyvar, I would like to extend something to you again. I know you don't have many stones left. But I want to still offer you the same arrangement without cost."

"Immortality?" I ask.

"To be like me." He holds up his pasty hands.

Khal laughs.

"I know I am not much to look at, but I offer you our state of existence—the ethereal."

"What?" Ayera asks.

I shake my head. "We honor your existence, and much appreciate you saving us *again*, but we choose our current state of existence."

Behind him, I see additional fighters and more cruisers entering the fray. A Vidor ship explodes and lasers blast all over the place.

"Very well." He nods. "One more thing. When I was in your head, I learned something about you."

"He was in your head?" Ayera whispers.

"Mind-melt," Khal whispers back.

"What was that?" I ask Ackbray.

"The tragedy you experienced in your heart when you father died."

I scowl at him. "What?"

"The only thing I can tell you is that all will be explained in time. It is not mine to explain." The feed ceases.

Whatever.

The screen reveals the devastation of the Vidor. The remains of their fleet huddle around the protection of ten capital ships. The Gaxi barges cease fire for other vessels to close. The solar platforms single out the Vidor capital ships, and fighters attack the Vidor center.

Caman and CSX vessels target the individual capital ships, one at a time, until they are isolated and destroyed. The wide arc of fire and encirclement reveal static effects in the cabin. Periodic explosions provide lighting in our dim area.

Hydrobot brings me another drink. I am thinking about a meal when the remaining Vidor vessels surrender—a protocol forbidden in Vidor culture, the word not even in their vocabulary.

A space tug from Sidon comes to take us home. As we hook up, I ask *Resilience*, "Are you still displaying the stones?"

"Yes, Captain."

I am in awe. Not a single Holox square shows on the screen. The entire battlefield has been mined.

"Not a single floater," Axton mumbles.

I give him my best wry smile. "I never believed in floaters."

CHAPTER FORTY-THREE

ZEBULON STARFLEET BASE, SARDIS NEBULA

Khal stumbles out of the diplomatic lounge. "The boys are legendary at mixing drinks."

I laugh. "I can't believe no one knew it was Ox Ale."

Ayera strides next to me. "What was up with Nashtech?"

I remember it vividly. He repetitively came up to speak with me and walked off every time we spoke of our journey. It was as if he wanted to share something but couldn't. I shook my head. "He acted dodgy all night."

"What about vSteven?" Axton walks behind Khal.

Ayera steps ahead. "I would have never guessed he was a double friendly."

Khal looks at Xander. "You should have blasted him right there."

"I should have," Xander agrees. From behind me, he asks, "Can I?"

I glare at Khal and back at Xander. I shake my head. "No. You can't just vaporize him."

Xander hangs his head.

"You children." Ayera starts to walk away to her shuttle, turns, and walks backwards. "Kyvar!" she yells.

I smile. "I know ... the cosmos is calling."

She returns the smile. "No. Get some rest."

I nod. I am tired, very tired ...

"The cosmos *will* be calling," she replies as she turns away.

"I hope not, for some time." I move off toward the landing platforms.

"Where are you headed, Kyvar?" Khal asks.

"I plan to meet Valerie at the Isles. I'll leave you with the *Resilience*, but I'll power off the vessel and grab my gear. Enjoy the rest of the night." I look at the rest of the crew, minus the Shivyuns who have already departed. "I will see all of you when I return."

Xander salutes. "It's been a pleasure, Captain."

Axton salutes as well. "Next time, we'll stay away from Navarians and phasma charges, right?"

"Right." I hold my jaw almost unconsciously.

"And turning over 5 BURN?" Axton adds.

"Wrong." I smile. "I will *always* turn over 5 BURN."

"In the meantime, I'll refit the *Resilience*." Khal gleams from the excessive quantities of Ale in his system. "You know I can fix anything you break."

"Yes, Khal. You are the best engineer."

"But the worst pilot," Xander adds.

We laugh.

I head back to the *Resilience*. I need my things, but I feel like something is missing. As I approach, I see Nashtech. He looks like he is talking to someone and his face is flush from the Ale.

"What are you doing?" I ask.

"Saying goodbye to an old friend," he mumbles.

"What?" I stare at him, thinking he's said something else.

"Saying goodbye to an old friend." He runs his hand on the side of the *Resilience*. "You know, Kyvar, you're a lot like your old man." He starts to walk off.

Oxylium Ale does strange things to people.

"Nashtech, are you all right?"

He smiles. "We negotiated new business deals and ruined old ones." He laughs. "I have pockets full of Helix stones and I got to see an old friend. I'm doing great."

You strange thief! I walk onto the *Resilience's* bridge.

"*Resilience*."

"Yes, Captain."

"You ever gonna tell me how you ended up at Oxylium?"

Silence.

"I didn't think so."

I walk to my cabin and pack up my personals. I have no plans to go back to space for some time. I do plan to sleep for many leaps, visit the beach, and try not to do anything stupid or hurt anyone for a long, *long* time.

I grab my gear, walk onto the bridge, and sit in the captain's chair.

"*Resilience*. Are you sure you aren't going to dig into that huge memory bank of yours and tell me how you got to Oxylium?"

Silence.

I open the control panels and prepare for a shutdown of all systems. I flick off the power to the engine defaults, the weapons systems, and engineering. I pause at the onboard panel and look at the screen. "Last chance?"

Silence.

I reach for the onboard control panel. My fingers are on the switch.

The screen flickers and I turn around. My father's face is there, and he begins to speak.

"To my son, Kyvar, my first-born, I have given you everything that a father can give—"

This is the file he recorded. The same file from the black hole dream. "*Resilience*, where did you get this?"

Silence.

"*Resilience*, acknowledge. Where did you get this?" I demand.

"It comes from my archive."

"Your archive?"

"Yes. Would you like me to continue to display the feed?"

"Yes."

My father's feed resumes.

"In so many ways, you have failed me and in so many ways, you have stunned me. You are one of the most fiercely loyal individuals I have ever known. Your curious heart seems to always get you in trouble, but there is a tactical genius in you, a cleverness that scared your students and teachers, and even me. An inner brilliance that forgets the practical at times. A showy bravado combined with an inward humility that defines you. I will miss our times away from it all when it was just you and me."

I wipe my eyes. I cannot believe what I am seeing and hearing.

"I must confess I made the admiralty promise to not promote you too quickly, because I wanted you to learn the hard way. Character is more important than promotion. You will understand one day. You will have your chance to save the galaxy, and you will perform greater exploits than I." He coughs, then breathes deeply. "Your name will be the one remembered. My heart—" He coughs again, harder this time. "My heart will go forward with you. Goodbye, my son."

His eyelids lower, and his head moves slowly down and out of view. The feed continues, autospliced by *Resilience*. My father slumps in his chair. On the floor at his feet is a rounded stone. It appears to be a core sample. He must have been holding it to help with the stabilizers.

The feed shows his life readings close to ten percent in the dim light from the Hgate. The vessel drifts through the wormhole into Vidor territory. The feed shifts to reveal Vidor vessels and a CSX cruiser. The CSX vessel must have been on a trade mission.

More spliced feeds reveal a shuttle docking on my father's vessel. Vidor officers enter the vessel with a CSX officer. I pause the feed and zoom, yet cannot see the CSX officer's face. I resume the feed. The officer walks up to my father and stands over him. I pause again and zoom in. It's Nashtech. His dark hair, attire and posture are unmistakable.

Nashtech turns to the Vidor officers, speaks with them, and they leave.

The feed shifts. Doctors are working on my father's body. The feed changes to multiple-cut scenes. Nashtech is disappointed with the doctors. Another feed shows Nashtech trying to remove him from his vessel, but his life readings decline. Father's life readings remain consistent only within the confines of his own ship.

Another feed shows Nashtech speaking with Ackbray. *Ackbray?* I didn't think they knew each other. *That liar!*

The audio feed increases.

"We found him in this state," Nashtech declares. "He virtually died in hyperspace and no one can revive him. It's been leaps since we found him. His vitals deteriorate if he leaves the vessel. You can see his scores go down when we try to remove him. If he remains within the ship, his vitals remain at ten percent. It's like he bonded with it. He basically died in hyperspace, yet he has no resting place."

"No one has ever died in hyperspace," Ackbray processes out loud. "Have you tried to jump his heart?"

"Yes," Nashtech answers.

"How about a rejogging of the memory cords to stimulate his brain?"

"Yes, and we even took him back through the same Hgate to see if we could reverse it. Nothing. The only changes in life readings occur when we attempt to remove him from the ship."

Ackbray scratches his head and broods. "His consciousness remains, while his body is virtually dead. No one has ever died in hyperspace."

Heard that before.

"What are the onboard's specs on this vessel?"

"Look for yourself." Nashtech points. "Engineering is over there."

Ackbray walks over and thumbs with the controls. "AC3 dynamic personality chip."

Nashtech walks over. "That doesn't make sense. Let me see."

"They stopped making that model—it had too much spirit, too much independence. The mode was outlawed."

Ackbray scans the specs on a Holox pad. He smiles.

Nashtech stares at him. "You scare me when you smile like that. What is it?"

"I can make him like us."

"You mean like you?" Nashtech asks.

"Yes ... an Asatruan."

"Oh, anything but that ..." Nashtech moans.

"I can take his consciousness and merge it with the ship. You said they were bonded."

"No!" Nashtech shouts. "He always hated bots and AI. That's a horrible, horrible idea."

"What is your other idea?" Ackbray asks.

"I don't know." Nashtech starts to pace.

"That's what I can do," Ackbray thinks aloud. "Let's process this together. The doctors can't save him. You can park the vessel somewhere and he can rest in perpetuity, or you can remove him and he dies. Or we can merge his consciousness into his vessel."

"I don't mind the idea, but I know he would hate it. We could just remove him and let him die."

"No. We can save him."

Nashtech shakes his head. "If you can't bring him back as a human, I am not interested."

"But we can bring him back to life," Ackbray pleads. "What is it to be human? He virtually died already. We can raise him back to existence."

Nashtech crosses his arms. "Ackbray, give me another reason why we should do this."

"His son. He said he has a son."

Nashtech groans and walks over to the captain's chair. He sits and closes his eyes.

"His greatest joy was his son," Nashtech muses, "and he wouldn't want to leave him."

"Correct." Ackbray agrees.

Nashtech remains in the seat processing his thoughts. "And the Vidor are striking deep." He pauses. "This would help the Sidonians, and he could help his son."

"Correct." Ackbray repeats.

Nashtech's eyes remain closed. "He couldn't return as some sentient vessel. No ... that wouldn't work."

"Agreed. Not in *this* cosmos."

Nashtech stands up and breathes deeply. "There would have to be rules." He paces. "We couldn't just have sentient craft everywhere."

"We could put limitations in the programming," Ackbray concedes.

Nashtech looks up. "He wouldn't want this."

"It's for his son and the children of his galaxy," Ackbray responds. "I know he dwells in the ethereal now, but his heart is with his son and his people."

"You know we are breaking every galactic covenant?" Nashtech asks.

"I don't think so. I believe this action will eventually bring a greater peace to the galaxies. The planetary councils have made exceptions to keep the peace."

Nashtech stares at him. "And you believe this will bring peace?"

"I do. I can't explain it, but somehow this action will bring us peace. You've said it yourself. The Sidonians must be saved, regardless of the cost."

"And you believe bringing him back in the midst of his people will fulfill this purpose?" Nashtech asks.

"I believe his presence alone will empower his people and revive their spirits with vigor and strength."

Nashtech sits down, closes his eyes, and breathes deeply for at least ten mSEGs. "Very well ... do it."

Ackbray nods and starts to punch away at his controls. "What are the limitations to the programming?"

Nashtech looks up for a few mSEGs. "He can only intervene in his son's life in emergency situations, and he can only reveal himself after the Vidor are defeated."

I pause the feed and sit in silence. *This can't be real. This is unreal ... Where is his ship?*

I ask it out loud. "Where is his ship?"

"You're on the bridge," *Resilience* responds.

"No, this is not his ship. This one is modern, slick, with Holox controls."

"Those are all cosmetic," *Resilience* says. "Everything was upgraded. The name was even changed from the *Resolute* to the *Resilience*."

"Then where is my father?" I demand.

Resilience does not answer. The entire ship is silent.

"*Resilience*, acknowledge! *Where is he?*"

"Son." The voice is no longer that of the onboard—it is my father's voice. Something inside me shivers. I feel comfort, warmth, joy, and fear.

"Father? Where did you come from?"

"I have always been here."

I stand. "I don't believe this. This is insane!"

"Haven't I always been with you? With your mother and your sister. Through your days at flight academy. When we reminded you that you are a true Astilius."

"But you left me at Mrunal!"

"But I came back," he replies.

This is ridiculous. I start to pace. "Then how did you get to Oxylium?"

"Nashtech completed the upgrades and reworked some of the lines, but he couldn't edit the infrastructure. My plan was to come to your aid, but you came to Oxylium yourself in the *Impetus*. I allowed myself to be captured by the Kanvarians. I know you hate them, and when you lost your craft, I figured you would jump them."

I do hate those guys. "Nashtech released you to be found by us at Oxylium?"

"Correct. I would have never considered blowing up Oxylium. Brilliant, son. I wouldn't have thought to do that."

"I know."

"I saved you when you turned over 5 BURN the first time."

Yeah. That was stupid. I lower my head. "Thanks."

"I wouldn't have gone to Ackbray the way you did, much less have a meal with him or drink Ale with him."

"I did enjoy that."

"The idea of using Helix stones on the missiles was also brilliant."

I manage a smile. "Not my idea, but who would pay a million illirium for a warhead?"

"And the Shivyuns. They're my old friends from long ago. They joined me."

I sit down and breathe deeply. Shivyuns have always been a soft spot for us. "I should have known. And Xander?"

"Nashtech planted the military bot on the vessel to watch over you."

I groan, considering Nashtech saw everything we did through Xander's eyes.

"He was there to protect you, as he did in Navaria. I wouldn't have landed in Navaria," Father adds. "That wasn't the smartest."

I grip my jaw. The phasma shock had been terrible. "It was you and Xander that saved us."

"Khal said he saved you, but we all know he's a horrible pilot."

I laugh. "Father, *you* protected me."

"I only stepped in when you failed. I always let you make your own calls. It's who I am."

I pause. The realization hits me. The *Resilience*, the Shivyuns, and Xander were all sent to assist us. Ackbray's intervention was all intentional, and the contribution of plasma lasers was a part of the story. Father's hand was always there. I can't deny it.

"I gave my life for you to escape at Mrunal," he says. "When you were weak and unable to defend yourself, I was there."

"You shouldn't have left us." A tear streams down my face. "How could you leave us all?"

The voice pauses, and I hear what sounds like a deep sigh. "How can I make you understand, son? I did what I had to do so you would have a better life."

I wipe my eyes on my sleeve.

"The Voice showed me how to help you when I could not be at your side. It was the Voice that protected you, and helps me to protect you still. It was The Voice that sustained me at ten percent, so that I could watch over you. It was The Voice that sees and knows everyone and everything." My father's voice pauses. "The Voice stands behind me always, instructing me in how best to guide you."

I nod my head, acknowledging the wisdom.

"This is *your* journey, your adventure," Father's voice says. "Your exploits have already exceeded mine. I would have never detonated a dwarf moon for stellar rocks, or picked fights with global starfleet carriers, or transnavigated wormholes and Hgates, let alone transnavigate a black hole. I would have never put Helix stones on warheads and taken on entire fleets on my own." The voice chuckles. "You may possibly be the bravest, most reckless, most stubborn, greatest starfighter pilot in the cosmos."

I hold my fist to my heart in the honorable Sidonian way and bow my head. Silent, not-so-honorable tears run from my eyes down my chin to my shirt.

"Thank you, sir."

My father's voice is comforting and encouraging. It is true. He never left us to our own devices. He never left us to manage the impossibilities of life on our own. He was always there. He always will be.

He gave up his life for us to live a better one—to fulfill a greater purpose. It was his design to set us on an inevitable course, to be heroes in our own right.

"I was always there, my son. I always will be."

ABOUT THE AUTHOR

Brett Heaston is the creator of the Message to Kings Podcast (www.messagetokings.com). Married twenty-three years with five kids, he currently works as a Senior Manager in Finance and is the Treasurer of the Northwest Christian Writers Association. He lives in the Pacific Northwest, where he enjoys hiking, skiing, and watersports.

Brett is currently taking a break from rushing around the cosmos. He is finishing a children's chapter book, with his eldest daughter Madelyn, titled *Flora of Amoria*. Flora will demonstrate great honor in her quest to redeem the Kingdom of Amoria. *Flora of Amoria* has a target publication date of early 2022.

In addition, Brett is working on a historical study on the major global conflicts of the past 150 years. After studying all the battles in the Bible, he plans to apply this Biblical Worldview and understanding to the great conflicts of the past few generations. The work, titled *Cities Built on the Sand*, takes a Biblical Worldview examining spiritual cause and effects of global events. *Cities Built on the Sand* has a target publication date of mid-2022.

If you enjoyed this book and/or you would like to keep up to date on future publications, please connect with Brett via facebook: https://www.facebook.com/brett.heaston.3

LETTER TO THE READER

The Voice is the one who spoke all things into existence—the sovereign, preeminent power in the universe, all-powerful, all-knowing, and above all galaxies and universal planes. The Voice is the one that holds all things together and works all things for good.

Atilio, like our Savior, gave his life for us. He was willing to pay the ultimate price to save our lives and our souls. After his return, he was always before us, and will never leave us or forsake us.

Nashtech, Akbray, and Regulus are like pastors or friends who come alongside to assist us on our journey. They have their ambitions, yet they put them aside, like guardians and watchmen to cover us in time of need.

The Vidor and the Kanvarians represent evil in this world. They are the darkness that rages. Their assignment is to steal, kill, and destroy.

We are sojourners like Kyvar and his crew. Some believe and others doubt, yet there is a power at work in alignment. A friendship, a comradery, a loyal strength, like family, when we work together toward a common goal.

Kyvar's journey is our own. We must decide whether or not we will listen to The Voice. We must not be foolish like Kyvar and fall for the many ruses of the enemy. We must not reject wisdom for the sake of our own gifts, yet we should challenge the status quos of our day, and the rules set forth to limit our potential.

Most of all ... we should not reject The Voice that calls out to us to pursue authentic connection to the God of the Universe. He is The Voice that created everything, and he is calling out to each one of us.